Katharine Susannah Prichard ... Fiji where her father was a newspaper editor. ... she was three years old, the family moved to Australia. After leaving school, Prichard worked as a governess in outback Victoria and New South Wales, and later as a tutor in Melbourne.

In 1908, Katharine Susannah Prichard wrote her first novel, *The Wild Oats of Han,* not published until 20 years later. Her first published novel, *The Pioneers,* was written during eight years living abroad; it was a runner-up in the Hodder and Stoughton All-Empire £1000 Novel Competition.

Prichard married in 1919 and settled on a small property at Greenmount, Western Australia. During the next 36 years she published literary and political articles, twelve novels, five collections of short stories, a children's story, her autobiography, plays and verse. She researched *Haxby's Circus* by travelling across the country with Wirth's Circus.

Katharine Susannah Prichard died in 1969 and her ashes were scattered on the slopes of Greenmount.

By the same author

THE PIONEERS
WINDLESTRAWS
THE BLACK OPAL
WORKING BULLOCKS
THE WILD OATS OF HAN
COONARDOO

INTIMATE STRANGERS
MOON OF DESIRE
THE ROARING NINETIES
GOLDEN MILES
WINGED SEEDS
SUBTLE FLAME

ANGUS & ROBERTSON PUBLISHERS

*Unit 4, Eden Park, 31 Waterloo Road,
North Ryde, NSW, Australia 2113;
94 Newton Road, Auckland 1,
New Zealand; and
16 Golden Square, London W1R 4BN,
United Kingdom*

*First published by Jonathan Cape Ltd,
London, 1930
A&R Classics edition published by
Angus & Robertson Publishers in 1973
Sirius paperback edition published by
Angus & Robertson Publishers in 1979
This Sirius paperback edition 1988*

*National Library of Australia
Cataloguing-in-publication data.*

*Prichard, Katharine Susannah, 1883-1969.
  Haxby's circus: the lightest brightest
  little show on earth.

  ISBN 0 207 16115 1

  I. Title.

A823'.2*

Printed in Australia by the Australian Print Group

HAXBY'S CIRCUS

the lightest, brightest little show on earth

KATHARINE SUSANNAH PRICHARD

SIRIUS

To my good friends of Wirth's Circus
in memory of our time together and
their "assistant lion tamer".

CHAPTER 1

VERY dusty and jaded, the circus waggons and horses moved slowly along the wide dusty street of the little up-country town, between scattered houses and weatherboard, sun-bleached shops with verandah posts over the footpaths, on that hot summer morning, although, there was Dan Haxby, fat and jolly as a sultan, riding his elephant, and the dwarf on a pot-bellied Timor pony behind him.

Cowboys beside the animal cages had red shirts and goat skins over their trousers. An Indian in feathers and war-paint walked solitarily behind the buck-board; while Rabe, the band-master, on the seat of the cart driven by Mrs. Haxby got up to look like a squaw, blasted harsh wild music from his cornet and two small boys banged away on drum and cymbals beside him. Gina and Lily Haxby, on white horses, riding astride, fringed leathern skirts over breeches, waved their hats to the townsfolk, laughing and trying to look gay and jaunty, as they distributed pink and white papers among the men, women and children who, running from every direction, stood to watch the procession go by.

Everybody knew the circus had travelled during the night from Mallee, twenty miles away, making by wide unmade roads through shorn wheat lands, round the undulating stony hills to Narran. It had taken the place by surprise so early in the morning, although for weeks past red and blue bills plastered on trees and fences along the road and about the town, had announced the coming of 'Haxby's Circus and Menagerie. The Lightest, Brightest Little Show on Earth.'

Men and boys who were in Mallee the night before, going to their morning milking, or to bring the cows in, when they saw the circus waggons and horses, moving at sunrise through dust towards Narran, had yelled:

'Good show . . . damn good show, Mr. Haxby!'

'You bet,' Dan shouted, congratulating himself on having taken a new road through these little towns of the wheat growing district.

The harvest in, farmers were ready to spend their money, and enjoy themselves after their hard work. Some of them had driven miles in their high four-wheeled buggies and spring carts filled with women and children, drawn by horses from the plough teams and harvesters, great shaggy draughts, light, rusty, half-broken colts, or quiet old mokes doddering along. And how everybody laughed at the fat, funny little dwarf who was a grown man but no bigger than a child of five, exclaiming with fear and admiration as pretty Lily Haxby flew among the high trapezes, or Gina danced on the bare back of her white horse!

Some of the small towns scattered through recently settled country had never seen a circus. So that Haxby's did good business and Dan Haxby put up his prices, determined to make hay while the sun shone, shining though it might be with its summer brilliance and intensity.

Everybody growled, and worked, fagged and complaining at the way Dan Haxby was pushing them, but work they did from the moment the waggons and horses arrived on a lot, beside recreation grounds, railway siding or river, until the show was on the road again, when the men dozed as they drove or spelled horses in the shade of trees by the wayside.

The circus procession trailed now, through the dust it raised, to a paddock by the river, opposite the low-built, white-washed pub of mud brick beside the bridge.

It was Saturday. Those pink and white papers Gina and Lily threw out lay and fluttered about the wide empty road, announcing a matinee, and from the moment the lot was reached no time could be lost if the show was to be ready for the afternoon performance.

Haxby's was more or less a family affair, a show in which the artists were all Haxby's children or relations, with the exception of Jack Dayne, the trapezist, and Rocca, the dwarf. And it was a case of all hands on the job when there was pressure of business as there was this day in Narran. Particularly after the three tent hands who were also grooms and animal keepers, as soon as they had thrown off their parade costumes, deserted to the pub and refused to leave it. They were not going to work themselves to death for Dan Haxby, or anybody like him.

Dan swore they could rot in the fly-blown parlours of the Narran Bridge Inn, as far as he was concerned; and got all the help he needed for unloading, spreading and hoisting the tents, from men and boys who flocked down to the riverside paddocks to watch the circus unpack its gear.

The ground had to be measured and a place dug for the king pole. Dan himself bossed measuring of the ground for the tents, spreading the canvas, setting the king pole and stakes for the menagerie and circus tents. Rabe, the band-master, and Jack Dayne worked with him,

3

the onlookers hustled and jollied into lending a hand, but Dan saw to it that they undertook the heaviest pull, without knowing it, when the canvas was hoisted to its tall pole.

'Now then, you chaps,' he yelled, heartily, 'all together——'

And the tent sailed and bellied into position, its dingy white canopy under clear blue sky, against grey and green of the river trees.

In no time the peaked tents were all there on the summer-dried grass, the circus tent, the tent for the menagerie and the men's dressing tent. The horses stood haltered to the fence in the shade of trees. Queenie, the elephant, hauled animal cages on waggons with red and blue wheels, into the menagerie; and near the buckboard with its weathered white roof, Mrs. Haxby had made a fire. A heavy, ungainly woman in drab clothes, she moved about, washing clothes, hanging stockings, two or three shirts, and a clown's bags of white cotton stuff on a line stretched between two gum saplings. A smell of meat cooking, onions and potatoes in a stew, wavered over the open paddocks.

When the tents were up and the cages in position in the menagerie, Dan thanked his helpers heartily, and without squandering a single free seat, for their labours of the morning. He invited two or three of them across to the pub for a pot; and over the drinks was so jovial and chatty about the work and adventures of the circus that everybody was more eager than ever to see the show.

Monty and Les, the two elder of the Haxby boys, took the horses to water in pools of the river, and brought them back to the shade of trees beside an old fence of

4

posts and broad-slabbed rails, while the two younger boys went off to the township for bread and vegetables.

Under the big tent, in the hot mellow sunshine, the girls had set-up and arranged the seats. Gina was fixing pegs to run the red and white striped canvas round for the ring, while Jack Dayne tested the trapezes, ropes and guys he had slung to the roof of the tent.

'I'm fair beat,' Lily exclaimed, glancing at the light swings with their silvery bars gleaming against the roof of the tent. 'How on earth Dad expects us to go on like this, I don't know.'

'Go and have a lay down,' Gina looked up from the peg she was banging with a wooden mallet. Hard and brown her hands and arms were: hard and brown she was, a gypsy creature, bright-eyed, rough-haired, blood blooming under her swarthy skin. 'We're all right now. Everything will be ready in time. Aye Jack –' she glanced at Jack Dayne working among the lighting ropes and wires, 'make Lily go and have a bit of a rest now. You could get down under those shady trees by the river. The old man'd never see you.'

'Right!' the man called from mid air.

'I ought to give Mum a hand.'

Lily watched her sister tightening the ring pegs. A year or so older, she looked slighter, lighter, more sinewy and graceful than Gina. Her eyes, shallow grey, glimmered under fair hair peroxided a deeper gold. She looked older than she was, her skin withered and dried by the constant use of cosmetics. No more than nineteen, she might almost have been thirty. Her face had a worn expression, despite its pretty childish wistfulness.

'I'll give Mum a hand,' Gina said. 'I'm just through

here. And then there's only those damned monkey cages to see to.'

'But you've had no rest at all, Gi,' Lily exclaimed fretfully. 'You're always last down and first up. I don't know how you do it. Jack says Dad's crazy to work us like this. Flesh and blood won't stand it. Jack's not going to stand it . . . and neither am I. We'd oughter have decent tent hands and grooms. It's not fair to make us toil like this, and then expect us to go on as if nothing had happened.'

'Oh, me, I'm tough,' Gina replied sturdily. 'Besides, to-morrow's Sunday. I'm going to sleep all day on the road.'

'I like your chance. Forty miles between here and the next one-horse town.'

'Oh well,' having fastened the striped canvas round its pegs, Gina got up from the ground, 'you get a bit of shut-eye and tucker, and you'll feel better.'

'How about you Gina?' Jack Dayne asked, when he had slid down a long rope and stood on the ground near her.

'I'm all right,' Gina said.

She went to the back of the tent and returned, dragging a heavy bag, set it beside the ring and thrusting her hand down the open neck, drew out a handful of fragrant red-gum sawdust. She threw the sawdust on the ring until the grass and broken dry ground were covered; then, going across to the other side, lifted the flap which separated the two tents and went into the menagerie.

Dan and Rabe had left the menagerie, and gone off to the hotel as soon as the animal cages were wheeled into position. Sunlight made a hot yellow mist under the dust-stained awning over the half-dozen cages of wild beasts on blue and red waggons. Gina glanced round them, and at the elephant chained to a peg near the entrance, rooting at the dry grass and red earth and tossing it from her trunk over her back to keep the flies away. The stench was heavy and sickening.

A flare of anger rushed over the girl as she crossed quickly to a bundle of tools thrown down beside the monkey cages. Taking a long iron raking hook she pushed it into the nearest cage, where half a dozen little grey and brown Indian monkeys crouched miserably, and scraped the filth and rubbish which had accumulated on the floor of the cage to one side. Out into the sunshine for a kerosene tin, her anger carried her and back to rake out the cage.

Ordinarily Dan Haxby made a great fuss about cleaning out the animal cages. He boasted his beasts were better kept than most people's children. You could eat your breakfast off the floor of their cages. He was supposed to look after Hero himself. The old lion, who had been the pride of Haxby's for years, was almost toothless, had to have his meat beaten-up for him and be fed with soup and slops for fear he would die of starvation.

When she had scraped over and raked out the floor of the cages, Gina plunged her hand into the bag of red sawdust she had got from timber mills by the river a few days before, and threw handfuls of sawdust over the floor of the monkey cages. From one cage to the other she went, raking and scattering sawdust.

As she threw back folds of the tent to carry out buckets of evil-smelling rubbish, the animals blinked at each flash of blue sky and yellow paddocks in dazzling sunshine.

Two small Malayan bears lay panting in one small compartment. Next to them lived a long lean grey beast on whose cage was written 'Siberian Wolf.' Gina knew

B

there was much more wolf hound than wolf about him, and was sorry for the confinement and humiliation he suffered. He was more savage and untameable than any of the other animals.

Gina did not know what had come over the old man to neglect the animals like this. Perhaps he thought Charley or Lord Freddie had attended to the cages before they cleared out. Not much. Not likely. Gina promised herself to give the men a bit of her mind when she saw them. Her face was dripping and she worked so furiously that she did not see the edge of the tent lift and Rocca come into the menagerie.

Dan Haxby had picked up Billy Rocca, as he was called on the show, in Melbourne a few months before. His name was Guglielmo really; but that was too hard to say every day in the week, Dan declared, and too classy a name for the circus programme. So as William might be considered a free translation of Guglielmo, Rocca was christened Bill with a little sawdust and enjoyed the popularity the little name brought him. He had been ill and left by a vaudeville company in the city when he signed a contract with Haxby, for the sake of his health, he said ; to get into the country and have some outdoor life for awhile.

'Miss Gina,' Rocca exclaimed, 'you should not be doing this!'

His voice was the mature pleasantly modulated voice of a man of culture and breeding. Coming from that small misshapen body, it was a surprise, with its slightly foreign inflection.

Gina, lifting a bucket to take away across the paddock, pushed back the hair from her wet forehead.

'That's all very well, Billy,' she cried. 'But somebody's got to look after the animals. I'll give Lord Freddie and Charley a bit of my mind when I see them. Dad thought they'd done this, I suppose. We'll have the R.S.P.C.A. down on us, if we don't look out . . . and quite right too.'

Rocca let himself down on to the grass, pale-golden, and smelling like hay, beside the wall of the tent.

'I hate to see you work like this,' he said. 'It is too bad! And you so fine artiste, Miss Gina.'

Gina went out of the tent and came back again.

Rocca tried to fan himself with a panama hat he was carrying. Very dapper and elegant, he lay there in a suit of assam silk with a white silk shirt, blue braces and tie.

Gina knew Rocca much better than most people. She was so accustomed to the sight of him that she never thought of him as they did. He had travelled and read a great deal, and he talked so interestingly about things and people he had seen that she almost forgot when they were together what he looked like and how odd he was to most people.

No more than three feet in height Rocca was broad; his head that of a man of thirty or thereabouts, a rather good looking man with hazel green eyes, and a well-cut, sensitive, sensual mouth. Teeth white, well-cared for and tinkered with gold, gleamed against the sallow bronze of his skin. But from broad shoulders his body tapered to the legs of a child, his arms and legs were those of a boy of about five years old, small, plump, absurd. Grotesque his body was; its grotesqueness Rocca's means of earning a living.

No one knew perhaps the suffering of his mind: the despair, misery and loneliness which went on in the fine brain under Billy Rocca's big head, broad low brow.

Not that he was without professional pride in his appearance. Nothing more droll than those baby arms of his, those legs which trotted and gambolled with such a mockery of infantile grace and gaiety could be imagined. Rocca kept his body with scrupulous care, was always well washed and as daintily turned out as a baby although almost as helpless. Usually he had one of the tent hands to valet him. As the plaything of princes and oriental potentates, he had become accustomed to luxury, scented baths and fine linen, he said. He liked them; could not accustom himself to do without them.

"What a place . . . what a country,' he groaned, stretched there on the grass. 'I have been in India, Africa, Burma, the hottest places in the world, Miss Gina. But never anywhere has it been like this! So stifling! No ice . . . no punkas . . . no cooling fountains. How do people live, the country people? Why do they not make some comfort for themselves?'

'I don't know. I suppose they haven't got time,' Gina replied impatiently.

Rocca looked cool enough lying there on the grass doing nothing. A diamond winked from the knot of his blue tie and there was a diamond ring on his little finger. Yet what troubled him was that he could not offer to help her, Gina realised. That was what he was growling at really. He hated to see her working and not lend a hand. But what could he do?

Gina knew Billy suffered more than he admitted, by every exertion. His work looked simple; but he practised painstakingly, and his acrobatic stunts were exhausting really. Rocca liked to think he was a comedian of the first quality and had transformed his disabilities into natural advantages. To make people laugh by the drolleries to which he could put his body; to mock his own tragedy constituted for him the highest form of his art.

He had his conceits, aristocratic prejudices. His hands were white, his nails manicured. He had read a great deal, spoke several languages, and talked music with Rabe all night sometimes. Oh yes, he was clever, Billy Rocca, everybody agreed, 'the perfect little gentleman,' although nobody knew much about him.

Rocca said he was paying for the sins of his forefathers. He was the curse which had come home to roost. Only he refused to roost. When a local *enterpreneur* suggested to his parents in some small Italian town that there was a fortune in the boy's deformity, they rejected the idea with pride and indignation. But Billy had taken the law into his own hands, and by making a laughing stock of himself, wandered about the world, leading a gay grasshoppery existence, until he came to grief in Australia, where Dan Haxby had found him, penniless and broken in health by an absconding director.

'Did you know Miss Lily and Jack Dayne are talking of clearing out,' Rocca enquired conversationally, as he watched Gina stirring up the sleepy old lion to get out of her way whilst she cleaned out his cage.

'They've been talking, for years,' Gina said.

Rocca watched the sway and fling of her sturdy thick-set figure.

'I saw your beau in the town,' he said.

'My beau – what beau?' Gina asked.

'Oh, the young man who has been following us round these country towns and met us on the road with those grapes this morning.'

'Him!' Gina paused in her work to stare at Rocca, her eyes smiling. 'Has he been following us around?'

'As if you did not know,' Rocca scoffed. 'I let him buy me a lemon squash and pump me about you. Said you were so fine artiste, should not be with this dud show. And he asked me if you can cook and do you like cows.'

'Oh lord, Billy!' Gina gurgled her amusement.

'And were you straight, or could he take you to supper?'

'Bill!'

Gina laughed; but Rocca plucking at the grass, muttered and swore to himself in a variety of languages, Italian, Dutch and Malay. Then he caught Gina's eyes and laughter, and laughed too.

'What did you tell him?' she asked.

Gina was pleased and flattered by the way a good looking young farmer had followed the show from town to town since Haxby's had showed in Bendigo a week ago. It was the first time this sort of thing had happened to her. Young men had followed the show about to see Lily often enough, although Dan Haxby was so strict with his girls, a strange youth was rarely able to get a word with them. Lily might blow her young men kisses from the ring, or throw them a flower, but Dan Haxby would never allow any loitering about the tents after the show. He himself saw the girls had their supper and went to bed as soon as the waggons were loaded or under way for the next stopping place.

'What did you tell him Billy?' Gina asked smiling.

'I tell him: No! No! No!' the dwarf exploded violently. Getting up from the grass he shook himself and trotted out of the tent.

'Gina!'

Before going in answer to the call, Gina glanced about the tent she had been working in.

The menagerie looked trimmer; smelt better. The

cage floors at least were clean and strewn with fresh sawdust. The animals dozed peacefully, all but the monkeys who were still chattering and running about excitedly as they always did when Rocca went near them. One of the bears scratched the floor of his cage with ceaseless furtive movements of his long-nailed claws. The green eyes of the wolf-hound had half closed on their savage unfathomable rancour; and the yellow eyes of the old lion, half asleep, blinked at her gratefully.

'A poor old lot,' Gina told herself. 'But improving. There's the bears . . . and Rocca. He's a draw. The kids love him. He's got the crowd by the wool, Dad says. If business keeps up like it's been doing, we'll be able to get a tiger soon and a lioness. Then we could raise a couple of cubs, maybe. I could rear them . . . and work them myself.'

'Gina! Gina!'

That harsh exasperated voice called again.

'Where are you Gina?' A small boy lifted the flap of the tent. 'Mum says she can't keep dinner hanging round any longer. When are you going to get a move on and come and have something to eat?'

'Coming,' Gina called good-naturedly. 'I'm just coming, Mum.'

CHAPTER 2

AFTER mid-day meal in a limp shadow the covered cart threw on the grass, Dan and Rabe who had returned, refreshed and in good spirits from the pub, went off to prepare the animals' food and to see that everything was in order for the afternoon performance. Dan and the boys would have to be the band since Bruiser, Charley and Lord Freddie were past expecting anything from in the back parlour of the Narran Bridge Inn.

In odd moments on the road and in camp Rabe, who knew his way about any instrument, was teaching Syd to play popular airs on the trombone and Monty was learning to work on Rabe's own old fiddle. Dan himself took the cornet in an emergency and prided himself on his double stopping, while either of the younger boys could be trusted with drum, triangle and cymbals.

Everybody on Haxby's had to have two or three strings to his bow. Bruiser and Charley were not only tent hands, groomed the horses and fed the animals; but Bruiser whose other name was Stewart could make a fairly recognisable noise with a flute or tin whistle, and Charley performed on the barrel organ with pride and enthusiasm. To-day, because neither Rabe nor the boys could be spared for the band, the parade being short of three men, an urchin, who had been hanging round the tents all the morning, was commandeered to turn the handle of the organ for the grand march.

Before the parade and afterwards, Rabe and the boys, with Dan on the cornet, would be responsible for selections by the band. But the parade would look too skimpy without them, so that Rabe had to get into Lord Freddie's clown overalls, and make the best of it.

The boys ran off to wash their faces and hands in a bucket of water beside the cart, climbed up into it to put on their tights and trunks, hung from nails along the wall. They brushed cocoanut oil over their heads until their hair shone as if it were lacquered, rubbed a little rouge on their high cheek bones, and slipping shabby little old coats over their finery, came down to get trays of peanuts and programmes they were to sell before the show began.

Already people were beginning to wander down from the town, and the roads which led into Narran, swarmed with sulkies, spring carts, heavy horses and high buggies, loaded with women and children. Two or three of the first motor cars in the district raised whirlwinds of dust and made a great noise as they buzzed along.

Gina scraped dishes, dipped them into a kerosene bucket of hot water before the fire and stowed them away in a box for the next meal. She put the food away in a hanging safe under a tree, while her mother hustled the boys off with their programmes, little bags of peanuts, lollies, and wallets for change.

Mrs. Haxby herself went down to the ticket box Dan had set up for her outside the menagerie; and Gina was left to get ready for the parade.

She went over to the bucket beside the buckboard and sluiced her face and hands as the boys had done. She scrubbed her hands with the bar of hard yellow soap her mother had left there. They were ingrained with dirt and refused to come clean; there was not time to spend on them so she went on into the cart, stripped, and dragged on her breeches and blouse, knotted a red handkerchief round her neck and pulled on her long boots. Standing a moment before a small dingy mirror hanging against the wall, she plastered her face with grease, rubbed a patch of rouge on either cheek, and on her chin, mopped it with a scrap of soiled swan skin dipped in powder, marked her eyes with blue pencil and reddened her lips in half a dozen, steady, business-like strokes. Gina boasted that she could make-up in the dark, crude business though it was when she had done with it. Snatching up her wide felt hat and whip, she glanced about to see Lily's gear was ready for her.

The dressing whistle shrilled, and Lily came up to the buckboard. Jack and Rocca shared a tent at a little distance from the big tent. Good artist that he was, Jack usually gave himself plenty of time to dress. He was never late on parade, and nothing made Dan more bad tempered than to have the grand march kept waiting, hanging about, because Lily was late, or Rocca playing-up.

Dan Haxby was a stickler for punctuality and everything going with a dash, to the tick, exactly as he had arranged.

'I'm not going to make-up on an afternoon like this . . . and for a damned matinee,' Lily gasped, coming into the cart. 'No idea it was so late.'

'Had anything to eat?' Gina asked.

'Jack brought me some sandwiches. It was so cool and nice down under the trees . . . we near went to sleep. Oh hell, there's the old man roaring!' Lily was struggling into her trousers and boots as Gina went down into the

16

blank sunshine. 'Where's my hat? Oh, Gord, Gi, have you seen my hat? Look if Jack's got Beauty ready will you? And make Rabe hang on to the band!'

Ordinarily the grand march made its entry to stirring strains of 'The Turkish Patrol' by the band which consisted of Rabe and the two younger boys, or Rabe and the barrel-organ, as circumstances decided. Gina did not wait to explain that Rabe was taking Lord Freddie's place as clown for the grand march to-day, and ran off to saddle her own and Lily's horses.

The wide hat set rakishly on her fair head, Lily added red to her lips and blued her eyelids. Matinee it might be, and nothing but a swarm of kids, farmers and their women folk, for her to take her life in her hands for, but the gush of admiration and wonder sight of her caused was the breath of life to Lily Haxby. She had been so long the brightest star of Haxby's, that now Gina was beginning to attract attention by her riding and wild gypsy beauty, Lily could not forego a cry or gesture of the applause she had been accustomed to so long.

Very pretty and graceful Lily was, and clever too in the trapeze and aerial stunts Jack Dayne had taught her. But no good with horses. She could not work them; and Dan Haxby, infuriated at last, had washed his hands of her. Surprised and delighted, he watched her training with Jack, and had to admit, after a time, that Lily in mid-air showed a daring and agility he would never have dreamed could be got out of her. Jack had given her confidence and pride in her work, and Lily's swallow-diving and tumbling, Dan swore, were as dainty as any he had ever seen.

Gina was too heavy for the trapeze, but a good acrobat and so strong that she stood the strenuous practice and exercise needed for stunt and jockey riding without turning a hair. Besides she loved horses and was quite fearless with them. She had worked the white mare, Beauty, since she was a child. Dan had taught all his children trick riding on Beauty; and now Gina was helping him to train a good-looking young white horse they found in a milkman's cart, bought for a few pounds, fattened-up, groomed and broke-in to circus work.

An envious worm had pried its way into Lily's brain as she watched Gina running and vaulting to the back of the new white mare, standing poised with pointed toes throw herself easily, gracefully from Bonnie's back to the ring or turning a somersault from the back of one horse to the other, stretch up on her toes again, blow her kisses and retire.

Dan was proud of this trick of Gina's. He used to do it in his young days, he said. He had taught and trained Gina. She was young, gay and strong. She loved her work. Never was there a more apt pupil.

But even the circus people themselves, watching Gina's flip-flap from the back of the moving horses, were glad when it was over. They knew the danger: that this was the most dangerous trick in the show, this ride of Gina's. Only she never seemed concerned about it. She had come two or three busters while she was learning and practising, but without hurting herself at all. And she was so good at her work, went through it so easily, gaily, people as often as not did not realise how difficult and dangerous what she had done really was.

On this hot summer afternoon, the tent from inside glowed like parchment. Where it was folded back for the horses and performers to run in, a panel of blue sky gave a gout of fresher air.

Under the tent, wooden seats packed with women and children in light summer clothing, small boys, youths and men, made a wide variegated border to the ring. An eager, excited chatter and clatter of exclamations, clapping of hands shook it, from the moment the grand march swung the circle of the red sawdust mat, until Dan and Rabe were blasting 'God Save,' about five o'clock.

The children had shrieked at Rocca and his antics; the heavy, fat faced, or weedy, thin and melancholy farmers and their wives laughed till the tears ran down their faces, to see the dwarf trying to imitate Jack's and Lily's feats on the trapeze. Rabe in Lord Freddie's white clown sack, his face whitened, with red gash for a mouth, had made the time-honoured jokes and booted the little man out of the ring to the hilarious enjoyment of everybody.

The boys' tumbling and Risley acts, the way Monty balanced a ladder on his feet and Syd hung by one leg from the top, their juggling and sleight-of-hand tricks together, filled all the country lads with envy. Women had gasped and clutched at their men folk when Lily in her pale blue cotton tights and spangled trunks dived and tumbled, catching Jack's hands as he swung from the trapeze opposite. Then Dan worked Phil, the piebald pony he was so proud and fond of. Phil waltzed, sat down on his haunches, bowed and answered questions like a Christian, nodding or shaking his head for yes, or no. He was, Dan proclaimed, 'The octo-miraculous wonder of the world.' The eighth wonder of the world that was – a horse almost human.

And Gina drove her team of six horses from the Indians, turning and sitting back to front on one of the leaders, to fire at an Indian. Leaning from her saddle, when she had released the other horses, she picked up a wounded comrade, the youngest of her brothers, and as her horse cantered round the ring, shot away the rope by which the Indians had strung her cowboy lover to the roof of the tent. She used blank cartridges and the rope was cleverly faked. The turn never failed to please. Men and boys whooped delightedly when it was over.

Very dashing and reckless Gina looked as she waved her hat to the youngsters. Much more so than when she threw those gay somersaults from the backs of the moving horses, later, in yellow flowered trunks with a coloured handkerchief tied round her hair.

But everybody had worked flatly, tired by the day's journey and the business of getting ready for the performance. The tent was sweltering in the hot sunshine. Dust beaten up by the horses' hoofs hung in the air and already the place breathed the musty, fetid smell of caged wild beasts, sweaty human beings, rank tobacco, and peanuts.

When the eager, happy and excited crowd drifted away over stretches of dried summer grass, to the township, their carts and buggies were jolting along the road and over the bridge into the country beyond, Dan counted his money with Mrs. Haxby. He tied it in a little bag of unbleached calico and giving it to his wife to stow in some safe place, strolled across to the pub with Rabe for their beer and yarn with local worthies.

Gina changed into an overall of dark blue print and went over to rub down and water her horses. Whether there was a groom, or not, she liked to do this herself, and to feed Beauty and Bonnie with pieces of carrot as a reward for the afternoon's work.

The sun was westering; that dry smell of summer dried

grass on the paddocks, lying still and far before her, tasted sweet to her mouth and nostrils. Gina lingered under the trees when she had tied her horses to the fence again. A slender rough-barked gum tree had masses of downy white blossom. There were bees in it making a dull murmurous melody. Gina picked a branch of the blossom; it smelt of honey and the bees flew about her. She had intended to carry the blossom back with her; instead, she thought now, she would lie down on the grass there and rest a little. It was so quiet, so beautiful, under the wide, mild skies, beside that clump of slender young trees. A faint bluish haze of bush fires stood among trees along the river and the grass was sim and golden: fading pink of the sky above the trees, the trees themselves, smoke, mists and grass fused and hung together in the half-light.

Gina threw herself down, and stretched against the earth. She would take a couple of minutes.

'Gina! For Gord's sake, Gina!'

So sharp the cry, Gina sprang to her feet almost as quickly as it rasped.

'Coming,' she called.

She could see her mother, a gaunt darkly clad figure beside the fire near the buckboard. Lotty Haxby was standing curved, as she had set down a blackened kerosene tin from the fire. Her arms were folded across her body.

Running from the trees, Gina came up to her.

'What is it, Mum,' she asked anxiously.

'I must have strained myself . . . or something, Gi', the older woman said, her face torn by the pain which wrung her. 'It's the heat . . . and being that way I suppose.'

'Go and lie down,' Gina begged. 'I can see to things

now. There's an hour before you need go down to the ticket box.'

'There's such a lot to fix up, Gi –'

'I'll look after it.'

Gina led her mother towards the cart.

'Stay here,' she said as they stood beside it. 'I'll get a blanket and you can lay down.'

'That bit of cold meat 'll do for tea,' Mrs. Haxby gasped as she let herself down on to the grey blanket Gina spread on the grass for her. 'The boys had better have something to eat now. You could send Monty for your father and Rabe.'

'Mont!' Gina called to the elder of her two brothers as they came from the menagerie where they had been going round the animal cages with bucket and raking hook again, 'go over to the pub and tell Dan and Rabe tucker's ready . . . and if they don't come at once they won't get any.'

'All right,' Monty replied. He finished what he was doing, took his bucket and hook back to the tent and turned off across the grass to the hotel.

'He's a good kid, if ever there was one,' Gina remarked, watching the wiry, slow figure of her eldest brother. 'Did Dad give the boys anything from the peanut money this afternoon?'

'Not a bean,' Mrs. Haxby replied wearily.

'Where is it?' Gina asked.

'In the cart, under my bunk,' Mrs. Haxby said.

'Hi, Monty, you might get a couple of bottles of lemonade while you're about it,' Gina called.

The boy came towards her. She went into the cart and re-appeared presently with a couple of shillings in her hand.

'And you stick to the change, Mont,' Gina said as she gave him the money.

'Dad's counted the money, Gina,' Mrs. Haxby exclaimed fretfully.

'Oh well,' Gina replied, 'tell him I took it. I'm going to take what I want these days. We work hard enough goodness knows, and when there's money about, I don't see why we shouldn't get a bit of the good of it.'

She went across to the fire and the box of plates and cups nearby, spread them out on the grass, and cutting thick slices of bread, slapped butter on. A tin of jam and a piece of cheese wrapped in greasy paper she put beside the bread, and from a hessian bag took bunches of grapes, gold, green and purple, and laid them on the grass too.

Then sitting down nearby, she set to filling small paper bags with peanuts, and arranging the bags on trays which the boys wore slung by a strap around their necks.

'Where's Lil?' Mrs. Haxby asked, 'The lazy hound! She ought to give you a hand, Gina. She's always sneaking out of things and prowling round with that damned trapezist . . . having meals with him in the towns. Your father's real mad about it. Says he won't stand it. He won't stand that feller making-up to Lil.'

'Oh well,' Gina replied tranquilly, 'he'd better let them get married and be done with it.'

'He won't do that.' Mrs. Haxby moved uneasily.

'They will, anyhow . . . and if he doesn't want to lose them both from the show, he'd better put up with it.'

'The show – the show! It's all the show with him,' Mrs. Haxby grumbled. 'Gord damn the show I say, sometimes, Gi.'

'Go on, Mum.' Gina's hands moved busily as she talked. 'You're a bit done-up to-night. It's not a bad life—

c

ours. You've said so yourself, often enough. And what would we all do in a town, or one of these farms for the rest of our days.'

'You're getting as bad as your father, every bit, Gina. You don't care about nothing but the show.'

'Oh I say, Mum –' Gina protested.

The men were coming from the hotel on the opposite side of the road, Charley, Lord Freddie and Bruiser, the Haxby boys, as well as Rabe and Dan.

The tent hands slouched away together to where the horses were tethered. They had slept off the first bout of their spree and were going on with their night's work. Rabe's tall figure swayed and straggled beside Dan in the twilight. He had already drunk as much as he could carry; but Dan strutted jauntily, towards the fire-glow, assured in his cock-o'-the-walk air, a bottle in his hand, and in such good humour that he shouted to Mrs. Haxby he had brought a drop of stout for her.

'Thought you was looking a bit used up with the heat, Mum,' he called, opened the bottle, poured a mug full of the dark frothing brew and took it over to her.

Monty, Syd, Les, Bob and Rabe sat down on the grass beside the food Gina had spread out for them. She passed plates of corned beef to her young brothers and put Dan's ready for him. Rabe said he did not want anything to eat: a cup of tea would do him. Gina made it strong, black, sweetened it with sugar and set the quart pot down beside him. For herself she took a couple of bunches of grapes, muscatels and flame Tokays. Filled with sunshine, rose tinted, the grapes hung along their stalks, some of them mauve and burned dry, as they turned to raisins, others pale green and cool as iced water.

24

Gina had been teased a good deal about the young farmer who held up the circus waggons that morning to present Dan with a sack of grapes. Rocca called him her 'beau' because he had been following the show around. From Bendigo and Southern Cross to Mallee he had been at every performance for a week, and this morning, just after sunrise, had ridden out from an old white-washed homestead among trees. Gina on Bonnie looked out to see the young man streaking across paddocks, gilded with early sunshine. He had waited at a long white gate for the circus waggons to pass, given Dan a cheery 'good-morning,' and presented the grapes.

'Thanks. Thanks very much.' Dan had taken the bag of grapes and stowed them away on the buckboard. ' See you at the show to-night?'

'I'll be there,' the young man answered heartily, and stood staring at Gina as the waggons moved on.

'Go on, give him a wave, Gi,' Lily teased. 'It's good for business and Dad's not looking.'

Gina turned in her saddle and waved back to the horseman standing beside that long white gate in the fence round his paddocks. She had seen his hat fly off and watched him canter away over the stubble fields again.

Dan pulled up after awhile and handed out bunches of grapes. Everybody had eaten grapes as they rode along. Gina gave handfuls to Beauty and Bonnie. Even the bears and monkeys had a cluster or two.

The sky was the colour of grapes now, flame of the Tokays and gold of the muscatels, clear pale light washing high up into the faded blue; mists among the trees like bloom on the purple and black grapes.

Coming through vineyard country, Gina had seen men and boys in blue trousers, limp felt hats, picking cartloads of grapes like these. Standing among rows of vines, under bare blue skies, they snipped off great bunches and piled them into spring carts drawn by staunch, slow-going, ruddy-brown, bay or roan horses. Sometimes the circus waggons passed these carts on the road, and men or boys driving gave the girls bunches from their flamy, green and amber load. As often as not Jack or Rocca brought a case of grapes. But Gina thought she had never tasted grapes as nice as these, 'her beau' had brought her; all liquid sugar and sunshine, they were.

She wondered who the young man was as she lay on the grass beside Rabe and the boys, happily conscious that the day had been permeated by a faint odour and taste of grapes. Who was the young man, she wondered. What was his name? It was real nice of him to bring the grapes like that. Her hands sought the used mugs and plates. She started to clear away after the meal.

Dan and Rabe went over to the tents to light up for the evening performance. Mrs Haxby got ready to go down to the ticket office.

'I'm all right now, Gi,' she called. 'That rest and the drop of stout did me all the good in the world.'

CHAPTER 3

CARS and buggies, far away on the dark roads flickered like fireflies, coming into the town, converging round the restless spangle of lights in the paddock beside the river where the circus had camped.

Under starry skies, across the dim plains, gay blare and tinkle of the circus band flew far and wide.

The tents erected during the morning, glowed like a crop of luminous toadstools. Smoking flares showed gaily caparisoned horses, fantastically clad riders moving in and out from the dark behind the tents. Crowds of men, women and children from the town and surrounding farms, seethed across the dark paddocks towards them. Cries of the peanut sellers and of Dan Haxby calling attractions of the show went up, with now and then a shrill whinnying of horses. Queenie trumpeted and the old lion yawned and roared obligingly in the rising excitement.

All day the township had been in a ferment with sights and sounds of the circus. Everybody had been saying to everybody else: 'See the circus has come? Are you going to the circus?'

From the matinee in the afternoon, men had gone promising themselves to see the show in the evening, as well, Dan having promised a change of programme. Narran was agog with laughter and yarns of the droll doings of Rocca the dwarf: full of exclamations at the riding and horsemanship of Gitana, the gipsy, the doings of Phil, the octo-miraculous pony, aerial feats of La Lilla, the tumbling, flip-flapping and double somersaults of the boys – Dan himself looking like an emperor in a fairy tale, as he put the lion and elephant through their tricks.

Dan and Rabe had enjoyed the hilarity and rural tributes to their greatness when they went along to the old white-washed pub for their pot in the evening. They blew their bags about the marvels and merits of Haxby's which really was the lightest, brightest little show on earth, they swore, and their hearers agreed with them.

Charley, Bruiser and Lord Freddie had gone about their jobs as usual before the evening performance. Dan threatened to sack them on the first opportunity. He always threatened to when anything went wrong; but was glad to see them sober enough to-night to be going about their work as usual. To-morrow they would get the length of his tongue; to-night he was satisfied for Rabe to devote himself to the band, tune-up for the grand march, work the contraption he had fixed so that he could use drum and cymbals with his feet while he blew away on his cornet, and that proud small boy of the town set the barrel organ going.

The grand march launched itself with a swing to the gay loud jargon Rabe put up, Dan himself leading off on the elephant, in turban, jacket and trousers of a rajah flashing jewels; Lily and Jack Dayne riding behind him in their wild west rig-out; Gina sitting sideways on her white horse in spangled ballet skirts; Rocca in the pink satin jacket and cap, tiny white trousers of a jockey, on the big grey draught horse, used for pulling the monkey cages.

How the crowd laughed, rocked and yelled to see him,

the smallest jockey Narran had ever dreamed of on the largest horse. The boys in their big felt hats, red shirts, goats-skins over their trousers, whooped and yelled wildly. Bruiser blackened with charcoal to look like a negro, walked beside the lion's cage, and Lord Freddie in his clown's bags with white plastered face and red gash of a mouth ran after the procession crying: 'Stop! Stop! Wait a minute, wait for Willie. Please wait a minute for little Willie!'

The procession circled the ring twice and went out through the back of the tent against a back screen of starlit sky.

Then the lion's cage was wheeled into the ring and Dan himself put Hero through his tricks, cracking his whip and swaggering valiantly, while Lord Freddie pressing his face against the bars yelled:

'Come out! Come out I tell you! Many's the man that lion's killed and eaten before breakfast!'

The crowd bellowed applause, though the old lion just strolled round his cage, sat up on his pedestal, yawned, blinked, roared as he was supposed to every night, then thoroughly bored, stretched at Dan's feet and went to sleep again.

The boys ran in for their acrobatic turn. Tumbling and somersaulting, building figures, jumping over each other and standing on their heads, they pulled very well together. Monty lying on his back took Les on his feet, Syd stood on Les's shoulders, and Bob, from Syd's shoulders threw a double backwards which brought down a shower of hand clapping and exclamations. It was really a clever turn and very popular with men and boys who knew how difficult these light and graceful gymnastics were.

Lily and Jack appeared next in their pale blue and silver spangled trunks, blue tights. Very slight and pretty Lily looked with her fluff of fair hair, as she stood rubbing her feet in powdered resin on a board at the foot of the rope to her trapeze. Then she shinned up the rope, caught the trapeze, swung and hung there, turned and flying lightly, caught Jack as he hung with outstretched hands from his trapeze. Very nimbly and gracefully they disported themselves among the high wires and descended again to the pattering and clapping of eager hands.

The Mallee Derby was what Dan called his special item for the programme that night. Gina and the boys dressed as jockeys rode their horses in for it, while the ring-master and clown played book-maker and punter. 'I'll lay the odds! I'll lay the odds! Any price runners. The field a pony!'

'What price Beauty?' Dan asked.

'Beauty, Mr. Haxby? I'll take ten to one.'

'Oh go on,' Dan jollied. 'Beauty's not in it with a moke I know.'

'A dark horse? You got a dark horse, Mr. Haxby?'

'Sure, I've got a dark horse. I'll lay you any money you like, Grey Dawn will win the Derby.'

'Grey Dawn?' the clown doubled and screeched his laughter. 'Grey Dawn . . . here he is.' The crowd yelled exuberantly as Billy Rocca on the grey draught horse broke into the ring.

'Hi! Hi!' Dan called, 'where are you going?'

'Going?' Rocca pulled up, 'I'm going to win the Mallee Derby, Mr. Ring-master.'

'You're going to win the Derby – on that?'

'My oath,' Rocca boasted. 'She's a dark'un this mare, mister. Fastest mare in the Mallee.' Roars and guffaws of laughter shook the roof of the tent. 'I don't mind telling you . . .'

Rocca slithered down the big grey's massive quarters and Dan stooped for him to whisper in his ear.

'You don't say,' Dan pattered. 'Think she's good enough to have a bit on. Well, I don't mind telling you she looks more like as if you'd nicked her out of one of the plough teams about here. She looks the champion heavy weight of a racer . . . and you're the champion light weight jockey, aren't you, Mr. Rocca?'

'That's me. I can talk horse.' The dwarf strutted away and made several futile, footling attempts to mount his great steed while Jack fastened the lunge round his shoulders. As the mare lumbered off Billy ran after her. Catching hold of her flowing tail, he hoisted himself by it, sustained by the lunge, and crawled on to the middle of her back again. He clung to her neck, tried to throw his arms round it, bouncing up and down like an india-rubber ball.

'She's the chance of a life-time,' he yelled. 'The biggest bloomin' monty ever started on a racecourse.'

'What did you say her name was?' one of the boys called from the audience.

'Grey Dawn,' Rocca called. 'She was got by "Moonlight" out of "Paddy Murphy's Plain."'

The countrymen roared heartily. This was their way of saying the mare had been stolen.

The Derby consisted of Rocca racing round the ring with Gina and the boys three times.

'I'll lay the winner! I'll lay the winner!' . . . the clown pranced and yelled. Men from the audience threw him a bet or two.

Rocca tumbled from the grey's broad back, climbed up

by her tail, held on the lunge worked by Jack Dayne.

The horses went three times round the ring, Rocca galloping the grey to pass Gina and the boys.

'Last lap to go,' the clown yelled, 'I'll lay the field. Ten to one on Beauty. Two to one against Bonnie and Beeswing. A hundred to one the Grey.'

As the fun and excitement grew louder and rougher, Gina and the boys held back their horses, and Billy on the grey draught mare cloppered past them to the winning post.

People laughed till they wept, shrieked helplessly. All the stolid red faces split in half, mouths gaping and bellowing, emitted strange helpless cries of glee and exhaustion. A woman had to be taken out in hysterics and a fat man in the front row shook and howled as if he would never stop laughing.

It was sweltering in the crowded, one-poled tent. The crowd seemed to have melted and run together like a large piece of pink and white cocoanut ice. The kerosene lamps smoking, filled the yellow-lit enclosure with acrid fumes. The boys cried their peanuts and boxes of lollies between the acts in which they appeared, and Rabe, a little more drunk than usual, struck his tunes, high, low, flat, and in so many keys, that Dan had to go and remonstrate with him.

When the melody of the Blue Danube drooled seductively, Beauty, the beautiful white mare cantered into the ring, led by Lord Freddie, her neck arched, a bearing-rein through the ring on her roller. Gina in pink tights and a spangled ballet skirt ran in after her, whip in hand, and skimming from the side of the ring as the mare went by, jumped to her back, landing sideways on the broad hindquarters.

The red faced young man in the front row, who had clapped and applauded vociferously all the evening, stirred and leaned forward. The crowd clapped delightedly at sight of the girl who was down on the programme as Gitana, the gypsy.

Gina dropped to her feet, ran and vaulted again, this time arriving on her feet on the Beauty's back; she danced pointing and moving her toes as she tossed kisses.

A kiss fell in the direction of the young man who had brought the grapes to the white gate in a fence near his home that morning. He half-started as if to catch it. Gina smiled as Beauty loped on in her slow, easy stride. She slid to the ground, turned a hand spring and running caught the mare again and swung to her back as if this were the easiest way in the world to mount a horse.

There were 'Bravos!' and loud cries of admiration when she had jumped through the hoops and gone half round the ring, standing on her hands on Beauty's back, legs drooped over her head. As she ran out to dress for her turn with both the white horses, Gina called to Lord Freddie:

'A bit more resin for her back, Freddie. She's sweating like a pig.'

Dan and Rocca went on fooling with the elephant while Gina shed her ballet skirt, tied a coloured handkerchief round her head and took a breather.

Billy humped a swag for this act. He had tied on a flaxen wig and painted his nose red.

'Tell you what, Mr. Ring-master,' he said, 'what you want for this show is a tiger.'

'I do.' Dan agreed. 'Can you tell me where I can get a tiger.'

'Course I can. I got a tiger.'

'You got a tiger?'

'Yes I got a tiger. You can have him cheap.'

'Cheap? What do you call cheap?'

'One hundred pounds.'

'Well, that is cheap for a tiger – dirt cheap for a good man-eating tiger.' Dan reminisced about the ferocity of tigers he had known and handled, and what a mess the last one Haxby's bought had made of his keeper and trainer.

He and the dwarf struck a bargain. Dan handed over his cheque for one hundred pounds and asked for delivery of the wild beast as soon as possible.

'He's here. I got him now,' Billy cried, and produced from under a bag on the ground a stuffed toy of yellow velvet with black stripes, about the size of a puppy, which he pulled along on a string.

The children clapped and shouted happily while Dan chased the swaggie out of the ring.

Lord Freddie brought in the white horses, Beauty and Bonnie, their reins knotted. They cantered round the ring and Gina ran in after them, her brown limbs bare but for trunks of a red and yellow figured material, a waist-coat of the same stuff laced across her breast, large brass ear-rings in her ears and a handkerchief over her head. Usually she enjoyed this turn more than any other; it was her pride and joy. The horses had little jangling bells on their breast plates and swung at a steady canter. But to-night she was tired and Rabe was giving their waltz tune with uncertain rhythm, making strange hoots and blares which upset the horses.

Gina ran and jumped, stood laughing, on Beauty, arms curved above her head. She jumped to Bonnie's back; the mare was frightened and jerky, quickened her pace.

Gina slid to the ground; let the horses run, then took her leap again, landing on her feet on the broad flat back of the older mare. But still the horses were moving too fast for her to throw the somersault she was waiting for. Trying again for her position, Bonnie rooted; Gina's foot slipped. She saved herself to the onlookers by turning a handspring as she hit the sawdust.

'What the hell's the matter with you, to-night,' Dan muttered.

'She's all of a sweat,' Gina gasped.

Rocca gambolled and made some silly game of her hand spring to divert the audience. Freddie ran after the horses and rubbed resin across Bonnie's back under pretence of petting her.

Dan flicked his whip and the white horses took their customary gait around the ring again. Gina ran from the side of the ring for her leap, sprang and landed on Beauty as she always did. A wild graceful figure, she stood a moment poised with pointed feet and stretched for her balance before Bonnie could hump her back as she had been doing. She flung for her somersault and took it neatly on Beauty. From Beauty she had to poise and somersault back to Bonnie.

What happened it was hard to say; the horse against the ring seemed to have shied. Gina threw short and fell.

The band should have held its breath for that moment; but it blared on as Gina crashed between the horses. They galloped, maddened by the shrieks and yells which went up from the audience. Jack caught the horses as they dashed to the exit. Dan shouted: 'Sit down. Keep your seats please!'

Lord Freddie and Rocca ran to Gina where her limp,

brown body in its glittering trappings lay on the saw-dust.

The crowd surged, yammering excitedly:

'Is she dead? What's happened? Is it all right? She isn't killed is she?'

And Dan kept on vociferating: 'Keep your seats, please. Sit down. Sit down, everybody.'

Jack, Charley and Bruiser ran in with a mattress. The young man who had watched Gina all the night from a front seat, was in the ring beside the girl almost as quickly as Rocca and Lord Freddie, as if he had a right to be there.

Gina could not move. Was she conscious? They did not know. There was a bloody gash on her forehead where a horse's hoof had struck her; but it was her back that seemed to hurt most.

People stood up on the seats to see what had happened, swayed and heaved out of their places; but awed by Dan's shouting, kept back from the ring.

'I've got a car,' the young man said, 'I could take her to the doctor.'

He helped Jack, Lord Freddie and Bruiser to carry the mattress with Gina on out of the ring, while Dan Haxby, sweat pouring from his forehead, addressed the audience, apologising for the unfortunate accident which had marred their night's entertainment.

'An accident, a slight injury to one of the riders,' he explained, trying to restore calm. 'Nothing serious. Please take your seats, ladies and gentlemen, and we will continue with our programme.'

Some of the women and children went out; but most of the people sat down in their place again and in a few moments were laughing and clapping Rocca who in the robes of a baby was being presented to the ring-master by Lord Freddie as the latest addition to his family.

Billy was furious with Dan for going on with the show, although he knew the showman's motto: 'Keep going whatever happens.' It was all in the luck of the game. A showman had to keep faith with his public. He had guaranteed certain items for an evening's amusement, had been paid for them, and must deliver his goods.

There were still two acts to be gone through. Rocca shrieked at the audience in Italian and Malay, dancing with passion.

Dan knowing what was the matter, cursed and threatened him under his breath; but the crowd, thinking Rocca was playing the baby, as he squalled and threw himself about like that, laughed unrestrainedly. The more he screeched, the more they roared their great helpless laughter.

'Devils, damn swine,' Rocca yelled, 'devils and swines!'

The crowd had melted and swollen together for him. He could see through the blood-mist over his brain, only rags and faces, simmering and swimming as it were on top of a pot, swayed this way and that by their laughter; laughter as harsh and explosive as the gases of a sewer; gross easy laughter, rumbling, and chuckling. Shouts and screams of laughter, sobbing and snuffling to tears, giggling, gurgling and guttering away.

Laughter, Billy got it, in every tone and key, guffaws and roulards of laughter. He had only to stand before the crowd for it to laugh; that raucous blare to lash round and scourge him. If he fell, or sat down, people laughed the more, and to poke out his tongue, or pull faces provoked a many-throated baa-ing frenzy and ecstasy. So droll the little figure of the man, its strut and toddle. Caricature of man though he was, Rocca got back on the crowd, by caricaturing the airs of its most respected citizens.

'Who are you?' Dan asked, when Rocca first entered the ring in a town of any importance.

'Oh me,' Billy would reply, strolling about and smoking a cigar made of brown paper, nearly as big as himself, 'I am the Gord Mayor of this town.'

There might have been some shame and pity in the laughter which inundated him; but Rocca never caught those notes. He was made to be laughed at, and lived on the laughter he stirred, though he cursed laughter and hated the crowd that laughed, as all men hate the gods whose puppets they are. His face was a suffering mask, under its paint, on nights like this when the hard-working country folk laughed themselves to hysterics and tears. He was Life's joke at itself, he believed. His mind as fine and straight as the bodies of these people. Their minds as deformed, childish, undeveloped, paddling soft and helpless as his limbs.

But that night as he saw the faces he loathed, blurred and boiling together with laughter across the ring, beside himself with rage and grief, Rocca shrieked and screeched at them in all the languages he had ever heard, one of those tempests of insane fury to which he was liable, shaking and overwhelming him.

'Is she dead or dying?' he howled. 'What do you care? Does it matter to you? You laugh. Devils . . . mean devils . . . worms of devils. May you roast in hell! Boil in everlasting damnation. God Almighty blast your putrid souls!'

And the crowd rocked with laughter, roared and yelled

at the fury of the little man. It was titanic; but his arms and legs so absurd as he ran about shouting and spluttering.

Dan had to grab Rocca by the back of the neck and trot him out of the ring finally; and Jack and Lily ran on for their last turn with the boys on the trapezes. There was terror in their hearts. With trembling limbs, nervous apprehension in every movement, their minds full of Gina, the stifled agony of her cries, they went through their act, descended, bowed and skipped out through half-hearted clapping and applause. For, despite the way people had laughed with Rocca, at him rather, the accident had cast a gloom, and the crowd drifted away gratefully, to gossip about it and the girl who had fallen between the two white horses.

39

CHAPTER 4

THAT crying, eerie and unconscious, the sobbing moan arrested in agony!

Through the warm starlit darkness, Will Murray steered, sweating with each bump and jerk the car gave on the rough, unmade road, each cry wrung from the girl stretched on the mattress behind him. She was lying there on the floor of the car, scarcely conscious, as she had lain under the smoky flare of the circus lamps.

Will thought he knew every twist and turn of the road into Mallee where the doctor lived; but he had never realised it was so rough; never known it was so full of ruts and old roots. He cursed the road and the darkness, the long wheel tracks through shorn harvest fields the circus had come over that morning. His own home standing back among river gums, their silvery grey trunks clear in the starlight flashed past; he saw the glimmer of whitewashed sheds about the old house as if they did not belong to him. His thought and feeling were all with the girl lying there in the car behind him; his dream of her.

He had never suffered as he did with each jolt of the car; each cry Gina uttered. A nightmare of a drive it was. He had not waited for anyone to come with him, but had brought her in to the doctor as fast as he could.

Lights of the township, glittering there on the edge of

the plains were like sequins on the girl's dress. How glad he was to see them. Mallee. He had begun to wonder whether he had lost his way. It seemed such a long time before they winked up from the distance. And he was so rattled, unnerved. It was hideous to think of what had happened and this bumping on interminably over the rough road.

'Why Will –' the doctor's sister exclaimed, when he drew up before a buff-coloured, wooden house in the township, jumped out of the car, and went to the open door.

'There's been an accident at the circus,' the young man said, his broad pleasant face wrenched with horror.

'Geoff's up the river. Was called out an hour ago,' she explained. 'But he ought to be back any minute.'

'She's here . . . on a mattress. Can we put her in the hospital?'

'Of course. I'll light up. The place is empty. There's no nurse; but we're expecting one by to-night's train.'

'Here, you chaps!' Will hailed a couple of men who were standing around the pub a few doors down the street. They helped him to carry the mattress with Gina on from the car into the small clean room of Dr. Geoffrey Heathcote's cottage hospital in Mallee.

After laying the mattress gently on a bed against the wall the men got out of the room, as quickly as possible, swearing a dazed pity and consternation.

'God, but it's awful!'

Gina was crying out and moaning. Her dark hair pushed back from her forehead, showed the brass rings still in her ears. Her face was wet with sweat, the painted red lips fluttering over the breath of her agony, all the beautiful young brown body bare but for the spangled, red and yellow trunks round her thighs, the waist-coat over her breasts.

'If only I could stop yelling,' she cried. 'But it's all right, isn't it? It will be all right, Lil?'

'She thinks you're her sister,' Will explained. Miss Heathcote pulled a sheet over the girl.

Gina looked at Will with the brilliant eyes of her pain and bewilderment, taking him in. He seemed to have been with her a long time; to have been standing beside her, giving her something to hold on to through all the suffocating unconsciousness, the strangling agony of the pain at her back.

She did not know him, and yet she felt as if she had never known anyone better than this young man. He seemed to have been with her for hours, suffering with her; wrestling against the pain with her.

'You're . . . very kind,' she gasped. 'It's . . . awful good of you.'

Will Murray had never suffered as he did this night, suffered with a physical and mental anguish which was strange to him. It was not so much that this was the girl he had been sweet on a few hours ago; but that she was a creature in pain; such pain as he had never imagined. The doom beyond he foresaw vaguely. He would have shot an animal who was suffering like that; could not sleep in the winter if his beasts were not fed and sheltered for the night.

'It's all right . . . it'll be all right,' he muttered, giving the only soothing he knew.

As the pain attacked like some fierce animal, invisible, racking and devouring, Will put out his hand and Gina clung to it. Every tremor of her lithe, strong body went through him.

'By God, she's plucky,' he exclaimed.

'It's all right,' Gina cried, . . . 'it'll be all right . . . It's only . . . a crick . . . in me back, really . . . It's not broken. My back's not broken, is it Lil? Where are you Lil? . . . It's not that . . . me back's not broken, is it?'

'No, no,' Will murmured, consoling her.

'I was so tired,' Gina breathed. 'It was . . . awful hot in the tent . . . Must've slipped or something . . . Lil? Oh, tell her . . . to give Mum a hand . . . won't you?'

Will realised that the hand he was holding was as hard and work-grimed as his own.

'Don't let them tell Mum about me . . . She's six month's you know . . . It'd be bad for her.'

Will drew his hand away.

'I promised to go back and bring them,' he said, his voice breaking.

'You're not going?'

Dazed, through her pain, Gina's eyes clung to him, as if in the torment and break-up of her world, there was nothing else to cling to.

'No,' Will said. 'I'll stay as long as you want me.' To hell with her people and the cursed show they would not leave, if she were dying, to save her this agony, he thought. Except her mother, of course. She would have come; but Gina herself had cried in her first moment of consciousness:

'Don't tell Mum . . . keep Mum away. I'm all right . . . Tell her I'll be all right.'

Will had understood when he saw the poor woman on the edge of the crowd, clasping her hands and crying: 'Gina! Oh, Gi, what's the matter? Whatever's happened? Won't somebody tell me what it is?'

Lily had hustled her mother away to the covered-in cart.

'Here's Geoff!' The doctor's sister moved from the open window, as a car slowed before the hospital with the low droning hum of a drowsy beetle. A moment later Geoffrey Heathcote, shedding his dusty driving coat and hat on the hallway table, stalked into the room, all his lean sensitive face strung to the need of the girl before him.

He threw back the sheet which covered Gina. Will went outside the room. Gina's quick, wavering cry went up:

'It's all right . . . it'll be all right, won't it Doctor?' And the Doctor's muttered soothing lie: 'Yes, yes, it'll be all right.'

'I've cricked me back . . . it's not broken . . . not that. It couldn't be that, doctor?'

'No. It'll be as right as rain in no time.' The doctor's fingers closed over the wrist of Gina's work-worn hand. He was watching the face of his wristlet watch. When he came out of the room Will met him.

'Broken right across,' Geoffrey Heathcote said, opening his bag and taking from it the black case which held his hypodermic syringe and needles. 'There may be a shred of the vertebra intact; but that's all. X-rays the only chance, if we can get her into Southern Cross.'

'I'll drive you doctor,' Will said.

'Thanks Will, but where are her people? How did it happen?'

Will Murray had never seen this quiet long-headed man who was the only doctor for a hundred miles in every direction, so upset and at a loss.

'This is the only thing I can do.' Dissolving a pellet

in water, he drew the fluid into the fine hollow needle of the syringe. 'Keep her under morphia until we get into Southern Cross. They've got X-ray at the public hospital, and can operate if there's a chance.'

He went back into the neat green and white room, the hypodermic syringe in his hand. Suddenly Will felt queer and sick himself. He walked into the garden and put his hands and head under Miss Heathcote's garden tap.

The doctor came after him.

'How about a drink, Will?' he asked. They went into the house; a wire door banged behind them.

'What a damnable business,' Geoffrey Heathcote exclaimed. 'A beautiful young thing like that – to be broken . . . thrown on the scrap heap of life. And she's got grit, Will, to be sticking it out the way she is.'

'She's got grit all right,' Will agreed. He felt heavy and torpid. Ordinarily he drank whisky circumspectly; the stiff nip Heathcote poured for him had clouded his brain at once.

'Where do you come in, Will?' the doctor asked.

'Me?' Will replied. 'Oh, I was just at the circus.' Then shaken out of himself, 'I was shook on her all right, Doc . . . been following the show around. From Bendigo to Southern Cross, Eagle-hawke, Oldbridge and Narran. But they're awful strict, the circus people. Never got a word in edgeways with Gina until to-night, driving her over.'

Heathcote glimpsed the irony of the boy's confession. He smiled to think of the stolid young farmer caught by this will-o'-the-wisp passion for a circus girl. Caught and crushed by it. A car buzzed down before the hospital. A loud hard voice was raised exclaiming and explaining.

'It's her father,' Will said.

Heathcote went out to the car. 'I can't have her disturbed now. You'd better get home and have a rest, Will. I won't be able to start before six in the morning. New nurse coming up by the express . . . a couple of patients I must see in the town first.'

Daniel Haxby was thanking the man who had driven him with Jack, Rocca, and Lily over from Narran. Noisely, jocosely, laughing and talking, he was assuring everybody that the accident was not serious. He was certain of it.

'Never have a serious accident on Haxby's – not in a dozen years. Of course, old Jumbo tossed Paddy, The Pig, to Kingdom Come a couple of years ago. But then Paddy had put one over on the elephant, fed him on orange filled with pepper, and Jumbo didn't forget – or forgive.'

'Not so much noise, please,' Geoffrey Heathcote said, coming from the garden before his house to the footpath. He was irritated by the frothing of this man who could take life so easily, break it and go on as if nothing had happened. He guessed the bluff behind Dan Haxby's blather; that the show man dared not face the truth. Geoffrey Heathcote, with the fastidiousness of a mind accustomed to deal with facts, disliked him the more for that.

'Oh, Doctor,'– Dan turned ingratiatingly.

'Mr. Haxby, I believe,' Heathcote replied.

'Yes, Mr Haxby of Haxby's Circus,' Dan preened himself. 'We had the misfortune to have an accident at the show to-night. My daughter . . . a young friend in the audience drove her over. Couldn't get away myself until the performance was finished, But it's not serious, I suppose, just——'

'Are you offering an opinion or asking for mine?' Heathcote interrupted frigidly.

'Asking your opinion of course, Doctor.' Dan struck a lower key.

'It's about as serious as it could be.' Conscious of the girl and Jack moving closer to listen, of their haggard, half-washed faces, Heathcote repeated more gently 'as serious as it could be.'

'She's not . . . going to die?' Lily wailed.

'I don't know,' Heathcote replied. 'Her back appears to be broken about the seventh cervical vertebra. If she lives . . . she may never walk again. There is just a chance that the fracture may not be as complete as I fear. An X-ray photograph would show. They have apparatus at the Southern Cross hospital.'

'Then for God's sake let's take her there.'

Heathcote examined the watch on his lean wrist.

'That is what I propose. But she is under morphia, at present. I doubt whether she could stand the journey. Eighty miles . . . over cart tracks for a case of spinal lesion . . . it's almost inhuman to subject anyone to it.'

'But you will go with her. You will administer morphia, Doctor,' Rocca said.

Heathcote looked at the dwarf as though he had not seen him before, surprised by the cultured tone, the mature mellow voice, the air of authority with which Rocca spoke.

'Yes,' Heathcote said curtly. 'I will go with her.' Unconsciously, his voice took the level of the little man's. Here was someone who understood suffering. 'Mr. Murray has offered to drive, and with her father's permission' – Heathcote deferred ironically to Dan Haxby – 'we will take Miss Haxby into Southern Cross hospital as soon as possible.'

As Rocca was going to speak he added: 'At about six in the morning. I can't leave until then. A maternity case in the township which has to be attended immediately.'

'Anything . . . anything!' Dan threw out his hands choked and abashed. 'This has knocked me endways, Doctor. Who'd have thought it. Gina . . . why, she was about the last one you'd ever have thought it could happen to. She was so clever . . . best bare-back and acrobat rider for her age ever I seen in my life. We just thought she couldn't fall . . . nothing could happen to her.'

'She was tired out, that's what was the matter!' Lily cried shrilly. 'Been working night and day for the last week –'

Heathcote smiled at the girl with her frizz of upstanding straw-coloured hair, the paint and chalk-white powder barely washed off her face. Her bitterness and grief attracted him.

'If it had been her sister,' Dan continued, 'nobody 'd have been surprised.'

Anxious to avoid anything in the way of a family quarrel Heathcote interrupted: 'We will leave at about six in the morning. Meanwhile – I must ask you to excuse me.'

As he turned to go away, he caught the misery of Lily's slight figure and following eyes. 'If you would like to sleep in the hospital, my sister will arrange it,' he said. 'But do not go to the patient unless she is restless and asks for you.'

'Dr. Heathcote,' Rocca went on in his clear exquisite English, 'permit me to say how grateful we are for what you are doing. Please let everything be done for Miss

Gina which it may be possible to do. We circus people, it is thought, are sometimes . . . forgetful where money is concerned. I will guarantee the expenses.'

Mechanically Heathcote had taken out his notebook. Amused, he looked down on the dwarf. It seemed absurd to take him seriously. The little man looked so absurd in his dignity. Then ashamed of his amusement, Heathcote saw something of the man behind his mask.

'What name?' he asked.

'Guglielmo Rocca.'

'Thank you, Mr. Rocca,' Heathcote said. 'Rest assured, everything possible will be done for Miss Gina in Southern Cross.'

CHAPTER 5

FLUSH of dawn was in the sky, a smoky haze lying across the horizon of widespread, sun-bleached land as Will Murray swung his car before Dr. Heathcote's cottage hospital in Mallee, next morning.

When Will helped Dr. Heathcote to lift the mattress from the hospital to the car, he scarcely recognised the girl on it. So wan and sleepy looking, she lay, half-conscious, the paint all washed from her face, the gypsy rings gone from the lobes of her ears, her rough coarsely waving dark hair thrown back from the forehead. Yet the eyes, with brilliant, black-ringed and freckled irises were the eyes which had clung to his the night before.

The nurse, who had arrived by train at midnight, in her blueprint frock and white cap fluttered about Gina, arranging pillows, blankets, making her as comfortable as possible. Miss Heathcote came down to the car with a handful of roses. Lily, a little further along the footpath, tears running down her face, was standing gazing at the car in which Gina was lying.

'She may not know you,' Heathcote said to his sister. 'Better not rouse her.'

Miss Heathcote put the roses down beside Gina, unable to speak.

Gina's hand moved. Her hard brown fingers closed over the flowers. She smiled faintly.

'It's awful good . . . of you,' she murmured. 'So kind.'

The doctor laid his well-worn bag containing emergency gear and instruments on the floor and took the seat beside Will. The car moved off, stirring a cloud of light saffron dust. Beyond the scattered white wooden houses of the township, the stubble and paddocks of sun-dried grass stretched far and wide, or the fallows lay bare, ruddy and brown. Ibis, plucking over them, raised the scimitars of their ebony beaks and flew off with faint whistling cries.

Eighty miles over long winding, rough hewn roads, it was, into Southern Cross. Ruckled by heavy rains and baked into hard ridges, the road wound round low rocky hills and over dry river beds. Ordinarily Will would have made the distance in a little over three hours, bucketing along carelessly; but driving as he was this morning, slowly, straining every nerve and sinew to avoid bumps in the roughest places of the road, it was two o'clock before poppet heads of the mines and shafts, slag heaps of the mining township struck the pale blue of the sky before him.

At first Gina had not seemed to feel movement of the car; she had lain very quiet. Heathcote watching her had seen the pain gaining on her. Morphia losing its power, sweat gathered and beaded on her forehead and upper lip. The brown hands were flung out, clutching and grasping sides of the mattress, making their little frenzied efforts at restraint. Low moaning cries broke from her.

'We'll have to stop a moment, Will,' Heathcote said once, and getting out of the car took the girl's wrist between his fingers. He reached for his bag, quickly took out, charged a syringe and injected restorative. He sat beside Gina then and Will Murray drove as he had never done in his life, steadily, and as fast as he dared, knowing every moment counted in the agony of the girl behind him. At last through the town, the hospital loomed before him. He swung past the gates, round the hospital garden and lawns.

It seemed an age before Heathcote came from his interview with the resident medical officer, and stretcher-bearers lifted Gina from the car and carried her away very slowly and carefully, through the arched doors into the wide cool tunnel of the hospital. The place flowed down on Will's brain, the buff walls and green gardens, the hospital doorway opening wide and shadowy.

Gina had been unconscious as she was carried away, out of sight; she had not opened her eyes. Will Murray had seen her head fallen back, her face clear-cut like the face on a coin. Something went out of his life as they carried her away from him into the interior of the hospital: something as gay and beautiful as she had been. Will remembered a horse he had been fond of who broke her leg. It was like that. He had never got over Lady-bird breaking her leg and having to shoot her. He would never get over seeing Gina Haxby carried into the hospital.

Will was sitting crouched over the wheel when Heathcote returned. They were to drive straight back to Mallee.

'We'll have a bite to eat and get back, Will,' Heathcote said, when he stepped into the car and banged the door again. 'I've got a couple of cases I'm anxious about. She's stood the journey pretty well considering. Wonderful constitution. I'm inclined to think the fracture may not be as complete as we feared. Aarons promised to give me a ring this evening. He'll do an X-ray as soon as possible.'

On the long road back to Mallee, Will scarcely seemed to be driving consciously at all. The car skimmed along over ruts and mallee roots, skidding and missing trees and jutting rocks by a breath.

'Well,' Heathcote exclaimed as Will jammed on his brakes in Mallee, 'I don't mind telling you I'm glad to get here, Will. With a patient on board you're the best driver I ever struck. I'd send for you any time. But for a joy ride, I'd as soon take a ticket to Kingdom Come.'

'Oh, I say . . . did I step on it, Doc?' Will asked.

'Step on it? You waltzed all over the bloomin' auction.'

Heathcote wondered, when the young man did not call that evening to hear what the medical officer of the Southern Cross hospital had to say about their patient. Or next day, even.

Meeting him in the street two or three days afterwards, Heathcote pulled up to tell Will that Aarons of the Southern Cross hospital had rung up to say an X-ray photograph showed a thread of the vertebral column intact. He proposed putting Gina in plaster of Paris for three months. There was every possibility the fracture would knit.

'A lesion lower than the seventh cervical and above the sixth dorsal is far more dangerous,' Geoffrey Heathcote explained, betrayed into more or less technical language by his interest in the case. 'A patient usually dies of these injuries due to pressure on the cord. That involves the phrenic nerves which supply the diaphragm, tending to produce a hydrostatic pneumonia.'

'Thank you, Doctor,' Will said.

Heathcote was surprised the young man's face showed so little interest. The information had dazed rather than enlightened Will, he thought. The news did not seem to concern him: be of much importance at any rate. Will Murray looked as well-fed, self-satisfied as he had ever done, the pleasant faced, equable young man, Heathcote had always known, a little duller, perhaps. Flash of that will-o'-the-wisp passion for the circus girl had died out of him, Heathcote told himself.

'By the way, do you know where the circus is now?' he asked.

'Up Swan Hill way,' Will said. 'They're making south, then, I think.'

'Haven't heard from Haxby,' the doctor remarked, his wheel moving again. 'But the dwarf's been into Southern Cross, I believe.'

'Oh, he has, has he?' Will was mildly interested.

'Queer fish,' Heathcote exclaimed.

'I like him,' Will said decidedly. 'There's something about the chap gets me. He's most interesting to talk to. But it's not that. When first you see him, there's nothing to do but laugh at him. Afterwards when you know him a bit . . . the last thing you think of is laughing at him.'

Heathcote was interested Will Murray should recognise a quality he had sensed in the dwarf.

'An inferiority complex taking the disguise of mystery, sagacity,' he ventured.

But that was beyond Will Murray. A light film of rolling dust separated the doctor's car from Will as he glanced across wide tawny paddocks to where beyond the horizon's rim the mining township raised its scraggy works among bare low hills of red and yellow gravel.

CHAPTER 6

THE hospital which the people of Southern Cross boasted was one of the best equipped in the country-side, had an imposing entrance hall and office, under red brick neatly ruled and painted white. The wards were wooden sheds with roofs of corrugated iron, white painted to keep off the heat.

To Gina, the hospital was a place of pain. Pain which gnawed and chewed at her, resistlessly. Pain she fought breathlessly, brown hands doubled; pain that dived and jabbed clawing her over with electric needles, millions of them wringing, screwing, tangling, torturing and tugging fiendishly at every nerve.

For days and nights it was like that with a black-out of fear and unconsciousness. She only realised when she was awake by the pain flaying and devouring her body and brain until she could see and hear no more: drowned in darkness again.

In those pain-racked hours between spasms of a doped drowsiness Gina realised the hospital – a dim whiteness about her . . . other beds . . . the coming and going of sharp heels on a wooden floor . . . a click-clack-clacking . . . women in cotton frocks, blue and white, bending over her . . . a man . . . two men who bared her back and pressed their thumbs into it. Voices weighed down discussing her.

'Is the spinal column irreparably damaged?'

'Will she walk again?'

Wheeled away, she glimpsed the tall black instrument which was to decide her fate. A monstrous thing of wheels, and legs and arms, sinister, huge, it seemed.

After coming from a long darkness, a voice had whispered, a kind voice; and a pretty young face, drifting in a mist, far away, had come closer.

'It's all right . . . it'll be all right, Gina. The plate's a good one, quite clear. Shows the fracture not nearly as bad as we thought.'

So eager and sweet the voice, it made a little song for Gina. Over and over again, the words repeated themselves winding in and out of her consciousness. Her brain clouded, the mists of weakness obliterating everything, carried her away through the air. Yet it came again, that twittering of a little bird.

'It's all right . . . it'll be all right, Gina!'

The sound brought relief rather than the words. They twittered and sang so.

How did Gina know what it meant? That the fracture was not quite as bad as had been feared. That the vertebral column was not broken quite across. In this battle with blind forces in which she was engaged how could an ignorant girl know what words like that meant? Only sounds mattered. Those grave doubtful sounds the doctors had made to each other, and the nurse's voice letting fall soft sweet notes about her.

When she looked into Nurse Edie's sensitive, eager face, with the brilliant eyes of unfathomable suffering, Gina's gratitude unnerved the girl who was new to her work, a probationer, not used yet to purgatories the spirit suffers in its conflict with disaster and disease.

'You've just got to stick it out; be brave and Doctor

says you're going to be all right,' Nurse Edie Grey said.

'True, Nurse?' Gina begged in her aloneness and horror of the doom before her.

'You are brave, Gina,' the nurse's voice was not quite as steady as it might have been. 'We all think so. You're just the bravest girl we've ever had in here.'

Gina could not speak. Only the faint glimmer of a smile, the shine of tears welling in her hazel eyes with their wide black pupils told the watcher that she understood. There had been no tears in Gina's eyes before, only stark agony.

After that came an operation to fix the dislocated vertebrae, the strapping and binding down of shoulders and back into a plaster of Paris jacket which Gina was to wear for three months, lying flat on her back without moving.

Nothing but her youth and sturdiness, her grit and extraordinary vitality pulled the girl through the first of those awful days, exhausted as she was by suffering and the use of drugs. Heathcote had been impatient of the delay, resented the unnecessary dilatoriness of hospital doctors where a bone setting was in question. But hospital routine refused to be hustled or jostled out of its course. Gina was operated on after she had been in hospital three days, and laid-up in plaster of Paris for three months.

'Gord, not to move for three months,' she gasped, when they told her. But she could speak and smile then; see something of the ward about her, the long room with beds on either side, a table with flowers in the centre, floors that flashed up at her when the afternoon sunshine sprawled across them.

'Never been still three minutes before in all me born days!' she explained to Nurse Grey. And when Grey, interested, had wanted to know more, Gina went on:

'I was born on the road, as we say. Mum and Dad were with Wirth's circus then, before Dad started on his own. He was riding and training horses, and she was doing wardrobe . . . mending tights and making trunks. She's real good at costume, Mum. Does all of ours.'

A shadowy thoughtfulness had taken her mind from what she was saying Nurse Edie guessed. Gina was wondering about her people on the road now. Where were they? What were they doing? The nurses had been surprised there were so few enquiries from her family. Only the dwarf had come to see her and he had not been admitted, because Gina had just been given a sleeping draught. The Heathcotes rang up every day, the doctor or his sister.

'Oh, I forgot to tell you,' Nurse Edie lied cheerfully, 'there was a long distance call for you last night.'

'Where was it from?' Gina asked.

'Duck Creek, I think. Somewhere up river.'

'Have they got as far as that?' Gina realised she must have been in hospital much longer than she imagined. 'It's Mum,' she said after a moment. 'I'm a bit worried about her. She was six months you know . . . had a bad time when Bobbie was born. That's why I didn't want them to let her get upset about me.'

'I see,' Nurse Grey was brushing out Gina's rough burnished hair. 'I suppose they've told her you're all right. And they don't want her to think they're worrying about you.'

'They're that busy. Not a moment to breathe,' Gina said slowly. 'Lil would do what she could. But if anybody rings up again, would you ask how Mum is?'

'I'll tell them in the office to be sure to,' Edie Grey said.

But when she was off duty herself that evening, remembering the frown and brooding look which had overcast Gina's face at thought of her mother and the expected baby, Edie Grey sent a wire to Lily Haxby.

A week or so later, there was a letter for Gina, a letter card bearing the stamp of a post office nearly a hundred miles from Duck Creek. It was from Lily, a few lines in a scrawling, round, childishly-unformed handwriting.

'Dear Gina,' it said. 'Just a few lines to let you know Mum's all right. She had a baby last week and it's a boy. It's what they call a seven months' – and getting on fine. We're staying here over the week-end, show in Murray Town, Monday. All well and send love. Hoping you're better, love and kisses, Lil.

'P.S. It's hot as hell here and business gone to pot. Jack wants me to clear out as soon as you get back.'

Gina was very happy to have received a letter; although the brightness of her face faded a little as she went over it again.

She knew the words almost by heart before she read them to Nurse Edie, all but the post script.

'You don't mean to say your mother and the new baby are going on with the show?' Grey exclaimed.

'Oh yes,' Gina said, 'Mum can't bear hospitals. Once she stopped in town to have a baby. But most of us have been born in the waggon, or on the road.'

'Goodness. And you're all alive to tell the tale!'

'Two babies died,' Gina said, wondering at the nurse's amazement. 'But Dad says it brings us up hardy, being born and reared in the open like that.'

'I wish he could have babies and see how he likes it!' Nurse Edie exclaimed indignantly. 'Why, women come into our maternity wards and have a week or fortnight's rest at least afterwards. It gives them and the babies a chance.'

Gina looked at her with troubled eyes.

'Mum's fair worn out,' she said. 'I don't know how she stands it. There's six of us and two dead. She's always up and about at the end of a week.'

Nurse Edie cleared away her washing gear and mopped down the small white locker beside Gina's bed. Her hands flew about briskly. She could not allow herself to speak. Gina, understanding that she was indignant, disapproving, resolved to know more of this.

The world of the hospital was so different to any she had ever known. But then she had known nothing except the world of the circus. The world of the dirty white tents, the waggons, cart horses, show animals, wild beasts in the menagerie, a world of acrobats, contortionists, wire walkers, clowns, tumblers, wild beast trainers, performing dogs a.d elephants who stood on barrels, waving short legs in the air. A world of wandering mushroom tents, spawning on bare paddocks beside some small town and then off again; trailing the long dusty roads between harvest fields as they had lately; camping by rivers to fish, crossing blue tumbled mountain ranges and coming on green valleys with farms about them, farms and herds of cows; places that smelt of milk and wheat, where the farmer people gave you milk and apples, or melons; you got fresh water to drink and a bath sometimes. A dirty, strenuous world. Cruel, courageous, a hard, hungry world for all the glitter and flare of its laughter; but a good world, her world.

Gina was sick with her longing of it; her being surged restlessly. She would have given anything in the world to be moving with the show to-night: to be packing up, hustling and scolding everybody to get a move on. To hear Dan and Rabe after their drinks for the night, quarrelling good-naturedly, count the cash, and go round to see the animal cages were all locked and the waggons loaded to start at once, or first thing in the morning.

This world of the hospital was so different, a well-ordered, antiseptic world of pain and cleanliness where everything happened in just the same way every day. People spoke in careful, pleasant polite voices. They smiled like that too, with measured tepid glances; the nurses' heels click-clacked on the polished floors. The white dress of the sisters and the blue print frocks of the probationers were so spotless, so uncrushed, always.

You ate, slept, said good morning to the matron when she made her tour of inspection. Thermometers, bed pans, all the comings and goings of the wards were regulated in the same precise, implacable fashion. Only cries of pain and delirium, the moans and whimpering of unconscious suffering, defied the rule of the hospital: the smells of dressings, disinfectants and anaesthetics persisted.

There was something behind and beyond all this systematic way of living, Gina realised as she lay watching, studying all that went on about her. She wished to get at it. Her energy, the eager enquiring brain which had survived those first weeks of torture, was alert and avid.

She had fought her way through the days when she lay in her plaster waist-coat, with such grit, a cheery smile refusing to acknowledge defeat. Sturdy, uncomplaining, she faced through days and nights when everybody knew how weary she was; how almost at the end of her power to endure.

'I'm fine, Doctor,' she would gasp. 'I'm getting on fine. Soon I'll be able to start practising again . . . won't I? Never do to get stiff on it.'

No one had the courage to tell her it would be a great thing if she were able to walk again; that the days of her riding, vaulting and somersaulting from the back of a moving horse were over.

She began by asking the meaning of words she heard the nurses use often and quite ordinarily. A-sepsis, antiseptic, cerebral, haemorrhage. Then it occurred to her that she might make good use of the months before her.

'Never been to school,' she explained to Nurse Edie one evening with the brilliant smile everybody found so irresistible. 'Do you think I could have some books and learn a bit, here?'

'Of course,' Edie Grey agreed. 'What would you like?'

'Oh something to tell me about the sort of things you know,' Gina said. 'A-sepsis . . . and all that.'

Edie had given her a few pamphlets, the sort of leaflets which were handed to mothers leaving the hospital, as to the care of their own health and their children's. Gina consumed them quickly, eagerly, asking innumerable questions. Edie Grey lent her a text book on physiology. Still Gina asked questions, demanded explanations. The nurses exclaimed at the way she read; her brain seized on so swiftly, and retained what it read.

'If I could remember things like you do, Gina, I wouldn't be a bit afraid of my exams at the end of the year,' Nurse Grey said.

Gina had been in the hospital nearly a month when Edie came from the end of the ward, smiling, one afternoon.

'Here's a visitor for you, Gina,' she said.

Gina looked up to see Will Murray walking between the rows of beds towards her.

Awkward and self-conscious, his sun-red face very serious, the young man stood beside her bed, and Gina knew she was blushing for the first time in her life. Will only knew she had been pale, went red suddenly, and did not look in the least like the girl he had known. He would never have recognised her; and said so. He felt stupid uncomfortable.

Edie brought him a chair and chattered cheerfully. 'Gina did not expect a visitor,' she said. 'You must not stay very long.'

'It's awful good of you,' Gina said. It was the only thing she seemed able to say to him, 'You're very kind.'

'Not at all.' Will cleared his throat. He was wishing he had not come. Why had he come, he asked himself. He had heard from the Heathcotes all there was to know. The chances were she would be able to walk, but never ride or turn a hand spring in her life again.

The ruddy brown of her skin was pale biscuit-coloured now; her hand flung across the white cover of the bed, quite clean and lady-like.

In the next bed, a patient just come from the operating theatre was vomiting desperately. The smell of ether and chloroform hanging about enveloped and sickened Will.

'Where's the circus? Have you been lately?' Gina asked desperately, as he did not speak.

'No,' Will said. He held himself back from saying 'I never want to see another circus . . . not as long as

I live. Cripes,' – he jumped up, as the patient in the bed nearby was sick again – 'I can't stand it. You'll have to excuse me.'

He walked quickly away down the narrow track of cocoanut matting between the beds.

'Swob,' Nurse Edie said indignantly, as she saw him go. 'He didn't even ask how you were.'

'Oh well,' Gina parried. 'It was good of him to come, wasn't it? And he was good to me you know that night . . . God, how good he was!'

CHAPTER 7

THROUGH those long months, as Gina lay in her plaster jacket, she became almost as familiar with the life of the hospital as she had been with the life of the circus. Everybody gossiped and joked with her, wards-maids, nurses, workmen, even the matron, doctors and secretary whose office was near the entrance door to the hospital. An over-worked, pale young man, with large round paned spectacles, he kept the records of the hospital, wrestled with problems of up-keep and expenditure, looking out upon everything and everybody as if they caused him nothing but worry. Scurrying through the wards, now and then, he stopped to tell Gina where the circus was, give her a letter from Lily, or a bundle of magazines.

She knew what was going on all over the hospital every day. Had learned the routine of kitchens, laundries, and out-patients' departments. If an operation was being performed, she knew who was operating, and why; which nurses were in the theatre. Who was on, and who off duty, she remembered as well as the nurses themselves; heard stories of illnesses, and the life histories of patients and their families, as well as yarns of quarrels, love affairs and minor intrigues, shaking the hospital staff itself. There was a feud between Sister Jones, who was in charge of the male surgical ward, and Mac, as the Matron was called. Jones was the surgeons' pet, it seemed, and making a fool of herself about the junior resident; nearly every day brought some tit-bit of Jones's or Matron's hostility to each other.

Gina gurgled over and hoarded every confidence chattered away by the nurses or ward-maids, as they worked beside her, making herself one in spirit with the interests of the hospital. She was as pleased to hear that Charley, as Dr. Charles Bell, the junior resident was called, had backed a winner at the races on Saturday, as the nurses themselves, and as surprised that he had given his ladies' tickets to a pretty little girl, in the tobacconist's shop, beside the railway station.

Everybody took Gina magazines, newspapers, books to read. She had poetical, theosophical and religious pamphlets, Christian Science journals, children's comics and novels with gaudily coloured wrappers. Dr. Aarons lent her *Wonders of the Universe*, and Wells' *Illustrated History of the World*, Matron Mackay some little suede covered books of poetry.

Poetry, Gina decided, she did not like.

'It's silly, I think,' she said, 'to say things like that. Why do people? You have to wonder what they mean. And then poetry is always talking about the scenery.'

'What do you like best to read, Gina?' Matron Mackay asked.

'Oh, these and these,' Gina replied, fingering Dr. Aarons's copies of *Wonders of the Universe* which lay beside her, and Edie Grey's text book on anatomy, biology and psychology. She had made herself very popular with the nurses by telling their fortunes, after reading an article on palmistry, in a magazine, too.

Her sturdy cheeriness and response to kindness won everybody who came in contact with Gina. She had sympathy for everyone, the rare irresistible smile of a sunny, exalted character. As she became accustomed to lying there in her bed near the big window at the end of the ward, and the ache of her back subsided, something of the old gay charm of her circus manner returned.

'She's intelligent and witty, a most interesting girl,' Matron remarked to Dr. Aarons, one morning as Gina's term of convalescence was nearing an end. 'We shall be quite sorry to lose her. I don't think she suspects yet, that she won't be able to go on with her circus work.'

'Better prepare her for disappointment,' Aarons said.

'I'll tell Nurse Grey,' Matron replied. 'She has a real affection for Gina.'

During those first months when she was becoming accustomed to the life of the hospital, Rocca had come to see Gina.

It was Grey's day off, and the girl who was taking her place hurried up to Gina, smiling.

'Another visitor for you, Gina,' she said, 'the funniest little man.'

Rocca had walked into the ward, carrying a bouquet of flowers almost as big as himself.

Women in the beds about Gina craned their heads to see him, gasping and exclaiming, giggling and turning to stare again.

'What is it?' they asked each other.

Gina saw Rocca in a new grey suit with the flowers. Never had he looked so grotesque to her. She was so used to him that she had never thought much of his unusualness; his deformity had been something for the show ring; one of the assets of the circus. Billy Rocca as a star performer held the respect of brother artists. There were those like Rabe who thought he earned his crust easily; but Jack and the boys recognised he made the most of himself and worked for his living, like the rest of them.

Here it was different. In the hospital, toddling towards her in his coat, waistcoat and trousers of light grey tweed, hat and flowers in one hand, sight of Rocca struck Gina with a stab of revelation.

Would she be like that – deformed, a monstrosity?

In the agony of the moment, she lost sight of Billy. And then, he was standing beside the bed, looking at her, his face ghastly. He had guessed her thought with that quick sensitive brain of his, and his trouble was greater than hers. An anguish of mind shook him, as he leaned against the bed, the flowers in his hand trembling.

'I shouldn't have come,' he cried, when he could speak. 'I'm sorry. I wouldn't have if I'd thought. If——'

But Gina put out her hand, so thin and ladylike now. 'Billy!' she laughed shakily. 'I'm that glad to see you. You see nobody's been . . . and . . .'

'I thought . . . I thought – he muttered brokenly.

Nurse Peggy had brought a stool, seeing the little man's distress. He sat down, putting his hat of dove grey felt on the locker beside Gina, with the flowers. Wiping his forehead with a handkerchief in which there was a thread of mauve, the same colour as the shirt he was wearing, he stared at her unhappily.

'Tell me all about everybody,' Gina begged. 'How's Mum . . . and where are they, Billy? How did you come and what have you been doing?'

It was what he had come to do; to give her the news of the show, gossip and 'cheer her up a bit,' as he put it to himself. He had hired a car and driven over a hundred miles and would have to face the hundred miles over rough roads back to join the show again.

In a suit case he had brought fresh clothes, bathed and been shaved before presenting himself at the hospital, and bought roses and carnations to bring her, in the township.

Exerting his powers of an entertainer, Rocca told Gina all that had happened in her absence. How the bears got loose: what a chase there had been for them through Duck Creek. Lord Freddie had distinguished himself and caught Mujik who, maddened by perfumes of the bush and some bee-hives the waggons had passed, standing out under trees in a paddock along the road, made off out of the ring during a matinee. Bruiser and Monty had captured the smaller bear, but Lord Freddie would wear the gash on his cheek from Mujik's nails for many a day.

Then there had been a fight with rowdies at Long Reach. Bruiser laid out a couple of miners at the pub one night, and the next night half a dozen men from the shafts and claims about set on to him and Charley while they were loading waggons after the show. It was an all-in go-as-you-please for a while, with Lord Freddie, Dan and Rabe taking a hand. If Rocca himself had not hailed the local policeman on to the spot to stop the fighting, goodness knows what would have happened. As it was Bruiser was beaten-up a good deal, Charley had an eye like a thunderstorm for a week, and there was as much blood about as if someone had been killing a pig.

Gina laughed but was concerned: 'That Bruiser's a damned nuisance,' she said. 'Dad ought to sack him. He gets us into more rows than he gets us out of. It's all very well to keep a man who's a bit of a pug – to deal with drunks and put up a fight if there's a brawl, occasion-ally. But I reck'n Bruiser's over the fence. He *makes* trouble.'

Rocca agreed with her and laughed again.

'Well, he says he is clearing out if you don't come back soon. The show's nothing without you. Business has fallen off, Miss Gina, it's a fact: though your Dad swears we're doing well. Several of the horses have had the strangles too . . . Beauty's been pretty bad. Thought we would have to leave her at Little River, but she's better now. I cut up an apple every day and give it to her for you.'

'Do you?' Gina's eyes filled. 'That is good of you, Billy.'

'I'd have asked Miss Lily to come,' Rocca said reluctantly when it was time for him to go. 'Only there'd have been no one to help your mother.'

'Of course.' Gina understood.

'Next time,' he bent over her hand, as he was saying goodbye, in his courtliest manner, 'next time I will send her – and stay myself to mind the baby.'

Gina laughed. How she laughed! It was worth everything to Rocca that she could laugh like that.

'Oh, Billy!' she cried.

'You see,' he promised. And toddled off down the ward again to the accompaniment of tittering, suppressed and whispered exclamations.

'Isn't he,' Gina said when Nurse Peggy came to put her flowers in water, 'the perfect little gentleman?'

'Is he?' the nurse asked.

'Oh,' Gina explained, back in her world again, 'that's what we say, on the show. But he's better than that, really, Billy Rocca. There's something in him, deep down. I don't know what it is . . . good and kind . . . really good and kind . . . not only pretending, though he's a little devil when his temper's roused . . . and——'

She did not add, as they usually did when Rocca was being discussed on the show, 'he's mad about women.'

They would not understand that here, Gina guessed. They would not be able to make allowances for Rocca as Haxby's could.

Gina remembered how her father had said once, in Billy's hearing, and when she and Lily and her mother were there:

'Oh, Rocca – he's a great man for the ladies, aren't you, Bill? Mad about women!'

And how angry Billy had been. Not that it was not true. Rocca was mad about women, Daniel Haxby had told his wife when Billy joined the circus: and she told the girls. They knew all about the parties Rocca gave in the cities sometimes; parties where everybody got drunk, and the largest and fattest women he chose for himself, made love to Billy. Gina and Lily could not imagine anybody making love to Billy Rocca, although they had no illusions about men or women.

There were men who would do anything, they knew: women also. Rocca? You could not blame him for taking any woman who would take him, if he was like that – mad about women. It was the only thing anybody could say against him anyhow. On the show, he was very distant and respectful to the girls; more a gentleman than anyone they had ever come in contact with, rather a dude of course. He would not do any rough work; his little fat hands were white and always manicured.

He belonged to a different world, to cities and theatres. It was evident. He had never travelled before with a ramshackle show like Haxby's. But he liked it, he said; liked the open air and wandering about the country, sleeping under the stars. It did him good. His health

71

was better; and he had thought he was going to die when Dan Haxby found him in a city hotel, his heart shattering itself against the walls of an exhausted body.

Rocca was grateful to Dan Haxby for having lifted him out of depths of misery and despair. And Dan was grateful to Rocca for the new life he put into Haxby's when he began to work with the circus. In some of the country districts life was so hard and meagre, pleasures so few, people had almost forgotten how to laugh till Haxby's came along, and with Haxby's Billy Rocca.

But Billy had resented Dan's betrayal of his passion and humiliation before women.

'If ever . . . you speak to me in that way again, Mr. Haxby,' he said, his face sallow and quivering, 'I will leave this show immediately.'

'But Billy, I say. I never meant——. I never intended,' Dan stuttered.

'What you meant . . .what you intended were perfectly clear, Mr. Haxby,' Rocca replied sternly. 'But always have I had respect for the women of your family, and I will not permit that you revile me before them.'

He strutted off with his rage and dignity.

'Did you hear that, Rabe?' Dan exclaimed to the bandmaster who lumbered up with Lord Freddie just then. 'Rocca says . . .'

'Poor little devil,' Lord Freddie mumbled, following the blob of the dwarf's small grey-clad body across the yellow grass. 'I suppose he's got feelings like the rest of us.'

Gina herself did not hold what was known as Rocca's weakness, against him. Men were like that she believed. She had no sentimental illusions about them. Gina did not want to have anything to do with men, herself, except as grooms or partners in her acts for the ring. They were all right to put up tents, lumber gear about, she thought; but she could not endure them when they came near her, making soft eyes and wanting to maul her.

Lord Freddie tried to take hold of her once or twice when he was drunk.

'Here, hands off,' she had said, sharply, 'Keep your hands to yourself, Freddie!'

Gina told the nurses about Rocca, Lord Freddie, and Bruiser. She liked talking about them and they liked to hear about the everyday life of the circus.

'Lord Freddie? Is he really a lord?' Nurse Peggy asked.

'Oh yes. Dad gets letters from his mother now and then . . . and money to buy him socks, wool singlets and things,' Gina said. 'Freddie's not all there – and drinks like a fish. But he likes working with horses. His mother's a real nice lady. She came to see Freddie while we was in Adelaide, couple of years ago, and wanted him to go away with her to England. But Freddie didn't want to go. He wouldn't. And she said she thought he was really happier here with us. And so, she left him . . . and went back to England. Sad, isn't it? And him her eldest son. He wasn't always like this . . . had a fall from his horse, or something when he was a young man, his mother said, and has never been the same since. His brother manages his place . . . and all that. And Dad says he's married Freddie's wife. There was a divorce, it was all fixed up after Lady Despard went back to England . . .'

When Dan Haxby first came across Lord Freddie, he was working as yard-man in an up-country hotel, Gina explained. A lanky, cadaverous, unkempt, destitute, half-daft creature living for drinks, he did anybody's bidding in a scared, dazed, spiritless fashion.

'It was cruelty to a dumb animal, that's what it was, Dad said,' Gina told the nurses. 'And Dad can't stand cruelty. You should hear him go off if he catches anybody ill-using an animal on our place. And people think circus folks are cruel to animals! Why you see more cruelty in a town or city any day than you'll see on Haxby's in years. You got to be firm of course, when you're training a beast, or a horse. But you do ten times more by kindness than by getting an animal frightened and nervous. It's sugar and carrots does the trick. And Lord Freddie looked like a cat with a tin tied to his tail, at that pub. Everybody roused on to him. It was: "Lord Freddie!" here, "Lord Freddie!" there, all day . . .'

'Tell us about it, Gina,' the nurses begged.

'Sandy Dawson, who kept the Southern Star Hotel, was a fair pig of a man,' Gina went on, 'he liked to run Freddie around and give him the dirtiest jobs to do because he was a lord and down and out. Made him scrub the bar floors, wash dishes, empty slush buckets and run round after the Chinese cook. Dawson thought it was dead funny, Dad said, to yell: " 'Ere, Lord Freddie clean out them lavatories, damn you, and look sharp about it, or I'll want to know the reason why!" It made his blood boil, Dad said. So he put it up to Freddie he could come along and look after our horses, if he liked . . . and Freddie came.'

'But did they know he wasn't just making it up about who he was?' Nurse Edie asked.

'Oh yes, they knew all right!' Gina said. 'Somebody'd written to the old country and got the strength of it. There was photos and letters from lawyers. And funny

74

thing – Freddie 'll never talk about himself . . . where he came from; why he's out here . . . as if he didn't know or couldn't remember. Only if anybody says to him: "They tell me you're Lord Frederick Despard of Despard and Annersley?" He says: "That is my name," quietly – as if it was the only thing he was sure of, could not forget.'

'Do you like him, Gina?'

'Lord Freddie? Oh, he's all right,' Gina replied. 'Never puts on side. Acts just the same as Bruiser or Charley; goes round with them. If they get drunk, he gets drunk. He's different to when he joined us though. You'd never know he was the same man really. He doesn't look starved and he's lost the tin from his tail. Was as pleased as Punch when Dad gave him a bit of clowning to do, fixed him up, and taught him a few lines, and now he's an artist – like the rest of us! Of course, you can't depend on him. He's a bit moony, and gets on the booze now and then . . . Mum and Billy Rocca both say Lord Freddie may be a shingle short – but there's many shorter who think they're all there!'

'And Bruiser, tell us about Bruiser, Gina!' the nurses begged.

'Bruiser? His name's Brown, and he's our strong man,' Gina laughed. 'Sometimes we blacken him up to look like a negro and tie a skin round his middle, Dad keeps him really to take on any rough who makes trouble at a performance. But he's more trouble than he's worth, Bruiser, I think. He loves fighting . . . can't keep out of a scrap. Everywhere we go, as soon as he gets a few drinks in, Bruiser wants to take on anybody who's willing. If it wasn't for Charley, I don't know what we'd do. Charley and Bruiser's great mates. They go everywhere together, and Charley soft-pedals Bruiser out of all the shindies he can.'

'And what about Charley?'

'Charley? Oh he's one of those weedy-looking fellers, grows a cigarette on the side of his mouth, been a jockey. It's funny. He's "got an 'abit," Bruiser says. You could leave a bag of sovereigns about, and he wouldn't touch 'm, but let it be a gunny bag - and he'll pinch it every time. He can't resist gunny bags, Charley. Any old corn sacks or chaff bags left lying around, he picks up and makes off with. And you know how farmers are about their bags. Charley's done time for stealing gunny bags. Every time, he sees a bag Bruiser shepherds him past it. "Now, then, Charley me boy," he says, " eyes right!" But Charley gets the bag every time. Sometimes he's caught and sometimes he isn't. It was Charley put the others up to going off at Narran, the other day, I bet——'

'The day you were hurt, Gina?'

'Mmm,' Gina brooded, a shadow on her young face.

'Perhaps, if they hadn't gone off like that . . . if you hadn't worked so hard -' Nurse Edie began.

'Oh, no!' Gina stirred. Quickly, loyally she broke across what the nurse was saying. 'It wasn't anybody's fault, really. Just the luck of the game. When can I get up, do you think?'

CHAPTER 8

GINA took it very quietly that she could walk, but that she would never be able to work as a circus rider again. After the long months of her waiting and lying stiff bound in plaster of Paris, she could walk slowly, with pain and uncertainty at first, for all the massage, re-education of muscles she had been given.

Everybody in the hospital seemed very pleased and satisfied that she could walk. Gina did not say she would rather have died than live as she was. She tried to smile; but her face would not work.

How bitter her disappointment after those months of pain and hope, lying waiting and thinking, she tried not to let the nurses and doctors know. It would have seemed ungrateful when everybody had been so kind; done their best for her. Perhaps some few people guessed it was worse than death to her, this; that the doom of her world had descended upon her. Among her own people she would soon become a hated shadow; a thing of ill omen, hidden away, dreaded, kept in the background.

They all knew it, her father and mother, Lil and the boys as they stood in the Hospital entrance hall waiting for Gina. They wished she had died rather than come back to them like this, halting and maimed, leaning on a stick. They understood she would be a drag on them; and they knew she knew what they were thinking. Haggard, with Gina-eyes trying to smile, but nothing else that was Gina about her, except some old clothes she had worn, three months ago, it seemed years, she came towards them.

But Daniel Haxby was a good showman. He bluffed out the meeting before the hospital people. Kissed Gina, said they would soon have her looking more like herself again.

'Healthiest life in the world, ours, Doctor,' he assured Aarons, genially, 'Look at mother and the kids here. Never a day's sickness in their lives. Never an ache or pain, you might say. It's the out-of-doors and exercise . . . plain wholesome food and hard work. Plenty of hard work, Doctor.'

Aarons agreed with him, though Matron Mackay, looking over the gaunt and work-worn woman, the thin brown children, hard and wiry though they were, was not taken in. She caught the wry smile of Lily's thin reddened lips; the aged withering and tightening of her slender youthful figure and pretty face.

'It will make all the difference to Gina,' Mac said. 'She ought really to be on her back for another two years . . . with the least possible exercise. The more rest she has the better her back will be, the straighter and stronger.'

Daniel Haxby gasped for breath. Gina on her back for another two years, in a waggon. My God, what did they think a circus was? A damned convalescent home? But they were all mad, hospital folk, doctors and nurses, he fell back on his pet idea. Had a bee in their bonnets about what you should eat; what you should drink; germ bugs and all that.

Rest? Gina smiled, she knew how much rest there would be for her on the road.

'It's no good trying to thank you,' she said to Dr. Aarons and Matron Mackay.

She could hear the secretary giving Dan a bill for the time she had been in the hospital; listened to Dan exclaiming, apologising. He 'didn't think he'd got all that on him!'

'What is it, Dad?' Gina asked.

'The bill for this little stunt of yours,' Dan said. 'Twenty pounds.'

'There's no hurry . . . no hurry,' Mr. Smith explained, nervously, conscious of Gina's discomfiture and embarrassment. He had rather reckoned on a bad debt.

'Well, this'll have to do for the present.'

Dan handed him a note for five pounds.

'It'll be paid,' Gina murmured desperately. 'It will be paid. I'll see that it is.'

Dan promised to send Mr. Smith instalments of five pounds from time to time.

He shook hands with Mr. Smith, Dr. Aarons and Matron Mackay, Nurse Edie and one or two others of the nurses standing about the hospital door, thanked them with jovial and blustering heartiness for their goodness to his little girl, and went over to the circus waggon. As the tents were up and everything in readiness for the show that night in a mining township eight miles on the other side of Southern Cross, Dan had harnessed up a couple of horses and driven over for Gina.

Gina said her good-byes and the family followed Dan to the waggon. Nurse Edie went with them to see her patient as comfortably seated as possible. She fussed about a cushion and rug for Gina to sit on and ran back to the nurses' quarters for her own. There were only boxes on the floor of the waggon. 'Good-bye. Good-bye, Gina. Don't forget to write!' she called.

Gina fell into her new place on the circus very quickly.

In a few days she was doing the cooking and washing her mother had done for so long. She took the baby to sleep with her so that her mother might get some rest and be able to feed him better. Mrs. Haxby had suckled the child for the first few months and put him on bottles of artificial food when he did not seem to be thriving. He was a sickly wailing little creature.

Gina remembered what she had read in the hospital leaflets about sick babies. She began to do for Lin what she had read should be done for babies. She bathed and fed him, herself, keeping his bottle and teats scalded and wrapped away from the dust and flies. She got fresh milk in each township where the show stopped, and would not let anybody give Lin biscuits or sips of tea at meal times.

Dan Haxby laughed at the hospital ways Gina was introducing to the show; but her mother would not have Gina interfered with. The child improved under her care, at any rate. Gina weighed him every week and wrote down on a card how much he weighed. The boy began to get some colour in his cheeks; not to cry so much, and Mrs. Haxby busied herself with her sewing, mending and making clothes. She looked happier than she had been for a long time. Life was easier for her. She attended to the box office and made new clothes for everybody, although Gina would not allow time to be wasted on sewing for her.

'What's the good of making clothes for me,' she said. 'Nobody sees me. I don't want nobody to.'

She kept out of sight as much as possible, working all day at the back of the waggons, washing dishes or clothes, peeling potatoes, packing and unpacking. A drab, stooping figure, beside the fire, behind the buckboard, scrubbing pots or carrying kerosene buckets, was all anybody ever saw of her, with the child, asleep in a bag hammock she had rigged up for him, or playing, near-by.

She had lost any interest in her appearnce. The bow of her back, which had been slight when she left the hospital was unmistakable now. Gina slumped as she walked, moving with a heavy weariness; her arms hung beside her, long and ungainly, with hands hard and work-blackened. Her rough burnished hair was brushed back from her face, anyhow.

As often as not she slept on a rug on the ground. Nobody seemed to care or bother much what Gina did, and Lin slept beside her. While the show was on sometimes, and everybody busy over at the tents, she read by the light of the fire, or a smoky lantern; more often, stretched on the ground, lay listening to laughter and cheers from the tent, gusts of applause, the rattle and clatter of hands beaten together.

Eyes closed over the ache of her back, she lay, deluged by an unbelievable weariness and suffering. She never spoke of them. She did not give in to them. But her face became old and haggard with her endurance. She talked to nobody but the child now. She seemed to have become a stranger to everybody.

Rocca sought her out and tried to reach her on the old friendly footing. But she could not bear his pity and sympathy. Gina herself did not understand why, but he did. She had to find herself, Billy understood, get used to this sort of life, work it out for herself before she could talk to any one.

'We're different from the rest of them, here, you and me, Gina,' Rocca said to her once when they sat talking beside the waggons, 'We've got better brains than most of them. We think and feel more.'

'Oh, I don't know, Billy –' Gina objected apathetically.

'I hate the sloppy insides people have, the way they bluff, hearty and kind, and are cruel as sharks beneath. Think Gina . . . and act hard, steer straight – it's the only way for us.' He talked earnestly, eagerly, to stir and comfort her; help her to see the way ahead.

'Don't go looking for justice in the way things happen. Where was the justice in what happened to you? There you were, a beautiful young thing. As sweet and unselfish a girl as ever lived! You worked yourself to death helping your mother, doing Miss Lily's tasks as well as your own. And what did you get for it? A knock-out. No. You have got to stand up to things. You must not let life do what it likes with you. You have your brain. Make the most of it. You can make it pull you out of any hole you are in. And you must.'

Gina listened without seeming to absorb the meaning of what Rocca was saying. He continued, the clear swift torrent of his speech claiming her attention at last.

'Once you were young and beautiful. Now you're young; you've got a brain. Don't let them smash you the way they're doing . . .'

'Don't seem to want anything, but to be smashed-up and go out,' Gina said.

'But there's the kid.'

'I suppose I've got to stay and look after him,' Gina agreed. 'Dad's looking to him to learn my work. The others are all too scared to try, now. I'm a Jonah . . . A cripple on the show always brings bad luck, you know. But they say, Lin will grow up without knowing about –

the accident. He won't have his spirit broken to start with . . .'

Billy had come to her again one night when she was lying on her back behind the covered-in cart.

He sat down at a little distance from her, dressed for his jockey turn with the grey draught mare.

'Did you know I was going away, Miss Gina?' he asked.

Gina did not look down from her gazing among the stars.

'Dad said something . . .'

She remembered vaguely having heard Dan growling that Rocca was talking of leaving the show, hoping he could be induced to stay on.

'Did he tell you why?'

'No.'

'It is . . . because . . . I am afraid I shall kill him . . . if I stay.'

Gina stared at her in surprise. His face was a mask of fury, like one a Japanese conjurer had carried about with him.

.'I never felt it before.' Billy's voice hurried. 'I never felt I could kill a man . . . But I am afraid now . . . I hate your father so. He drives me to madness.'

Gina sat up. She could not imagine what had come over Rocca.

'But what has he done? Why——'

'Oh,' he cried, 'it's you . . . it's because of you, Miss Gina. Who is to blame for what happened but him? He worked you to death. He gave you no rest. He took your beautiful young body . . . all your youth and grace and radiance. He was reckless with them. He has been

83

a showman all his life. He knows how careless he was of you. He knows I am right. I told him that night.'

Gina remembered now, she had heard something of a row between her father and Rocca, after the accident. Lily told her that Rocca had thrown a knife at Dan Haxby, and called him a murderer. Billy had been ill for days as a result of the rage he got himself into; and had refused to more than walk sulkily through his turns.

'Oh, I don't know, Billy,' she said. 'It was an accident. Nobody's fault as far as I can see.'

Rocca swore, words which spluttered and spattered about; although Gina did not know what they meant.

'He took your life . . . broke it and threw you aside. If I could have forgiven him . . . I can't now. Never. Never will I forgive that man the damage he has done. To the day of my death will I curse and revile him for what he does to you now. I cannot stay . . . and see and not . . . kill him some day.'

'But Billy – –'

There was no stemming his rage and grief.

'I have no right to think or feel about you so . . . abortion of a man that I am. But to me you are always that girl you were. I would die to serve you.'

Gina was silent. She did not know what to say.

Rocca continued more quietly.

'What I want to say is. I am going away. Will you come with me? It is absurd I know to suggest such a thing . . . but I . . . we could live quite easily . . . pleasantly. There is enough money in my bank. This isn't a proposal of marriage. I could hardly dare that . . . or putting the hard word on you, Gina. Let us be companions . . . partners . . . brother and sister . . . anything you wish . . . if only you will come and let me give you some rest and comfort in your life.'

'Rocca! Rocca!'

They were calling him from the tent. Rocca ran away over the grass in the moonlight. A moment later the tent ballooned with laughter; the blether and cackle of people greeting the droll figure of the dwarf on the great grey draught mare.

Laugh, how they laughed! Was it any wonder Dan Haxby said Haxby's could not afford to lose Billy Rocca?

How everybody would laugh if they knew what he had just said to her, Gina reflected. Even Lily and Jack, her father and mother. The hunch-back and the dwarf to elope together? But that was not the way to look at it. It was quite right what Rocca had said, Gina brooded. He could give her an easier, more comfortable life. She would have time to read and think.

'You're clever, Gina,' he had said. 'You've got a good brain. Goodness knows what you might do with it.'

They had thought in the hospital that she had a good brain, Gina remembered. If she went away with Billy, she might be able to study, learn to be a nurse, perhaps.

Lin stirred, crying fretfully. A mosquito had found its way under his sleeping net. Gina went to the bag hammock under a tree, and chased a frail gauzy-winged insect from under the green net she had hung over the child. She knew that she would not go with Rocca when she went back to the place where she had been lying and threw herself down on the grass again.

To escape from the doom settling down on her, wander about the world, seeing strange countries and people, or live on some tropical island in blue seas, the dream had attracted her for a moment. Gina did not know whether she was really tempted. She had not considered, weighed the idea at all. It had flashed and pleased her for a moment, as a parrot flying across the road with the scarlet, blue and green of his breast and vagrant wings might have. But there was Lin! Thought of escape, of an easy, luxurious life recoiled before the child's demand on her. Only Gina knew and could foresee what that would be. She had a sense of obligation and responsibility towards him; as though her life had cast a shadow on his. She must be there to fight the shadow always, distance and keep it away from him.

She tried to explain something of this to Rocca. 'It's all right this life – our work, you know, Billy,' she said, 'when you're fit, and know it. I loved it. Never felt happier in me life than when Bonnie and Beauty were going sweet as nut together, round the ring, and I was jumping out of me skin . . . could throw a flip-flap as easy as kiss your hand. But I've got to see Lin gets his training proper, is led up to things. Dad's a bit inclined to rush the boys. I won't have Lin worked without the lunge till he's sure of himself.'

'You've got something to live for then, Gina?'

Gina smiled into the deep, welling hazel and freckled eyes of the dwarf's buried self.

'I'll miss you, Billy,' she said. 'But it's like that . . . There's Lin.'

CHAPTER 9

ROCCA left the show as soon as his contract was up. Daniel Haxby used every argument and threat within his power to induce him to remain. 'With the right of renewal for a year' a clause within the terms of his contract read; but Rocca refused to be bound by it. He knew Haxby had no money to fight him, and could not even try.

He had made up his mind to go; and if Rocca had made up his mind to go, that was all to be said about it. Billy Rocca could be obstinate as a mule, Dan swore. But Rocca had told Dan Haxby why he was going. Dan roared as though it were a joke Billy was making, the best he had heard for a long time, translating it into a dim perception that Rocca, as he told his wife, was sweet on Gina.

He had even asked Gina to soft-soap Billy a bit, in order to get him to stay on, 'seeing he's worth a few hundreds to the show.'

'No. I won't ask him to stay,' Gina said with a cussedness she could not explain.

Loss of Rocca added to the grudge her father was accumulating against Gina. Sight of her, and the acid of what Billy had said were eating into his consciousness. She was a constant reproach to him, a reproach he would not admit to himself. Gina had never reproached him. She never hit back when he reproached her with every misfortune, every piece of bad luck the circus encountered.

87

'That comes of having a cripple on the show – a bloomin' hog-fat,' he said.

Whatever else she was, Gina was not that, a hog-fat, Lily or her mother hit back.

'Oh, go on, Dad, nobody works harder than Gina.'

'There'd be no show, but for her,' Lily cried contemptuously. 'Who'd look after things when you and Rabe are on your ear, clean the cages, feed the animals? Jack does what he can.'

'Does what he can!' Dan exclaimed. 'God-damned nincompoop, that he is! Does what he can? Yes, he does what he can all right.'

'Oh well, you know your remedy,' Lily replied with an indifference which infuriated him.

No one knew better than she and Jack that theirs was the only turn worth looking at on the show these days. They were only biding their time, practising hard and perfecting themselves in their work, so that when the chance came they could take it and leave Haxby's together.

'See here, my girl, if you think I'm going to allow you to take up with that blasted Yankee——'

Lily's little laugh flickered derisively.

'Tell him,' she said. 'You're not game!'

'For goodness sake, Lil, don't go aggravating your father like that,' Mrs. Haxby expostulated.

Five years moved slowly. The circus waggons creaking along country roads covered hundreds of miles, travelling through wheat growing districts of the Mallee to Swan Hill and Mildura. From vineyards along the Murray, they had crossed the river into New South Wales; treking east, had roamed over the wide plains, capturing small towns for their race meetings and agricultural shows.

Swept by heavy rains, battered by gales, crooked and wayward as a moth in its flight, the circus had alighted on small towns along tributaries of the Billabong, and Murrumbidgee, and flitted on.

From Hay, Narrandera, Cootamundra to Wyalong, Haxby's had gone, and back by way of Goulburn, Yass, Junee, Wagga to Jerilderie and Deniliquin, zig-zagging to Albury and trailing down through the yellowing vineyards about Rutherglen and El Dorado. Through old mining settlements and station lands where the grass was bleached and almost the colour of dirty wool on the sheeps' backs, the circus had come again to the orchards and wheat fields between southern flung creeks and rivers of the Murray, such a happy hunting ground a few years ago.

The show held together but was never again what it had been then. Rocca had gone and with him the good luck and prosperity which had shone on Haxby's that season. There was no girl either to take Gina's place, do bare-back and jockey riding, and a circus without a girl rider was no circus at all, Dan found the country people were saying.

So Bob was put into Gina's old spangled ballet skirts and given a fair fluffy wig. Powdered and rouged, with eyes and lips painted, he made such a pretty girl that Dan billed him as Miss Kitty, and as Miss Kitty, Bob was a success he had never been before. Young men all over the country side rode miles to see him and tried in all manner of ways to make Miss Kitty's acquaintance.

But Dan was as strict as ever about allowing outsiders to come into the everyday life of the show. Few people ever got a chance to speak to his wife or children. In the tent, on the programme, they belonged to the public; but afterwards, on the road, or in camp, no sultan more zealously guarded his harem. The circus lived a life separate and apart in all the country it travelled through. With the pride of a wandering race, the circus folk held themselves aloof, knowing that people who stuck fast in towns and on farms regarded them as freaks, curiosities, thieves and chicken stealers, and with the ethic of a nomad and adventurous people, despised and were contemptuous of the stick-in-the-muds.

That the show still held together was something of a miracle. During a wild night at Swan Hill the tents had been torn to ribbands. For days all hands were to be seen, sitting about, stitching the bits together; and it was a poor patchwork edition of the menagerie and circus tents which went up in the next town.

Then too, during the following year on the long stages of a journey across the Riverina, the whole circus had been marooned by a flood. It had been raining for days when the waggons left Moula. Dan had been warned of the danger of the creeks coming down when he left a township thirty miles away but pooh-poohed it. Haxby's was accustomed to danger and taking chances, he said.

Bruiser, who knew the country well, induced Dan to camp for the night on the high ground of a slight rise some distance from the river. The backwater of a creek passed a few hours before was running a banker. During the night when Queenie began to trumpet, Nero muttered and growled, pacing restlessly, all the monkeys were making a noise, gibbering and running about their cages, Dan got up to see what was the matter. And there was the water stealing out over the countryside, pale and silvery in a moonlight drenched by the rains which had been falling all day and for days.

He wakened the camp and everybody turned out to

harness the horses and move the waggons and animal cages to the highest ground. Even there they were so little above the level of the river flats that the flood waters, rising steadily all night, flowed over the wheels and floors of the waggons. All hands took to the top of the canvas and gear waggons, and seated there watched themselves surrounded by the slowly moving, wide-spread sea of the flood waters. The rain stopped; but it was very cold, the air saturated with moisture.

In the morning, the flood waters spread out for miles in every direction. As far as anybody could see lay the lake of yellowish still water. It was up to the horses' girths. Queenie, chained to a tree, trumpeted restlessly; the monkeys huddled, shivering and chattering miserably together, on a rafter in the top of their cage. During the morning Dan pushed a packing case into Hero's cage, and the old lion climbed on to it. Thrashing about in water up to their waists Dan, Bruiser, Charley and Rabe sorted out gear and provisions, putting the largest boxes into the bear's cage and one for the wolf to jump on to.

Dan Haxby's chief concern was for the wild beasts and the horses. How was he going to feed them? Hero already had rheumatism and was hungry. During the day the old lion got all the meat there was. Travelling light as Dan made a rule of doing, he had expected to pass a station next day where he could buy a sheep and some hay. The horses usually grazed along the roadside, or bank of a creek where they camped, and got two hard feeds a day as well as grass. Dan prided himself on the condition of his horses, fed them well, but carried as little fodder as need be between towns.

For three days, Haxby's lived on biscuits, cheese and

jam which had been salvaged from the buckboard, and a couple of bottles of beer Charley and Bruiser had stowed away. Gina managed to make a fire in a kerosene tin, and by boiling some of the water which had settled in another tin was able to warm Lin's milk and give him something to drink. The tin of wheaten biscuits she carried for him was safe too. Later Mrs. Haxby made some tea, very black and strong and tried mixing the sodden flour for a damper.

When Dan was at his wits' end for food to give the beasts, a dead lamb floated by. Charley went after it and raked it in. The horses suffered most: but each day the water subsided a little and on the third day was low enough for the men to wade through to the river.

Dan had determined to swim across and go to a homestead whose roofs and sheds could just be seen in the distance, to get food for his family and animals. Bruiser offered to go; but although stronger and the younger man, he was not much of a swimmer, and Dan thought he himself had more chance of staying the distance.

He stripped, fastened a light rope round his waist and dropped into the thick muddy water swirling along the bed of the river; was carried some distance down the bank, and Bruiser and Charley ran along, following him and paying out the rope as they went. Thrown by an eddy against the further bank, Dan clambered up and lay there exhausted for awhile.

'Oh, my Gord, he's killed. He's drowned, Gina!' Mrs. Haxby cried, as she and the children watched Dan disappear down the swift current of the river.

'Go on Mum,' Gina cheered. 'My money's on Dad.'

Despite all the antagonism between them, Gina had pride and confidence in her father. She knew his stuff. Dan was the sort of man who did things nobody else could do; believed he could do them and brought them off. She was sure he would not come to any harm. And presently he reappeared on the bank opposite Bruiser and Charley.

'There,' she said, 'didn't I tell you Dad'd be all right.'

Dan pulled over a block and tackle, fastened them to a tree while Bruiser and Jack and Charley fixed the other end of the rope with block and tackle to a tree on their bank. Then putting Dan's clothes in a kerosene bucket, Bruiser shot that over to him.

Dan dressed and climbed the river bank. The flood waters stretched as far as could be seen there also; but the ground was higher and he signalled jubilantly as he splashed off towards the homestead. Before nightfall he was back with a stockman, a couple of pack horses and provisions for man and beast.

Oats and hay, bread and meat were swung over the flooded river on the rope, and Dan himself returned on it to explain that folk at the homestead had promised to send food down until the circus could get across.

The following day a raft lashed together of stakes, poles and seating planks carried the family across. The waggons hauled down to the raft, were also safely steered to the opposite bank with Bruiser poling and Dan and Rabe hauling on to the tackle. Bruiser led Queenie, and the boys swam the horses, so that finally, without a single casualty or loss of a beast, Haxby's went on its way again.

The roads were heavy and soft. The waggons bogged again and again in the gluey mud. But, 'you can't keep a good thing down,' Dan said; and if he was in Santa Rosa a month later than advertised time, he made good use of the floods and his feat crossing the flooded river to advertise the show. Got a record house and boasted that Haxby's was none the worse –'not even by so much as a cold in the nose'– for its adventure.

A great washing day Mrs. Haxby and Gina had in Santa Rosa, hanging their clothes on lines behind the circus tents; and when everything was washed and dried again, the horses spelled and waggons restocked, the show went on by easy stages, steering away from the area of flood waters.

The weather had broken for that year. Farmers and pastoralists everywhere were celebrating the rains and promise of a good season; but the circus folk trudged wet and depressed from town to town of the route Dan had mapped out and sent posters ahead for. Haxby's played in dripping tents to handfuls of people for a shilling, two shillings and three shillings: then turned and went south again with the spring.

There were good as well as bad days on the road. Days of blue skies and glittering sunshine, when the waggons moved slowly, going thirty miles between towns. The horses in good fettle, grazed on grass and herbage by the wayside. The boys practised flute and cornet with Rabe, sitting on top of a waggon, as they went along. And always someone was whistling or singing.

Wild duck roasting on wood embers put spicy odours into the air from camp fires sparkling in the dusk, when the waggons had halted for the night near a swamp or backwater of some creek. Dan was a good shot and brought teal and black duck for the pot, in and out of season, whenever he got a chance. He liked fishing too, and if there was time would camp near a creek or river and stand fishing on the bank for hours, or get up at dawn in order to bring in a bag of fish for breakfast. Gleeful, singing and shouting for the rest of the day, he was, when he could dangle a Murray cod, all pink and silvery, exclaim at his weight and beauty, telling about the fight he had to land him, and the fishes he had caught in his day.

'A beauty, isn't he? You can't beat Murray cod fresh from the river, by God!'

Although, if there was not time to angle, he was almost as pleased to have got the fish from a basket of meat bones, with lines set in the water round it over night – though that was poaching according to the game laws of the country, and no sportsman would be guilty of it. But Dan had his family and beasts to feed. He would fish for sport, and poach if he had to. Those were good days along the Murray rivers in the spring and early summer. Gina and the children were kept busy plucking black-duck and cleaning fish.

Then in the autumn too, mushrooms gleamed along the roadside and in the paddocks beside them; tiny, rose-fleshed and white-satin-skinned with the brown gills of fish underneath. Further south rabbits were plentiful. The children could knock then over with a stick as they scampered across the road, and many a savoury stew of bunnies kept down Dan's food bill.

Through forests, under the deep shade of great eucalyptus, messmate and mountain ash, Haxby's had wandered, and gone on over the ranges, watching the rain lift in mist from dark timbered slopes, leaving the earth purple and dark where bush fires had passed.

From the blue mountain ranges, trailing across the wide plains between orchards in blossom, miles of peach trees, bouquets of pale pink petals on black sticks, the circus had steered its slow, irregular course, to the valleys where orange gardens stretched in squared-off acres of dark glossy shrubs with blossom thick as snow upon them; the air held their breath for miles.

And again the waggons would climb shingly ridges, coming down steep tracks to mining townships, rain a white mist before and drizzling all round. Past the poppet heads of mines and the ghostly dumps of shafts strewing the hillsides; the white, card-villages of old prospecting rushes scattered about.

Lights of a township, flickering out in the twilight, white plumes of smoke from its chimneys, hailed the wayfarers sometimes, and Haxby's trailed into a town, too late for a procession perhaps, but in time to show for the night. A roar from old Hero, and sight of an elephant perambulating the main street, could always be depended on to throw quiet up-country towns into furore; and although the show might have been delayed on the road, held up by rivers running too high to cross, or by waggons which had bogged, Haxby's always kept faith, showing to half-filled seats, as gaily and bravely as though it could live up to the boast of its posters and placards and was still 'The Lightest, Brightest Little Show on Earth.'

There were days when the men strolled singing beside the horses; days of sunshine and good living; and wild, wet days when everybody trudged, chilled to the bone, weary and dejected, the waggons bucketed about on rough roads, over mallee roots, like ships in a stormy sea.

It was after one such day, when a light spattering of snow had fallen along the track into a mountain township, that the greatest misfortune it had suffered for years struck Haxby's. Hero was found dead on the floor of his cage, when it was opened after the waggons came to a standstill on the lot where the circus was to show that night.

Dan was overwhelmed by the disaster. He cried like a child.

But the early twilight was closing in. It had been raining all day and was very cold. Everybody was wet and cold. The tents had to be hoisted, the horses fed and rested before the show, and although Bruiser paraded Queenie through the streets of Beaufort, and Rabe and Monty followed with a cornet and placard announcing 'the tragic death of Haxby's notorious man-eating lion,' – Gina having painted the placard hurriedly in large letters of red ink and washing blue – Dan's funeral orations over the dead body of Hero, who was laid out in state on a union jack for the occasion, was wasted on a handful of people scattered about wet, empty seats.

'Never,' Dan swore, with emotion and prodigious nose blowings, 'had there been such a lion. Never would there be such a lion in captivity again. Ferocious man-eater, though he was, Haxby's had tamed and trained Hero until he would eat from his master's hand like a great cat.'

All of which was true enough, in parts. Hero's death was a great loss to the show, if his man-eating propensities rather a myth. The lion was so old and helpless, went through his tricks with such lazy condescension, roaring obligingly whenever a whip was cracked, that everybody was sure Dan would never find his like on earth again. Gina, Mrs. Haxby and the children were as upset by the passing of Hero as Dan. His death cast a gloom over everybody. What was a circus without a lion or tiger? And Dan could not afford to buy even cubs these days. The show seemed to be going from bad to worse. And Dan's temper with it. There were only the performing horses, the boys' riding and acrobatic tricks, or Lily's and Jack's work on the trapeze worth looking at.

A few days later, a crowd of drunken miners let Dan know it. They roared riotously at the end of the show and wanted their money back because the man-eating lion who had been advertised on posters sent ahead, was not to be seen.

'Obtaining money under false pretences,' they shouted. 'That's what it is! Where's the man-eater?'

Cat-calls and yells of derision greeted Dan's story of the death of Hero in a snow-storm.

'Ladies and Gentlemen'– Dan wound up his explanation raging and sore, 'the pride of an honest showman is that he always delivers the goods. In my long and varied experience, I have never billed a turn that I do not produce. Our posters were sent ahead weeks ago. But you can't argue with Death. Our belover man-eater, Hero, the pride and glory of Haxby's, has gone to his last home. It's the worst bit of damned rotten luck the circus has ever struck. If you're the good sports we've always heard you are in this town you'll go into mourning with the rest of us – and take up a collection for the widow and orphans.'

The riot subsided with laughter and cheers. A collection taken up jocosely among the men resulted only in a few shillings; but Dan was pleased with it, as an indication of how to handle an audience when other methods failed.

CHAPTER 10

GINA no longer felt the grudge everybody on the show bore her in more or less degree. She was a constant reminder to all performers of the chance of disaster which might befall them: a fear in the background. She took abuse and blame, growlings and irritation when they came her way much as a matter of course.

For a long time she had drugged herself with work, and there was the child to love. That was sufficient to keep her going. She had become insensible to harsh words. Her mind acquired a film which would not let them through, as water-proof keeps off the rain. And under it a something dumb and individual was growing; a will that was herself, strong and stubborn which would be heard, would have its way some day. Already it was stronger than she was. It had said no to Dan Haxby about Rocca.

Some day she knew she would meet and beat her father again. Yet she bore him no ill will. She did not blame him although almost everybody else did for what had happened to her. She saw his point of view. It was the show mattered to him. Always, first and last, he lived for the show.

Gina understood that. She could see the thing as he saw it. She loved the show. Born within hail of the peaked one-poled tents, she had grown-up wandering about the countryside with them, seen them pitched and sprout by the wayside, a crop of dirty, fantastic toad-stools, glowing magically, lit by the flare of kerosene lamps inside, infested by gaudy glittering insects who were men and women in their circus clothes, while Rabe's band of cornet, flute, cymbals and drum, put gay, squalling tunes into the air. She was used to the racket of laughter, eager excited chatter, the shouts and yells of wonder and amusement which gushed and swayed out from the tents.

Gina had lived and worked for the show as Dan had done she realised after a while. Always she had spent herself so that Haxby's should be the brightest little show in the country-side, as Dan boasted. She had watched with a religious zeal to see that everything was in order for performances, seats, cages, gear, the ring sprinkled with red dust from the timber-mills. Gina sympathised with her father. She knew how hard it was for him to forgive her for the knock she had dealt the show. She felt that way about it herself.

And there was Lin. From the time he was five years old Dan had been practising Lin in the ring. But Lin was a nervous child. He never wanted to go into the circus tent, or near the ring. He cried and could not be induced to try even a hand spring except with Gina and the boys away from the tents.

Dan fretted and worked himself into a frenzy about it. He wanted to know whose child this was. There never had been a Haxby like this, he said, such a wailing, puking, miserable little mongrel. No ginger or spunk in him.

Gina and the boys taught Lin his first tricks and gave him confidence, without his knowing that he was being taught anything. Dan declared himself pleased enough with the result and put Lin into a turn with the other two boys at once. Quite happily Lin had gone through the Risley and somersault he had learnt to do with his brothers when they played together on a sea beach or under trees in the bush; but when it was a question of learning to climb to the trapezes, swing and fly from one to the other, he was too nervous. All his fear came back again.

The more Dan insisted, the more terrified the child was. There were scenes and rows every day, Lin crying and refusing to attempt the simplest tricks.

Ordinarily Dan Haxby was a good trainer, patient and even-tempered. He prided himself that he had never raised a hand to one of his children while he was teaching them to ride or tumble.

'But so help me Gord, I never had a child like this before,' he cried exasperated. 'What's to be done with him? He won't try . . . He won't even try. If he were trying, I wouldn't feel so mad about it. But all he does is hang there crying like a great baby.'

The day his father flicked a whip round Lin's bare legs, as he had often threatened to do, was the last he ever exercised the child unless Gina was in the tent.

She had lifted the flap and come into the tent next day when the boys were practising.

'What do you want?' Dan roared. 'You got no right here when we're workin'.'

'Yes,' the sombre level glance of Gina's eyes said much more. 'I've got a right.'

She sat there on the edge of the ring, watching the boys at work, shinning-up the rope to the trapezes turning, hanging, swinging from one to the other. Lin wanted to run to her.

'You stay where you are,' Dan commanded. The child broke into tears and threw himself down beside the box he had been sitting on.

Gina neither moved nor spoke. Lin climbed the rope to the trapeze; but he refused to do more than sit there, clinging to the ropes and crying.

Gina watched him go through his Risley tricks, springing quickly, cleverly to Monty's feet. As Monty lay on his back with feet in the air, Lin somersaulted backwards to land on his feet on Monty's feet. But Dan held him by the lunge – a safety rope run through a pulley hung up near the roof and fastened about Lin's little body by a leather belt. When the boys had run away to take off their calico boots and change, Gina rose and stood looking at her father. He knew she was ready to speak; but she did not. She stood there, that sombre gaze of hers on him.

'Well,' he fidgetted. 'What have you got to say?'

'It's you he's afraid of,' Gina said.

'It's you's made him afraid,' he accused harshly.

'No.' Gina was conscious of a stab she had not felt for a long time. Pain in her back. Lin. The spasm went from her thought of him to the vulnerable place. Could she so hurt Lin? 'He was born that way . . . afraid. You forget when he was born.'

'By God,' Dan blustered, 'am I never to get away from that? Am I never to be allowed to forget?'

'As far as Lin's concerned, no,' Gina said slowly. 'You've got to make allowances for it. He's afraid with you. You'll never make him forget his fear. He'll never do any good with you. Leave him to me and the boys . . . and he'll come along all right like he did before. Only I won't have him working without the lunge until he's ready to; and there's got to be nets while he's practising on the trapezes.'

'Whose show is this? And who's givin' orders? By God, it's too much!' Dan flung down his whip and rushed out of the tent.

Gina picked up the whip and put it in its place beside the king pole where he would find it when he came into the ring that evening. She went to the loose fold of canvas which fell over the exit, stooping more than usual, it seemed, dragging her feet; but there was a smile in her eyes as she glanced back about the tent, to see whether everything was in order for the evening performance. She was smiling at that other self sitting within her. A serene, steadfast self, who was saying: 'I told you so . . . You can do things if you like.'

The ring-pegs looked loose and crooked. Gina searched for and found a heavy mallet by the door and went back into the tent, to hit the pegs into place; she noticed how rough the track was, ruckled hard after rain, a paddock cattle had been in, although the herbage was thick on it, crow's foot, clover and cape weed. Cape weed daises spread yellow over the green mat. There was a faint fragrance in the tent, mellow as parchment under the hot sunshine. Golden mist filled the enclosed space; smell of cape weed daises and the dry harsh tang of red gum sawdust.

'My Gord, why do you rile him so, Gina?' her mother exclaimed when Gina went back to the waggon where Mrs. Haxby was sitting, mending the socks and shabby clothing spread out round her.

As Gina moved over to smouldering embers of the fire, a gust of smoke filled her eyes. She lifted the blackened kerosene bucket from stones on either side of the fire.

'Rile him?' she asked.

'It isn't as if I hadn't enough worries without you adding to them,' her mother went on irritably. 'I'm fair worried out of me life with the lot of you. Lily and the way she carries on! Not that Jack Dayne's not a decent enough young feller and why *he* can't make up his mind to letting Lil have Jack, I don't know.'

'Show can't afford to lose her,' Gina said.

'That's it I suppose,' Mrs. Haxby sighed, crossing her scarlet worsted, thread by thread, under and over. 'Jack'll hang on as long as Lily does. But Lord, they've been going together for over six years and don't seem in any hurry to get married. They're that settled down and used to each other, the funniest lovers ever I came across . . . You'd think they was married already . . .'

'Perhaps they are,' Gina said.

'Don't say that Gina.'

'Why not? And why shouldn't they be – if they want to?' Gina asked indifferently. 'Jack's real good to Lil . . . looks after her . . . won't let Dad work her too hard. Sees she don't do anything but her own job.'

'That's right,' her mother agreed. 'Ever since . . . ever since . . . he's been that careful of Lil and himself. I don't know what to make of things. Dad's that cross-grained there's no talking to him . . . and the show's going from bad to worse. It has been ever since your accident, Gi.'

Mrs. Haxby's brown fingers moved nimbly over the red tights she was darning, had made and dyed from a pair of men's cotton drawers.

'Never get the crowd now like we had then,' she stopped to bite a thread. 'Rocca's going too. That upset Dad . . . If Lily and Jack was to clear out I don't know what we'd do. There's all new wardrobe wanted. These tights of Monty's is darned and darned till they'll scarcely hold together. You'll have to do what you can about the mending while I'm laid up, Gina.'

Gina stared at her mother. There was no mistaking the significance of Lotty Haxby's glance.

'When?'

'Oh, in about four months,' Mrs. Haxby said in the same tone of weary irritation. 'And I don't mind telling you I'm fed up, Gina. Had as many babies as I want. A machine for churnin' out acrobats and bare-back riders that's all he thinks I am . . . It's the show all the time with your father – the damned show. That's all he thinks about . . . cares for . . . and my job's to supply performers.'

'Like Lin,' Gina said.

'Lin? Poor little Lin. But you know how broke up I was about you, Gina, before he was born.'

'I was thinking of that,' Gina said.

CHAPTER 11

GINA was haunted by thought of that few moments' talk with her mother. She watched Lotty Haxby's spare, burdened figure as they worked, packing and unpacking plates and dishes, washing clothes, preparing food for the meals. Mrs. Haxby looked weary and battered by the life of the roads; her face was shrunken, lines seamed about her mouth and nose. Her eyes, flat and unlighted, held only determination to keep going, a stubborn loyalty to the work and need of the moment.

Gina tried to understand, and realised that life had done to her mother what it had done to her, in a different way. It had beaten from her every shred of desire for herself; made of her an automaton, something which works, from habit, according to the demand put upon it.

She had taken her mother for granted always, much as everybody else was taking her. It had been Mrs. Haxby's job to dispose of all the food preparation, clothes making and mending, child rearing of the show. As long as Gina could remember her mother had looked work-worn like this, gone about talking in that would-be cheerful, querulous, fault-finding way. And most of the time there had been a baby.

But Lin was five. It was nearly five years since Lotty Haxby had had a baby. 'The longest spell on record,' she told Gina.

As Gina looked at her, she wondered vaguely that so

meagre a frame could still create another life. Mrs. Haxby was no more than forty-four; but she looked twice that age. Her small square face was weathered and tanned; her grey eyes so flat and unemotional usually, had a light from within now, the luminousness of another soul looking through her. Only the ear-rings dangling beside her tough, used-up face gave any indication of the woman she had once been.

A slight, pretty girl of eighteen, working in a milliner's shop, Lotty had fallen in love with Dan Haxby when he was riding for Wirth's circus. They were married in an up-country town, and had been on the road ever since.

Her mother still loved a bit of finery, Gina knew. She remembered the pink flower in her hat when the family came to the hospital for her. How Lotty had stood in a shabby old coat, and the hat with that pink flower in, nursing Lin, a sickly baby, in her arms. How dirty her hands were, and the rings on them, her wedding ring, a keeper with ruby and pearls, the big brummy diamond ring she was so fond of, and those old fashioned ear-rings of dull gold with fretted dangles beside her face.

Gina had kept all her little hospital books. She thought of them now. Lily said, she remembered, that her mother had been very ill when Lin was born.

Gina asked about it.

'Oh yes,' Mrs. Haxby said irritably. 'The doctor at Linton said I should never have another baby. Not before things was fixed-up any way. He said there ought to be an operation, by rights, Gina. But of course Dad won't hear of operations. Says –'

'I wish,' Gina ventured, 'you could go to hospital. Have a bit of rest . . . and be looked after properly for this one.'

'My God,' Mrs Haxby cried desperately, 'I wish I could. But he'd never consent. He says – But Lord, I wish he had it to bear. I wish a man knew what it was like, Gina, having children the way I've done.'

Gina's resolution was made. She rose awkwardly from the grass where she had been lying as they talked.

'It'll be all right, Mum,' she said. 'I'll fix it.'

Taking a kerosene bucket in each hand, Gina walked away towards the river for water. Mrs. Haxby looked after her, wonderingly. What had come to the girl? She did not know what to make of her. She did not doubt, unbelievable as it seemed, that Gina would arrange for her to go into hospital somehow. She began to look forward to those days of rest and being waited on, lying still in a cool clean place, sleeping, sleeping, sleeping.

Every day Gina relieved her mother more and more of the work she had been accustomed to do, would not allow her to lift the water buckets, or move heavy boxes and packing cases. She watched Lotty's food, insisted that she should have milk with her tea, and eat eggs, fresh meat, fruit and vegetables.

'I'm going to tell Dad you've got to go to hospital, Mum.' The waggons were moving over the plains towards Rainbow again, when Gina spoke.

'He'll never let me go,' her mother exclaimed, nervously. 'He'll never, Gina. He's used to me being around. Always before, I've been up in a few days . . . and after all, there's lots of things I've done for him, even you couldn't do.'

Gina's mouth set in taut lines.

'You're going, Mum,' she said firmly. 'I don't know how you're going yet. But you're going.'

'He wants a girl, Gina,' her mother confessed. 'Says

now . . . you're no use on the show and Lil's likely to run off any moment . . . and there's the four boys . . . we'd ought to have a girl.'

'I'll tell him,' Gina said, 'that if he wants the strong kind, he's got to give you a chance. If not the girl'll be like Lin . . . afraid of her own shadow.'

'He'll never let me go, Gina,' her mother wailed.

'Well, you'll go without the letting,' Gina said.

That was the only way she would ever go, Gina decided, after she had talked with Daniel Haxby, told him her mother ought to go to hospital and why. Gina explained she would do all the work her mother had done; and that after what the doctor at Linton had said when Lin was born, it might be really dangerous not to have skilful attention when the new baby came.

But Dan would not hear of it; pooh-poohed the idea of Lotty going to hospital. He believed in the old fashioned ways, he said, Nature's way, none of these new-fangled fusses for him.

'I'm not asking you what you believe in,' Gina said. 'That doesn't matter. You're not going to have this baby. I'm asking for the money to let Mum be properly looked after.'

'See here, my girl, you'll not get a penny out of me to throw away on doctors, hospitals and the rest of it,' Dan blustered.

'I thought not,' Gina replied, 'but I couldn't be sure till I'd asked you, of course.'

She walked away, while Dan strode fuming to his wife as she moved heavily about hanging some newly-dyed tights and parade dresses on a line between two trees. He stormed at her, wanting to know what mad ideas were these she had put into Gina's head.

'They're not mad. It's you're mad not to see the sense of them,' Lotty Haxby said, showing fight for the first time in years.

They talked angrily for awhile. Gina could hear her father's voice expostulating, indignant, from the little distance away she was. The argument came down to money. What would it cost? Where did Lotty think he was going to get the money to pay doctors and hospitals?

'Where you'd get it to buy a tiger or another lion,' Gina answered, coming behind him. 'You might as well shell out for a decent bare-back rider, once in a way.'

He threw out his hand as if to strike her. Gina moved back, staring at him with brilliant hostile eyes.

Dan heard no more of the hospital from either Gina or her mother. They went about their jobs as they had always done, except that Dan noticed Lotty was doing less than her share, Gina slogging away, silently, indefatigably with her stooping shoulders, back bowed right over nowadays.

He tried joking them both after awhile as to the bee they had got in their bonnets about the hospital and doctors. Was jocose over it with Rabe after a drink or two, several times, as if the thing were on his conscience, coming between him and his rest. But the joke fell flat where Gina and her mother were concerned. Their faces gave nothing away, though Dan sensed an agreement between them; some tacit sympathy and understanding. What had Gina got to do with it anyhow, Dan asked himself. What did she know about this business of child bearing, to get all these sentimental ideas into her head?

He had seen Gina and her mother sitting, sewing and talking together in the afternoons sometimes; noticed they were working on white things. There was little enough money on the show these days. He did not see where they could find any.

Lotty of course had charge of the programmes, peanuts and boxes of cheap lollies the boys sold. Dan allowed her to keep any profit for herself after she paid for supplies. But it did not to amount to much, a few shillings, that was all. However much Gina and her mother might like to defy him, Dan did not see how they could.

Neither did Gina. She lay awake for hours, trying to think out or discover some means of making enough money to provide for her mother the respite she had planned. Her mind did not budge from the fact that Lotty must and would have it. But how? Time was moving steadily, inexorably.

For three months Gina racked her brain, lying awake to think out possibilities. She had taken charge of the programmes, lollies and peanuts, trying by adding a penny here and there, to make them pay more. But these pennies went in buying fresh milk and eggs, fruit and vegetables for Lin and her mother. Gina could see no way out. She fretted and ached. She might have written to Billy Rocca; but it was too late for that now.

It would be no use to ask Lily or Jack for the loan of money. They were saving every penny they could get out of Dan for their flight together she knew. And who else was there? Lord Freddie? Rabe? Neither of them ever had more than the price of a drink ahead. There seemed no possible way for her to make money. She could not desert the show, to earn anything by washing or scrubbing and cleaning, as she had thought she might at first. That would mean leaving all the heavy work to her mother. Then unexpectedly, miraculously, it seemed to Gina, a way opened.

Black Wattle Creek was the name of the place where the circus was playing that afternoon, Gina walked into the township, taking Lin with her, to buy milk and vegetables.

The township was one of those old sleepy places in which houses of mud bricks, whitewashed, with pines and lichened fruit trees about them, told of long ago settlement, while an hotel of red bricks, and street of small shops, with a picture theatre and two or three banks, the bloom still on their roofs of corrugated iron, betrayed a younger generation refusing to slumber peacefully.

'Why, it's Gina!' an eager voice exclaimed, as Gina and Lin came from a shop.

'Oh!' The voice and the pretty, flushed and pleased face came between Gina and her troubled thoughts – 'Nurse Edie!'

'But I'm not now,' the gay little voice replied. 'My name's Newton. I married that young man you know, who used to come and see me at the hospital. And we've got three children. My baby's such a darling, not six months old yet! You must come and see him, Gina. Will you come to-morrow? Yes, do. I'm having a tea party. And tell our fortunes like you used to in hospital.'

The circus was showing for two nights in Black Wattle, so Gina borrowed a dress of Lily's, washed and ironed Lin's blue trousers and a white shirt he wore in one of his acts, and decided to go and have tea with Nurse Edie next day. Vaguely she felt that something would come of the visit: a way out of her difficulty. She intended to ask Edie about her mother.

Edie Newton's pleasure at seeing her had given Gina an almost forgotten sensation. That somebody really liked to see her: wanted to talk to her. So, comforted and a little shy, she went through the garden before the Newtons' house, a weather-board bungalow in a vineyard on the outskirts of the town.

In the large drawing-room, with its chintz-covered furniture and open windows, several women and girls were chatting together. Gina said: 'Good afternoon,' several times as Edie named her and rattled over several other names.

Edie Newton poured out tea, exclaiming and telling everybody how glad she was to see Gina; and how the children were looking forward to going to the circus that night. Everybody asked questions about the circus, wanting to know all sorts of things about the boys and Lily. Where they afraid? How did they get to be so clever? Who were they really?

Lin clung to Gina, gazing timidly at the soft, fat-cheeked, fair-haired children Edie brought to coax him to play with them, Mary, Rose, and George.

'But we're all wanting you to tell our fortunes, Gina,' Edie Newton cried. 'I've told them all here how wonderful you are. You know what you told me came true. He was a dark-eyed man all right . . . and Matron too, you were quite right there. She married Dr. Leigh and Jones is matron at Southern Cross now . . .'

'Please tell my fortune!'

'I'd love to have my fortune told!'

'Won't you tell mine too?'

The girls' voices besieged Gina.

'But,' Gina exclaimed in some embarrassment, smiling to Edie. 'I haven't done it since I was in hospital.'

'Oh well, just for fun . . . They'd love it, Gina,' Edie Newton begged.

Gina took a palm thrust towards her. She scarcely

looked at the sun-burnt, freckled face above it, as she told a story of hard work, honesty, faith and disaster that flashed to her from the small vigorous hand laid in hers. Over other hands, as the girls and women chirped and twittered about her, she wove fairy tales of love affairs, fortunes, letters and adventures to the satisfaction of everybody, using her small knowledge of the lines of the hand with an added sense of character, and an instinctive prophetic flashing of the future which came to her from each hand as she held it.

'You're a witch, Gina,' Edie Newton declared afterwards. 'And fortune telling's such fun. Everybody's enjoyed themselves. You were a dear to do it for me.'

But playing the old game she had learnt from a paper-covered book in hospital, meant much more than that to Gina. She was reprieved. Back by the open fire behind the buckboard, in her old clothes, she felt hopeful and light-hearted.

'I've got it, Mum,' she cried. 'There's some of my old things about still, isn't there? The handkerchief and ear-rings. D'you think you could rig me up a gypsy dress and I'll tell fortunes.'

Gina told her mother about Edie Newton's tea party. How, in the hospital, she had read what lines of the hand, shape of the fingers meant; and practised on the nurses' and patients' hands, making stories about them.

'They say I'm quite good at it, Mum,' she explained happily. 'And I could make some money that way.'

When he saw her in the gypsy skirt and jacket Mrs. Haxby had made, Dan imagined Gina was trying to smarten herself up so that she could sell the programmes and peanuts better. Then he saw her talking over the extended palms of boys and girls coming to the show;

watched them giving her money and wanted to know more about it.

Mrs. Haxby told him it was just an idea of Gina's to make a bit of money for herself. Gina had been quite good at fortune telling in the hospital. The nurses and everybody were quite crazy about her there: said Gina was 'real clever.' On the first two or three nights she had made about ten shillings a night.

'Old hog-fat beginning to earn a crust for herself,' Dan exclaimed jovially.

He had a tent put up for Gina, wanted to give her a fancy name and collect half her takings.

'You can call me what you like,' Gina said. 'But I'll handle the cash, thank you. Give you ten per cent, if you like.'

'Well, I'm damned——' Dan gasped.

But he and Rabe made a placard with the stencils to put on Gina's tent.

'Madame Zinga. The World Famous Seer. Come and See Her. She will tell Your Fate and your Fortune for a shilling.'

CHAPTER 12

As Madame Zinga, Gina regained something of her old footing on the show. Sometimes she made only a few shillings, sometimes ten shillings or a pound from the boys and girls who spread out their hands in the dim light of the striped awning Dan had put up for her near the men's dressing tent.

Gina fingered her shillings tenderly every night, counting them and handing Dan his ten per cent. Only her mother knew how much money Gina had collected, and the dreams she wove round it; but even she did not know where Gina kept her hoard.

For a long time Gina did not spend a penny of the money she made. She saved and hid it, calculating just what each shilling, each added shilling, and pound would do for her. It was Dan himself who suggested sending for a book on how to tell fortunes by cards. And after Gina had read it, and could 'spin the dope' as he said, her prices were changed to one shilling for palm or card reading, and two shillings for the double dose.

'You've got to have slippers, a dressing gown and a decent dress to go to the hospital, and come out in, Mum,' Gina told her mother one evening, 'some soap that smells nice and powder. We can do it all, easy.'

She went over to the camp fire and lifted the lid of a big black cooking pan so that the smell of onion, meat and cabbage broiling together, drifted out and mingled with the smoky mist and rosy glow of sunset about her.

'So long as the cops don't get me, that is. Dad says they can grab me any minute for telling fortunes. But why?'

'Gord knows,' Mrs. Haxby said.

'Lots of things I told the nurses at the hospital came true!' Gina soliloquised. 'It's funny Mum, but I do feel I know things about people. When I look at them sometimes, I know the sort of things that are going to happen to them.'

Everybody on the show had taken Gina's fortune telling for more or less of a fake. She was more serious about herself than anybody, and interested. At first she had been pleased chiefly at the shillings the game was giving her, and explained the lines of the hand as the book she had read interpreted them. But character in a hand assailed her, more and more, dominated and guided her ideas about people; the joys and sorrows which were likely to befall them.

Knowledge of character Gina had developed through those months of suffering and observation in hospital: the days of her bitter misery and loneliness. On the show she had known the loves and hates of wild beasts, horses, and men like Bruiser, Charley, Lord Freddie, Jack and Dan. The men and women who swam in spaces beyond the cosmos of the circus she had studied for the first time in hospital; but for a long time now, unconsciously, on the road and in towns she had been reading faces and saw people beneath the stiff placid masks they wore.

It was a different world she lived in as Madame Zinga, in the half-dark of her small tent, a piece of red paper tied over a hurricane lantern, a handkerchief over her hair and big brass rings in her ears. She almost believed in the Roumanian great grandmother Dan had invented for her. No one would have recognised her for the hunch-back in drab clothes who drudged about the camp fire and the circus tents. Gina did not want anyone to recognise her.

At Sphinx Hill one night a thick-set, red-faced young man and a fair-haired, jolly looking girl came into the tent.

'Oh Will,' she giggled, as Gina looked up.

The young man squeezed her arm.

'Silly,' he said, 'she won't eat you.'

Gina knew him at once, the pleasant lazy voice and eyes of a dog that loves and flinches from you. A man to love and to distrust, a fair-weather man who would fail you at every rough place in the road, yet was easy-going and good-natured enough in his way.

As Gina read the girl's pink plump palms when they were put on the box she used as a table, her voice sounded unsteady and far away, in her own ears. She gave the girl a good character, a peaceful, prosperous life, health, wealth and happiness.

'Go on,' Will Murray bantered, 'that's easy. Tell me will she run to beef . . . and rouse if a man has a drink or two.'

Gina's voice trembled. She was afraid he might recognise her. She was surprised to be so upset at seeing him again; she had not thought of Will Murray for so long, and yet the thought of him was always with her in a memory all gratitude, a lingering tenderness. She could not bear Will to see her like this, although he too had changed. He looked coarse and ruddy, like a score of other farmers she had seen, and as well-satisfied with life as any other of the domesticated young animals you see about farms.

'You will be married within the year,' she said quietly,

when his brown square workman's hands were laid out before her. 'The lines are clear and straight . . . not much fraying. Good health. Prosperity. You will be fat and well-to-do . . . have many children; go into politics, be member of parliament for the district, and walk with a stick when you are one hundred and four years old. Perhaps you will drink too much whisky, sometimes. There is an accident . . .'

She saw him flinch.

'Nothing serious. It will not hurt much. You will not be maimed or crippled.'

The young man had started away staring at the fortune-teller. He remembered her voice.

'Is it – is it really you, Gina?' he asked.

'Two shillings, please!' Dan was looming impatient in the doorway. 'This way. This way please for Madame Zinga – the world famous fortune-teller.'

'What is it, Will? What on earth's the matter?' the fair-haired girl beside Will Murray asked fearfully.

Will Murray blundered out of the tent, into the glare of lights about the circus. He had come to the show, hoping to see, or find out something about Gina, having heard vaguely that she was a cripple and went about with the circus still. He had brought the girl whom he was going to marry to disabuse himself of that old will-of-the-wisp romance of his. But it had all stirred again under the shock of hearing Gina's voice and seeing her bright eyes of pain and tenderness.

Gina herself wondered why she could not see the hands stretched out to her, a moment later, for the mist of tears before her eyes.

The waggons went on to a diggings twenty miles away the same night. Gold had been found and there had been a rush to Willingatta a few years before. A collection of wood and tin shacks, springing up in a few months spread among the dumps and shafts until they formed a fairly large town.

Travelling half the night through thick timbered ridges, to be in the township in time for a matinee on Saturday, Haxby's measured the ground for the tents and unloaded during the morning. There were fewer women than men in Willingatta, and only two or three women and girls, and half a dozen men sought out Gina's tent before the show, early in the afternoon, and spread grimy work-worn hands before her.

When the afternoon performance was over, as she went about getting the evening meal, Gina kept looking in an uneasy, absent minded way towards the pub, opposite which the circus had pitched its tents. Miners in faded blue and earth-stained trousers, grey shirts and old felt hats slouched, yarning and smoking about its open doorways.

As Dan, Rabe, her mother and the boys sat round eating their meal, sunset was wavering out above dark of the tree tops behind them, Gina said suddenly:

'Got the hand of a murderer this afternoon. First time I've even seen one . . . thumb and all.'

Rabe laughed that slow guttering laugh of his and Dan cried jokingly:

'Go on, tell us about it?'

Never before had Gina talked of her fortune telling. Nobody realised she took it at all seriously.

'It's not only that,' she said. 'But I've got it in me bones there'll be a murder in this town to-night.'

'Tell us about it, Gi,' Lily said lazily.

'It wasn't only the hand,' Gina said. 'I got it from the

man the minute he came into the tent. A little man with a big round head, all but bald, sharp nose and . . . mad eyes. Don't know whether he wasn't mad.'

'What did he say? Did he give himself away, Gina?' Jack asked.

Gina shook her head.

'But I could feel something ugly going on inside of him. Felt it, plain as if he had told me. All he said was: "Got something on. Tell me if I'll get away with it? Come on, if you're a dinkum fortune-teller you ought to be able to do that?" He must have seen from my face that I knew what it was . . . because when I looked at his hand, and tried to put him off, saying it was no good . . . he would fail in what he was trying to do, he snatched his hand away and went off laughing. It's fair given me the creeps.'

Everybody listened attentively and was impressed by the story, although Dan and Rabe still smiled and Dan winked across to the band-master.

'You got to be careful what you do these days, old bird,' he said, 'with a bloomin' thought-reader about.'

'Feel as if I should warn somebody,' Gina murmured. 'But I don't know who – unless it's a man who was this man's mate . . .'

'You're letting your imagination run away with you my girl,' Dan said.

But there was a shooting in the township that night. A man named Baldy Emerson shot his mate and himself. The two men had been working a claim together and were camped about a mile out of the town. But Brooks had jumped Baldy's claim on his wife. That was the way the miners put it, and this shooting was the end of the chapter.

Dan made the most of Gina's prophecy, telling all and sundry in the next township, how Madame Zinga had known and warned them there would be a shooting in Willingatta the night before; and sure enough a short bald-headed man had killed his mate and blown out his own light afterwards.

CHAPTER 13

WHEN they were in Jacob's Well the following month Gina and Mrs. Haxby took the afternoon train down to Eagle Hawke. Gina intended to catch a goods' train back to the circus. The goods' train left Eagle Hawke about midnight, and although she would miss the evening performance, the goods would pull into the Well in the early hours of the morning, and Gina knew Dan would want her to help pack-up before the waggons moved on again.

Everything was in her mother's suit case, as Gina had planned, scented soap, talc powder, baby clothes, a blue dressing gown and felt slippers.

'I feel like Cinderella going to the ball,' Mrs. Haxby declared happily.

And Dan, though he joked about Mum's spree in Eagle Hawke, raised no objection to it since Gina was paying. He even admitted that what she was doing might be worth while.

In a grey-green cravenette ulster, and blue serge dress she and Gina had made between them, Mrs. Haxby might have been a prosperous farmer's wife but for the earrings and rings she insisted on wearing, and the pink flower which she had transplanted to her new hat, and was sure gave the last touch of smartness to her appearance. Gina, herself, in a grey coat and hat of Lily's, looked quite decent, for her, it was agreed.

When she left Eagle Hawke for Jacob's Well on the

goods' train, Gina was still a little excited and vaguely exhilarated by success of the scheme she had planned for: worked so hard to make real. She slept coming along in the guard's van, jolted and bumped about; but she was used to that she explained, while the guard laughed at her hardihood.

Lily and Jack were there on the siding in the dawn to meet her. That was unusual. Gina took alarm at sight of them. What was the matter? What had happened? Every instinct swarmed to her anxiety. She could scarcely move when she saw that Lily was crying. Lil crying? Beyond Lily, Gina could just see the tents of the circus. The performance was over, and the poles not down yet. Lights and people about still.

'What's the matter?' she asked, as Jack came towards her. Lily hung back helplessly.

'It's Lin,' Jack said.

Gina knew then. The back-wash of so long ago inundated her. After a long time it seemed she could hear Jack saying,

'He would put Lin on the trapeze, Gina. And you know the kid was scared . . . He was scared stiff.'

Gina went over to the tents. She saw Lin lying on a mattress in the men's dressing tent. A limp, colourless little figure under a piece of soiled canvas, his face smashed and bloody; blood on his fair hair.

'The doctor said death was instantaneous,' Jack told her. 'He didn't suffer, Gina.'

'There were no nets,' Gina said.

'I saw to them, myself. The nets were there all right,' Jack said. 'But he bounced out of them . . . hit the seats, and . . .'

Gina closed her eyes. 'I see,' she said. When she saw

her father he was half-drunk and blubbering, with Rabe beside him.

Gina stood staring at him, nothing alive in her, the dark mass she made against the thin chill light of early morning, except her eyes. And her eyes were bare and wide to their anger and loathing.

'I knew when a man I'd never seen before was going to murder his mate; but I didn't know when a father was going to murder his own child,' she said slowly.

'Gina! Gina!' he cried, feebly, childishly.

'You knew he was scared,' she said, 'you knew he was scared stiff, and you did it to make a couple of hundred fools cry out and laugh . . . You killed him.'

She turned and walked out of the tent, away from the lot. Walked away and away. Where she was going she did not know. Could not think.

When the waggons went on next day, after there had been an enquiry, and Lin was buried in a small cemetery two miles out from Jacob's Well, the buck-board and waggons moved along the road north and east again. Haxby's was billed to appear in Kur-ur-rook the following night.

Dan expected Gina to rejoin the camp any time next day, or during the night. But she did not. They managed without her, he and Rabe and the boys; Jack and Lily refusing to take up the burden Gina had laid down.

Gina did not know where she was going that night, she walked out across the plains back towards the town she had come from. The earth stretched far and wide beneath a sky glimmering with the first light of day. Sky and plains rocked and wavered before her, so that she did not know which was plain and which sky. She seemed to be floating through the sky, drifting over the earth, falling through darkness.

She walked a long way over rough open country, stumbled against rocks, and then trees. It had been hot and she was thirsty. She heard dogs barking; cattle belching far-away cries round a dam where they came for water. Some time she had slept and walked on through blazing sunshine.

Lin! The thought of him was with her. But she was not feeling, not grieving, just wandering without him. She could not feel anything. She had always known this would happen, she told herself. Felt Death was lying in wait to snatch Lin. But she had watched and guarded him so. Death caught him when she was not looking.

'Lin! Lin! Lin!' a bird cried, flying across the plains. And there were trees. Gina could see stars above curdled darkness of the trees. The pulses of her body, a tiny clicking in her brain, said: 'Lin! Lin! Lin!' Such a stupid little broken face it had looked lying there in the tent – waiting for her. The torch Jack held threw a light over it, and Lily was snivelling. Why did they let Dan kill him? It was easy to cry when Lin was dead, but why had Lily and Jack let Dan work the child like that? Damn them. Damn them all.

There was nothing to do but walk now. Her feet followed the road.

Gina wakened to find the roofs of houses on the road before her, rusty shacks of tin and bags or wood, white-washed, and tumbled earth about old shafts, the tall smoking chimneys beside a mine in the distance; flocks of goats feeding among scattered dumps over the red earth.

What should she do? She sat down by the side of the road to think about it; realised she had left the circus; and that she was not going back. She had been walking for some time, sleeping and walking. She remembered drinking at the dam where the cattle were.

The township ahead was probably Star-of-Eve, a mining township, a few miles out of Eagle Hawke. The circus waggons had gone out of the town along this very road; it was vaguely familiar. Gina decided she would try to get work there, and find a room for her mother to go when she came out of hospital. Gina would take the baby with her and not let her mother go back to the circus. That had been in her mind when she left the tents beside the railway siding.

What work could she do? Washing, scrubbing? She determined to ask at the first hotel or big house she came to if there was any work she might do. If a woman came to the door, Gina resolved to enquire whether she knew anybody who wanted washing or scrubbing done; any cleaning or rough work.

She got up and walked on into the town, a slow stooping figure, hatless, looking half-crazy in her grey draggled frock. But Gina had lost consciousness of herself. How she looked did not occur to her. She did not feel anything she thought with satisfaction; even her back did not ache, though her feet dragged wearily. Only her brain kept saying: 'Lin! Lin! Lin!' She was afraid when anybody spoke to her she would say 'Lin.' That she could say nothing else.

At the first hotel, a long old-fashioned house with narrow verandahs slouched by the road, fowls scratching about, she went to the back door.

'Is there any work, scrubbing or cleaning, I can do for you, at all?' she asked the woman who came to the low open doorway.

'You been on the booze or what?' the woman exclaimed. 'You look crazy.'

Gina turned away as though she had been struck. The shock and dazed misery she was suffering reached the woman.

'Here,' she said, 'you might try at Bergen's, the boarding-house by the Star-of-Eve. Mrs. Bergen there wants some one to wash for her, I know.'

Gina walked on, past small wooden houses, tin sheds and shacks of old bags and rusty tin scattered over the low red shingly hills as if they had grown there, so earth-stained they were, so beaten into the ground by sun and dust storms.

At a little distance the whitened roofs looked like flakes of skin peeling from the bare rocky bosom of the hills. But on the main street, two or three large hotels of red brick spread verandahs on long slender legs of posts, over the footpaths. Rows of young trees made bouquets of green on either side of the footpaths. There were fruit shops, with grapes, apples, tomatoes and lettuces piled up in them, stores with food stuffs in coloured wrappings, drapers' shops, shoe shops and newsagents' windows gay with posters, books and magazines.

Gina felt comforted to be among people and houses. She walked on past the shops, towards the mine, at the end of the street. Its great mound of grey slag, the same colour as the sheds of corrugated iron, dominated the township. Thin sketchy outlines of the mine head pencilled the sky. Noise of the machinery, clatter, slash and batter of a stamper vibrated above all the subdued murmur of the wide, empty street.

Behind the row of shops and pubs, the wooden and galvanised iron huts of the miners scattered away again. There were a few trees beside some of them. Creepers trailed over trellises and wire netting, purple and magenta of bougainvillea flared against the pale blue sky: pink and red flowers stuck out from geraniums growing in kerosene tins and old pots.

Gina recognised the boarding-house when she saw it, a small wooden house with two rows of sheds behind.

'If it's work you're wanting, my girl, come inside,' a woman called from indoors when Gina stood in the doorway. 'But can you work? Are you strong enough?'

'I'm hard as goat's knees,' Gina said.

'Oh well, thank God for that,' Marie Bergen replied. 'You look a good girl. The men are wanting their washing done and me scarcely able to hobble about with the lumbago.'

In a few moments Gina was working at wash tubs on a bench behind the house. She lit a fire under an oil drum over a fire-place built of stones, and scrubbed at the dirty clothes, mostly men's things, shirts and trousers, dungarees and moleskins, carried them from tubs to the oil drum which was used for a copper; from the copper to the tubs again and hung the wet clothes on lines where she pegged them to dry.

Several times her head swayed; she felt giddy, but kept on with her work, telling herself the queer feeling would pass. And it did after awhile. Her brain stopped clicking. It was no longer saying: 'Lin! Lin! Lin!' as it had been all the time before she had something to do.

Mrs. Bergen brought her a cup of tea.

'I don't know what you been doing with yourself, but you look fair done-up,' she said.

Gina's circus smile flashed in her gratitude.

'I've walked a long way,' she said.

'A long way, have you? Where've you come from?' The

little woman was curious. Gossip was her chief interest in life.

'Swan Hill way,' Gina said, with some hesitation, and turned to lift clothes from the boiler again.

There was little news of the countryside that escaped Marie Bergen. She knew of no girl who would answer to a description of Gina at Swan Hill. Over a hundred miles away though that was. But she was glad enough to get her. You could not get a girl to do a hand's turn for love or money, in Star-of-Eve, she was tired of saying. The district lying about the great mine carried its name.

Gina suited Mrs. Bergen in every way. She was quiet and homely. Worked about the house unobstrusively, cleaning and tidying-up, washing dishes, was satisfied with the small wages and room suggested for a week's trial.

At the end of the week, Gina had to tell Mrs. Bergen she must find a room for her mother who was coming out of hospital with a baby. There was not a corner to spare at Bergen's and Gina did not know where she would find a room to which she could take her mother and the baby. Somewhere her mother must go to rest a little longer, Gina declared, and she herself must be near to keep an eye on the child.

In order to keep Gina handy, Mrs. Bergen offered to clear out a shed at the bottom of the yard and let Gina have that for her mother. On several occasions it had been let to a miner who came to Bergen's for his meals, and as there was a mulberry tree in the yard, and a bit of a vegetable garden which Mart Bergen tried to keep going, Gina was more than pleased to rent the shed and go to sleep there. Besides as Mrs. Bergen pointed out, she could make a little more money by washing for miners who did not board at Bergen's, if she had a place of her own.

Gina swept and scrubbed the shed, so that it would look nice and be as comfortable as possible.

She had been to the hospital in Eagle Hawke once or twice to see her mother and the new baby, a swarthy little girl, as dark as Gina had been, with brown eyes and soft dark hair.

Gina had never seen her mother so pleased with and proud of a child. Perhaps it was because everybody in the hospital made a fuss and said what a beautiful baby Max was. Mrs. Haxby had called the child Maxine, a name she had found in a book.

'It'll look well on the bills, by and by, Gina,' she said. 'Dad'll be pleased.'

Mrs. Haxby had cried and cried, and said she was heart-broken about Lin. But her baby was there. Her heart was not empty like Gina's. Gina felt as if her heart would always be empty because of Lin. She thought she could not care for the pretty little brown baby; that she had no caring left. But she resolved the new baby was to have a better chance than ever came Lin's way to be well and strong.

She told her mother what she had done.

'Oh, Gina, you've never run away. You've never run away and left the show.'

'I have,' Gina said steadily. 'And we're not going back . . . not until Max's old enough to stand the life. Not then if you don't want to——'

'But Gina——' her mother gasped.

'I've got a house for us,' Gina explained eagerly. 'Such a nice little house, Mum. Just one room and a lean-to at the bottom of Bergen's garden. I work at Bergen's and take in washing for the miners.'

'My!' Her mother stared wonder and admiration.

'You won't have nothing to do but just look after the baby. I make about two pounds a week altogether. *He* won't never find us. All you got to do is leave here with me . . . not say anything to anybody where you're going. And when Dad comes for you, if he does come, you'll be gone that's all.'

'But he's written already to say will I get back as soon as possible.'

Gina's smile was wry and bitter.

'He would. Well, you're not going. He'd have you slaving yourself to death . . . because I'm not there. And how'd the baby get on then?'

'That's right,' Mrs. Haxby said slowly.

As soon as he thought of it, Dan had rung up the hospital and asked a nurse to let Mrs. Haxby know he wanted her back with the circus as soon as possible. He was told she had given birth to a daughter; but that it would be a week at least before she could travel.

Dan had written then, telling Lotty where the circus was going and to rejoin him at Red Rock or Ballinyo. He told her about Lin and that Gina had gone off, 'good riddance to her.' Perhaps the show would have better luck now. She had been nothing but a Jonah for years.

When it was time for her mother and the baby to leave hospital, Gina was waiting for them: she had taken them away. So that nearly a fortnight later when Dan himself got down by train to know why Lotty had not come to Red Rock or Ballinyo, it was to find she had left the hospital. Gina had taken her away. No, the matron did not know where they had gone. Nor could Dan in the little time he had to enquire, hear or discover any trace of them. He did not care to put the police on their tracks, and expected they would rejoin the show in a week or two, after they had had a good holiday together.

Very proud and pleased with herself, Gina took her mother and Max to the home she had made for them. She had whitewashed the shed, inside and out, and hung blue cretonne printed with roses, birds and apples at the window. There was a bed inside for her mother; a wooden box lined with pink sateen and net over it for the baby. Mrs. Bergen advised staining the floor boards which were very rough and old, and Gina had painted them over with a solution of permanganate of potash. She had piled boxes on each other for cupboards, and tacked a few coloured pictures from magazines on the wall. A table and a couple of boxes for chairs completed the furniture. Gina herself slept on a stretcher made of wire netting, under the lean-to at the back of the shed.

Out from the lean-to she built herself a fire-place like the one at Mrs. Bergen's and had bought a large black copper. Then too, she arranged a couple of tubs and tar barrels to catch water, and used the same sort of tubs sawn in half to wash in. Mrs. Haxby, who had not lived in a house for years, was delighted with Gina.

'Well, I declare, Gina,' she said, 'and you've done it all in less than a fortnight.'

'We can get things, make it more comfortable as we go on, Mum,' Gina explained.

Already she had an air of the man of the house. Just at first with rent to pay, and so much to buy, all the money she had earned was used.

'My, I should think so,' Mrs. Haxby agreed. 'But what will Dad say? Won't he be mad? And what if he finds us?'

'He won't find us,' Gina said. 'If he does, I'm not

going back. And you needn't if you don't want to. It's for her really.'

'That's right,' Mrs. Haxby said. 'All the same——'

Gina knew her mother was wishing she could have said good-bye to Dan; got him to consent to what they were doing, which he would never have done. Gina realised that hers was the master will. Lotty Haxby was doing this against her own inclination. There was the tug of her long years of wandering and mateship; but Gina was very young and stern ruling against that weakness.

'It's for Max,' she said.

She worked hard. Day in and day out, week after week, month after month, year after year, she cleared-up and scrubbed for Mrs. Bergen and took in washing for miners.

She rarely went beyond the garden in Bergen's backyard and 'her place' as she called it. The pink ivy geranium she planted and watered, grew quickly beside the shed; a couple of lucern trees and dolicos screened and gave it a white-flowered coolness. Indoors too, gradually she had improved the room with a mat or two and an easy chair.

An old miner knocked up a cool-safe for her. He had seen Gina trying to make chairs of butter boxes and given a hand with them too. Mart Bergen shared his seeds with her, and Gina watered his vegetable garden; fed the fowls for him. When Mrs. Bergen was ill, Gina had looked after her and taken charge of 'the boarding-house.

Year after year, as she worked and lived in the same quiet absorbed way, people began to forget she had not always been there. She was as much a friend of Mrs.

Bergen and her son, Mart, as if she had always lived with them.

And Max grew from a bonny dark-eyed baby to a toddling urchin; then an elfish merry youngster, as like Gina as if she had been her own child.

Gina had come to love Max, but never as she had loved Lin. Always she was on her guard against the hurt a love like that would do her.

Only Mrs. Haxby was not happy. Shut away, with nothing to do but sew a little for the women about, she grumbled and wailed more than she had done when she was washing and sewing for everybody on the circus. She talked a great deal of her life with the circus and on the road: the costumes she had made, parade dresses, tights and trunks. She seemed to remember every piece of finery she had ever put together; and all the sights, dangers and adventures she had been through. There was nothing Mrs. Bergen and women of the mines liked better than to get Lotty talking about the circus.

It was from her they heard about Gina. From Gina nothing was ever heard of her old life. Some of the men on the Star-of-Eve, who had seen Gina ride, remembering the beautiful girl she used to be, would scarcely believe the sombre, heavy woman who was always stooping over a wash tub, or grubbing about in Bergen's backyard, was the same girl. Lotty could not keep her mouth shut. She talked endlessly about Dan and the show, Rabe, Lord Freddie, the boys, Lily and Jack.

She was very fed-up of sitting cooped in a backyard, dressmaking for strangers, she said, and pined for the noise and bustle of her old life. Mrs. Haxby told the Bergens why Gina and she were there, in the shed near the big mulberry tree. They had run away from Haxby's, from the show and from Dan, until Max was old enough to begin work. Not that Lotty did not want to go back; she would have rejoined Dan before this had she known where he was. But she did not know where the circus had gone; what had become of Dan. Could hear nothing of Haxby's. Nobody had seen or heard anything of the show for ages.

'Six years is a long time,' Marie Bergen said.

'You've said it,' Mrs. Haxby agreed.

'A man could easily get a divorce and be married again,' Mrs. Bergen remarked.

Lotty was aghast at the idea.

'Oh – but,' she faltered, 'Dan never looked at any other woman but me. I must say that for him.'

Her mother had wailed over the possibility with Gina. 'To think of it, Gina – your father could get a divorce and be married to another woman – for all I know about it. Where is he? What are they doing I wonder? I'd never have gone off like I did if you hadn't rushed me into it.'

'There's Maxie,' Gina said.

'Well,' Mrs. Haxby defended angrily, 'there she is! And I can't see she's anything more wonderful than you were at her age.'

'At her age,' Gina murmured.

'Gina I believe . . . you . . . you hate your father,' Mrs. Haxby sobbed. 'There's something so hard in you. It's as if you had it against him, and –'

'Not till Lin,' Gina looked away from her. 'I forgave him everything till Lin . . . and I'll never forgive him that.'

'Gord, it was an accident! You may be sure,' Mrs. Haxby exclaimed impatiently. 'It was an accident. I'm sure he was always a good father to you. Kind and generous . . . and proud of you. How proud he was of you, Gina, before – everything was for us.'

'And the show.'

'The show, of course. But he didn't drink, not what you'd call drink, or beat you.'

'He was only selfish and careless, like most men, only a bit more.'

'And there's the boys and Lil, Gina. I wish I knew where they are. What they're doing.'

CHAPTER 14

DURING all the years Gina worked for her in Star-of-Eve, Mrs. Bergen went away to the sea-side for a few weeks in the summer time and left Gina in charge of the boarding-house. Once or twice Mart had gone with his mother for a few days; but usually he took his holiday during the football season, and went round with the boys. He played half-back for Eagle Hawke, and came home looking the worse for wear with a sore head and empty pockets.

Mart Bergen was a miner, and the son of a miner. A lad of eight when his father died, Mrs. Bergen had let rooms to miners by way of making a living for them both. Later she arranged for huts to be built at the back of her own four-roomed house until Bergen's was accommodating twenty men for the Star-of-Eve. And although her boarders growled a good deal about the plainness and meagreness of the fare Mum Bergen supplied, there was plenty of it, and the men recognised you could not get more for the money anywhere else. The rooms were clean and Mrs. Bergen was a good sort, would wait for her money during a strike, or if a man were pushed for cash through sickness or bad luck at the races.

For two or three years, Mart and Gina barely crossed words with each other. She saw him coming and going about the house, shouting and whistling, turning out for his shift in earth-stained blue trousers and flannel shirt, coming in to shower, dress and go out again. A stalwart, well-built, good-looking, good-humoured young man, the core of his mother's life, he had watched her curiously at first, remembering La Gitana.

Gina had not noticed him or his glances, caring only to get on with her work and do it as well as possible. And he had become used to see her slaving about, a drab figure in old clothes. In those days Gina worked for the sake of working and to make money. It did not matter to her how she looked. She had put all thought of herself out of her mind. It never occurred to her to push a wisp of hair straight, or change her dress to please and attract anybody.

She drudged for and waited on Mart and his mother, doing any odd jobs that came her way. Every morning she went up to the boarding-house, swept, scrubbed and made beds there. Then down at her own shack in the afternoon and evening, washed and ironed for the miners who brought her their dirty clothes. Nearly every night in the week, for years, Mart saw this girl who had been a circus rider, ironing at a bench under the lean-to verandah of the shed at the bottom of the garden.

'Cripes, Gina, you're a terror to work!' he called sometimes. 'Don't you ever let up?'

She, looking towards him, smiled, without troubling to answer, as often as not.

More than once he had said: 'Doesn't that girl ever take a day off, Mum?'

'I've told her to, Mart,' Mrs. Bergen replied, 'but she doesn't seem to want to. She's glad to have work, I think, afraid to let go of it. Felt that way meself sometimes. I know what it means.'

When she was six years old, Max trotted off to the

State School in Eagle Hawke with the children of miners and other folk who lived round the Star-of-Eve.

A fleet agile little creature, she skipped, climbed and ran about, getting into all manner of mischief. There was nothing she liked better than helping Mart to paint the roof of the house and huts with whitewash to keep off the heat, or clean out the spouts before rain. She played about in the mulberry tree, chased goats and ran races with all the small boys in the neighbourhood.

Gina had seen her walking along the edge of a fence, balancing herself to the amazement and joyous enthusiasm of a horde of urchins as wiry, brown and eager as herself. She watched Max turning hand-springs with the boys about, but with a dash and grace none of them had. Mart had taught her some gymnastic tricks, and watching her somersault easily, gaily, one day, Gina called: 'Try it backwards, Max.'

The child tossed herself backwards and sprang up on her feet delightfully.

'It's born in her,' Lotty Haxby exclaimed, and Gina herself was surprised that without any teaching Max should know how to do these things so much better than the other youngsters.

More and more Mrs. Bergen had grown to depend on Gina. She liked the girl, trusted her, and chatted away to her, about every detail of her life and Mart's. Her son was the be-all and end-all of Marie Bergen's existence. She told Gina about Mart's father; how he had been killed by a fall of earth in an old shaft when Mart was about eight years old, and what a fight she had to make ends meet for them both at first. What a good lad Mart was, though a bit wild, earning good wages, and spending them all as he went along. And how could he help it, seeing how popular he was and the girls all running after him?

Mart wanted his mother to give up the boarding-house and live more easily. But frail and always more or less ailing though she might be, she refused to forego her independence, and the money she was making now.

'I won't never be a burden on him,' she confided to Gina. 'I've kept going so long, I can keep on a bit longer. I couldn't bear to think I'd come between Mart and the things he wants to do. And a miner's life's so uncertain. You never can tell what might happen. If only he'd put a bit of money by to go on the land. A man can't stick to the mines all his days . . . and then too, someday, he'll want to get married . . . and I'm not going to be a hanger-on in my old age – or let any girl think she's got to make a blessed martyr of herself on my account.'

They were very good friends, Mart and his mother. Mart teased his mother about the money she made and her investments, and she laughed at him about his smart clothes and the girls he was always flying about with. His tarts, she called them. There was a pretty little girl with a frizz of fair hair who rode behind him on his motor bicycle, and a dark-eyed one he took to dances sometimes.

'There's safety in numbers, Gina, they say,' Mrs. Bergen declared happily. 'I don't need to worry while Mart's tracking round with half a dozen girls.'

Gina agreed with her. After awhile, she found herself dancing attendance on Mart much as his mother did, putting his dinner away in the oven to keep hot, pressing and cleaning his clothes, hunting for a tie he had mislaid.

Once when she brought him a shirt newly-ironed for a dance he was going to, his mother had called:

'Who is it to-night, Mart? Poppy Lewis or Dorrie?'

'Guess,' he yelled, light-heartedly.

'Wish it was you, Gina,' he added with a quick glance as Gina handed him the shirt.

'Me?' The startled leaping of Gina's eyes surprised him.

'You shouldn't pull her leg like that, Mart,' his mother said.

'I wasn't pulling her leg,' he replied sulkily.

He found Gina more stand-offish, less easy to make friends with than any girl he had ever known. Not that he tried very hard. He watched her at work and was sorry for her. Carried a heavy basket or bucket of wet clothes for her now and then, or lit the fire in the morning. She said: 'Thank you,' but paid no more attention to him than that. This, to so good-looking and sought after a young man, was disappointing. He would have liked her to be more pleased when he did things for her. He was curious to ask about the circus and her trick riding; how it was done, all that; would have liked to talk to her about them. But Gina never gave him a chance. She was always so locked-up in herself. So set on her work.

'I don't think she likes me,' he told his mother.

'Go on, Mart,' Mrs. Bergen teased, 'Gina's got a lot of common sense. She's not making eyes at you, if that's what you mean. With her back and all, she reckons she's done with that sort of thing . . . and of course, she has, I suppose, poor girl.'

Through all those years, it was true, Gina regarded Mart Bergen as the superior being whose comings and goings were the important happenings of that small house. She dusted his room, hung his best clothes on their hangers or put his trousers between drawers in a chest of drawers to keep their folds, and smiled with Mrs. Bergen over the photographs of girls they found stuck round the mirror, or on the walls of Mart's room. But Mart had her under his eyes, and watched her with sympathy and grudging admiration for a long time before he tried to express them at all.

When he suggested, the year Mrs. Haxby was fretting so because she could not find out anything about the circus or where Daniel Haxby had gone, that Mrs. Bergen should take Gina with her when she went to the coast, his mother suspected some kindly instinct and approved of it. In fact why should not 'the family' go, Mart asked. He had adopted the Haxbys as part of the household these days, and was really fond of Max. Mart promised to take a fortnight off to go to Mallacoota with his mother; but declared he would not go unless she arranged for Gina to do the cooking and house-work.

'You're a bit used up, Mum,' he offered by way of explanation, 'and it's time I took hand bossing you now.'

Mrs. Bergen was too pleased at the prospect of a holiday with Mart to quibble about terms.

She had been a Gippsland girl, before she married Lloyd Bergen and went to live on the mines, and it was the joy of her life to go back to the great forests, and hear the sea pounding away on the ninety mile beaches. The hut built of shingles and slabs of bark, she had got an old fisherman to put up for her, was on land which had once belonged to her father. She had taken Mart to Mallacoota Inlet for his school holidays before he went into the mines, and any year since, when she could get him to go. They had lived fishing, swimming, and dozing in the sun, for weeks at a time.

Mart seemed to have thought over his proposition a

good deal. He suggested that Mrs. O'Keefe, a neighbour, could be trusted to look after the boarding-house. She had done so before. And when Gina wondered whether she could afford train fares and to do without her washing for a week or so, Mart decided Max was looking a bit peaky: the child really needed a change. Train fares would be his funeral because after all Gina was going to look after his mother. So there was nothing more to be said.

Traps and food boxes were packed, and after the long train and coach journey, dawdling across the wide, still Mallacoota lakes in a little motor boat, Mrs. Bergen threw open the door of the bark and slab hut which had stood waiting and empty for them since last summer.

The hut stood on a slope overlooking sheening waters of the inlet with mountain ranges and the high peak of Gabo beyond; that strip of golden sand separating quiet waters of the inlet from crested rollers of the Southern Ocean, and Marie Bergen was all delighted excitement and happiness to see it again; to be gazing out over the inlet and sea; have all the smoked and misty fragrance of the bush behind her, hear the bird warblings and callings she had loved as a girl.

'Oh listen,' she cried as a grey magpie threw his pure minor notes from a dead tree in the clearing. 'Isn't he a darling? He's calling to welcome us. You don't hear him anywhere else, like down here in South Gippsland, do you, Gina?'

Gina took the work of the little household out of Mrs. Bergen's hands at once. First to move in the morning, she made tea, lit the fire and cooked fish for breakfast; washed-up and swept sand from the wooden floors of the two rooms and verandah, round which Mart had arranged stretchers of wire netting and saplings, to sleep on.

Everybody slept out on the verandahs, using one room to dress and the other to cook and eat in.

For the rest of the day there was the sea and the beaches. Mart went fishing or duck shooting along the creek, with men who lived further inland or along the inlet shores. Mrs. Bergen, Gina and Max lived in their bathers; Mrs. Haxby preferred to dress more. There was no township for miles away, so for the most part the camp had to be self-supporting, eat fish and wild duck, or bunnies they caught. Mart brought in oysters now and then and Mrs. Haxby made damper and Johnny cake.

The hut was above a lonely stretch of beach, with moors behind, islands scattered about the inlet in front. Few people ever came that way, and sprawling in the sun, swimming, fishing and sleeping on the sand, Gina and Max from being raw with sunburn burned to a mellow brown. They played and ran about on the beach together. Sometimes Mart played and ran with them, turned hand-springs and raced Gina swimming to the sand-bank.

Gina was heard to laugh. A low rippling melody, like the uncertain song of a bird, flew and floated from her.

'It makes me want to cry every time I hear her laugh,' Mart exclaimed to his mother.

For those four weeks of summer Gina seemed to forget her back. There were no strangers with glances of shock and pity to remind her of her appearance. The people she was with had become so accustomed to sight of her that they had forgotten it; and because they had forgotten she slipped into unconsciousness for awhile. In the sea, she lost her sense of deformity. She moved with her old dash and grace through the clear glassy water.

Diving with Mart, swimming with Mart, Gina laughed

as eagerly, gaily as she had ever done. Her body cut the pale clear green water, she glided through the purple depths, brown limbs flexed, brown arms stretched and curving out and over. Her body in its dark blue bathers, barbed by clean-cutting brown arms, a feather of spray tossed from the sleek black head, she swam out with Mart. If they were racing, Mrs. Bergen and Max shrieked as they danced up and down on the beach: 'Go it Mart! Go it Gina!'

Gina loved the sea, loved it when it was still and blue as the sky, glittering at mid-day, cut into tiny flaked waves as the land breeze ruffled it, in the late afternoon, or when it lay misty and still as silk under the haze of bush fires. In the sea she had something of her old joy of life. She felt young and gay again. The sea hid her body from sight: she could go out into it as if she were folding its wonderful azure, or the wide shimmering green of the shallows round her.

She laughed and talked gaily, carelessly to Mart when they were swimming out in deep water together, or had stretched to sun themselves on a sand-bank, winking salt from her eyes, blowing salt water from her nose. Her eyes met his with a wide confident friendliness.

Awed and bewitched, they had watched a storm gathering on the outer beach one day. A strangely malignant storm, it looked, coming up from the sea, with purple and indigo clouds as if some great dragon had crawled across the sky and was filling the air with his poisonous breath. The sea cut into little metallic waves, green and brackish as the scales on putrescent fish, slapped the beaches. Light flashed from and played over dark clouds. Waters of the inlet were verdigris in their shadow.

The earth looked a livid thing beside the sea. Great

breakers came up from the Southern Ocean, flinging themselves at Gina's and Mart's feet as the fury of the storm broke. Electric flashes tore the ashy blue and purple murk of sky and sea, crackling and crashing into thunder. Garish, unreal, sea and sky looked.

Mart took Gina's hand and they stood watching the storm a little afraid, yet loth to go in out of it. Then Mart had pulled Gina to him, looking deep into her eyes. What magic held them through the deep stirring kelp dark pools of her eyes and his, indigo, storm-swept as the sea? Shaken, in the vague, earth-warmed, sea-smelling happiness of those days, Gina had swung to him on the surge and emotion of the moment. Mart held her with passion and tenderness in the storm all about them. He had kissed her. To that singing tumult of the blood what answer was there?

Mrs. Bergen called from the hut through the rain which lashed down from the sky. So heavy the shower, it had screened and hidden Mart and Gina.

As they scrambled up from the beach, a sea gull screamed shrilly, blown past over the dunes by the wind and the rain.

After a few days Mrs. Bergen began to realise how her boy's eyes went after Gina. She became aware of an undertow in his feeling for the girl.

She had not thought of that. Such good friends they were all together. On such good terms, Gina and she, and Mart and Mrs. Haxby. None of them seemed more intimate then she, herself and Gina, though Mart and Mrs. Haxby got on very well.

Mart liked to make Lotty talk of the circus when Gina was not there, stringing the little woman on to boast of the wonders and marvels of Haxby's, pretending to forget she was not a trapeze star or contortionist and had played with bears and lions in her spare moments. And there was the child between them. Max was full of wonder and delight at the sea and the beaches which she had never seen before. Mart taught her to swim and dive; they turned somersaults on the sand. Gina and Max wandered and picked wild flowers on the edge of the sand hills and in the scrub inland, sea lavender, late orchids, black wattle blossom.

It had all been such good fun, each one doing as he or she liked, going her own way; not bothering much about what anybody else did, just eating, sleeping, fishing, lying about reading on the sand, or chatting together. If anything Mrs. Bergen thought she and Gina understood each other better than any of the others. She had a real regard and affection for the girl. Gina was so sympathetic, so helpful and reliable in her quiet way.

Mart had been sorry for Gina, his mother imagined; interested in her; but Mrs. Bergen never expected to see the look in his eyes she found just now. She was satisfied to have Mart with her, enjoying the holiday. She had been easy in her mind about him: to know he was not wasting his money with other young men, boozing, and going to the races. But her heart felt like the fish she had seen in a giant shell on the beach the other day, when they wrenched the white china of its valves apart, quivering and wounded, at the thought of Mart caring for Gina, really caring for and set on the girl.

He could not want to marry her, she told herself. It was not that. No man would want to marry Gina, poor girl. Not a young man like Mart, so good looking and popular; a man so fond of life and gadding about as he was.

No, Mrs. Bergen assured herself, Mart could not be

in love with Gina, not really in love, for all her goodness and unselfishness. He admired the willing way she worked for everybody and was grateful for a companionship which made no demands on him; was there when he wanted it and just what he wanted it to be. Gina had fished with him, swum with him, yarned with him, sung with him through all the sun-filled, sea-dreaming days and warm sweet nights of those weeks. That's all there was to it, Mrs. Bergen decided. The being thrown together, no other young people about but themselves: a midsummer madness.

'Mart,' she said to him, having watched him bathing in the inlet with Gina, the pair of them splashing and playing about there together as happily as children, 'Mart, you're real fond of Gina, aren't you?'

His eyes quick to her, steadily, as if he had thought a good deal about what he was going to say, 'Real fond, Mum,' he said. 'Fonder than I've been of any girl.'

'Oh, Mart!'

Her wailing cry warned him.

'I know all you're thinking,' he added quickly. 'I don't know what I'm going to do yet.'

'You'd never marry her. You'd never want to do that, Mart?'

Mart stretched his brown legs, lying out on the sand beside her.

'I want to all right.' His mother had never heard Mart's voice so hard and old. She scarcely knew what to make of it. 'And I don't see why not, really, Mum. Gina's healthy and strong . . . stronger than most of the girls we know, really. She works harder. It mightn't make any difference.'

'It would. It'd make all the difference, Mart,' his

mother said. 'Oh, Mart, I know what a good girl Gina is . . . her nature and all that. But you can't do it, my laddie! You can't. It's not now . . . but by-and-by you'd hate her.'

'I don't see it,' Mart protested. 'I'd believe in her, always. We're such good cobbers, Mum.'

'Couldn't you go on being good cobbers, Mart?'

Mart smiled through half-closed eyes.

'I don't want to,' he said. 'That's it. Gina's got the stuff I've been after all my life, Mum. If I don't get her . . . I might as well take Poppy Lewis, or any other pretty little fool. It'd be all the same. If it was Gina, I feel there'd be something to rest on till the end of my days . . .'

'It wouldn't work, Mart. I know it wouldn't. After a bit . . . you wouldn't want to take her about with you,' Mrs. Bergen exclaimed. 'You'd be ashamed . . . not want to be seen with her. You'd hate it – and her, poor Gina. It's hard on her I know; I've never seen her like this, never thought she could laugh and look happy . . . though people say she was a bonny girl, on the circus. Oh, it's a cruel shame; but what's the good of talking like that! You've just got to take things as you find them and do the best you can.'

Mart was not convinced.

'You're not to say anything to Gina,' he commanded.

'All right.' His mother was depressed. She felt as if she were helping him to bind on some great burden. All her pleasure in the holiday had vanished.

Mart took his own way.

'I want to marry you, Gina, but Mum doesn't want me to,' he remarked casually, as they lay on the beach in the sunshine, next day.

'Oh, Mart!'

Gina looked down at him stretched beside her in faded black bathers, shrunken and tied over one shoulder with a bit of string; his arms and legs sunburned a woody brown, still showed pink petal of the underskin here and there. She had never thought of Mart saying that; was very humble about it: could see his mother's point of view at once. Mart talked in a matter of fact, quite commonsense way.

'I like you better than any girl I ever knew,' he said. 'I think we could make a do of things. We'd be good cobbers, always, at any rate . . . even after we were married.'

'Do you think so, Mart?'

Gina had watched sea swallows, skimming the edge of the sea as he talked, the satiny gleam of their little upheld bodies, arcs of their wings flashing as they drifted inland. She plucked at sea-lavender growing among the sandhills, crushing the small grey leaves, and loosing their frail, warm fragrance.

It was too much, what Mart had said. That, and the fragrance of sea-lavender, held her heart and brain in a trance.

Mart moved nearer, threw an arm round her and they sat happily beside each other with an understanding and consciousness beyond words. Gina lived in the glamour and tenderness of Mart's eyes, yielding her own to them. She was loth to try to be explicit about the miracle which had befallen her. That it could not last; would fall to pieces she was sure, yet for what it was worth, she was grateful and surrendered.

When she and Mart went back to the humpy in the late afternoon, still in their bathers, towels over their arms, Gina had a little bunch of sea-lavender in her hands, and some of a small woolly white flower like white coral that raised its head sniffing the salt air, beside the track they had taken to walk home through the sandhills.

Gina's dazed, joyous eyes told Mrs. Bergen that Mart had made his explanation. The nerves about her heart tightened and stung her. Gina saw and understood what Mart's mother was suffering.

'I know,' she said to Mrs. Bergen, when they were clearing away the tea dishes, 'you can't be glad. I can't either, really. It's not good enough for him.'

'Oh, Gina, my dear,' Mrs. Bergen had broken down and cried. 'You're such a dear, sweet girl, I wish——'

'I wish too——' Gina stopped her, unable to hear the hurtful thing said. 'But it won't last. You see. It's . . . just for here . . . and now.'

Mrs. Bergen felt comforted. She was able to endure Mart's air of an accepted lover; the way he and Gina went about together, their banter, familiarities and happy confident glances. But after a few days she began to fidget to go home. The holiday had lasted long enough, she said. It had run on from a fortnight to a month. Everybody was beginning to get collar-proud.

Mart was for taking another month, sensing why his mother wanted to go away, to break up this loafing and dreaming by the sea. Gina, too, at the end of a week, realised Mrs. Bergen was right. Time could not stand still for her any longer. Only Mart laughed at the shrewdness of their reckoning. It would not make any difference to him where he lived he told his mother and Gina so long as he could see something of 'his girl'. He was sure of himself, had got something he had been looking for all his life, and was not going to be done out of it, no matter what anybody said or did.

CHAPTER 15

DURING their last days at the seaside, Mart and Gina went about with the assurance of sweethearts. Only Mrs. Haxby had not been aware of it, so accustomed was she to the idea of Gina as something life had broken and set aside. Gina begged Mrs. Bergen and Mart to say nothing of what was between them to her mother, just yet, fearing explanation might be bitter for her later on.

Before long, life was moving again at its customary jog trot about Bergen's boarding house in Star-of-Eve. Gina scrubbed and cleaned about the house and huts: took up her washing and ironing again.

Mart went down in the evenings to talk to Gina; but she was always so busy. It irritated him to find her at work; to see her dowdy and bent at tubs of washing, or sweating over flat irons beside an open fire. For a while he renounced all his old friends and acquaintances to hang round the garden and yarn with her while she worked. But Gina did not seem able to think of anything but what she was doing. The sea magic had left her. She looked older, duller, more work-worn now.

His old mates and the girls he used to take out began to ask what had happened to Mart Bergen these days. A rumour got about, spread by men who lived at Bergen's, that Mart was going to marry the hunch-backed girl who worked for his mother. Mart had never found the courage to ask Gina to go out with him, which would have been acknowledgement of the rumour. She would not have gone; but she knew why he did not ask her.

It was as his mother thought, she realised; as she herself had expected. By the time the football season came round, Mart was caught up in the whirl of his old ways, except that he went out alone or with other men. Since the summer no one had seen him about with a girl and it did not agree with Mart not to be made a fuss of by some girl or other, his mother said.

'Mart's that grumpy and bad-tempered, I don't know what to make of him,' she grumbled. She seemed to have forgotten more easily than Mart any reason for his loss of confidence in himself just then.

Mart had not forgotten, Gina knew. He was struggling against memories of the summer; out of conceit with himself because he wanted to forget. He realised, as his mother had said, what it would mean to marry Gina; and Gina had worked, absorbing herself in her work so that he should realise, showing him only her drudging exterior and nothing of the gay, buoyant spirit which had revived for a little while in her at the sea and on the beaches.

A rind of sunset, blood orange, lay along the horizon, at the end of the street, the evening Gina went to the Bergen's gate to call Max. White sun-bleached huts and humpies, the pent houses and high dumps of the mine were huddled together; tall workings etched in fine lines against a sky limpid, pale winey yellow in the waning light; a new moon awash in it.

Miners who had come off shift were lounging about their doorways; goats wandering behind the cottages after they had been milked. Children playing in the street a little distance away laughed and shrieked happily, Max among them. Gina could hear the lovely staccato of their exclamations and calling to each other. She saw Max turning hand-springs with the boys; then walking on her hands, legs curved over her head. One of the boys tried to imitate her and sprawled in the dust.

Two men, strangers in the neighbourhood, who had been looking on from the foot-path, walked over to the children. Gina did not mind the miners beside their gates, watching and talking to the children; but these men were not miners.

'Max!' she called.

The child ran towards her. The two men followed. As they did so, the familiarity of that short rotund figure reached Gina, and the tall straggling one beside it. Could it be? Yes. There was not much doubt about it. The tall man was Rabe and the short stout man, her father.

Gina took Max's hand and went quickly down the path beside Bergen's and past the huts. What were Rabe and Dan doing in Eagle Hawke? Why were they there? Had they come looking for her mother and her? It was show week in Eagle Hawke. There were a great many strangers in the town, but not many of them had wandered so far. Star of Eve lay on the outskirts of the larger town, forming a scattered suburb at the foot of the Star of Eve and several other mines near-by.

Absorbed and disturbed by her own thought, Gina did not notice what the child was saying at first. Then she heard Max, in an excited babble, telling her mother about the man who had spoken to her while she was playing with other children in the street.

Max had been with the rest of the school children to the agricultural show in Eagle Hawke the day before. Gina had washed and ironed her pink print frock for the occasion. And Max had been chattering ever since about the trained monkeys she had seen at the show. Monkeys who sat at a little table and ate a meal, cleared away, then undressed themselves and went to bed.

'It was the monkey man, at the show, Mum,' Gina heard Max explaining to her mother. 'And he said I'd make a real good circus girl. Watched us just now when me and Clary was doing hand springs and walking on our hands. And he asked me my name——'

'Did that man speak to you just now?' Gina asked fiercely.

''Course he did, Gi,' Max replied wide-eyed.

'What did he say?' Gina demanded.

'Asked me my name,' Max prattled, 'and I said Maxine Haxby, and——'

'My God,' Gina groaned.

The gate beside Bergen's had clapped. She heard feet on the gravel, men walking down the path towards the huts. Gina glanced back at them.

'It's Dad and Rabe,' she said to her mother, and went out to the back of the shed.

Mrs. Haxby scuttled out of the room, dropping the sewing she had been at work on. Gina heard her scream of joyous exclamation.

'Oh, well,' Gina's hand went to the irons on her stove, 'it was bound to come, I suppose. And it doesn't matter now.' A basket of ironing was waiting for her to deal with.

Outside on the path, she could hear her mother crying and talking.

Gina lifted an iron, felt the heat against her cheek and began to press out the damp crumpled cotton of a miner's Sunday shirt. She felt weary and at the end of her tether.

But then, she had done what she promised herself, she remembered. Max was well and strong. She was ready for training, eager for it. Gina knew it was time for her training to begin even. The child was a born acrobat. That was all right. Gina had no fault to find with Max's prospects now.

Only she must go where Max went to watch over her. See that all went well for her. As Gina guessed, Dan had recognised there was good stuff in the child. She would be a credit to his training. Fearless, a gay, supple little creature, Max might become famous. Gina had never seen anybody as clever for her age.

And perhaps it was time to go away; to leave Star of Eve. Mart. She thought of him with all the glamour and tenderness of that sea dream which had faded in the hard work-a-day life of the mines. Never mind, Gina told herself, she had had those days of storm and sunshine among the sandhills, and never believed really there would be more to them. Mart still looked at her sometimes with a resurge of his troubled desire. But he knew himself now; that he would never have courage to face life by her side. Perhaps he would be happier if she went away? Gina thought so. She imagined Mart reproached himself because he had not come up to his own estimate of himself. She was a thorn in his self-respect. Perhaps he loved her. But he did not want to be laughed at and pitied because he had married a woman with a broken back.

The voices outside were coming nearer. They entered the house, Lotty Haxby's voice, eager, excited and tremulous; Dan's resonant and bombastic, good-natured, a little more subdued than of old. Gina set aside her ironing to make tea.

Mrs. Haxby took charge though, arranged and explained everything. Gina coming from the lean-to with a tray and cups of tea, nodded to her father and Rabe as though she had seen them the day before.

'Hullo, Dad,' she said. 'How's things, Rabe?'

'Well, Gina, I do think you might give your father a kiss, considering——'

'I'll give him a cup of tea, instead,' Gina said.

'Thanks, Gina,' Dan replied. 'Which is not to say we wouldn't rather have a pot of beer, eh Rabe? But you don't keep beer in your house, I suppose, Gina?'

'No,' Gina replied unsmiling.

Dan was staring at Max, quite taken-up and in love with her.

'By God, she's a bonza kid, isn't she,' he exclaimed. 'Near jumped out of me skin didn't I, Rabe, when I asked her her name, and she said, Maxine Haxby? Cripes! And then all we had to do was follow her here.'

'It's time for bed, Maxie,' Gina murmured after awhile.

Max demurred, thoroughly enjoying being made a fuss of and talked about, sitting on this new-found Daddy's knee and hearing all the wonderful things he had been doing, and she was going to do in the future.

When she was too sleepy to keep her eyes open any longer, Gina took her away to put her to bed.

'What is it, Gi?' the child whispered seeing the thought and misery of Gina's eyes. 'Aren't you glad Dad's found us?'

Gina looked down at her, all the deep love of her being stirred.

'I don't know. It'll be all right, Max, I think,' she said. 'But I'm not going to leave you, ever.'

Max pressed her little brown face and soft hair against Gina's.

'No, Gi,' the child snuggled against her contentedly.

'Not till you're old and happy and don't want me any more.'

'But you're crying, Gi?'

It was true. The tears had rained and splashed down Gina's dark tired face almost without her being aware of them. Why was she crying? She hardly knew herself. Max clung to her, patting Gina's hand and kissing her. Max had never seen this big sister of hers cry before, and she was just beginning to realise what she stood for. Gina had done so much for her, as long as she could remember; Max could not imagine being without her.

When Gina returned to the little sitting room where Lotty Haxby was sitting with Dan and Rabe, the conference was well under way. Lotty had forgotten that there was anything to forgive Dan. For the past few years, she had been upbraiding herself, regarding herself as a runaway to be forgiven and received back into the fold if ever there was a chance.

'It was a mistake, I know, Dan. I should never have done what I did. I've told Gina that lots of times. But – –'

'We'll let bygones be bygones, Mum. Don't let's talk of it any more,' Dan agreed.

And Gina in the bitterness of her understanding had nothing to say.

Dan told the story of the misfortunes Haxby's had suffered during the past few years. How the circus had gone to West Australia after Gina and her mother ran away. The break-up had been all their fault you might say. Bruiser and Charley had deserted after receiving their wages one night. Jack and Lily cleared out soon afterwards.

The tents were torn to shreds in a storm soon after Dan returned to Victoria. He had advised the boys to try to get a job and they had been touring with Wirth's for awhile; but were out of work again now. After the tent was destroyed, it was no good hanging on to the waggons. They were sold, and the menagerie, all but Queenie whom Dan loaned to the Melbourne zoo. The monkeys, Rabe and he had been taking round the country districts for shows, and from being down and out were doing quite well now. Lord Freddie had been left on a farm at Three Springs only a few weeks ago.

Some of the horses were sold, but his trained pets, Dan had hung on to, he said, always hoping that some day he would find his missus, his children would come back to him, and he might be able to start rebuilding the show again. There were tears in his eyes as he spoke. Phil, Beauty and Bonnie were eating their heads off at his brother George's farm in the Dandenongs. Dan could not bear to part with them, if they never did another tap in their lives. The wild west team was there also.

'I know a chap would give me tick for the tents,' he said, 'we could go out to George's place and start training again and be ready in a month – if you'll come, Lotty. You and the kid. But it's no good on the road without you. There'll be no Haxby's unless you come along.'

'Dan!' Lotty trembled to her delight and pride.

This was something like being alive, having a man beside you, wanting you to work with him, telling you he could not get on without you. And she knew he could not.

'I may have me faults,' Dan boomed. 'I don't say

I haven't me faults, but women's not one of them. There's never been any woman but you, Lotty, since you went away. And that's the truth, isn't it, Rabe?'

Gina knew her mother would go through all the years of wandering, child bearing and hardship, again for him, after that. What did she know of this husband-and-wifeness which made you go through so much for a man?

'You stick to me, Lotty, and I'll stick to you,' Dan said.

'I'll stick, Dan,' her mother quavered.

'How about you, Gina?'

'Yes, what will you do, Gina?' Rabe croaked.

'I'll go with mother and Max,' Gina said.

Was it an end to the revolt of Gina? Dan chuckled but Rabe did not think so. Dan was in a fever of happiness and excitement at thought of getting the circus together again. Lotty confided to him she had £20 put by and would get busy with wardrobe at once. Lotty and the kid were an asset in themselves and to have captured Gina as well, a feather in his cap. Dan did not deceive himself. He began to realise valuable quality in the girl, intelligence and determination. Besides Lotty had whispered of a nest egg Gina must have, which was all to the good.

Dan did not intend to run foul of Gina again. She was much harder metal than he cared to run up against. He intended to make the utmost use of her. He was beginning to see her point about the kid; conceded she had been right about that and was willing to humour her.

With Max, Dan was too delighted for words, played the indulgent parent, spoiling her and showing her tricks all next day. He would not leave Eagle Hawke without his wife and prodigal daughter, he declared. No, nothing would induce him to. Lotty wept at the flowery eloquence of his sentiments, freely expressed to Mrs. Bergen and men at the huts where a room had been found for Dan and for Rabe.

He was so good, Dan, Lotty told everybody. However she had come to leave him she did not know. She felt that she did not deserve such magnanimity.

Mrs. Bergen and several of the miners and their wives and children were there on the railway station to wave good-bye to Gina and Max and Mrs. Haxby when the train drew out. They had brought little presents, and were full of excitement about this romance in real life they were taking part in. Mart did not put in an appearance. Neither had he gone down to say good-bye to Gina, the night before she and her mother left the shed at the bottom of the garden which had been home to them for so long.

Silent and withdrawn in the eager chatter of friends, Gina looked out towards the mines. 'Mart! Mart!' she cried within herself, 'it couldn't last! But I'm glad it was true for a little while.'

When Mrs. Bergen kissed her good-bye the little woman was trembling: 'I can't ask you to forgive me, Gina,' she said.

Gina's smile was as bright and friendly as it had ever been. 'Don't worry about me, Mrs. Bergen.' Her voice frayed and broke. 'You've all been very good to me. So kind. With us circus people it's come one day and gone to-morrow. And now there's the show – we'll be so busy getting the show going again. And it's all the show with us, you know.'

CHAPTER 16

FROM Eagle Hawke, Dan Haxby intended taking his family, Rabe and the cage of monkeys to his brother's farm at the foot of the Dandenong Ranges. His idea was to collect the horses and put them into training again as soon as possible.

He had wired Monty when to meet him at Spencer Street railway station, and told him that Haxby's would be on the wing again in a month. The last time Dan saw him, Monty was talking of working his way to America and trying his luck there. Les had a job with a ship's chandler down near the wharfs, Syd and Bob had been selling newspapers and race cards in the streets. There was a fine affection between the brothers and they had held together even when the rest of the family broke apart. They were all there at the railway station, in answer to Dan's telegram to meet their mother and Gina, when the train drew in at the up-country platform.

Very happy and excited Lotty hugged and kissed her boys again and again. Dan, as happy and excited as she, bought tickets and hustled his family into the first train for Dandenong. The grass was not to grow under his feet these days. George Haxby had driven into Dandenong to meet them and took them all back to Yowan, Rabe, the monkeys and all, in a cart stacked with his empty milk cans.

Yowan farm was one of the oldest in the hills, a large dilapidated house settled down among cleared paddocks marked off by hawthorn hedges, on either side of a creek with willows along the banks. Foothills on which a forest of dead trees still stood, rose behind it and went off into the blue ranges.

Mrs. George Haxby had no children and was a little in awe of her circus relations. She was afraid they would be wild, loose people, with no morals at all, and she would not know what to say to them.

George's hankering for years to rejoin his brother on the show had been suppressed on her account. She came of farmer folk. Yowan farm was hers really, and although she and George eked out a poor living milking cows, selling eggs and raising ducks for market, Ada Haxby loved the house her grandfather had built, every aged apple tree in the orchard beside it, and eye-full of hills and grassy paddocks.

A shy little wood pigeon of a woman, very plump and kindly, she had captured George while he was suffering with a strained heart and supposed to be resting at the house of a friend nearby. George Haxby had travelled with the show as strong man, weight-lifter and bottom in acrobatic feats during Dan's first years on the road. When he married a farmer's daughter George had not intended to be a farmer; but at last becoming rooted in the soil he was almost as fond of Yowan as his wife.

After Dan wrote to his brother, telling him of the disasters which had overwhelmed the circus and asking him to paddock his trained horses for awhile, Mrs. George had been a little apprehensive of what was to follow. When a year or so later, Dan and his family arrived with only a few days' warning, she was even more so; but she bustled about making room for them in her old house.

Auntada, as Dan hailed his sister-in-law from the beginning, was surprised to find her worst fears unrealised. She could not have believed Lotty Haxby would be so homely and unassertive a person. Gina she loved at sight, and Max, with her sprightly wild grace – who could resist her? Not a childless woman who loved children. Not Auntada at any rate. Of Dan, she was not so sure, a little afraid. And as to Rabe and the monkeys, she reserved judgment. He looked such a queer, melancholy, half-starved bird of a man, and she had heard from George of his capacity to drink beer till the cows came home.

George had told her too of the way Rabe and Dan had hung together ever since they first met when they were both young men. For what reason, no one could tell. They seemed to have nothing in common. Rabe, a forlorn friendless creature, loved music and Dan. No one knew anything else about him, except that the first part of his name was Johann. Rabe never lost sight of Dan if he could help it, and Dan, with the same affectionate regard for him he had for any other of his performing animals, saw Rabe was fed and taken care of: would not allow him to be ill-used in any way.

When everybody had settled down in the places she managed to find for them, Mrs. George was thrilled and thoroughly enjoyed her hospitality. Gina helped her about the house, Max sang and danced everywhere, cuddling all the young animals she could catch hold of, poddy calves, little pigs, kittens, even the ducklings which were running under the blossoming apple trees at the moment, flecking new green of the grass with yellow floss of their small toppling bodies.

Auntada found Max in bed one night with a dead duckling beside her. Max had seen Auntada bring up ducklings, and put them in a basket near the kitchen fire, to warm them back to life again. They were dying of cold, she said, because their mothers would not cuddle them up and keep them warm. So Max was trying to cuddle and warm this little dead duck back to life again.

'Oh, George,' Auntada cried, tears brimming in her mild brown eyes, 'if only we had a little girl like that!'

So when the boys brought in the horses, Dan said he must up-stick and get nearer the town to buy canvas for the tent which Gina and Lotty were to start making at once, while he exercised the horses and taught Max to ride, it was Auntada who demurred.

'But Dan,' she protested, 'couldn't you stay a bit longer. There's the apple-barn for making the tent. And I could give Lotty and Gina a hand with the stitching. Wouldn't the stockyard do to start training the horses in?'

The invitation was too good to be resisted. Dan was very grateful for it, considering all the expense it was likely to save him.

'Too right we could, Auntada,' he declared gleefully. 'And you're a real sport to ask us. I was afraid we might be outstaying our welcome.'

Dan and Lotty went down to town to do some shopping, buy sailcloth, thread and needles, material for wardrobes, and a couple of instruments for the boys to practise band pieces on with Rabe.

The canvas was spread out on the floor of the apple-barn when they had brought it home. Dan measured it off, cut out segments for the women to sew, although he, Rabe and the boys all took a needle and set to work in every spare moment.

Auntada thought it the funniest thing in the world to see men sewing like this, although Gina and Mrs. Haxby told her that stitching and repairs to the tent were always considered men's work on the road. Mrs. George declared she had never enjoyed anything so much as these sewing bees in the barn, where apples were graded and packed in the autumn, and still lay strewn about for use during the year.

Dan worked his horses in the stock-yard every morning, and for two or three hours in the afternoon, before the tent was finished. Phil he decided was too old to go on the road any more. He must be left to end his days peacefully in Yowan paddocks. The Wild West team had to be re-educated though, and Dan took each horse regularly and in turn for thirty minutes at a time, putting him through his part, before Monty was allowed to drive them together.

Auntada was amazed to see how, though he carried a whip and cracked it, the lash rarely touched a horse. And after every trick Dan petted and patted his horses, feeding them with pieces of apple or carrot when they had done well.

'I had no idea you people worked so hard, or made so much of your horses,' she said. 'I don't know anybody else makes such a fuss of their horses.'

Auntada laughed too, at the way Dan coddled and petted Phil: the old pony followed him round the paddocks and came snuffling in his pockets for bread and sugar.

'Goodness!' she exclaimed. 'I've heard about him

often enough from George. He's the pony you called after Mr. Philip Wirth, isn't it, Dan? But I'd never have believed a horse could be so knowing.'

'Knowing?' Dan chuckled, as the old pony nuzzled up against him, 'he's as knowing as a cageful of monkeys, aren't you, Phil?'

'Look at them!' Lotty teased happily. 'There they go the pair of them – smoodgin', I call it. Dan never made as much of one of his children as he's made of that pony.'

'Aw, go on Mum,' Dan protested, ' a man can have half a dozen kids – but there's not another pony like Phil.'

As soon as she arrived on the farm, Max had been given Auntada's own pony to ride, and presently was scampering headlong all over the wide open paddocks. The monkeys too were a new toy to her, and she was never tired of watching them at play, feeding them, or putting one or other out on the end of a chain to run about in the grass.

Monty soon had the two white mares moving at their old steady pace. Bonnie was still young and fresh, but Beauty eighteen or thereabouts. Such a pretty docile creature, though, worth her weight in gold for teaching Max to ride on, Dan declared. Bonnie had never been so well behaved.

Monty, who Dan described as 'our equestrian director,' had clipped both the mares, and groomed them so strenuously that in no time their hides looked as if they were woven of the finest white silk, while their manes and tails, after he had washed, blued, plaited, and combed them, flowed in lustrous plumes.

Les and Syd practised leaping and vaulting with Beauty and Bonnie round a ring in the open paddock, while Dan in the yards schooled a grey pony he had taken a fancy to and bought for a few pounds at Dandenong market one day.

The grey pony, a spirited handsome gelding about fourteen-two, stone grey with darker dapples, and silky white mane and tail was being trained in what Dan called liberty stunts. That meant tricks requiring intelligence and memory to be performed by a horse without a rider.

After teaching Yarraman, as the pony had been named, to canter easily round the ring, first one way, with a flick of the whip always at the same place and word; and then the other way, to stop when he was told, come up and stand; with infinite patience and ' perseverance Dan coaxed him to bow. Fastening pads to his knees, and strapping up one leg so that he had to go down when he tried to walk, Dan taught Yarraman to fall on his knees. 'Down! Down!' he commanded. Every time the horse went on his knees, the boys hung on to him, at first held him down, petted and fed him with pieces of apple.

The trick was repeated until the animal was no longer frightened when he went on his knees. The strapping was taken off. 'Down! Down!' Dan commanded, and the boys forced the pony to his knees until he realised what the word meant and went down easily of his own accord, and was petted, caressed, and fed with apples, lumps of sugar or carrot as a reward. After a rest he was brought in again an hour or so later, and made to rehearse the same trick; applauded, caressed and fed with apples or sugar when he had learnt to do what was required.

'By God, he's intelligent,' Dan boasted. 'One of the smartest ponies ever I handled, George. Phil, of course, is on his own, but this chap's a ringer all right.'

To teach him to lie down when he was told, Yarraman was thrown; Monty sat on his head, the three younger boys on his hindquarters. Dan petted and encouraged him to keep still and get used to the position, until finally the gelding would lie down of his own accord and remain still until he was fed and permitted to get up. He was trained to buck picturesquely as he galloped into the ring, and to pick up Max's handkerchief when she dropped it, and go after her with it.

A week after his training began Yarraman was doing several tricks as if they were the most natural things in the world for a horse to be doing. By the end of three weeks, when the tent was finished, and the boys and Dan had cut stakes of stringy-bark saplings and a king pole of mountain ash, the grey pony could give a performance which surprised and delighted everybody.

'Sweet, isn't he? Sweet as a nut,' Dan warbled.

King pole and stakes were set and the tent sprang up in the green paddocks behind Yowan Farm, as if it were a great mushroom, thrust fresh and white from the soil.

Then Mrs. Haxby and Gina busied themselves with wardrobe, making tights and trunks for Dan and the boys. As often as not if it was fine they took their sewing down to the tent while Dan was practising the horses or teaching Max.

Every morning he exercised the Wild West horses in the tent, with Monty, Les, and Bob, putting them through their riding, shooting and lassooing act, went on with the schooling of Yarraman; and worked the Snowies, as he called the white mares, with Max and Monty.

While Les and Monty were doing their turn, Max, in a practising suit of red Turkey twill, turned hand-springs, jumped hurdles, bounced on the trampalene, a canvas sheet Dan had rigged over a wooden framework for her. She practised dance steps, rougon, high kicking, back bending, pirouetting and running tip-toe in ballet shoes with padded toes.

It was Dan himself who warned her to go easy.

'See that child doesn't overdo it,' he called to Lotty and Gina, keeping an eye on Max while he was working the horses.

Gina looking up from her work, every now and then would say quietly :

'Take a rest now, Max. You don't want to knock yourself out.'

Dan liked to take Max for his instruction while her muscles were hot, running like elastic, he said.

He taught her first of all to run from the opposite side of the ring, and jumping from the spring board placed beside the track, land on old Beauty's back. Monty manipulated the lunge with a rope run through a pulley to the roof of the tent, holding Max by a leather belt under her arms so that she could not fall whatever happened. At first she misjudged her time, jumped short or lost her balance quite often; but Monty was always there on the lunge and the leather belt held her up like a scarlet spider in mid-air when anything went wrong. Max laughed, shook herself, and tried again. She was quite fearless learning to run and jump, and determined to get the better of the trick.

'Hands off the rollers,' Dan called, as she grabbed for support when she jumped, at first, and clutched at the hand grips on the surcingle. 'You'll never learn to ride if you hold on to the rollers, Max.'

Again and again: 'Hands off the rollers,' he called until Max had mastered the knack of the run and jump; could land on Beauty's back, throw up her arms, unconscious of the lunge, get her balance and keep it.

She was so eager, so quick to learn, Lotty who had seen Dan training all his children knew he had never been so patient, so careful, as he was teaching Max.

She had to learn to run and jump to a standing position on the back of the old mare then, and Monty worked with her for awhile, riding Beauty and holding out his hand to support Max when she alighted beside him. With a turn of his whip on the earth, Dan would send the mare along at an easy canter, and Max take her flying run and leap.

'That's it . . . Get your balance . . . keep moving your feet,' Dan called. 'Arms out, over your head now . . . A few kisses! Like this——'

He posed and gestured as if he were a pretty young thing throwing kisses to an imaginary audience, and not a short, stout man in a faded shirt with old grey trousers held under his belly by a leather belt. Auntada tittered; but Dan and the rest of the family were much too absorbed in the lesson to notice how funny he looked.

Max shifted and poised so daintily, with such a grace, he was beside himself with joy. Soon she was working without the lunge, sitting and sliding about old Beauty's withers and rump.

'By God, did you ever see anything so pretty,' Dan exclaimed, as Max posed, toes pointed, doing her little dancing steps and Beauty took her easy canter round the ring. 'I've seen Gladys Wirth and the best women riders in the world, but our Max is going to beat the lot of them I tell you. There's not goin' to be a lady rider anywhere to beat Maxine Haxby.'

Gina watching with her eyes of love and knowledge

agreed with him. Max looked so bonny and fearless on horseback. And Gina had no fear for her, only joy and admiration of her spirit and grace.

'Did I do all right, Gina?' Max would ask eagerly after her morning's practice.

'All right,' Gina replied, with the deep sweet smile of her assurance, and sometimes she would give Max a tip that was helpful.

'Get your balance . . . throw yourself back and keep your feet moving, Max,' she said. 'You don't want to let a horse feel your weight over her kidneys. Beauty's all right but Bonnie'll root if you do.'

Work of the farm went on as usual. The boys gave a hand with the milking and wood chopping. Monty ploughed the orchard and he and the boys put in a couple of hours before breakfast ring-barking and clearing some of the hill-side paddocks in which old stumps had suckered-up during the last few years. Gina and Lotty Haxby helped Auntada with the cooking and house cleaning; and George and Auntada spent every moment they could down at the tent watching the boys and Dan at work with the horses.

They loved to watch Max learning to ride, or feeding Beauty with bits of apple or lumps of sugar when her morning's work was done. A vivid little figure Max made standing beside the old white mare in her red practising suit, made like a baby's romper, with ballet shoes tied round her bare legs.

'Got the airs of a circus queen already,' George chortled.

'She's good, isn't she?' Dan cried delightedly. 'Chip of the old block, a real Haxby, if ever there was one! It's a treat to train her. She's not as strong as Gina at her age, but dainty and graceful, by God. The way she poses and throws out the kisses, eh George? That'll get the crowd.'

'If she don't get swelled head, the way you're all going on,' Mrs. Haxby said.

'She won't get swelled head will you Maxie?' Dan cried, grabbing the child, hugging her against him and ruffling the rough dark curls. 'It'd spoil everything if you went and got a fat head, Max.'

Max twisted away from his grasp.

An elfish, undemonstrative child, she did not like being grabbed and held tightly like that. Restraint of any kind she could not endure. She was not used to it. Her mother had fussed over and petted her to be sure; but Max was conscious of a grudge she bore her for being the cause of having left the circus. And Gina, the child was puzzled always by a reluctance in Gina's affection, something withheld. She had heard vaguely of a little brother who died when she was a baby and how Gina had loved him. It was on his account Gina would never love her altogether, Max reasoned in a childish way, although when Gina thought she was asleep, Max had heard her whispering as she tucked the bed clothes round her sometimes:

'Little precious . . . little precious darling.'

Max knew that of Gina. Knew she meant more to Gina than anybody else on earth anyhow, and tyrannised over her accordingly. Max was born knowing how to tyrannise, as she was born with that subtle grace and dash, an urchinish impudence and daring. She had been spoilt by the devotion Gina and Mrs. Haxby lavished on her in those days when she was the centre of their existence, although it was so matter-of-fact always: they had never kissed and hugged her as Dan had.

Gina herself felt a little out of all the bustle of practice and preparation. She helped Auntada in the kitchen and about the house, and stitched at wardrobe all day; but she was so accustomed to everybody on the show doing two or three things, having more than one string to their bow, that she was troubled to think there was nothing else she might do.

In the evenings the boys and Rabe practised with cornet and flute, drum, cymbals, and triangle in the barn. Dan brought up his cornet sometimes and played airs from the operas with variations for George and Auntada, by the kitchen fire.

'I wonder could I do anything for the band?' Gina asked Rabe hesitatingly.

'Course you could, Gina.' Rabe was always willing to break in a recruit.

'Remember when I was a kid . . . and you were teaching me to play the fiddle?' Gina asked.

He nodded.

'You were coming on fine, but——'

'There wasn't time to practise, I had to give it up.' Gina said, reluctantly. 'When the others have gone to bed, I'll go down to the barn and see what I can do – if you'll lend me your fiddle.'

'Good.' Rabe left the fiddle and a hurricane lantern in the barn when he and the boys finished their evening practice.

But a few days later, Gina shook her head when he asked her how she was getting on.

'It's no good,' she said, 'my fingers are stiff and lumpy as wood.'

Rabe lifted her hands.

'No,' he said sadly. 'You could not play the fiddle now, Gina. How about trombone or——'

'I've tried Monty's flute,' Gina replied drearily. 'But it's no good. There's no music in me. Feels like as if my soul was dead.'

'But you are artist to say that, Gina . . .'

'Oh I don't know,' Gina moved away from him. 'I'm better as a beast of burden, I reck'n.

Dan had taken a day or two off to go down to the Zoo and reclaim Queenie, leaving Monty in charge of the horses and practice. Syd went with him and they brought back a couple of waggons, seats, lighting gear and an Afghan hawker's covered cart for Lotty and Max and Gina to travel in during wet weather. Dan decided for the time being that the circus should operate in a small way, not bother about menagerie; stock up when business was good again.

Between them, Dan and the boys had worked out a route and fixed up the programme. Haxby's was to open at Dandenong on its way down from the farm and show again in outlying suburbs until Flemington was reached during show time. A lot had been rented on the show ground, and although during August squalls and heavy rains were to be expected, sometimes the days brought the balmiest of spring weather.

With his congenial optimism Dan gambled on sunshine, but steeped his tents in raw oil and kerosene before leaving the farm, taking advantage of a sunny day to dry and stretch them before loading and 'making tracks,' as he said.

A day or two before the circus was ready to move off there was a grand rehearsal in the paddocks at which George Haxby and his wife were the only on-lookers. And how thrilled and excited they were to see Dan in his rajah costume of cretonne with turban and jewels on, riding Queenie. Max in the white spangled ballet skirt she was to wear, pirouetting gaily, altogether in love with herself. Bob talked of clearing out and leaving the show when he heard he was to play girl again. But professional pride ousted his boyish sulks. Dressed in pink tights and fluffy pink skirts, a flaxen wig, blue ribbon round it and a rose over one ear, powdered and rouged, with red lips and dollied eyes, he held himself so shyly and gracefully, throwing coy fluttering glances to convince Auntada and Uncle George he could look like a girl, that they laughed until tears ran down their cheeks. Bob was such a pretty miss, more girlish really than Max, who, in her urchinish way, just gambolled through her tricks, quite as pleased with herself as anybody was with her.

'Oh, Bob!' Auntada cried, weak with laughter.

And George, hugging his wife, exclaimed: 'Lord, mum, if it weren't for you, I'd be gone a million on the minx.'

The rehearsal went off with 'the zip' Dan insisted on. The four boys doing their wild West turn with their own horses and three youngsters they had trained during the last few weeks. Dan himself got into a clown suit while Monty acted as ring-master. Max went through some simple tricks with Monty on Beauty, and Bob in his pink skirts and Monty worked the two horses together.

Monty's juggling on Beauty was probably the cleverest turn in the show. He was a perfect horseman, as good a jockey rider as there was in the world, Dan considered. Monty had modelled himself a good deal on Alf Clark who was riding for Wirth's, tossed oranges in the air, and speared quoits. Then Dan brought in Queenie, the elephant, to stand on her hind legs, sit on a tub, wave her front feet in the air, waltz round the ring and play football with him. The monkeys presented their little drama. There was an acrobatic turn, a magician and a strong man act, by Dan himself, and the boys went through their trapeze, double trapeze and polandric ladder exercises, with Max assisting, prettily, though she did nothing much.

When the circus waggons, newly painted red and blue, packed and loaded, turned out from Yowan paddocks, Dan led off with Queenie drawing the heaviest load, tents, poles, seats and all the ropes and lighting gear piled up behind her. Les drove the second waggon and the monkey cages, drawn by two of the younger horses, Gina the covered-in cart, Monty and Syd followed with the rest of the horses in the rear.

George Haxby and Auntada went down to the long white gate which had 'Yowan Farm' in black letters across it, to see the show on its way. While everybody was kissing and hugging everybody else, saying how sorry they were to be going; how good Auntada and Uncle George had been; Auntada was crying and telling Max and Lotty and Gina to come again and write to let her know how they were getting on; Dan was thanking his brother; the boys trying not to look self-conscious and impatient to get it all over; even Rabe, joining in the clamour of gratitude and good-byes, half a dozen kooka-burras flung a cackle of hoarse rowdy laughter from a tall dead tree on the other side of the road.

They seemed to be laughing at the red and blue waggons and the elephant on the road.

'There's a good omen,' George Haxby exclaimed. 'Even the Johnnies are going to laugh at your show, Dan.'

As the waggons moved off along the road in spring

sunshine, for the first time in her life Ada Haxby understood the lure that life of the show had for her husband and how difficult it had been for him to settle down on the farm.

'Oh, George,' she cried, 'I feel as if I'd like to be going with them.'

Then she looked at the old house with wisteria drooping along the grey verandahs, apple trees in blossom beside it, her cows wandering in green paddocks, a bull calf baaing beside the orchard fence where she had tied him; and her heart failed her.

George glancing down at her guessed the farm had it. He knew the life of the road and the circus too well to believe it could compensate Auntada for her cosy rooms, furniture that was each piece like a friend, poddies and well-filled jam cupboards, bowls of cream and family photographs; the trees she had planted and watched grow.

'Perhaps we'll take a holiday some day, and go round for a bit with them,' he said.

Auntada nodded, relieved he understood she did not really mean what she said. She could never leave Yowan to go far away, or for long at a time.

The circus procession trailed away down the road into Dandenong, among the light growing trees, myrtles and saplings, young green and golden, with the rolling back of the hills, blue and purple behind. Sweet briars straggling beside the road had wide-open roses of pale pink and the air after rain was filled with their fragrance. But the rain was not over. It flashed from ravelled clouds as the cavalcade was a mile or two from the market town at the foot of the ranges.

Dan and the boys had to work in the rain getting the

tents up. They mustered as many interested on-lookers to help as usual, but rain fell steadily all the afternoon.

The new kerosene lights flickered bravely in the humid atmosphere, split and spraying against veils of the rain. It was sale day in Dandenong and a goodly crowd in town had promised itself a night out at the circus, after seeing the posters Auntada and Gina had painted with washing blue, along the roads and about the town and the sale yards. But the prospect of a cold wet night sent many people home early who had been looking forward to a night out.

Only Dan refused to be downcast. He was too cock-a-hoop at having got the show together again for anything to daunt him. It was bad luck to have struck rain for Max's first night; but he would not show a white feather for all the rain in the world, he said. His pluck kept everybody going.

'You can't have all the plums, all the time,' he told the boys. 'We're dead lucky to be here, I reckon.'

No more than a score of men, women and children sat huddled in overcoats on the brand new seats as the grand march swung round the ring, for despite its oilings and careful preparation, the tent let in the rain at a good many places. But Dan whipped up his team in the best of good spirits.

'It's easy enough to give a good show on a good night when the weather and everything's with you,' he told his audience. 'The test of a good show is a night like this, friends, and if you don't reckon Haxby's is a damned good show when you go to bed to-night . . . well, I'll reckon Dandenong folk don't know a good show when they see one.'

So brisk and buoyant, he flung on with his showman's

job, flogging laughter from the few solid bundles of men
and women, packages of bodies and clothes spread along
his seats. Gina never remembered having seen her father
work harder, do better. Watching people straggle away
from the tents after the show, when the rain had cleared
and a fine starry sky spread over the dark paddocks and
wall of the mountains, she heard two men laugh and
exclaim to each other:

'Good show.'

'Damned good show, I reckon.'

And something of Gina's old secret pride in her father
and Haxby's stirred again.

CHAPTER 17

AFTER giving two or three performances on the way down from the hills, the waggons reached Flemington a day or so before the great agricultural show opened. For that week, every day, Dan put on an afternoon and an evening performance, and the weather and crowds brought the grist to Haxbys, he had gambled on.

To be sure high winds caused him a good deal of anxiety, and he dropped the tent after the show one night so that it would not be blown away as all the tents on the show ground had been one wild night, a few years before. Three hot, dusty days drove women and children into the circus; and Dan went on his way at the end of the week, well satisfied with his luck and the money he had made.

In Melbourne, Gina took Max to the Zoo on Sunday and a keeper confided to her that he was at his wits' end. A lioness had given birth to a litter of five. He did not think she could rear the lot, wanted to get three cubs away and leave her the chance of making strong beasts of the other two.

'Would you give them to me?' Gina asked.

'Give them?'

'Sell them?'

Dan was mad to have the cubs when he heard of them. 'We could rear them on the bottle,' he said, 'with goat's milk or . . .'

'Used to get a bull bitch at Hagenbeck's,' Rabe said.

'We'll rear'm all right,' Dan promised.

'I'll buy the cubs,' Gina said, 'if you'll let me look after them . . . and work them, by and by.'

'No,' Dan was emphatic. 'I won't have a girl of mine working lions. It can't be done. Not in my circus. After all they are wild beasts . . . and what would people say? Puts his own daughter in the lions' cage – his cripple daughter – No, it can't be done.'

'But they're kittens, Dan. They wouldn't hurt her,' Lotty protested, marvelling.

'There's a good deal been said about me being careless with other people's lives. Well, they aren't going to say that any more. Gina's not going to say it. No. No. That's flat.'

'It's just to nark me,' Gina declared.

Even Rabe spoke for her. What harm could it be for Gina to buy the cubs, rear them, teach them to sit on stools, do as she bid? It would give her an interest in the show and was the chance of a lifetime. After all if they got out of hand, by and by, a trainer might be found to take charge of the young lionesses. Dan was obdurate. He bought the cubs, but anybody rather than Gina was allowed to play with and feed the baby lions, as he billed them, with their fluffy yellow faintly spotted fur.

The waggons had taken the wide road over the Werribee plains to Geelong then, moving slowly between the paddocks marked off by stone walls, towards outlines of the You Yangs, with glimpses of sea by the way, and camping grounds under wide blue skies on which the clouds gathered and spread in high piled fleeces, or drifted grey as the feathers of geese about the farms. And from Geelong the circus went west, making for Camperdown and larger towns of the sheep lands back from the coast.

Business had not been as good as it might have been, and Gina watching and brooding thought she knew why.

Dan was full of energy and never happier than when he was going from morning till night. Travelling by easy stages, after the tents were up, he never missed a morning's practice with Max and the boys, if he could help it.

Before leaving Melbourne Sailor was 'put on the pay roll,' as Dan said. The pay roll had to be invented for the purpose. But that was by the way. Sailor, who said his name was 'Olmes – you spelt it with an H – had insisted on embracing Queenie after the show one night. Said he had fallen in love with her. She was a girl after his own heart. He had worked elephants in Burmah: knew all about them, although for the last few years he had been a sailor, trading among the South Sea islands on a schooner which was wrecked off the Great Barrier.

Just then his coarse black hair was cropped close to his head. He was only a couple of days out of gaol after doing a stretch for laying a man out.

'It was this way, mister,' he explained, 'a bloke in one of those pubs down by the wharves started calling me a Kanaka, and a few other things – and when he thought I was goin' to hit him, crayfished . . . lay down on the floor, and said I couldn't hit a man when he was down. I lay down on the floor alongside of him, and let him have it. They say he's in hospital still . . . won't ever use his jaw proper again. But I done three months – blast him!'

A powerful blackguard, tattooed over every inch of his body, with some dark blood in his veins and pale blue shark's eyes, Dan saw possibilities in Sailor 'Olmes and offered him a job as rouse-about and keeper to Queenie.

Sailor jumped at it, thoroughly pleased with the idea of joining a circus, and perhaps doing some strong man turns with the boys. Dan put him through his paces as soon as the waggons moved on.

No one was happier than Lotty Haxby in those first days on the road again. With the stored up energy of her years at Star-of-Eve, she set about setting her covered-in cart in order. It was wonderful how she managed to pack and arrange it with bunks on either side, cupboards and shelves, nails for the calico bags which held show dresses on either side. She and Gina and Max slept in the buck-board in wet weather. The men had a tent, or rigged a tarpaulin over one of the waggons. It was always very snug and trim inside the buck-board. Lotty fussed and tidied endlessly to keep it so.

'T'any rate,' she said, 'we've got clean comfortable beds, and that's more than we could be sure of, staying at some of these little up-country pubs.'

'If only Lily and Jack were with us!' That was her one wail.

Gina looked at her mother. Had she forgotten Lin altogether, she wondered.

Among the tents, in all the bustle of preparation for a performance or packing up for the road again, she thought of Lin more than she had done for years. She had almost forgotten him in Star-of-Eve; but now, he was everywhere beside her, a frail little fellow with his frightened grey eyes.

'Never mind, Mum, shouldn't be surprised if they don't come askin' for a job, some day,' Dan said. 'You see. Wait till we get on a bit.'

On the road again, it was almost as if the years between were a dream to Gina. The tents and waggons moved off before her as they had done since she was a child. Some vague satisfaction of her youth grew again when, driving a waggon, or walking beside it, the circus travelled slowly along the country roads: plains and hills unfolded.

In the early morning, after rain, diamonds flashed from leaves of trees by the roadside; mists rising through sunshine, over the glittering green bosom of the earth, lay blue as smoke from the camp fire among the trees. A butcher bird threw his full pure notes through the clear air. The horn of magpies was heard warbling and winding; strings of the robins, wrens, native thrushes, silvereyes and honey-eaters wove their reiterated refrains. Kookaburras laughed mellow and subdued far away, and with a harsh brassy blare of cornet throats. The harping of a pallid cuckoo flew mournfully. As the bird music sank to a muted murmuring, or rose to its full blast in sunshine, Gina cried sometimes:

'How's that for a band, Rabe?'

Places she knew reformed themselves from the distance. Country towns into which the circus went with band playing, as it had done in the old days. It was good to camp on the paddock near a creek, or in some square among small shops beside a railway station. The rush to put up tents, everybody working hard, lending a hand, brought the old zest and excitement.

An eager and excited child, most of the time, Max took to the life of the circus as a duck to water. She loved work in the tent when she practised with her father and the boys, and sang in a shrill childish voice all day as the waggons blundered along the rough roads. Jumping down from the buck-board she picked wild flowers, trailers of scarlet runner, orchids yellow and brown, freckled white spring flowers and scyllas blue as the sky, exclaiming at the birds and bunnies who crossed the track.

It was all a picnic to Max although, young as she was, she was beginning to live for excitement of the ring. She worked hard, was never tired of practising to perfect a trick; but greedy of praise, looked for the lighted eyes and clamour of admiration from people who watched her.

With Dan and the boys, Rabe and Sailor to dote on and applaud everything she did, was it any wonder Max was learning more and more to get her own way, and never troubled to do anything for anybody? Mrs. Haxby asked. She blamed Gina most of all for making Max lazy and selfish. It was Gina who would not let her help with odd jobs when everybody else was going hell-for-leather to get ready for a performance, or packing up to move on to the next town.

Curiously selfless and selfish, the child practised with a passion to out-do everybody in their performances, working the horses with Dan in the morning, tumbling with the boys, practising Risley, wire walking and trapeze stunts in the afternoon. But she would do nothing else; neither wash dishes for Gina, nor sew with Mrs. Haxby. She lived for excitement of the ring; the adulation Dan and the boys gave her before ever she faced an audience.

'No,' she said one night when her mother asked her to help Gina wash the dishes after a meal. 'I'm not going to wash-up. I'm an artist.'

'Will you listen to that?' Mrs. Haxby exclaimed.

Dan roared with laughter.

'Wasn't Gina an artist, and didn't she wash dishes? And a better artist than you'll ever be,' her mother enquired.

'That's right Max, you stick up for yourself,' Dan said.

Gina looked up from slopping the dishes through hot water and soap suds.

'You won't ever have to wash dishes while I'm about, Max,' she said.

There had been a kind of armed truce between Gina and her father since reorganisation of the circus. Gina was not offered any place in it. She just went on as she had for so many years, taking over rough and dirty jobs about the waggons and tents, as a matter of course. She and Dan rarely spoke to each other. She never addressed him, and if he alluded to her sometimes, threw a remark at her, biting and hostile, she took no notice. Trudging about the camp, helping to load or unload the waggons, she worked as indefatigably as she had ever done.

But Gina had her dignity these days. She did not allow herself to be treated anyhow. As often as not when Dan asked her, as a matter of course, to do something for him, she answered: 'Do it yourself. I'm busy.'

And Dan, while he grudged her the independence, realised she had earned it. She was entitled to her dignity. He could not treat her as he liked. And he did not want to lose Gina. She was more valuable in her present labouring capacity than a groom or a tent hand. She did any odd job, uncomplainingly as a rule. And she understood every detail of circus work, could turn tent boss at a moment's notice, measure off ground for the tent, pack and unpack the waggons and direct hoisting of the tent, work out routes and the roads to travel, towns to show in, take the horses to water and buy fodder. Dan had been using her to write letters, arrange for lots and advertising of late, and found her shrewd and implacable in her dealing with business men.

Besides there was that nest egg of hers Lotty had

talked of. It created a respect for Gina in Dan's mind, the queer empty shelves of that cupboard of his schemes and ambitions. Gina's nest-egg was something he contemplated having the use of. He did not mean it to escape him.

When the show reached Three Springs, Lord Freddie was waiting for it, and waylaid Dan, begging to be taken on with the horses again.

'He's one of the best grooms ever I had,' Dan said. 'Sailor's a darn side too heavy-handed with horses. He can work Queenie, and Lord Freddie'll give the boys a hand – same as he used to.'

Two years petered out, as the tents and waggons steered a winding irregular course among prosperous towns of the western district of Victoria and went north from Warnambool.

But although it was a fairly good programme Haxby's put-up, as Dan said, the circus never seemed to do more than pay its way. There was nothing he could bill as 'octo-miraculous' and that in itself was depressing. These days, what with picture shows and motor cars, the visit of a troupe of acrobats and riders, such as Haxby's, did not attract the crowds in up-country towns it used to. Besides there was nothing new or original about the show. It was very much what it had been ten years ago, second or third rate as compared with great circuses like Wirth's which travelled on its own train, using ten elephants, an imposing menagerie and company of performers, tent hands, keepers and grooms.

Dan realised that the day of road waggons, and of a little show like his was over; but did not know what he could do to improve matters. He thought a menagerie, and a few sensational stunts with wild animals would make all the difference; but he had no money to buy animals. He had been teaching the lion cubs, fine healthy young beasts, to sit on pedestals, and jump through hoops. He would have to make the most of them, and of Queenie and the monkeys until the luck changed, he told everybody. When it did, he intended to buy a tiger, and bears, a couple of leopards perhaps, and a camel, though camels were nasty smelly beasts to have about a show.

'Listen,' Gina went to where Dan and Rabe were standing discussing the shortage of cash after a bad night in Nihill. 'I want to talk to you.'

'Right, Gina,' Dan said. He guessed she wished to make terms with him, and was curious to know what they were.

'I've got a hundred pounds,' Gina said. 'I'll put it into the show, but I want to work with you. Look after things on the business side.'

'Your money's your own, my girl,' Dan said. 'I haven't asked for it.'

'I know you haven't,' Gina replied. 'And I'm not talking of giving it to you. I want to map out our routes better, to fall in with country shows and race-meetings, send one of the boys ahead every now and then as advance agent, fix up advertising, distribute the posters, rouse a bit of interest, before we arrive at a place!'

'By all means if you can figure it out. You got time on your hands.'

The cut brought colour to Gina's face.

'And I want a share in the show,' she said.

'A share in the show. Haven't you got it? Haven't you all? Isn't this Haxby's?'

'That's all right,' Gina agreed. 'But I want things put on a business footing. To keep books, all that. How many of us are there? Seven. Well, I think if we reckoned the show was worth ten shares, we each took one, Mum, the boys, Max, Rabe and me – and you two, that would be about right?'

'Do you now? What do you think of that, Raven,' Dan glanced at Rabe.

'Above a certain amount, I think we'd all agree to pool our share to improve the show. I've had a word with Monty – and he thinks it's a good scheme.'

'You have, have you, Gina?' Dan laughed. 'Well, have it your own way! You're right, I dare say. Never pretended to be much of a business man. My heart's in the show – and that's all there is to it.'

He hardly thought anything would come of Gina's proposition, but did not like the idea of letting her hundred pounds slip through his fingers, once she had offered it to him.

'There's one thing more,' Gina said, in the steady, slightly contemptuous tone she assumed speaking to her father. 'And that is . . . if ever . . . at any time you take risks with Max. If ever I find any harm comes to her, through carelessness, on your part – working her too hard – not giving her safety nets, then I warn you . . . I'll burn the whole show down and clear out with her.'

Dan laughed.

'You will, will you? You hear that Rabe? If we don't play fair by Max, Gina'll burn the whole show down and——'

'I'll do it, don't worry,' Gina said.

Dan laughed genially, jocosely.

'You're a bigger fool than I took you for Gina,' he said. 'Am I likely to take chances with the kid? Isn't she the best thing in the show? Why wouldn't I take every care of her?'

'That's all right, now,' Gina said. 'But you know there's times when the showman runs away with the rest of you. You think people can do things they can't do. You try to make them . . . just so as the crowd will roar and gape. It gets you like drink gets Rabe. You're a showman . . . first and last. You love Max because you can show her off.'

With his genius for organisation, for making the most of every scrap of material, live or dead, which could contribute to success of the show, a bit of wire picked up in the street, the air of a popular song, an idea for an act, Dan conceded the practicality of Gina's suggestion. Not that he took the idea of the family becoming share-holders seriously. That was a sprat to catch the mackerel of Gina's hundred pounds.

Gina set to work immediately, however. She had collected a lot of useful information about agricultural shows and race meetings, roads and railway time-tables, and in a few days showed Dan a map and calendar with events and dates marked, explaining how by shipping the waggons on a goods train, now and then, more towns might be reached for their gala days. Her first innovation was to point out that if the waggons were put on a goods train next day Mirram could be reached for its annual races, while she went ahead to select a stand and placard the town.

'Our business manager,' Dan called her: Gina did not mind what he called her, so long as her plan succeeded.

Even Dan had to admit its success after a few months. Everywhere Haxby's went that summer people flocked, and crowded the small one-poled tent to see the show, until Dan began to contemplate a large tent, more artists and animals.

'The truth of it is,' he said, 'we're all pulling better. Max is coming on great. And the boys is doing real well. Do you know what an old josser said to me in Laanecoorie. 'Well, Mr. Haxby,' he said. 'I seen a lot of circuses in my time; but you got the cleverest little bunch of riders ever I see in all me born days.'

'Our business manager's got something to do with it,' Rabe reminded him.

'Too right she has,' Dan agreed.

'If only Lily and Jack were with us!' Mrs. Haxby sighed.

'Oh, they fancy themselves working at the Hippodrome. But there was never a rider like Gina.' Dan threw his peace offering. 'I suppose I won't never forgive her for going back on me and getting smashed up like that . . .'

CHAPTER 19

LONG before she ever spoke of it, Gina knew her mother was to have another child. Lotty looked afraid to tell her, Gina told herself. Her father too, looked afraid and resentful of her. Gina smiled over the realisation.

It was funny. What were they afraid of? That she would run off with her mother again? Lotty did not intend to be run off with. That was clear, although she was worried.

'Oh well, Mum,' Dan Haxby broke the news by saying, 'you and Gina'll be clearing off again soon, I suppose. If you clear off this time, though, you can stay. Blowed if I'll go scouring the country-side, lookin' for you – Bust-up the show and everything.'

'Who said I was clearing off?' Lotty snapped.

Gina walked away, as if the discussion had nothing whatever to do with her.

'Oh well,' Gina heard her father go on, 'you can't take Max, if you do go. A father's the legal guardian of his own child and I'll have the law of you, if you touch Maxie.'

When everybody was sprawling round the camp fire for the evening meal, one Sunday, a week or two later, Dan opened out again.

'Oh well, Rabe,' he remarked jovially, 'suppose Mum and Gina'll be clearing out and leaving us again presently.'

'Who said so?' Lotty struck in sharply.

'Said so? Nobody said so. I was supposin', that's all.'

'No more hospitals, doctors . . . and rubbish, for me,' Lotty declared.

'Good on you, Mum,' Dan applauded lazily. 'That's the spirit. Isn't that what I told you, Rabe? Lotty's all grit. That's what she is, my Lotty. Never made no fuss about babies. Just took 'em as they came along. Same as any other good, strong, natural female – until Gina got all these notions.'

Gina knew that she was being baited. That the dice were weighted against her. Dan had worked on her mother's pride and affection with his jeering at hospitals and doctors until she was afraid to go against him. He had exploited her grit, devotion and loyalty. Gina got up from where she had been lying and walked away from the little crowd round the cloth spread on the grass.

The boys and Max joined in the laugh against her. Gina heard the bubbling gurgle of their mirth.

Memory of her effort for the life of the child who was so bonny and sturdy now, seemed lost in ridicule. The boys could laugh. They did not know what they were laughing at – nor Max. And Dan Haxby? Nothing else was to be expected from him. But that her mother should forget – resentment and confusion cover her memory? Gina could not believe it.

She understood how it was. That inveterate appetite of the woman for the man with whom her fibres were woven, prevented her going against him. The things Dan Haxby said had soaked in and grown until they became part of his wife. Lotty was eager still to make amends for some injury she thought she had done her husband, unable to realise the selfish blindness of all his demands on her.

Gina's pity survived her pain. 'Poor old mum,' she reflected, 'she's got the rough end of the stick after all. And what does it matter what anybody does to me?'

She went back to clear away after the meal, pack the tucker-boxes and stow them in the provision waggon.

For days, whenever he thought of it, Dan Haxby twitted Gina about hospitals and doctors, and when she was going to clear out. But Gina, it appeared, did not hear, at least took no notice of him.

'Aw, go on,' Lotty replied testily. 'This isn't the first child I've had on the road.'

The weather was hot and dry. Out from small towns the circus passed through, round about Black Wattle, and Sphinx Hill, folk were harvesting. On the wide plains, moving from one township to another, the circus waggons and horses passed through miles of country pale gold with ripening wheat. Although no word had been said between them, that her mother was suffering more than she admitted, Gina guessed. Mrs. Haxby's face was drawn and sallow; her legs swelled with the least exertion.

Gina waited on her patiently. She took over all the work her mother was accustomed to do and made her rest as much as possible.

'Gord, you're good to me, Gi,' her mother murmured wearily, one day.

'Listen, Mum,' Gina said. 'You're ill. Let me talk to him. It's not right for your legs to swell up like that. You could stay here in this town . . . It can't be long now. I'll look after things till you're all right and then you can join-up. I won't clear out again, I promise. Beside there's Max.'

'It's no good, Gi,' Mrs. Haxby shook her head. 'He's got it into his head this child's to be born on the road.'

'He hasn't got to bear it,' Gina exclaimed angrily.

Her mother smiled.

'That's my job. Never thought I'd be having another baby, Gi – I've gone fifty now you know. But I feel as if it'd be funking not to go through . . . like I've always done.'

Gina had it out with her father all the same.

'She's not as young as she was. I'm scared . . . and that's flat,' she said. 'Mrs. Newton, a woman I know in Black Wattle, said it's a bad sign her legs swelling, she ought to be having treatment.'

Dan Haxby was inclined to laugh; but Gina frightened him sufficiently to consent that when the circus reached Sphinx Hill, Lotty should go to a midwife in the township.

A fortnight before the time expected, early one afternoon, Gina found her mother crying helplessly. She was sitting crouched on a bunk in the buckboard, and let out sharp, piteous screams as spasms of pain clutched and wrung her. The cart was moving along rough roads, twenty miles from a township on either side.

Dan went off to a farm house he had passed a few miles back to ask if his wife could have a room there; and one of the boys and Gina followed with their mother in the cart.

Her father went on to talk to the farmer, a dour elderly batchelor who declared there was no place to put a sick woman except his cow shed. He was furious at being asked to take in a woman in the throes of child-birth and looked on circus folk with dislike and suspicion. Why had they not taken the proper precaution? What did they

197

mean traipsing round the country with a woman in this condition?

The barn was big and clean looking. Gina helped her mother into it. There was a bed against one wall on which a harvest hand had been sleeping. Gina asked the farmer for a couple of clean sheets and a blanket.

'I'll pay you anything you like for them,' she said. Grudgingly he gave the bed clothes and Dan rode back into Table Top where the circus was to play that night. He said he would send out a doctor.

Through hours of horror and anguish, Gina did everything she could think of to lessen the pain her mother was suffering.

'Tell me what to do, and I'll do it, Mum,' she cried desperately.

She invaded the farmer's kitchen and begged for hot water from his stove. Begged in a way that would take no refusal. The cross-grained old man who had lived there alone for so many years, to escape women, was shamed into carrying buckets of hot water to the door of the barn for her.

A baby was born dead towards sunset and Lotty seemed easier for a little while. Then she writhed in pain again, and a haemorrhage began which Gina tried everything she had ever heard of to staunch.

'For God's sake come and help me,' she called to the old man; but he had gone off to the end of his paddocks so as to be well out of the way if she needed assistance.

'It's so dark, Gina,' Mrs. Haxby wailed. 'If only you could get a light, somehow!'

Gina threw back the door so that late brilliant sunshine flooded the barn. Her mother murmured querulously:

'It's so dark . . . so dark, Gina.'

She collapsed then, and in a little while Gina knew she was dead.

The doctor Dan Haxby had sent out from Table-Top arrived and was clearly annoyed to have driven so far for nothing.

'Why on earth you people want to do a thing like this I don't know,' he said. 'It's asking for trouble.'

When the doctor had left, Gina told the farmer she would have to go into the township to tell her father and arrange for the funeral. She closed the doors of the barn; and tramped off along the long dusty road winding over low undulating hills and harvest fields to the collection of white-washed and corrugated iron houses at a little distance from a tributary of the Murray.

Music of the circus band drifted to her across the wide quiet country. As she was coming to the town, loud cheering and the clamour of applause, drowned it. Rabe was beating out the Blue Danube. Max's turn that was with the white horses.

Gina quickened her steps unconsciously. She followed the music to where, beside the river, the circus tents glowed with their string of coloured lights and gay little flags.

Always her nerves stirred painfully under the drooling rhythm of that melody Rabe was so fond of. Her back ached and her brain swayed to flickering confused visions of flying horses, darkness, the crowded tent, uproar and herself, like a snake with its back broken, on red sawdust of the ring. Gina wished Dan would not give Max the same tune to work to. The horses were used to it, of course. It was their music. They would never work as well to any other. The minute she heard it, Beauty began to fidget and was all excitement and eagerness to get into the ring.

Gina trembled and stumbled so that she had to sit down by the roadside. A moment of unconsciousness overwhelmed her. She moved suddenly, startled by a vague apprehension for Max; wondering how long she had been sitting there by the road.

The circus programme had gone on by two or three items. The band was giving the tune for Dan's turn with Queenie, as Gina went on towards the tents.

She had not thought of Max until now. So devastating, mopping out everything else, had been the time she lived through with her mother in the barn, a few miles away. Walking all the way beside the dusty road under a night sky, suave and tender blue of faded wild flowers, pricked with stars, Gina had thought only of her mother lying there on a bed of straw, in that big bare shed where they milked cows. The stark quiet figure, its fight over and the garish business of life, which Gina herself had to go on with. She had been sunk in a brooding over her mother's pain and death: the load she had carried all her life, plodded along with so doggedly.

Confounded, and in sullen revolt, Gina wondered why a life should be used and yielded like that? Lotty had bred circus riders, trapezists to feed her husband's ambition. Was that all there was in being alive for her? Dan seemed to have been fond of her in his own way. He had not sought other women. Was it just that a man went his way? He could not see anything but his way. Pain and death? What did they mean to him? Was it true that the outside world knew more of sorrow and disaster than the world of the circus? There were the mines: the back streets of cities? Gina could not answer her own questions.   All the suffering and death in the world seemed to have swooped down on her, darkened and shut her off from the place she was in, other thought, for the time being.

Then she had heard beat and whine of the circus band again. Rabe blowing a melody from his cornet, banging drum and cymbals with that foot contraption of his. Max – thought of the child was like a star shooting across the sky. It was her turn on the trapeze with the boys, Rabe was playing now.

Gina hurried forward, fear for Max pressing her. She had no faith in life, except its infinite capacity to hurt unless you were watching, placating, guarding against misadventure at every turn. She was afraid, when she had reached the tent, to go in.

She stood there against the weathered canvas, arrested, unable to move, to look into the tent even. What was she afraid of? She could not tell. She could feel the crowd on the other side, almost see through the thick grey sheeting how the country people were sitting hunched along the seats, gazing up at the boys and Max as they swung and flew from trapeze to trapeze. Breathing of the crowd was suspended a moment. A muffled exclamation, and then with a sigh of relief, the surge of delight and excitement went up. Clapping rattled and clattered noisily. It was all right. Gina had almost suffocated in her consternation.

She had feared sight of her, any slight deflection of attention, might put Max, or the boys, off what they were doing, Gina told herself. At the clapping, she went in at the back of the tent amongst the men and children standing there.

Max and the boys were making their bows just before running out, and Dan, striding the ring, had started to patter again, and fool with Sailor and Lord Freddie, who in their clowns' bags, had flung themselves tumbling and shouting beside him.

There was no net beneath the trapeze where Max and the boys had been working. Gina stood staring at the place where it should have been. An anger, like nothing she had ever known, ploughed her. Max and the boys ran past, going out of doors to change. Gina caught Les's arm as he went by. She had forgotten her mother, the horror and grief which had overcast her.

'Where's the nets, Les?' she asked hoarsely.

'I couldn't help it, Gina,' he gasped. 'Told Dad you'd be mad.'

'Did he . . . did you . . .'

Gina was scarcely able to express herself. She could only croak and grunt incoherently.

'We was that rushed,' Les said. Bob and Syd came to stand beside him. 'It took us all our time fixing up to be ready in time to-night. And he said never to mind about the nets. It'd do us good . . . give Max confidence if she worked without the nets now and again.'

'She took off from the high swing?' Gina asked.

Les nodded. 'He said we was to go right through. I didn't like to tell Maxie to keep off – of that. It might've made her nervous, and, of course, she's right as rain while she isn't funky, Gi. How's Mum?'

'Mum's dead,' Gina said.

Moving away from the boys she went over to the covered cart where Max was taking off her tights and trunks. The band was playing its last number as the crowd sauntered out from the big tent. Gina could hear the laughter and exclamations of the people as they went off to the town.

Max looked up as Gina stood in the doorway of the cart. The blued eyelids and painted lips on the childish face made her look so much older than she was. She was singing as she hung her trunks and tights on pegs along the wall.

'Oh, Gi,' she cried, when she saw her sister, 'how's Mum?'

Gina could not reply to her as she had done to the boys. She scanned the child's face with her sombre passionate eyes. The jaunty, delicate little body seemed strung up before her, as half-naked Max stretched for her night-gown and wriggled herself into it. Then she reached for an apple which stood on the shelf beside her jars of make-up and sat down on her bunk, munching it.

'I'm that hungry, Gi,' she said. 'We didn't have any tea to-night. Monty brought me some biscuits and a cup of milk. But I had to sell programmes before the show, and——'

Dan's voice was nearing, blared and unsteady. The boys were with him. They had told him, Gina guessed. She could hear them talking and bent over Max, kissing her head. The waters of grief would break over the child presently, she knew, and must tell her.

'Mum died this evening, Maxie,' she said gently.

'Died!' Max had sprung from Gina shivering. 'Died . . . oh, Gi!'

'Gina? Where are you, Gina?'

Dan was calling, his voice rough and broken. Gina went down from the cart. The boys and Rabe were standing there at the foot of the steps with him. 'Gina,' her father demanded, 'what's this the boys are telling me. Mum——'

'Yes,' Gina said. 'The farmer says you must remove

the body before morning.' She spoke brutally. She felt hard and brutal to the man standing there looking at her. He was dumb under the shock; looked unwilling to believe what she had said.

'Gord! My Gord!' he gasped.

Max ran to Gina, crying, and clung to the heavy stolid figure of her sister.

The boys still in their trunks, stood staring, their faces wrenched; and Rabe began to cry, with guttering rusty sobs. He was drunk and so sorry for everybody. Dan walked away from the little group then. Gina put her arms round Max and led her back to their bunks in the cart. Wiping the make-up from the child's face with a grease cloth, she soothed and petted her.

'There, there darling!' she whispered.

She was remembering Lin and his smashed body, that small white body in blood-stained rags. Later Gina heard Dan taking one of the horses to ride out of the town. She heard him telling the boys and Sailor to start pulling down the tents, get everything ready for the road, and move on towards the next town.

The circus was billed to appear in Crewe, a town twenty miles further on, next day, and Gina knew well enough that Haxby's would keep faith with the public whatever happened.

What if her mother was dead? She still had Max. There was that to be thankful for. Max was still living and with whole bones.

When Max was asleep, Gina collected her clothes, folding and packing them into a small suitcase. There was not the slightest hesitation in her mind. She had given her word to Dan that if ever he worked Max without every precaution for her safety, nets and tested gear, it would be the last time he worked her. She intended to keep her word.

Her mother was dead. No one could do any more for her but bury her. And it would not matter much how that was done. There was Max to think of.

Rabe came to the cart seeing Gina had not put out her light yet. He had taken a few more drinks and was crying easily, muttering and crying; yet not so drunk that he had not a clearer sense than anybody of what was going on in Gina's mind and how it would affect Haxby's. He knew Gina's bargain with Dan; had guessed when he saw her in the tent that last moment before the boys ran from the ring what she would have to say about this business of the nets.

'You don't ought to be too hard on your fader, for this, Gina,' he said. 'You don't ought . . . it will be a lesson to him. It will not happen again.'

'I told him what to expect,' Gina said coldly, 'and he'll get it whether he expected it or not.'

Dan was calling at the undertaker's on his way out to the farm. He would ask the man to drive out and bring the coffin back to the township, and after the necessary formalities, enquiry and death certificate, make arrangements for burial as soon as possible.

Her father intended to follow his wife's body to her grave; and catch up with the waggons, or join them in the evening at the neighbouring town. He had not spoken to Gina again, or told what he was going to do; what he expected her to do. She had heard him talking to the boys, and knew how Dan Haxby worked. There was no need to explain to her what he was going to do.

Her mother would be buried as quickly and at as little cost as possible. The circus waggons would move along the road as usual: the routine of the circus would go on – except that perhaps there would be no practice for that day.

No time would be lost in useless fuss or grieving. Dan would grieve. Give him his dues. In his way he would be broken-up about Lotty. He would miss her, and want her beside him; he would bear her a grudge for leaving him in the lurch after so many years. It was too bad of a woman to go back on a man by dying like that. Dan would never forgive her for it, really. Always he would have it against her in his thoughts, that she had died on him without a 'by your leave,' or 'kiss me behind' and – without so much as a word of warning or regret.

Gina had no argument in her mind for her father. That was finished with. Long ago she had decided what she would do when this happened. She realised it would happen, some day, knowing Dan. She had not reckoned on her mother's death. That made it easier now. Max was not going to be sacrificed.

Gina thought out ways and means carefully. She must act quickly and silently, she knew. If Dan suspected what she was going to do, he would make it difficult to take Max. He could obtain legal injunction, and Gina knew would be quite equal to having her followed by detectives, so that he could take Max away from her.

She knew she must be unsparing; ruin him financially so that he would have to let her alone, and Max. Gina could be unscrupulous where her father was concerned; she would be, she assured herself. She did not intend to spare him. He had not spared Lin, or her mother. His showman's instinct had demanded all he got from them.

And now, Max. He was not going to get Max. Gina aroused herself. Max must have her chance. Her life should be her own at any rate.

Gina put out her light, but did not sleep when she lay down on the bunk beside Max. She had not quite decided how she would go away. There was the railway; but no train until mid-day. The river? They might take a boat and row down to the next town. Max could not walk the long way to Black Wattle. There was a motor car in the township; Gina had noticed the placard in a shop window: 'Cars for hire.' She would go along and ask if a car could come for her in an hour. That would be best. Expensive, but it would give her a quick get-away. The boys and the waggons would be moving early that morning.

She got up at once. Everything was quiet about the camp, the tents dismantled and waggons standing loaded in wan light; the moon going down, dinged and yellow. Gina glanced about her quickly. She could hear Rabe snoring under one of the waggons, Les and Monty lying near him. She went over to look at them: find out whether they were really asleep.

Neither of the boys moved. Gina bent a little nearer. She tucked a couple of notes under each boy's blanket and moved away again.

Hovering about the waggons of stacked gear, ready for going on in the morning, she raked little piles of grass and leaves against them. Then she went down the wide street of the township to where in a shop window a motor car was advertised for hire. It did not take long to waken the owner of the car and arrange for him to drive to the nearest train town.

'How soon can you be ready?' she asked.

'In about ten minutes,' the driver said.

'I'll just get my suit case, then,' Gina told him and went back to the cart where Max was sleeping.

Max moved crying in her sleep, as Gina stepped into the cart again.

'Oh, Mum! Mum!' the child sobbed.

Gina bent over her.

'Darling,' she whispered.

Max wakened.

'Won't I never see her any more, Gina?'

'She's better out of it,' Gina muttered.

'But she didn't mind . . . she liked it on the show, Gina,' Max said. As Gina turned away, took Max's little coat and hat from the pegs, an awed, stubborn expression grew on the child's face. 'So do I. What are you doing, Gi?'

'We're going away, Max,' Gina said. 'We're going to see Lily, and then. . . .'

'But I don't want to go away, Gina.' That curious obstinacy settled about Max's mouth; her eyes were old and resolute. 'I know . . . it's about the nets. You're angry. But I didn't mind really when I knew, I just made up my mind nothing could happen because . . . because . . . it would hurt you so.'

'Maxie!' So she had known all the time, Gina thought, and gone on with her work, saying nothing, letting them all believe she had not noticed.

'I promised Mum, Gina,' Max said slowly, 'that if this happened, if ever you wanted to take me away, I wouldn't go with you. I'd stick to the show . . . for Dad's sake and the boys. And I've got to, Gi.'

Gina sat down on the edge of the bunk, dumb and frustrated. She could find nothing to say. After awhile she began to tremble. Hoarse breaths shook and broke from her; Max crept close to the big heavy form of her sister, nestling and clinging, crying too.

'Oh, Gi! Gi!' she whispered.

She understood vaguely what Gina's love and suffering for her meant.

'It's quite true, Max,' Gina said at last. 'I meant to set fire to the grass round the waggons and clear out with you, to-night. But I suppose we'd better stick it . . . and do the best we can.'

The storm of her anger had blown over. Presently Gina told Max that she must go and tell a taxi driver in the town not to wait for them. They would not be needing his car that night.

If she had felt vindictive before, glad to strike back as she said she would; keep faith with herself and make Dan Haxby suffer a little for what he had made others suffer so much, that was over. A new frail comfort sprang through all her grief and desperation; a happiness which was like the twittering and tinkling of little birds beginning to sing among some tall slender trees in the first light. She was not to leave the show after all. She and Max would go on working out their lives together on the circus.

When she returned, the boys and Lord Freddie were putting horses to the waggons, Sailor was bringing Queenie to pick up her harness and yoke herself for the start off. Mud larks flew up from the river with sweet eerie cries spreading their black and white chequered wings over the dim flat land. It was good to be on the move again: to have no emotion, joy or sorrow, away from the roads stretching into the distance, and the busy life of the circus tents.

CHAPTER 19

MAX was asleep when Gina went into the covered cart again, and lay down on the bunk below her.

The waggons moved slowly over the road, Gina raised herself and drew the little lace curtain her mother had hung across the end of the window in the covered cart. Les was driving on the seat before her. She could see Queenie lurching ahead, heavy shabby red and blue vehicles stuttering behind. Monty had taken the roadside to let the loose horses graze as they travelled. Not wishing to disturb Max, Gina lay down again and was lost in a heavy drugging sleep until the cart stopped. Then, as Max was still sleeping, she rose quietly from the bunk on which she had been lying, and dressed as she had been the day before, let down the steps hooked at the back of the cart and went across to where the boys were making a fire.

It was nearly mid-day and the waggons had halted on a stretch of open ground near a creek which still held pools of still water along its dry bed. A clump of black wattles, downy with pale yellow blossom, filled the air with a warm musky incense.

Les got the fire going. Monty brought two kerosene buckets of water from the creek. The horses were grazing tethered under the wattles nearby. Syd pulled the tucker boxes from under coverings on the provision waggon.

Gina took some of the water to wash her face and hands in and went about getting a meal ready as usual.

'Dad said to go on, Gi,' Monty said as he put a big blackened billy of water over the fire. 'Came into camp before daylight and said we'd better push off. He'll ride on . . . afterwards.'

'Did he?'

Gina put out the mugs, knives and forks, bread and cold meat, cheese and jam for a meal; cut pieces of meat and bread for the men. Syd and Les sat down on the grass to eat. Only Bob looked sick and was shivering under his freckles.

'The kid's been sick all night,' Les said.

Gina went over to where the lad was lying beside a straggling wild currant bush.

'What's the matter, Bobbie?' she asked tenderly. 'I've brought you a cup of tea. Drink it and you'll feel better.'

She sat down beside her youngest brother. He was such a gritty, self-reliant kid. No one had ever made much fuss of him.

'It's awful, I know, Bob,' Gina said, realising that he was grieving for their mother. 'But worse for Max than any of us. She's the youngest, after all. We've just got to do the best we can for her.'

'That's right, Gi,' the boy's teeth chattered as he spoke. 'I must have eaten something bad. It's given me a stomach-ache. I'll be all right, presently.'

Gina understood, as did the others, that he was suffering from shock as they all were.

When some sort of a meal had been made in the hot sunshine, the waggons went on again. The men, Rabe, Lord Freddie and Sailor, had not spoken to Gina, eating their meal in silence and slouching off again. The sense of loss was heavy on everybody.

Max slept on. At a homestead, not far from the road, later in the day, Gina bought milk and eggs. When Max wakened Gina gave her a mug of milk and beaten-up egg. The waggons were late on the lot; and while Monty and the men set to work to get the tent up, Gina went into the town for fresh meat and vegetables so that her brothers should have some hot and sustaining food before they went into the ring that night.

Ordinarily they did not eat a heavy meal before going into the ring, the evening meal was a light one; her mother liked to provide a mid-day meal as the substantial feed of the day. But this day everything was upset. Gina did the best she could to make up for the scratch meal everybody had taken at mid-day. She was stooping over the fire, serving a hot stew for Rabe, Lord Freddie and Sailor, when Dan rode on to the lot.

As he came towards her, Gina knew that the night had aged her father more than all his years on the road; any hardship or bad luck he had ever encountered. His stout, short figure had lost its spring, its jaunty lurch and sway. As he stood beside her with the stubble of a night's growth on his jaws, Gina thought she had never seen Dan look old before. The jowls of his face sagged: his eyes were apprehensive. He had probably not eaten anything all day; his breath smelt of whisky.

'How's Max,' he asked, looking into the fire, as if he were uncertain what to say.

'She's been sleeping most of the day,' Gina replied. 'She's all right.'

No more was said between them. Dan went over to the tent to see everything was ready for the evening's performance. He came back with the men. Gina called him to have something to eat. He sat down on the grass near her, and ate all that she put on his plate with a queer, humble docility.

He remembered very well what he had promised and what Gina had threatened. He was in for it, Dan told himself. And he did not feel equal to dealing with Gina just now.

This was a heavy blow Fate had struck him. Let her think what she liked, Gina with her heavy accusing eyes, Gina sour and unrelenting. Her eyes drove through him, making him cringe and recoil from her: his belly writhe and turn in on him. What the hell was he made of to put up with it? Why did she treat him like this, her own father? She was his daughter. Afraid of her, the damned hump-back? Not he! Let Gina get out of his way, if she did not like it. He was not going to be brow-beaten, dictated to by a chit of a girl.

Gina could be useful, of course, damned useful. She had got her head screwed on the right way. Dan did not know quite how the show would get on without her, particularly now Lotty was gone.

The band put up its racket of popular airs. The boys dressed and set off with the programmes and peanuts, and Gina herself went down to the ticket office when she had seen that Max was ready for the grand march.

While the show was on everybody worked with desperate energy and gaiety. Gina, watching from the ring, was sure no one would ever have guessed the gloom depressing each and every member of the Lightest, Brightest, Little Show on Earth, that night. The turns were presented with a finish and verve, which did not permit a dull moment to creep in. And watching Dan as he went through his business as ring-master, or clowning with Lord Freddie and Sailor, Gina's old homage to his spirit and nerve defied the deep surge of her hostility and anger against him. She knew he was broken; something vital had gone out of Daniel Haxby that night. He would never be the same man again. Yet he played the game; he played it to the limit.

There was no one now to take charge of youngsters found prowling round, after the show had begun, trying to get a peep or crawl under the tent. Dan used to chase them off, if he found them; but Lotty always smuggled in children who had no pennies to see the circus, when she found them standing disconsolately about outside or trying to get a peep through the tent anywhere. Dan and she had many a row about the way she would trot in after the first turn sometimes, and plump down a horde of small boys in the front row, even if they had to sit on the ground.

'Oh well,' she said. 'I'm not going to be Mrs. Haxby of Haxby's circus for nothing. And children can't see at the back.'

Everybody teased and laughed at her about it, but Lotty continued to smuggle urchins into the show just the same. And that first night after her death, Dan missed those eager childish, unbelievably happy faces of Lotty's freebooters from his audience.

'Oh well,' he said to Gina and the boys, 'Mum's brats'll always have to come in now. You look after 'em will you, Gina?'

So Gina went round the tent when the show had started after that; and Dan had always a smile for Mum's brats as he called them, when the children settled down like a flock of hungry sparrows beside the ring.

As the days went on, the circus in its orbit played dozens of small towns before it came to the Ninety Mile desert, and turned south again into the sheep country beyond Black Range. Dan was surprised that Gina did nothing, said nothing; that she had taken up her mother's work on the show and was going about it, dumbly, uncomplainingly. He could not make it out; her acquiescence, above all her failure to let him know about the neglect of those nets for Max. He was wary still, not altogether convinced Gina had nothing up her sleeve. Rabe had told Dan of his talk with her, and that he was sure Gina meant to leave the show on the first opportunity. Dan was surprised himself to find her going about her work as usual.

In the tent all hands worked up to standard, doing their best; training went on in the morning, when the tents were erected early enough. Dan put the boys on to new stunts; and Max was practising with hoops and a flock of white pigeons which her father was teaching to circle about her and take grain from her hands as she rode. But the shadow of Lotty Haxby's death was on everybody.

Even Sailor exclaimed every now and then:

'Gord, you miss her, don't you?'

And it was true something had gone out of the show, something that had been cheery and unifying, stimulated and upheld everybody.

'Dad's only half the man he was. He's growing old,' Monty said.

Monty was more concerned than anybody about the way Haxby's was just ekeing out an existence. Monty was young and ambitious.

'It's no good to me, Gi,' he said several times. 'The

215

show's going to pieces and there's no way out of it I can see. The old man's done his dash. If we was on wages there'd be none. It's all we can do to keep Sailor going on a quid a week. Your idea of shares in the show was all right, only shares in Haxby's are not worth two bob, these days.

'Oh, things'll look up presently, Mont,' Gina said. 'We been over this track too often. That's what's the matter I reck'n. If we strike new ground up in New South Wales, go on to Queensland, maybe, business'll be better.'

'Perhaps you're right Gi,' Monty agreed. 'But it feels to me as if the spirit's gone out of the old show since Mum's death. It's knocked Dan endways. He's never been the same since. Bluffs hearty and all that . . . but the stuffing's out of him. It was the same before when you and Mum cleared out. He just lost grip. "It's no good to me," he said, when we broke up. "I won't never go on the road again without your mother, boys." '

'There's Max,' Gina said.

Monty nodded, 'She keeps him going. But he's losing heart, Gi. Can't you see yourself, the way things are going.'

'I see all right,' Gina admitted.

CHAPTER 20

GINA was concerned at the work Max was doing, during that year after her mother's death.

'I think you're taking her too fast,' she told her father angrily. 'She's too young for so much riding and tumbling. Not strong enough.'

'Go on, think I don't know what she can do?' Dan jeered. He had lost some of his fear of Gina since she had failed to keep her threat to him. 'You're jealous. That's all that's the matter with you. Think Max'll be beating you on your own stunts presently. And so she will.'

Gina eyed him steadily.

'You know it's not that,' she said. 'Max'll do all I did and better. But I was older and stronger and it knocked me out. I won't have Max trying somersaults on horseback till she's older.

'Won't you?' Dan cried exasperated. 'We'll see about it.'

That she was right Gina knew. She had seen a curious drawn expression on Max's face when she threw herself down to rest after her morning's work that year.

'Are you tired, Max?' Gina would ask anxiously.

'Lord no,' Max replied restlessly. 'Don't fuss, Gina!'

But she lay about more and more, after a year or so. There was less spring in her movements except when she was in the ring. The birds had it all their own way on the road; and when Max was flat, out of sorts, her temper flashed fiendishly on the least occasion.

Gina had seen her using her whip on Bonnie after the mare balked in a trick once. Max had thrashed Bonnie in a frenzy of rage as she had seen Monty thrash a bad-tempered piebald pony he was training for an act of his own.

The unwritten law of the circus that every man or woman was boss of his or her own horse, Gina respected. Nobody was entitled to interfere between them. But Max had vented her fierce temper on Bonnie and another white horse Dan was training to take Beauty's place. Max sobbed herself sick and hung round Bonnie's neck, petting and caressing her, afterwards, whispering how sorry she was, and feeding her with sugar, although she bragged that she had broken two whips on the darling.

'That's it, Max,' Monty upheld her. 'You got to be firm.'

Dan laughed though he did not approve. He thought it rather a joke Max should take the law into her own hands like that, and he did not want to hurt her pride by refusing to allow her to run her own horses as the boys did theirs. But Gina gave the child a piece of her mind.

'I never saw Dad thrash a horse the way Monty does,' she said. 'That's why Dad's the horse-master he is. He never loses his temper with a horse. Monty'll never be the horseman his father was, if he goes on the way he's doing.'

'Didn't you never thrash your horses, Gi?' Max asked.

'No. I never did,' Gina replied. 'I thrashed Charley once, for laying a stick on Beauty.'

'Oh, I'd never stand a groom ill-using one of my horses,' Max declared airily. 'I told Lord Freddie, I'll make Dad give him the sack if ever I saw him hustling the Snowies about again like he was the other day. And Sailor's real cruel to Queenie sometimes, Gina. Heard her squealing the other morning when we was loading for Shallow Lakes.'

Gina's face hung, heavy and thoughtful, for a moment. Then she smiled, remembering how she had seen Max run across and stand screaming, furiously, beside the great grey beast and the brawny blackguard who was supposed to be Queenie's keeper.

'I gave Sailor a bit of my mind!' Max said. 'Told him Dad wouldn't stand for that sort of thing, and he'd get the shoot, sure as God made little apples, if he poked Queenie with the hook under her front leg again.'

'That's right, Max,' Gina said quietly. 'You see he does too.'

'I will,' Max agreed.

Victoria was really the hunting ground of Haxby's. Dan had rarely taken his horses and waggons further north than a few miles across the New South Wales border, although he talked of trailing further north and west in the future.

That summer the circus went south into Gippsland, showing in Warragul, Korrumburra, and Alberton. Dan put the waggons on trucks to take in towns along the railway to Sale, Bairnsdale and Orbost. Distances of thirty and forty miles ·had to be covered between towns in South Gippsland sometimes; but Dan took them by easy stages, going off for a day's fishing now and then. Feed was good for man and beast along the roads, the herbage green and sweet, black swans, snipe and wild duck plentiful on the rivers and lakes. When Dan and Sailor went fishing on Corner Inlet one Sunday they brought in a boat-load of flat-head.

Flitches of home-cured bacon from farms, in the maize-growing valleys of the Tarwin and Snowy, replenished the circus stores, and four-gallon tins of wild honey, scooped in dark shapeless combs, from hollow trees in the bush. The country folk were generous with apples and ripe pears; the boys gathered sacks of windfalls for the monkeys and Queenie, in orchards about Sale and Bairnsdale. Gina and Max picked blackberries along the rivers, and Gina made jam over the camp fire, filling all the tins and jars she could lay hold of with the sweet-smelling crimson pulp.

Roads over the ranges from Orbost were as bad as roads very well could be, in those days. Dan would never have attempted them except in the summer time. He had to put eight horses to a waggon negotiating a stiff pull, as often as not; and there were days in the great forests when no clearings or habitations of any sort were passed. Bell birds could be heard dropping their sweet notes through the deep stillness above gullies. Tree ferns threw the green umbrellas of their delicate fronds over creeks, chattering crystal clear between timbered hills. Only a few late spikes of pink heath and wild fuschias were out by the wayside; but Christmas bush fleeced with mauve and white bloom pressed out from tangles of scrub and ferns about the track, and black wattles under pale creamy blossom wafted warm smoky odours of musk and hay.

Gina and Max, of course, knew this road. They had been over it as far as Genoa, on their way down to Mallacoota with Mart and Mrs. Bergen. If they went down the lakes to the coast perhaps they would find Mart and his mother there on the beach in bathers, Gina thought, swaying again to the illusion and tenderness of those days. But she did not suggest delaying Haxby's on its way, to go down to the coast.

Dan was beginning to fret at the time which had been wasted on this journey, although he apologised for it by saying that the family had earned a holiday, and loafing along like this was as pleasant a way of taking it as any other.

In Eden, Haxby's had a great reception. People came from scores of miles about to see the circus which had trekked over the Southern Alps to show there. Motor cars were few and far between on the road then; but Gina had arranged for the mail man, Jack M'Alister, to take a parcel of posters with him when he left Orbost, and as he made his trip with three or four changes of horses, he was in Eden and nearly half-way home again before the two circus waggons and the covered cart trailed slowly down the steep track beyond Kiah into the old settlement on Twofold Bay, not far from the whaling station.

From Eden, the circus went on over Monaro to Bega and Cooma, playing to fair houses and making good money for awhile in towns of the dairying, sheep and cattle country round about. Turning east from Nowra, Dan prowled towards the Murray rivers again.

The worst luck of those days was finding Beauty dead in long grass at a little distance from the waggons. The horses had been restless during the night. Dan and Monty got up to see what was the matter; but could find nothing more disturbing than a flock of white cockatoos roosting among the riverside trees. In the morning, though, there was Beauty lying blown and prone. Crows already flecking the clear blue sky, in every direction uttered their raucous cries, and hovered in the trees nearby. It looked like a case of snake bite, Dan thought. The boys had killed nine snakes in about two hours, the day before, black snakes mostly, four or five feet long, looking like the lashes of bullock hide whips as they lay across the road or in fallen timber near the river.

'Snake bite, it was,' they decided at the homestead Dan called on that morning, when he told of the bereavement the circus had suffered during the night. The station had lost horses through snake bite, at one time and another, and they were always found like that, dead and blown-up, in the morning.

Dan talked of Beauty: must have been twenty-two or twenty-three if she was a day, he said, but such a pretty docile creature. The number of somersaults his girls had thrown on her back. Thousands at least! How he had found and trained her when she was a two-year old. The cuteness and reliability of the old mare. How she danced with excitement to get into the ring as soon as she heard her music, and had never missed a turn of her tricks in all the years Dan had known her, although she would not work at all without a clown in the ring to fool round and give her a breather now and then. The manager of Tara Station wondered to hear this fat well-set up little man who looked such a hard-doer, so wrought up about a horse. It was the way with theatricals and circus folk to be emotional, he imagined, although he recognised true feeling in the way Dan's voice trembled as he talked of Beauty.

Max was heart-broken by the death of the old mare.

'Oh my dear Beauty!' she sobbed. 'What shall we do without her? Mum gone and now Beauty!'

Max still had Bonnie to work and the younger white horse Dan had broken in for her. 'Princess,' Max called her. But everybody had loved Beauty, and she was the oldest horse on the show.

'Oh well,' Dan offered consolingly. 'She couldn't live for ever, I suppose. And it's better this way than if she'd just died of old age – crocked-up and had to be shot perhaps.'

No one dared to tell him that Phil was dead. Before they left Gippsland, Uncle George wrote to Gina: 'the old pony's teeth were as long as your arm. I rasped them and did all I could for him. But he went poor as wood. To save him from the ants and flies had to get a neighbour to put the merciful bullet into him. Couldn't do it myself. Poor old Phil, he must have been as old as the hills. Dan will be cut up. You'd better break the news to him, Gina, my dear.' Gina gave the boys and Max the letter to read, but none of them could bring themselves 'to break the news' to their father. He knew somehow, Gina thought, because he rarely mentioned Phil, these days, and no one liked to speak of the pony to him.

Max screamed and talked of snakes in her sleep for two or three nights afterwards. Nobody slept on the ground for awhile, and Dan was glad when the next town hove in sight, to get the tents up and busy himself practising Max and Princess again.

CHAPTER 21

WINTER on those inland plains that year was a god-send to the country, but hard on any shorn lamb of a circus that happened to be wandering about. A drought had broken, and Dan thought the rain would never stop. Several times the show had to be abandoned when there was no ground in a township to pitch the tents on. Rainwater lay about everywhere in wide shallow lakes. Once or twice, too, after the tents were up they had to be pulled down again, heavy rain having laid two or three inches of water all over the lot.

Now and again a town hall, or Mechanics' Institute, was hired and some sort of a performance given so that Haxby's could pay its way. But Dan disliked these indoor parties. The horses could not be used and he was put to it to provide an evening's entertainment without using his trained horses and riders.

Soggy and dispirited, Haxby's kept on its way, taking advantage of every flash of sunshine to dry the mildewed tents and revive its drooping spirits.

Everybody was pleased when Dan decided to wander north to Condobolin, playing Booligal, Cargelligo, Mt. Hope and a dozen other small towns, make a butterfly flight across country to Cobar turning north-west to Burke, and north along the Darling to Brewarrina and Walgett. Then by Wee-Waa and Narrabri, zig-zag among mining townships and pastoral settlements, across the plains to the coast.

Dan had never been along these tracks in the back-country of New South Wales before. He thought new scenes would shake things up, enliven the boys and do everybody good.

From fair crowds around Cargelligo and Condobolin the circus fluttered through towns scattered across drought-stricken country towards Cobar. The rain which fell in such torrents further south, the year before, had drifted inland only in a few stray showers. West and north of Cobar the earth was red and bare for miles, with a sparse covering of blue bush, cotton bush, only here and there.

Dan found he had to pay a shilling a gallon for water in mining townships that year, and feed was scarce. With a dozen horses, an elephant and a company of eight men and boys and two females to provide for, maintenance cost him more than it had ever done. A bumper audience in Cobar filled the till however, and the waggons were making their way towards Burke when trouble was struck near Yanda Creek.

Bob had been playing girl so long that the family did not notice how brawny his legs were getting and how his arms jutted at the elbow. He had forgotten himself to be careful about details. His gait had a manly stride and swing when he was not watching it. Then too when he was doing his acrobatic turn with Monty, Les and Syd, sometimes absent-mindedly Bob threw a girly pose and gesture in the same way as he did when he was Miss Kitty.

It was at Yanda that some 'smart boots' as Dan said, 'took a tumble' and a mob of shearers who had come in from stations west of the Darling, and were having 'a beano' at the local pub, began calling for Miss Kitty.

'Miss Kitty!' they yelled. 'We want Miss Kitty!'

In no time there was an uproar.

'A bloody fake! A dud show. Give us our money back!'

'Gentlemen! Gentlemen!' Dan protested, trying to make his voice heard. But the shearers were out for a bit of fun that night.

'We're decent toilers here,' a tall bearded man yelled. 'And we haven't seen a pretty woman for Lord knows when. We come to see her!'

'Miss Kitty! Where's Miss Kitty?'

'Trot out y'r little twist!'

'Haven't you had a fair crack of the whip?'

Dan tried to make himself heard above the uproar. Monty made Bob jump on Yarraman and ride off to the next town. The men surged into the ring. Sailor taking on the first who attempted to get through the exit to the boy's tent, knocked him down. Instantly there was a riot. The men grabbed seats, started to smash them up, and use them as waddies, Lord Freddie swung a stool round his head and Dan defended himself with the butt end of his whip as best he could.

'The lights,' he yelled. 'Put out the lights, Mont. They're at the guy ropes.'

The boys shinned up ropes to the roof of the tent and extinguished the big kerosene lamps. An instant later, as the ropes were cut, side walls of the tent wavered and fell in. Had the lamps still been burning the place would have been ablaze.

As it was Lord Freddie and Sailor hustled Dan from under the tent.

'Look out! Look out, the pole's falling,' Monty shouted, as the king pole wavered and shook against the struggling mass of men fighting their way in the darkness under the tent. The shearers crawled from under the swaying canvas and ran on to attack Rabe, Monty, the waggons, anything belonging to the circus in sight.

Queenie raised a shrill trumpeting in the din, straining at the peg to which she was leg-roped. Gina and Max, terrified, watched the rough and tumble from the covered cart in which they had taken refuge.

Gina had seen brawls before when a crowd of larrikins and rowdies had some grouch against Bruiser or Sailor, but never a mob like this intent on wrecking the show. The circus people were hopelessly outnumbered. She saw Rabe knocked down and wanted to run over to him, but was afraid to leave Max.

Then a smoky flare where the tent lay on the ground caught her eyes. One of the lamps guttering had set the old canvas alight.

'Dad! Monty!' Gina yelled, 'the tent's on fire!'

Picking up a corn sack, she ran across to where. flames were flashing up from the fallen stakes and canvas. She bashed at them with the heavy bag.

Instantly every man belonging to Haxby's had turned from his assailant and run over, seizing anything he could lay his hands on, bag or branch of a tree, to beat the fire out; and the shearers stood off, for lack of stuff to grapple, watching the circus folk trying to save their gear – like so many ants, scurrying backwards and forwards, with wet bags, tossing all the water they had in their buckets, even coffee from beside the camp fire, on to the flames. Some of the men who had been fighting a moment ago lent a hand, such a foolish, desperate attempt it looked to put out the fire, as flames leapt and blazed on the worn oiled rags of the tent. Others laughed and strolled off to the pub again, satisfied to have got the better of their argument.

When the fire was out, and the last of the Yanda folk had wandered away, Dan sat down on the ground. His hands were burnt, his nose had been bleeding. His head and face felt bruised and battered.

'Forty years on the road,' he said, 'and that's the dirtiest mix-up I was ever in. Years ago, when our boys and some of the lads in a town got going, there was some pretty fast goes. But Lord, we hadn't a chance in life with this crew.'

It was a night of heavy still darkness; stars dim in the heat. The boys lit lanterns to investigate the damage. Syd and Les had not been hurt at all; but Monty had a gash on his left cheek. Lord Freddie's clown overalls, blackened and in ribands, hung all round his tall straggling figure, and Rabe was unconscious.

As soon as the fire was under control, Gina went over to him, sent Max for her dressings and bandages in the buckboard, and bathed Rabe's head with a little water left in one of the water bags. A nasty scalp wound had knocked the bandmaster out, and Dan was as enraged about the injury to his old mate as to the tent, one side wall of which had been burnt right away. Almost every section would have to be patched and repaired; charred and broken stakes and ropes replaced. The wonder was that any of the old top survived.

Sailor, dancing mad about the whole shindy, and black as a stoker, had nothing else to show for his night's work. And he had been in the thick of the fight all the time. He had been the fight almost, as far as Haxby's was concerned. His blows cracked hard and straight. He had given several of the cows something to remember him by, he swore, and would give a tenner to have a fair three rounds go with the best of them.

Dan was anxious to get out of the town before any of the shearers came to try conclusions with Sailor again. If Haxby's heard any more of them, it would be on Sailor's account, he reckoned, so determined to load the waggons and make tracks as soon as possible.

Fuming and disgruntled that he was not to have another scrap, Sailor went about his job of loading; harnessed Queenie and in an hour or so waggons and horses were on the road again.

The circus was a day late in the next town it was billed to appear, and Dan a little apprehensive of his reception; but Bob had got in before him and told the story of the row at Yanda in the local police station and newspaper office.

Macquarrie was one of those quiet, old fashioned centres of a pastoral district and local hotel and store-keepers knew the ways of shearers on the bust, so that there was some sympathy and a good deal of indignation when the way-worn and battered waggons, still bearing their legend: 'Haxby's Circus The Lightest, Brightest, Little Show on Earth,' wound slowly and wearily into the town, Rabe seated on the buckboard blowing away on his cornet, despite bandages round his head and one eye, and the boys beside him banging a cheerful accompaniment on drum and cymbals.

All that day the circus folk spent repairing damage to the tent and seats. The townspeople came round to watch Gina and Sailor, squatted on the ground, sewing away at the canvas spread out before them. The men's dressing tent had to be taken for the new side wall, and canvas bought in the township stitched over burnt-away holes in the roof. Dan and the boys with hammer, nails and fencing wire, 'the cockie's friend,' mended seats and fixed up stakes. Children saw Max feeding the lionesses who were huge dappled cats, these days, and playing with her white fantails, as they came to eat out of her hand and fluttered about her.

Macquarrie gossiped eagerly about the circus and the circus folk, agreeing that they looked a quiet inoffensive lot; and when Dan told his story in the biggest hotel in the town, he was assured of a fair spin as soon as he did get the tent up, and his seating accommodation in order again. At the same time, he was warned, it was more than likely the shearers on their way home would pay the show another visit and a repetition of the night before was to be expected, if they did.

Dan declared he was not going to be intimidated, and the show would be given as it was advertised. Bob's turn, he promised to show Macquarrie, and what the men at Yanda had taken exception to.

It was evident that some of the leading spirits in the disturbance were in the audience when the show began next evening. Everybody, strung-up and concerned, wondered what would happen when Bob appeared, to go through his turn in ballet skirts and wig as usual.

There were a few cries of:

'Miss Kitty! We want Miss Kitty!' But Bob's leaping and riding were clever enough to rivet attention; and then as he pulled off his wig and stood grinning before people, the clean-faced, good-looking boy he was, the applause was hearty and good natured.

As he thanked the audience for its patronage and apologised for the show being a day later than advertised, Dan explained that never in his forty years on the road had Haxby's been treated to the kind of demonstration it had got two nights before at Yanda. He hoped never again might it be his fortune to encounter a similar experience. Although Haxby's was going on its way a good deal the worse for wear, every member of the company had been cheered and heartened by the good-will of Macquarrie and he wished to thank the townsfolk for their cordiality and hearty response to his efforts, and those of his company, to entertain them.

It was Monty who discovered the greatest bit of good luck that had ever happened to Haxby's, the unbelievable, fairy tale luck you dream of and never dream could really happen.

In Walgett, when the waggons had just arrived, Monty slipped off to see that posters advertising the show had been distributed. He returned with a newspaper in his hand, his face stretched and colourless with excitement.

'Gina! Gina!' he called.

Busy unpacking, Gina turned as he called her.

'Gina!' Monty yelled, and at the sound of his voice everybody stopped what they were doing, unloading the waggons, feeding the horses. 'Rocca's died . . . and left you £100,000.'

'My God,' Dan gasped to Rabe. 'The boy's off his head!'

Monty had been so moody and depressed lately that everybody was concerned about him.

Gina stared at her brother's pale ecstatic face.

'Mont!' she said quietly. 'Take a pull at yourself.'

Monty laughed a queer, high, shrill quavering laugh.

'Look,' he cried, waving the newspaper. 'It's here . . . it's all here. That bloke over at the shop where I went to see if our posters are up . . . said: "My word you're in luck, aren't you? Haxby's have struck it rich this time." "How's that?" I said. And he said: "Well, folks don't die leaving you a hundred thousand every day do they? Do you mean to say, you don't know?" he said. "Don't know what?" I said. "We've been on the road nearly a week." Then he broke it to me. . . .'

Dan and Rabe came up.

'Broke what?' Dan asked impatiently.

'Broke it, that it was in the papers about Rocca dying and leaving Gina £100,000. My God. . . .'

Monty dropped down on the ground. And then they were all round her, Max, the boys, Rabe, Sailor, Dan and Lord Freddie as Gina read slowly:

'Guglielmo Rocca, better known as "Billy" Rocca, the film star who was a dwarf and celebrated for his impersonation of grotesque and comic characters, died recently at his villa in Hollywood. Rocca had a varied and variegated career. Reputed the son of an impoverished noble Italian family, a man of character and culture, by shrewd investments in real estate and rubber, he amassed wealth in his later years. Although extravagant and luxurious in his way of living, he was able to restore the fallen fortunes of his family some time ago; but returned to the stage and the silver screen after having lived in retirement for several years. The bulk of his fortune has been left to Miss Georgina Haxby of Haxby's circus in Australia. "The most perfect soul I ever met in my life's wandering," will of the deceased states. It is understood that Rocca had a romantic attachment for Miss Haxby dating from the time he worked with Haxby's here.

'Haxby's Circus disbanded some years ago, and the whereabouts of Miss Georgina Haxby are at present unknown.'

'Well, I'm damned,' Dan exclaimed, looking at Gina who was standing bareheaded in the hot sunshine.

'It seems too good to be true,' she said at last. 'Poor Billy!' She was remembering that day when they had talked in the tent as she cleaned out the cages. And how he came to see her in hospital, dapper and so gallant with his bouquet of flowers. That night behind the tent when he had asked her to go away with him.

'He thought it would be as hard for me as it was for him,' she told herself.

How bitterly she had suffered, she thought, no one knew. Yet Rocca had known. This last thought of his for her was the gesture of his understanding and sympathy. And she had scarcely thought of him in all these years. It was not fair; not to have given him the same gentle and sorrowing thought he had given her. She had after all treated him like the rest of the world, Gina told herself. Billy had been a freak and a curiosity to her, just the same as to the others.

'He was right about one thing at least,' Max said. '"The most perfect soul." You are that, Gi. There's nobody like you are.'

Gina's eyes filled.

'Oh Maxie,' she said, 'don't say such a thing.'

In all the excitement and rejoicing, nobody imagined Gina's good fortune was not everybody's. She least of all.

Preparations for the evening performance went forward with something like the old enthusiasm. The tent was packed and Haxby's never put up a better show than they did that night in Walgett. News of the windfall which had come to the circus got round the town, and the way Ted Blake, the tobacconist, had given Monty Haxby first word of it. At the end of the programme with yells, cheers and thumping of feet, clapping of hands,

Gina had been called for, and although she begged to be spared, Dan took her by the arm, and in her old coat, she stood in the circus ring and bowed her acknowledgement to an eager, curious crowd.

She seemed less excited than anybody.

'I can't believe it,' she said, drinking a cup of coffee beside the camp fire with the boys after the show.

Sailor, Rabe and Lord Freddie had all drunk her health, long and frequently, at the nearest hotel, and Dan, between drinks, had talked of Billy and of Gina, the beautiful girl she was, the wonderful rider, until that accident.

'It's true all right, my girl,' Dan exclaimed, overhearing Gina, as he returned to the camp fire and hugged her, hilariously. 'Now we can get a menagerie – build up the show. Have a dinkum circus. Eh?'

CHAPTER 22

Monty wired the newspaper in which he had found news of Gina's windfall, that Miss Georgina Haxby was at present touring the back country with Haxby's circus, but would be in Sydney at the end of the week to consult with her solicitors.

A country photographer lay in wait for the circus in the next town, took pictures of the waggons and one-pole tent, a family group of the Haxbys and a close-up snap of Gina which he dispatched to a city newspaper so that 'The romance of a circus,' as the story was headed, pre ceded the show everywhere.

Monty was for scrapping the show and getting to Sydney as soon as possible so as to make the most of the advertisement Gina's news would give Haxby's. But Dan would not hear of it. 'Haxby's keep faith' had been his text for so many years that he could not depart from it or cancel performances which had been advertised a day or two ahead. It was ten years since Haxby's had left Yowan farm, and although there had been changes of horses and wardrobe, the tents would hardly hold together, so patched, travel-stained and red and grey with dust they were. The whole show was shabby, way-worn, and the horses had lost condition; but Dan insisted on showing to Narrabri, beyond which no announcements had been made.

Since her mother's death, Gina's publicity arrangements had broken down a good deal. Monty had done what he could. But owing to the great distances between towns, and because neither he nor she could be spared from the everyday work of the travelling horses and waggons, advance agent business had been reduced to telegrams and bundles of posters dispatched to local publicans and store keepers.

Curious, eager audiences awaited the circus in towns where it appeared for the next three nights. On its last legs Haxby's might be; but Dan swore that it justified his boast of being.'The Lightest, Brightest, Little Show on Earth,' on those last nights of its existence under the old top. Everybody worked with gaiety and vigour.

Dan himself pattered and made his little jokes, bubbling over with pride and rejoicing. Gina had to appear and bow every night at the end of the performance, and Dan never enjoyed himself more than when he was announcing that 'Haxby's' would be going into dock at the end of the week. The old show was going to be overhauled and rejuvenated. Folk would not recognise it when they saw it on the road again, though it would endeavour still to live up to its reputation as 'The Lightest, Brightest Little Show on Earth' – only more so. He always thanked ladies and gentlemen, not forgetting the children present, for their patronage, and promised to visit the district again in a year or so with a programme and attractions which would make their hair curl.

Monty and the boys were left to truck the waggons, horses, monkeys and Queenie, with all the paraphernalia of the old show, and take them to a farm a few miles out from Sydney where Dan had arranged to quarter them. Sailor and Lord Freddie were to be left in charge, and the boys to join their father and the girls in Sydney.

Dan installed himself, Rabe, Gina and Max at the

Burlington Hotel in the Haymarket. He always put up at this roomy, cosmopolitan hotel down near the markets, when he was in Sydney, and saw no reason now to alter the habits of a lifetime.

Before leaving Narrabri, Gina received a letter which had been chasing her all round the country. It was from Smith and Dreary, a Sydney firm of solicitors, informing her that they were in communication with the lawyers of the late Guglielmo Rocca in California and had been requested to interview her, establish her identity, and arrange all formalities in connection with the will of the deceased.

A junior partner, Mr. Jesse Dreary, called on Gina and her father as soon as they arrived in Sydney, and with shrewd courtesy put the resources of his firm at Miss Haxby's disposal, pending wind-up of the Rocca estate. That, as Dan joyfully interpreted it, meant ready cash, within reason.

It is true Mr. Dreary explained that Rocca's assets being chiefly in stocks, the bequest might not work out as considerably as was at first anticipated; but to Gina and Haxby's it still represented a windfall of fabulous dimensions.

And so in a few days Gina had more money to spend on clothes for herself and Max, and to give her father to buy things for himself and the boys and Rabe, than she had ever dreamed of coming into her hands.

Among the telegrams of congratulation waiting for her had been one from Lily and Jack; another from Auntada and Uncle George. Other wires from old friends all over the country, Dr. and Miss Heathcote for example, Edie Newton, Mrs. Bergen, and above all Bruiser and Charley, were a surprise and delight. How Gina smiled and exclaimed over them! Wasn't it nice of people to send her good wishes like that? A cheque for the hospital at Southern Cross was one of the first she wrote.

Lily and Jack she wired to at once, asking them to join the family at the Burlington as soon as possible, and offered them any contract they liked with the new Haxby's. To Auntada and Uncle George she wrote, enclosing a cheque for their train fares, and saying they must come at once to take the holiday of their lives in Sydney.

For the next few days, notes and comments on sawdust and spangles, the luck of the ring, circus ways and days were to be found in almost any newspaper. Gina was photographed and interviewed. Dan reminisced and denied that there was ever anything in the nature of an engagement between Rocca and his daughter. The story of Gina's accident was told and of Billy's distress for her. Gina herself did what she could to destroy the myth of 'the perfect soul' she was supposed to possess.

'It was Billy who was good natured and kind to me,' she said. 'I never did anything for him.'

There was a sketch of her in an evening paper describing her brown gypsy face, thoughtful dark eyes, hair with its touch of fire turned back from a broad forehead. Her gaze had freedom and strength; the well-cut mouth was held firmly. There was nobility in the proud passionate face in respose. Virginal, untouched by turgid emotions, Gina looked out from a photograph by Cazeneaux; and yet in her very austerity was the depth from which her being might move to its dissolution.

Gina herself hated the talk about her, the congratulations and questions which sprang thick and fast wherever she went.

'What was she going to do with her fortune?'

It would keep her and her family in comfort and idleness for the rest of their days. But none of them wanted that. Their ideal of life was a strenuous and daring one. Miss Haxby, it was understood, had decided to put most of her newly-found wealth into equipping and reorganising the circus.

In all the happiness and excitement, Gina was still a little overcast.

'If only I'd done anything for him, Max,' she brooded. 'Poor Billy. I didn't really, you know. He was banged about so. Everybody laughed at him. "What is it?" you'd hear them say if he walked down the town. Like they've done to me, sometimes.'

'Oh, Gi.'

'I've seen his face wither, and twist up, and sweat, Max. Then he'd laugh . . . stare and laugh more. And when he was in the ring he'd do all manner of silly things to make people laugh more and more.'

The following week Lily and Jack arrived, and with them an American boy who had been working under engagement to them since they returned from the States. His name was Laller Hayes although he passed as Jack's younger brother. A good-looking youngster with a girlish complexion and blue eyes, there was nothing girlish about Lal except his clear skin, and he was clever at his work.

'Not a bad youngster if only the women would leave him alone,' Jack said.

There was a woman in Melbourne, one of these barefoot dancers, crazy about him. She wanted Lal to partner her in her dancing, Jack told Gina; and thought Lal would probably go away with the dancer if she followed the Daynes to Sydney.

Jack and Lily still had a month of contract to work off at picture theatres in and about Sydney. Neither of them looked much older, rather thin and hard after the years of their life together; but they had worn well.

Lily's hair was a lighter drier gold, perhaps; her blue eyes made up with mauve and grey shadows, had still their vague, childish dissatisfaction. And Jack exhaled the same faint odour of kerosene and olive oil he plastered his hair with, to keep it looking black and shiny, prevent the grey hairs showing.

Very pretty and elegant, a woman of the world, and experienced by her tour of the United States and Great Britain, Lily took Gina and Max in hand at once; managed their shopping, and decided what clothing they should wear, and what they could not possibly be seen dead in, as if being the elder sister, so travelled and knowledgeable, that was what she was entitled to do. And there could be no two points of view on the subject.

Max and Gina submitted contentedly to her verdicts and were rather in awe of their appearance when Lily had done with them. Gina bought frocks, shoes, under-clothes and hats for Lily too, in the exuberance of their first days together. Such an orgy of spending money the sisters had never imagined.

For although Jack and Lily had earned good salaries wherever they went, their living expenses were high and Jack had watched expenditure scrupulously, banking a fair proportion of their joint income, so that rainy days should not find him napping; and Lil would be well provided for if defective gear or any unforeseen mischance disabled him.

He was as careful and devoted to her as he had ever been, and Lil as self-centred and indolent as ever. The

240

excitement of her nightly performances left her flat and exhausted. She had trained hard for years, dieted and practised, to keep up her form – but was really tired out – now. Strung-up, eager and vivacious, she went through her act on the wire and the trapezes at night; but lay about most of the day, could not be bothered to tidy her room even, or wash her silk stockings. It was time for them both to retire, Jack said. He thought of buying some nice quiet little pub in a seaside town and taking it easy for the rest of their days.

But the scheme for a new Haxby's lured and dazzled him.

'You don't mean to say you're going to put all this money into the show, Gina,' he said. 'Hand it over to the old man, and –'

'Not quite that,' Gina explained. 'I'm going to buy Dad out. Put him in as general manager and ring-master. But it's to be my show, Jack. I want you with me as adviser, business manager. You've got the experience, and can do that sort of thing. Lil's tired – you're neither of you as young as you were. Can't keep going much longer. We'd all be keen on making the old show go.'

'Lord, yes,' Jack brooded. He looked older than usual in the morning light, spare and keen; but his hair was thinning, and for all the oiling and kerosene, silver threads were showing through it. 'Lil'll hate to give up . . . but neither of us is getting younger as you say, Gi. I've been wondering how long we could keep going. The pub'd be all right as a money maker: but I can't see myself pulling beer for the rest of my days.'

'Think it over, Jack,' Gina said, 'and have a word with Lil. If you'll come in and stand by me, we'll make a do of things I think.'

The more Jack thought out the idea to rebuild Haxby's the better he liked it, and at the end of the week he decided to throw himself into the enterprise. It took Dan some time to understand his was not to be the only word in reorganisation of the new show. Jack and the boys put it to him he was needed to train horses and youngsters and could not be expected to undertake business responsibilities as well. Gina's idea of buying him out and putting him in as manager, he treated at first as a joke; but as the proposition read extremely well in terms of hard cash, he pocketed the deal with good grace.

'Ah well,' he said. 'I've always been a showman. Not a financier. Have it your own way, my girl. So long as it's Haxby's, and I've got a finger in the pie, I'm satisfied.'

'Everything'll be just the same, Dad,' Gina consoled, 'except that we'll all share in profits – and there have got to be profits.'

'I see.' Dan grimaced; but was too beside himself with importance and enthusiasm to make difficulties about anything. To restock the circus and get it started was all he cared about.

'There's one thing though,' he said, 'we aren't puttin' up any opposition to Wirth's. I learnt all I know of handling horses from Phil Wirth and I reck'n there's not a finer horse-master in the world. Many's the hole Wirth Brothers have helped me out of in the old days. We was down and out in the Western district in 1902, after Jumbo laid out Paddy Hannigan. What with the weather and floods – if Phil Wirth hadn't lent me a few pounds and an elephant we'd never've got away.'

Dan went about extraordinarily busy, making enquiries as to tents, waggons and wild animals; had his hair cut, shaved almost. It stood up over his head in white bristles, and his moustache shorn to a tooth brush gave him the air of a successful stockbroker. Very prosperous, energetic and alert he looked in a new suit and fawn-coloured felt hat he wore a little to one side, a tie of gold and purple poplin Max had chosen, and patent leather boots which made the most of the small feet he was so proud of.

In the exuberance of his self-respect and good spirits, he reassumed an attitude of authority over his family. Even Lily felt he was presentable and likeable enough to own as a father. It gave an air of stability to Haxby's, to point Dan out in the hotel lounge or dining room, as Daniel Haxby of Haxby's Circus. And quick to sense his social success, Dan made the most of any parental airs he could display.

'Lily, my girl, your dresses are too short,' he remarked one morning after lunch, 'far too short for a respectable married woman.'

'Well, I'm damned,' Lily replied, staring at him.

With Max he was more successful.

'Maxie, my dear' – he held Max's face up one afternoon as they were starting off for the pictures – 'I won't allow you to put rouge on your lips. Go and wipe it off. What would your mother have said? I never saw your mother put rouge on her lips in my life.'

To Gina's and Lily's amazement, Max went meekly and wiped the red from her mouth.

In innumerable other ways, her father exerted a discipline where Max was conce..ed, with severity and success, that neither Gina nor Lily would have dreamed of. He sent Max to bed early every now and then. Stopped her chocolates before breakfast, and insisted on putting a nip of salts in her morning tea.

As for men, Dan was as strict with Max as he had been with either of the other girls. When her father was about, no young man approached Max with the familiar patronising air which annoyed Gina. And Max seemed to take it all as a matter of course. She was more childish and docile with him than she had been with anybody. 'Right, Dad,' she said, very sweetly and quietly, to most of his demands.

It was certain Dan had a very good effect on his youngest daughter. He was fond of her; as proud as a peacock when they went out together. She looked such a credit to him, this vivid young thing. Dan took her little trips on the harbour, to the zoo and the pictures – which Max was childishly delighted with. He even allowed her to go to the horse bazaar with him sometimes; and they chased every creamy or piebald horse they saw in the street, to discover whether he had a good back and was suitable for the new show.

Between them Max and her father bought a beautiful white mare for sixty guineas, more than Dan had ever paid for a horse, and decided to call her 'Lotty.' Dan promised that Max should work her some day and sent her out to the farm with the other horses.

In a grey suit and blue shirt, Rabe was less of a success sartorially than Dan. He spilt beer on his new clothes as if they were not new at all; and his hair and moustache remained limp and unregenerate however clipped and brushed. His blue eyes, faded and dreaming, never seemed to be looking at anything less than a hundred miles away; and he stooped and slouched about, forgetting to tie his boot laces as usual.

Rabe alone was unable to escape a frugal habit of doing things and horrified at the idea of buying new instruments when good second-hand ones could be found. He had combed the second-hand shops for instruments he needed and collected half-a-dozen performers.

The only fly in the honey of his happiness was that Max insisted on a saxophone for the new band. Rabe loathed the saxophone and all its works. He said it gave him a stomach-ache, churned up his insides and made him want to howl like a dog. But Max had made up her mind. Nowadays you could not have a decent band without a saxophone, she said; and Gina left them to it, having no doubt Max would have her own way in the end.

'No! No!' Rabe protested. He would not have that howling niggers' *geshreierei* in his band. *Gott in Himmel*,' what did she think he was? What did she take him for? It could not be done.

'But why do you want a saxophone, Max?' Gina asked.

'It's not me, it's Lal,' Max confided ingenuously.

She and the American boy had struck up a gay kiddish friendship. Although they were supposed to be on holidays, Jack and the boys were so afraid of becoming stale, they had rented a shed for practising in, and Max had been exercising with them every morning for an hour or two. For the sake of old times, Lily and Jack decided to appear with Haxby's for a few weeks, before retiring, and Jack had been putting Max through some new turns with Lily, Laller Hayes and himself. Lal and Max had invented a new turn themselves, from watching a cage of monkeys at the Zoo. 'The Last Links,' they called it; and got no end of fun out of seeing how like the monkeys they could play about and swing among the trapezes.

'Lal wants awfully to learn to play the saxa',' Max explained. 'They're awfully expensive – he can't afford to buy one. But of course – if there's a good instrument in the band, he can learn on it. And we ought to have a saxophone, shouldn't we, Gi?'

Gina smiled, thoughtful and a little uneasy.

'Oh well, if you think so, Max,' she agreed.

And was not surprised, when she heard that Lal and Max had taken Rabe out to lunch one day. Laller, who was quite a good musician really, had talked all Rabe's pet music to the old man, flattered and complimented him, while Max wheedled and coaxed, so that they led him straight to a music shop afterwards and had brought home the coveted instrument. Lal had taken lessons immediately and enrolled himself for the band, as well as for his aerial and acrobatic work with Jack and the boys.

Gina worked out and thought over every detail for the new show. She had gone with Dan to a tent maker's whom he dealt with once in the old days and ordered a grand two-poled tent of red and white striped canvas with 112 stakes; and another not quite so large for the menagerie, requesting that the best material and work-manship be put into every bit of stuff designed for Haxby's. A padded barricade for the ring was also one of her specifications because it minimised danger in case of accident. She kept estimates for all the work ordered and undertaken; and insisted on a careful accounting for every expenditure, consulting with Jack on propositions involving legal and financial responsibilities of any significance.

Lily was put in charge of wardrobe, the ordering and making of uniforms, parade dresses and costumes. It was decided that attendants should have blue and scarlet uniforms with gold braid and brass buttons, which although they might not wear well would look showy and

246

make a splash for the debut of Haxby's. The waggons were to be painted and have blue and scarlet wheels to match the uniforms; the bandsmen wear saxe blue uniforms with gold braid, and the keepers, scarlet.

'Some turn-out,' Dan chortled, the dream of his life fulfilled, by this equipment of a show in proper style.

Gina and Jack agreed that the road was out of the question for an up-to-date circus. Haxby's would travel by train when it took the road again. There was a special train to arrange for, a route to map out, and facilities and dates to be discussed.

Dan remembered weather conditions in every State for the last fifty years. He urged going north for the spring, west during the winter, showing back through Adelaide and Victoria, and laying up during the hottest of the summer months in Melbourne or Sydney to practise, and re-condition, or try out a visit to Tasmania, New Zealand or Noumea. An itinerary was worked out to make the most of shows and race meetings in the country districts, and dates fixed for visiting them.

Out near the farm where Dan had sent the horses, there was a disused quarry and its sheds, and this was rented to exercise and train the horses in. Dan had the horses he bought in Sydney sent up to McNamarra's, and Monty drove him out there every morning in Gina's new Chrysler.

Dan was anxious to start training the new white mare he called 'Lotty' at once, and to teach Les and Monty all he knew of handling horses; what nerves to press for certain tricks, the importance of regular and persistent practice, wielding the whip smartly when necessary, and using a good supply of carrots or sugar, as rewards –

R

carrots rather than sugar because sugar destroyed a horse's teeth in time.

Dan, with Monty and Les to help him, Sailor and Lord Freddie to hang on to the horses, spent all the morning breaking in and training the new horses to high school and liberty stunts, exercising Princess and Lotty or his favourite Yarraman. Bonnie, he decided, had earned a rest and was to be left to graze peacefully on McNamarra's paddocks till the end of her days.

The boys practised running and jumping from the spring board to the back of their horses every day and all day. They bounced on the trampalene, went through their horizontal bar and acrobatic exercises for strengthening and keeping the muscles supple. Max and Lily worked with them in the afternoon, and Jack took charge of them as trainer.

A menagerie was the difficulty. Dan was for 'nipping over' to the Malay States or Singapore for wild animals. 'You can pick up a couple of elephants and a keeper . . . a tiger and perhaps a couple of leopards dirt cheap over there,' he said. 'There was a man I knew used to be an agent. If we could get hold of him—'

But neither Dan nor Monty could be spared. They were needed to train the horses. Jack and Lily had to fulfill their contract, so that in the end it was decided Gina herself should 'nip over' to Singapore. She was anxious to take Max with her; but Max did not wish to go. She had been practising with Jack and Lily and the boys in the mornings, and neither Dan nor Jack were in favour of it. They said it was better for Max to keep on with her training. Jack had arranged tentatively for her to appear in their turn at the Tivoli. Lil was tired out he said. It would give her a let-up if Max went on for awhile; and it would do Max good to work with Laller and himself.

'All the years we've been working together we've never had an accident,' Lily said. 'Jack's that careful, Gi, and we train like hell. Every morning Jack and Lal do a couple of hours and I go down in the afternoon and work with them. My nerve's not what it was. Jack doesn't let me risk anything. But Max is young and pretty. She doesn't know what fear is, I suppose. We'll be glad to have her, Gi, and I'll look after her.'

Jack had cabled to Hagenbeck's for a lion tamer and it would be three months before the tamer, and the young lion and couple of lionesses he proposed to bring with him, could arrive. An American trainer with his pretty wife and performing bears had been engaged, and Dennis, a French clown with a couple of performing dogs. A strong man, and a trick cyclist of international reputation with his wife, were also booked for the new show by an agent in Hamburg whom Jack had wired to negotiate the business.

CHAPTER 23

WHEN Gina returned from Singapore in a cargo boat with half-a-dozen cages of wild beasts, six elephants, and a pair of young king pythons in a card-board hat box, her arrival caused something of a sensation on the quay.

The family was all there to meet her and inspect the animals, Dan, Rabe, Lily and Max, Jack and the boys – with two new sisters-in-law who were a surprise for Gina. And such a chattering and clatter of exclamations and greeting they made, that the officers and crew of the *Johore* said it was as good as a circus to watch and listen to the circus having a day out.

Everybody had been alarmed when one of the bears escaped from his cage, during a storm, after the steamer left Thursday Island. But Gina herself had caught him, when she found him wandering round the hold, and coaxed him back to the cage with a bunch of bananas.

'Reminds me of the yarn they tell on Wirth's about Johnny Rougal,' Dan laughed. 'He was a trainer they had, years ago, one of the bravest and best I ever knew, and a bear got loose in a storm at sea when he was on board once. Everybody was scared stiff and all the animals went mad, roaring, chattering and howling. The bear got to a cow and calf in a pen at the end of the deck, grabbed the calf and made off with it; Rougal, who was near dead with sea sickness, jumped up when they told him and went after the bear. He trotted her back to her cage. And when somebody asked Johnny if he wasn't afraid the bear might have done for him, he said: "No! Oh no . . . but I was afraid the cow might bite me because she had lost her calf!" '

Gina was full of her experiences in Singapore and native States of the Malay peninsula. She talked of crowded streets, small bright shops, tall trees, vermilion against dim blue skies, tropical nights, like immense jewels, strange and rare, Wajang dancers, snake-charmers, Chinese temples: a tiger fight she had seen: and her deals with European traders and dark-skinned trappers of wild beasts in the jungles. It was like living through a fairy tale, she said, to visit the palace of the Sultan of Johore, and stand in the great hall with its ancient Chinese jars, when the gold plate was spread and mauve and magenta orchids piled for a banquet.

In the absence of his father, Gina had been courteously received by the Crown Prince of Johore, the Tungku Makota and his wife. She had met, also, his brother, the Tungku Ahmad and his wife, and been captivated by the serene and tranquil beauty of these Malay Princesses. Their aunt, a very noble and dignified personage, the Sultana Fatima, had given the wanderer a little charm of Pahang gold 'to scare all evils from her path' and Gina was going to remember the only Sultana she had ever known with real affection, she assured everybody.

She had bought trappings for the elephants, native umbrellas, Chinese coats, lanterns and banners, lengths of gorgeous silks, sarongs, all manner of glittering fabrics of native weaving, for parade dresses and turbans: necklaces and ear-rings of jade and aquamarines for Lil; tiny seed pearls on a single string for Max, as well as shawls, kimonas and embroidered slippers for everybody.

But when the family saw Gina, a chinese shawl of black silk gorgeously embroidered with birds of paradise, flowers, butterflies and pomegranates, over a dress of some Eastern tissue with a glittering thread, amber beads and ear-rings beside her dark face, they could scarcely believe she was their own, their very own Georgina Haxby. Gina had come out of her shell, it was agreed. Her trip had done her all the good in the world.

Syd recounted the adventures they had been through together with boyish gusto. When he described a tiger fight they had seen at the palace of one of the native rulers up country, Dan was inflamed with the idea of staging one. But it was out of the question, Gina said, too brutal and bloodthirsty for words. Besides the tigers had torn each other to pieces and tigers were far too costly to be allowed to treat each other like that on a circus. Syd's story of how Gina pleased the Sultan of Jahlan by teaching a horse she had been riding to bow before him was a good one too. Syd himself showed what he could do on a pony he and Gina schooled in a week; and he had learnt a number of new tricks from a troupe of native acrobats in a Chinese circus touring the peninsula.

Dan was more than pleased with the animals Gina had selected, and the prices she paid for them. A hundred pounds for the young Bengal tiger, forty pounds for the leopards, fifty for an orang-utan family, father, mother and baby, ten for wolves, six pounds for a pair of Malayan bears and from one hundred and fifty to two hundred for the elephants, a pair of Capucin monkeys she had got for next to nothing and brought a silver gibbon as a present to Max.

The animals stood the journey well, with the exception of the elephants, two of which had died on the way.

Cages were loaded on to waggons on the quay and taken off to the circus camp at McNamarra's.

The family sprang several surprises on Syd and Gina too. Les and Monty were both married. Monty had married a widow with two children – a quiet homely little woman who had been staying out on the farm while Monty was living there to be handy to the horses.

Les's wife was Rene Morris, an American girl who had been dancing in a vaudeville turn at one of the picture theatres.

The circus tents and uniforms were all finished, and everything was ready for the first night which had been announced for the following Saturday. Paul Bach, the lion tamer, had arrived, Anna and Frank Molnar, the bear trainers, also; Dennis, the French clown, with a family of performing dogs, and Madame Dennis. Joshua, the strong man, Dan was furious about, had called a damned impostor and after a terrible row threatened to sack if he did not get more guts into his act. And Bruiser and Charley were back – had tramped down from Queensland and begged Dan to give them a job of any sort.

Only Max stood aside in all the excitement, chatter and curiosity with a little subdued air Gina was puzzled by.

While Lily and Max were resting, Gina talked to Jack.

'What is it, Jack?' she asked. 'What's the matter with Max?'

'Cripes, I'm glad to see you Gi,' he said. 'I've been worried to death about the kid.'

'What is it Jack?' Gina plumbed the depths of his anxiety.

'She's lost interest in her work and gone nervy, for the first time in her life. It's that little brute of course.'

'Lal?'

Jack's blue-grey eyes met hers, troubled and keen.

'You see, they used to play about like a couple of kids, joking and cracking each other. It never occurred to me. . . . I never thought there was more in it than that. I should have I suppose. I've been pretty strict with Max about fellers. Wouldn't have them hanging round or let her go out with them. As bad as your Dad, I've been. But it's the only way in our business Gi. There's some awful wasters chases a good-looking kid like Max, and they take it for granted she's years older than she is . . . knows all there is to know.'

Gina's hands twisted.

'But that little blighter – I'd let him take her to pictures, now and then, or for an ice-cream . . . and it seems to have been love's young dream for Max. Anyhow, the woman I told you about who does those statue poses and dances followed us here and to make a long story short, Lal lit out with her.'

'Oh Jack!' Gina could think of nothing but Max.

'Of course it was a devilish trick to play me. Max has paired with him ever since she went on with us, and they worked together like birds. Simply couldn't go wrong and Max was as happy as larry. I couldn't get anybody to take his place for a bit of course. The lad I've got now isn't a patch on Lal, a Japanese; and Max hates the sight of him. She cried herself sick, wouldn't eat and went to pieces generally, for awhile.'

Gina's troubled eyes held his.

'Rotten, isn't it?' Jack queried. 'If I could've got my hands on to that lad I'd have flayed him alive. She's a sweet kid, Gina, a bit selfish and lazy . . . all that. But honest and generous . . . and I'm awfully fond of her.'

Gina trembled. 'You've been good to her Jack, I know.'

'I've done what I could to keep the wheels running smoothly,' Jack smiled his old wise smile, 'but it hasn't always been easy. Lil's used to being the only pebble on the beach, you know.'

'I know,' Gina replied.

'Max seems to have got over it a bit. I wouldn't say anything, if she doesn't,' Jack continued. 'We'll see how things go after opening night and put her off the trapezes, if she doesn't feel better about it.'

Gina lay awake a long time, aching for Max and wondering about her. What should she do? Without her work Max would fret more. With all its danger, in the frayed state of her nerves, Gina wished Max need not go on with her aerial turn until she wanted to, and was as eager and happy in it as she had been.

Time she knew was the only cure for this hurt Max was suffering – and some other diversion. But Max was too young to be suffering at all in this way, barely seventeen. It was too bad. Gina wished she could spare her the hurt and disillusionment. She remembered Will Murray and Mart Bergen with some of the old yearning and pain it had been to go away from Mart, realising she was cutting this sweetness and magic out of her life.

It was nearly dawn when she went to sleep; and she wakened to find Lily in the room with tea on a tray, Max sitting up in bed, a box of chocolates and a book beside her.

Lily's exclamation aroused Gina.

'Max, chocolates at this hour! You'll be as fat as a pig if you don't look out.'

Gina took her tea from the tray Lily put down beside her.

'And those beastly novels she's always reading . . . I wish you would make her give them up, Gi.'

'Oh shut up!' Max stretched, lazily. She looked weary and withered in the early light, much older than she was.

'Sleep well, darl?' Max smiled to Gina.

'Like a log,' Gina replied.

Max selected a large chocolate.

'Have one?'

'No thank you, dear.'

'Don't let her be late for practice will you, Gi.' Lily hurried out of the room again. 'Eleven, Max, not a quarter to twelve.'

'Leave me alone, can't you?' Max threw back her head. 'Why can't Lil leave me alone?' she cried petulantly, as Lily closed the door behind her.

Twitching herself out of bed, Max went to her dressing table and examined her face seriously.

'Am I getting fat, Gi? Is that a spot on the side of my nose? I'll have to leave those darned chocolates alone I suppose.' Taking a cigarette from a little gilt case, she lit up and smoked. 'If it weren't for Jack I'd give up the trapeze. He's getting old and fussy, poor dear, and Lil's no earthly use. There's only me and Zuki . . . the little devil. But I'd hate to give up, Gi. It'd look so like showing the white feather – as if I couldn't work without Lal . . . I suppose they've told you Lal's cleared out.'

'Yes,' Gina said. She was afraid to say more and waited for the story she thought Max would pour out to her. But Max's face settled into a hard, stiff little mug.

'Oh well, that's that!' Max slipped into a pale pink kimono sprayed with apple blossom Gina had bought her. 'I can work as well – without him as with him. So they can put that in their pipe and smoke it.'

She went off to her bath; and when she returned sat down on the edge of the bed to manicure her nails.

'Must come out to the farm and be introduced to Anna Molnar, Bach, and the Dennises, Gi,' she remarked politely. 'The tents are all up, there. Oh, and a foal one of the new ponies had last week.'

Gina went out of the room for her bath. When she came back Max was still working intently at her finger nails.

'Anna's a darling,' she chatted, making conversation in a strained little voice, as she put a little pink paste on each nail. 'You'll like her, Gi. She's American. Such a good sort, pretty, got bright eyes like a bird. We're all gone on her, even Dad. Con's nice too, Monty's wife, you know, though Dad thinks Monty might have done better for the show. Married somebody younger and prettier, who could have been trained to do something. Still – there's the kids. And they're as keen as mustard to learn the business . . .'

Max rubbed and polished her nails, as if this really were the most serious and important business of her life.

'And Bach – Paul Bach . . . you say it as if you were howling. He's awfully clever, Dad says, but I hate him. Won't let me go near the lions – even Belinda. And you know, I've played about with Belinda ever since we brought her from the Zoo that day. "You go and play with your dolls, kindchen," he said to me, one day. "Don't be silly, Mr. Bach," I said. "I've never had a doll – only Belinda!" He did laugh, Gi. But I can't stand him all the same. He's a woman hater.'

'A woman hater?'

'Anna told me he was awfully mad when he heard a woman owned this show. Said he'd never have come

out if he'd known. Won't have a woman messing round
. . . giving him orders.'

Gina smiled.

'The Molnars knew him at home, say he's cut up rusty
about women because his wife eloped with a violinist in a
show they were on, years ago. She was a real beautiful
woman, had wonderful golden hair . . . used to ride like
me. That's why he doesn't like me. Though I haven't
got long hair – thank God. And he drinks, Gi . . . says
the lions like the smell of whisky. He wouldn't dare go
near them if they didn't get a whiff. But he's real clever
. . . and not a bit afraid.'

'Dennis is a dear, too, Gi,' Max gossiped, packing her
orange sticks, buffers and file into their silver case, 'but
his wife would murder you for two pins. They're both
mad about the dogs. You can't go into their room at
McNamarra's without stepping on one, or sitting on it.
They sleep on the chairs, and Madame's best silk dress,
if they want to. Bach puts his head in the mouth of one
of the lions. Dad swears Rosa'll get him some day. She's
the other lioness Bach brought out with him, boss of the
cage. Ugh! An ugly-looking beast . . . makes your blood
run cold the way she prowls round him in the practising
cage and watches him. Bach never takes his eyes off her.'

Practice was at eleven o'clock. But for all her coaxing
and urging, Gina could not get Max to the circus camp
before twelve. Jack had been working with Lily and the
boys for an hour then.

'It's too bad of you, Max! It really is,' Lily protested.

Max changed into her suit of black velveteen, and calico
boots.

'Sorry!' she called indifferently. 'I'll be there in a
jiffy, Jack.'

While Max was with Jack and the boys, Gina went off to see that the animals and keepers she had brought from Singapore were comfortably installed. She wandered into the menagerie tent where Bach, in the tall iron practising cage, with Syd and one of the cage hands in attendance outside, was putting the lions through their act.

She stood watching him for some time. He was teaching her own lionesses to answer to their names, each in turn, and to jump through a hoop he held up for them, feeding them a piece of meat after every trick was successfully performed.

A short, square-faced man with a broken nose and eyes of quicksilver, fiery and magnetic, Gina realised a solid worth and primitive force about Paul Bach she liked and respected immediately. When the lionesses returned to their cage he came to her and stood before her.

'I do not like to be watched when I am at work,' he said.

'Oh, I'm just home. I didn't know,' Gina apologised, smiling a little, her brown eyes of sympathy and friendliness speaking for her.

'It is distracting to know others are there when I wish to give all my mind to the beasts and what I am doing,' Bach conceded, feeling it impossible somehow to maintain so rigid and hostile an attitude to this woman with her bowed back and brave smiling eyes. If she wanted to watch him, why shouldn't she?

'Of course,' Gina agreed. 'They tell me you've done wonders with our beasts already.'

'They are all right,' Bach spoke slowly, carefully, but without any embarrassment for words. He had travelled in America a good deal, and used the vulgar tongue of Anglo-Saxon peoples with easy disrespect. 'You got them young, that is the great thing. They have not been hurt, made afraid. In some of our German circuses, the training is too harsh, spoils the temper of a beast. There are good lionesses and bad . . . as with women. My Rosa for example is not good. She is moody and jealous . . . though I like her. That is why I work her. There is always a battle of the wills between us.'

As they talked, Bach turned towards the cages in which were Rex, the young lion, and the two lionesses, Milli and Rosa, he had brought with him from Europe. One of the couched beasts turned her head and snarled, her fur fluffing along her yellow back.

'There she is, Rosa.' The lioness gathered herself up, her amber eyes shifted and glared as she slunk round the cage and lay down at the back.

'Here's the boss come to see what she thinks of us,' Bach remarked cynically.

'Oh – ' Gina's steady gaze met his. 'I suppose I am "the boss" – but I never thought of it before. This is Haxbys', Mr. Bach!'

Bruiser and Charley came up to have a word with her.

'Oh! Bruiser! Charley!' Gina exclaimed. 'So you thought you'd like to come back to the show.'

'Too right we did, miss. When we heard the news, Miss Gina,' Bruiser said. 'Me and Charley was sitting down on a sapphire mine, up in Queensland, but the sapphires wouldn't bite. So I says: "Come on Charley, me boy, let's go and congratulate Miss Gina." And so we humped it . . . and your Dad didn't see how the new show could start off right without us.'

Gina laughed. 'I'm sure it couldn't either,' she said.

During the week before Haxby's reopened, Gina and Bach established a more or less friendly relationship.

She prowled about the menagerie, watching him at work, much as she wished, asking his advice about the other animals and their trainers.

Dan was anxious to put the tiger in action and have something done with the wolves and leopards; but so far no one had been found to handle them. Bach promised to get busy with the tiger and wolves, as soon as he had finished with the young lions he was training, although lions were his speciality. He did not care about working other beasts. Bears, wolves and tigers he had trained before and understood. But leopards, no. They were the most treacherous beasts to have anything to do with, he said. You might work them for years, but could never trust them. The men were born, not made, who worked leopards; and it required one person's whole time and attention to teach them to go through the simplest tricks.

Bach himself thought that leopards were more intelligent than almost any of the wild animals. Their swiftness and intelligence were greater than most men's. That was why they were so difficult to train. Used to flying among the trees as over the ground, their fierce wild spirit was never tamed in captivity. They were superior to men in their swift cunning, lithe strength, and the electrical rapidity with which their brains worked. A man had to be something of a leopard to work leopards.

Paul Bach himself, fearless as he was with other wild beasts, had the respect of all able trainers for the man who worked leopards.

Bears, he considered almost as treacherous, but more manageable. Slow, stupid creatures; if once they learnt a trick they could be depended on to go through with it; they did not forget either rewards or punishments. But, like slow stupid people, they smouldered over their resentments. Their hatred was implacable once it was generated against you. Bears, like elephants, never forgave or forgot.

'But I could not work elephants,' Bach said. 'A man needs to know their lingo and country – like Sailor 'Olmes – to work elephants.'

He would not believe that a woman was working elephants in Australia.

'But she is,' Gina protested. 'Eileen May with Wirth's circus. She's wonderful. You must see her.'

He had no feeling for elephants, Bach declared. He did not admire them, had an antipathy for them, rather. It was their beauty, character and sterling quality he admired in lions. He was at home with lions and lionesses. He understood them, he said. That was why he was their master and they obeyed him. He could make friends with a tiger; get the upper hand of him. A tigress was a more difficult proposition – unlike most female beasts who were all easier to manage than the male of a species. Male elephants, for example, after maturity, were always liable to 'must.' Few circuses kept them; the females were much more docile, biddable, and not so delicate, lived a hundred years in captivity sometimes.

Gina liked to yarn with Bach about animals and his experiences with them; his years of training and travelling the world with various shows. He had known Mabel Starke, the American woman who worked tigers, and the Pallenbergs, whose trained bears were the best he had ever seen. Bach promised to train the tiger and wolves on Haxby's for an act with his lions later on.

'Hot iron, dope! What for?' he demanded scornfully. 'No, I never used them. The great thing, training a lion or a tiger is, to get him young, win his confidence, as you know. Make him understand what you want him to do – and insist he does it. Patience, perseverance – that is all there is in the game. But you must never be afraid of a beast, relax the iron of your will towards him or her.'

A peasant of the Rhinish provinces, Paul Bach had put in years as a cage hand in Hagenbeck's, the great German circus. At the death of a famous lion-trainer he was working with, Bach had taken charge of the beasts and put them through their tricks.

Success, travel, and experience of living among all sorts of people had given him the manner of a man who knows his way about the world, polished the surface of his mind to an easy cynicism. But he was still the peasant beneath it all, rugged and shrewd, a man of definite impulses, rooted in his appetites.

Thoroughly absorbed in his work, he gave most of his time to the young lion and lionesses, rarely left them.

Dan took Bach's advice in the menagerie. Bach did not approve of the way their keeper was cutting the bears' toe-nails. The beasts needed their long-nailed claws to scratch themselves and keep healthy, he said. Their fur would never be fresh and bright if they could not scratch themselves. Dan gave instruction that the bears' claw-nails should not be cut, and although the order did not make Bach more popular among the cage keepers, who had torn hands to show for it, that he knew what was best for the animals was generally conceded. They were fed according to his system, lions, lionesses and the tiger in doles of twelve pounds of fresh meat a day, and the bears and monkeys with chopped-up vegetables.

No animal was permitted to interfere with another's food allowance. The discipline Bach established in the cage of young lionesses was as remarkable to Gina as anything he ever did. Although three animals fed in the

s

same cage, each was given her share of meat and bones, and none dared encroach on the other's meal. At first if Belinda, who was boss of the cage, seized a bone from Polly or Sadie, Paul raked it away from her with a long iron hook he thrust into the cage, and scolded her sharply.

His discipline was stern and inflexible, and after a while even Belinda learnt to respect it and crouched gnawing her own bones without attempting to grab any others. Milli, Rosa and Rex, the young lion Bach brought out with them, had long ago learnt the rigour of this law.

On Saturday night each animal received a bran mash with cream of tartar, sweet spirits of nitre, sulphur and soda mixed up in it to keep them in good condition, sleek and bright-furred; and Sunday was fast day for the whole menagerie.

The only cloud in those days of ferment and preparation for the new show was Max's unhappiness. She was doing her best to hide it, riding herself on a tight rein, cracking hardy and throwing herself into her work with a gay and sprightly recklessness. Everybody admired her spirit. Young though she was, Gina realised, Max had the instinct of her breeding to keep going whatever happened: the courage which is the supreme virtue of circus folk who live gamely, juggling with life and death for the laughter and applause that are coin of their realm.

CHAPTER 24

FIRST night of the new show went with 'the zip' Dan was always talking about. The big two-poled tent, one hundred and twenty by four hundred feet and fifty feet high, so white and gay with its red facings, was packed. An eager, chattering crowd seethed and swarmed everywhere. There was standing room only half an hour before the grand march swung into the ring, with five elephants in gorgeous trappings, and gaily caparisoned camels, horses bearing retainers and veiled houris, keepers striding beside the animal cages, slaves carrying gaudy, glittering umbrellas, or standards, and a horde of snake charmers, dancers and native musicians. Described as 'a procession from the Arabian Nights,' every artist took part in the parade of the company.

Programmes in bright red, green and yellow showed lions and tigers leaping and rearing from their covers, elephants playing football, and Lily and Jack in the new Fire Flies act they had invented for the occasion; Max on Princess, and Dan in the most correct of dress suits, urbane and immaculate, bowing to tremendous audiences.

The ushers, decorative and obsequious in scarlet and blue, showed patrons to their seats, whisking about busily. The band, in new uniforms of saxe blue with gold braid, Rabe looking like a reincarnation of himself as he conducted for the grand entry and parade, distilled a wild luscious rhapsody of airs, worthy of Rabe as a musician and of the new show he was celebrating with all the vigour of wayward genius.

The story of Haxby's in a little red booklet, as a young pressman had written it up, with photographs of Gina and Rocca, and an account of the vicissitudes the circus had passed through, was sold with the programmes, pea nuts and boxes of lollies, boys were carrying about the amphitheatre, and on the lot outside the menagerie, so that a sympathetic and interested audience waited as eagerly and good-humouredly to give the new show a good kick-off, as Haxby's was to earn its goodwill and praise.

In her tent that night, helping her to dress, Gina watched Max put on her make-up, skin back her hair, rub a little cold cream into her face and tint her eyelids with purplish blue paste from a small black box.

'It's some stuff Lal gave me,' she said. 'You can't buy it here. He got it from America.'

Very assured and careful, she was marking her eyebrows, tipping her eyelashes, rubbing her cheeks and chin with rouge.

'Lil's got an awfully good lip-stick,' she peered at Gina from the mirror, the highly-coloured little face as though it were done in oils by an impressionist painter. 'I'll nick a bit when she's not looking. She gets awfully mad when I do, or mess up her powder.'

Bach's turn with the lions had been placed early in the programme, because erection of a large iron-barred enclosure in the ring necessitated some fixing; and the whole thing had to be taken to pieces and removed to leave the track clear for the horses and riders.

Gina went into the tent and stood among the keepers and grooms to watch Bach drill the three young lionesses,

Rex, and his own two older pets. He looked very dashing and impressive, among the great tawny beasts, in dark blue and gold braided jacket, white breeches and high boots of a cavalry officer.

The lionesses went through their tricks with surprising readiness. Cracking his whip and calling each lioness by name and in turn, Bach sent her to run the ring and return to her pedestal. They mounted high stools with Bach between them forming a pyramid, shaking hands with him. Milli licked his cheek – 'kissed him' – Dan said. Bach had laid his head between her open jaws for the fraction of a second. Rosa snarled and roared as she was expected to, lurched sideways and jumped through the flaming loop, held for her through the iron bars by one of the cage hands.

The lionesses yawned, stretched to sleep on the floor as they were bidden; but thinking better of it, Paul 'sent them home to bed,' and when the sliding door of the cage on a waggon beside the enclosure was opened, the great beasts under a volley of whip crackings, raced the ring and scampered off to their cage. Paul bowed himself out of the enclosure.

'Well,' he asked, as Gina joined the little crowd of artists congratulating him beside the men's dressing-tent, 'how did we go?'

'I'm sure everybody was thrilled,' Gina told him.

'It is enough that you are pleased,' Bach said.

'Pleased?' Gina laughed, a little uncertainly.

She had been, she admitted to herself, carried away by the skill and daring of Bach's work with the lionesses. He attracted her strangely, his fearlessness and virility: those freezing, quicksilver eyes of his.

Jugglers and clowns followed Bach in the ring. The

267

boys went through the first of their riding acts. Sailor showed his baby elephants at school, and Max ran in for her turn with Princess and Lotty.

Max had never done better than she did, working the 'Arabian ponies' as they were billed, that night with Monty. Gina herself joined eagerly in the clapping and exclamations of the ring side. And Max played and slithered about on Princess, who had spangled bandages above her fetlocks, as if the pretty little mare were a rocking horse, and she the lightest and gayest of fairy creatures, as she danced, pirouetted and gestured on Princess's broad back, or jumped through hoops of pink roses.

'You were wonderful, darling,' Gina cried, going into her tent a little later when Max was changing for her turn with Jack and Lily on the trapeze.

'Was I, Gi?' Max queried indifferently.

Gina went to see the Molnars with the bears. The two big Russian bears, and Mitzi, the young American grizzly they used, were well-trained, climbed and balanced cleverly; but such uncertain tempered beasts that working them in the open ring was the most dangerous and risky business of the evening.

Anna wore white satin and swansdown in a short skirt, gaiters and cap, to escort her Teddies through their manœuvres. She travelled with more dresses than any woman on the show, because so often the bears snatched at and tore her frocks to ribands. She had been hugged and badly clawed several times, and her husband, a big, quiet good-natured Dane, was always anxious for her. He would have been better pleased if she did not appear with him; but Anna liked her work and refused to be dispensed with. Besides she was so piquant and coaxing with the clumsy creatures that success of the turn was as much due to the contrast of her charm with their ungainliness and brute strength, as anything else.

'The public,' Dan said, 'likes to see a woman handle wild beasts like that.'

He himself took Yarraman for his feats of memory and intelligence. The pony was still his pride and joy. Hunted the slipper hidden in a barrel or in sawdust of the ring, bowed, answered questions by shaking or nodding his head, pretended to be dead, played-up, bucking and snorting wickedly, then was sorry for his sins. 'Never trained a more intelligent horse,' Dan said, 'except perhaps a piebald pony named Phil – and he was as human as a horse could be.' The beautiful grey, with his flowing white silky mane and tail, was applauded almost as much as any performer, when he trotted out of the ring.

Joshua and the boys went through their strong man and acrobatic acts; and there was a shuffle and stirring of excitement for the last item on the programme: 'The Fire-Flies Act, on trapeze and wires, by the world-famous Daniella Troupe.'

In her tent, Gina fixed Max's gauzy wings so that they would shed easily when she reached the swings. A small glittering figure Max was in her silver-grey silk tights, silver and Rhinestone tunic.

Lily came in from the tent she and Jack shared, a larger edition of the fire-fly, but very elegant in her silver hose and sparkling tunic.

'My Lil,' Gina cried eagerly, 'you do look well.'

'It's an effective turnout, isn't it?' Lily agreed. 'How's Max?'

'She seems all right,' Gina said.

'Wants to show you what she can do.' Lily was preening herself before the long mirror. 'But you know . . . she's been giving us a rather bad time. Swears she'll never be able to work with Zuki. Will miss her catch or something.'

Watching the turn from the darkened ring, Gina lived through every pose and gesture of the Daniella Troupe. No one knew better than she every twist and tremor of the four glittering figures who ran in to the light rhythmic music Rabe drew from violins and flute for them. What was palaver and what were really clever moves, Gina recognised immediately. But even she was thrilled at the daring and grace of the act Jack had arranged to be performed under blue and silvery spot lights. Lily did little more than pose gracefully, swinging and chaining with Jack. But Max, fragile and dainty, shot through the air, swung and turned, flying from trapeze to trapeze, and finally somersaulting in mid-air reached for and caught the hands of the boy hanging head foremost from the opposite trapeze.

Then Jack, Lily, Max and Zuki were all bowing, gesturing, throwing kisses. As they ran from the ring hands clattered, shouts of applause shrilled through by a whistling on fingers and drumming of feet, resounded; but the fire-flies vanished through the darkened alley of their exit.

In her dressing room, Gina helped Max to take off her make-up and fold away her clothes in their long calico bags for the next performance. Already the national anthem was winding up for the night.

'You were lovely, my pet,' Gina whispered.

A tragic little face looked out at her from the small mirror before which Max was rubbing her face with grease again.

'If only I didn't see that damned monkey every time I look out in front of me,' she cried fiercely. And suddenly flung herself against Gina.

'Oh Gi. I can't bear it. I can't bear it. Every time I look, I expect to see Lal. It was such fun when he was here. So different . . . and now I hate it. When I take off . . . I don't want to catch Zuki's hand . . . I hate him. I'd rather drop into the net.'

'Darling! Darling!' Gina soothed and comforted.

Max sobbed and clung to her.

Jack came to their tent.

'Ready?' he called.

Gina pulled Max's cloak down and wrapped it round her.

'Dad and Rabe have gone off to celebrate, Gi. I'll go and bring the bus round,' Jack called, and went off. In a few moments Gina had huddled Max into her clothes and coat and hat. A slight forlorn figure, she clung to Gina, looking wan and childishly weary, all the excitement and exhilaration which had kept her going before her last act, evaporated.

Jack and Lily knew too well what was the matter to make any comment. Jack said to Gina: 'Keep her quiet and make her sleep if you can, Gi.'

Gina undressed Max and put her to bed as she had done when her little sister was a toddler.

Max sobbed and clung to her.

'Oh Gi. Why did he go away like that? Why did he leave me and go away with that old cow? She's as old as Lil – and got dyed red hair. And we had such fun together . . . Look, this is what he wrote.'

She pulled a crumpled piece of paper from the pocket of her pyjamas, and read, tears streaming down her face:

' "Maxie, my darling little Maxie, I love you. I will always love you. I don't know why I'm doing this. I don't want to. It's as if I was drunk or somebody had put a spell over me. Some day you'll understand but you couldn't now" (that's all scratched out, Gi). "We couldn't be married for such a long time. I can't help it. Lal." '

Stretched against the bed, Max wept tempestuously, her voice rising into broken exclamations.

'I can't bear it. I can't . . . Oh, Lally, why did you do it? Why did you go away?'

Gina sat down beside her.

'It'll be all right . . . it'll be all right, darling, you see. He'll come back.'

In her wrath and consternation she could have brought the boy by the scruff of his neck and given him to Max to do what she liked with. But she could only comfort her now; try to help her over the stormy passion of her loving and despair.

Max sat up.

'If we could find him, Gi. He didn't know I'd mind . . . like this. He thought I was such a kid . . . But I'm seventeen, Gi . . . and I can't live without him. I can't . . . It's just as if something had gone out of life that kept me going. You know, just as if you couldn't get water . . . or chocks, or something, when you want them – only worse.'

Gina smiled, so woe-begone, so tragic and intense the childish grieving.

'And I hate that Zuki,' she cried. 'I don't want to go to him, or catch hold of his hands. I don't know how I've done it. It's for Jack's sake really. He's such a brick . . . he's been so good to me. I couldn't let the show down, either.'

'You couldn't let Jack down,' Gina said.

'No,' Max admitted.

'That's it. When he says: "Funking, Max?" I could kill him, but I've got to go on. And, too, Jack says, one of these days, Lal's sure to come back and ask for a job again. . "If you've done your dash, Max, thrown up the sponge . . . and can't do your work. I'd have to put someone else with Laller. How'd you like that?" I wouldn't!'

'That's right,' Gina assented. 'You've got to keep fit, Maxie . . . keep up your practice and we'll try to find out where Lal is. What he's doing. But Jack says he and Lil are going to take a holiday, presently. You can too. While we're up country. I'll get a troupe from somewhere to do trapeze work.'

'Oh Gi.' Max's face was pacified, almost hopeful, 'if only I could see him again.'

'But you will, of course,' Gina said. 'Only you must keep fit, and work so that he'll want you for a partner. Laller's real clever, Jack says.'

'Oh yes, he is. Oh, darling old Gi. I will, you see . . . I will work. I'll be so good you won't know me, and I'll pay him out, the damned little swine. I'll give him hell some day, you see if I don't – for this.'

When Max lay asleep, very wan and exhausted after her weeping, Gina watched over her awhile, all brooding tenderness.

She wished that Max might never have to face an audience and the ordeal of that flying somersault again under the dark impassive eyes of the Japanese boy, understanding so well what it had meant to Max to feel there, after her perilous leap, the fair good-looking face of the youth she loved.

All the danger and courage of the leap had been worth being caught and held by him, drawn into the atmosphere of their light-hearted intimacy in the high air. They had often kissed as they met on the trapeze, and Max's being had laughed and sung with the exhilaration of their playing about, the world at their feet: all the stupid hordes of men and women who could not spin and swing through the air like fire-flies, kiss and delight in the supple and gracious strength of their own lithe bodies.

'When Lal touched me, he made happiness run all over me,' Max had said. 'When he looked at me, I wanted to laugh and sing. And when he squeezed my hand and said: "Darling . . . darling Maxie," or kissed me – Oh, Gi——'

Her tears carried away all the rest of what there was to say; but Gina gathered up the undefinable of that hurt and sorrow and folded them away in the depth of her love and pity.

Newspapers reported the resurrected Haxbys', with the apostrophe after not before the 's,' 'a clean, bright and up-to-date show, with not a dull moment.' But Dan was disappointed. Only to those who had known the old Haxby's, members of the company chiefly, something was missing. The show had not got the response from the crowd he hoped for.

The crowd was duller, flatter somehow; it had not given spontaneous combustions of laughter and applause. That was perhaps because it was a city crowd made up of people used to sights and wonders of all sorts. But also, the show was not supplying the humour, Dan felt; something was missing. He thought the clowns were to blame. They raised a laugh with difficulty: could not get the crowd going in the jolly roaring way Rocca had.

Dan promised himself to tune up the clowns. Something had got to be done about it. The show was all right; it was a good show. But the funny business would have to be improved, vastly improved. Haxby's had got to get the laughs it was used to, or be out of conceit with itself.

'If you can get people laughing, good tempered, you can do anything with 'em,' Dan said. 'We've got the goods . . . all but the laugh-shakers. We got to get them . . . or Haxby's isn't going to be "The Lightest, Brightest, Little Show on Earth".'

Everybody recognised, as Dan said, there had got to be more fun in the show. People went away without the rollicking sense of a jolly evening. Laughter was flat and lukewarm. Dan racked his brain for ideas. He put on the grossest foolery and roused hell out of the clowns; but nothing went with just the spirit he was after.

The season ended as well as could be expected. Haxby's had not put up any record or dimmed previous records of bigger, more brilliant circuses which had showed in Sydney. But it had held its own, given several good acrobatic, aerial and riding turns. The Fire-Flies were popular, although Max and Monty with the white horses, or Max on Princess, always scooped the pool of applause and admiration.

CHAPTER 25

ENTRAINING for a tour of the country districts began after the show closed down on the last night of the Sydney season. Dan and Jack had worked out every detail of organisation. Tent hands, grooms and keepers each had their special jobs. As each act was completed the gear in connection with it was packed and loaded in its place on a particular waggon. Canvas, stakes and king poles were loaded and packed on waggons; and as soon as the show was over, elephants hauled waggons and animal cages to the circus train, where they were put on trucks.

Sleepers for tent hands, keepers and grooms were hooked on behind the trucks. Performers had first-class compartments: married couples a carriage with two bunks and a meal table, which they converted into a small living and sleeping room. Max and Lily hung coloured chintz curtains over their windows and bunks, and most of the artists carried small spirit stoves to cook by. Gina herself, Jack had insisted, should have the state room beside the dining car, which was the best room on the train: Dan and Rabe shared the largest apartment at the end of the first car.

The family was to take its meals together in the dining room and Monty's wife had arranged to cook for some of the male performers. Tent hands, grooms and keepers cooked for themselves at a dixie on the train: fed as they liked and where they liked.

There was a luggage van for personal baggage and provisions. Gina's motor car had a truck to itself, and Dan insisted on a crate of turkeys going on board the train because he said Wirth's travelled with a crate of turkeys, and Haxby's were doing things in style these days.

When the train was lined up in the railway yards ready to start at midnight on Sunday as had been arranged, the family assembled to look at it. There it was: Haxby's circus train. It was the great moment of his life for Dan Haxby. As long as two trains, the lighted carriages stretched, with all the animal cages and elephant boxes, two big L class engines tacked on. Dan was broken up at the sight of it. He looked old and colourless in the moonlight, as he stood in the station yard among the rails, his family about him, Lily, Jack, the boys and their wives, Max and Gina.

'Haxby's,' he exclaimed. 'Haxby's train at last! By God, eh Mont? If only your mother was here to see it.'

Gina herself felt the thrill of the moment. It was her train after all. This was her circus setting out on its adventures.

'All aboard!' the guard called, going up and down the long line of carriages with his lantern. Everybody scattered to their places on the train. Dan had given Bruiser the job of night watchman. He was supposed to go the round of the cages before the train left, see that all the fastenings were in order and report to Dan ten minutes before the train left.

'Leave in ten minutes, Mr. Haxby,' Bruiser called, standing with his lantern below Dan's carriage on this first night before the circus train started. 'The lashings are all fast, and all's well.'

'Thanks. Good night, Bruiser,' Dan called. The animals roared, now and then, at the unaccustomed jolting and disturbance of their slumbers, and slowly, carefully with all her trucks, waggons, animal cages, and carriages trailing behind her, the circus train moved off.

Although so much of her life had been spent on a circus, Gina had never before travelled on a circus train. They had trucked their waggons on the old Haxby's sometimes, but then there was no menagerie. This was different. This was the circus special train. Haxby's own train with guards and engines hired from the State government. Dan, Lily and Jack knew what it was to live on a train, move out of railway yards with the animal cages bumping and jolting along before them; but to Gina it was a new experience. She could not sleep for excitement and realisation of what it all meant.

She had watched the elephants loading waggons on the trucks in a heavy dream; and now at night when everybody had left her and she lay down to sleep, she could not, for wondering what would happen if trucks with the animal cages on broke loose, there was an accident, the engines pitched over an embankment, or ran off the lines, smashing open the animal cages, and lions, tigers and elephants roamed out over the countryside.

Gina laughed at herself for imagining such horrors. 'Must be losing my nerve, or something,' she thought.

The train rattled down steep hill sides, all its waggons and trucks bolting and jolting together, slowed up and whistled if the signals were against it, and then galloped on again through the darkness, tearing and banging its way across mountains and rivers until it slowed down at last in the chill dawn at railway yards of the big country town where Haxby's was to show that night.

No sooner had the train come to a standstill than Gina heard Bruiser talking to Dan outside his compartment. Looking from her window she saw the shabby buildings of a town laid out on either side of flowing rails, silver threads in the early light, converging further along before a gloomy railway station.

Dan, an overcoat over his pyjamas and his grey hair on end, was already making his way along the track with Bruiser towards the engines. The elephants were emerging from their high boxes, keepers standing off and calling them by name. Each elephant had his own keeper these days, and so strange the great unwieldly beasts looked against the dim shining sky.

'Hullo, Gi,' Jack called, swinging down from his carriage which was next to Dan's, 'sleep well?'

'Not a wink,' she replied eagerly.

Pulling a dressing gown over her nightgown, Gina went to stand on the platform of the dining car beside her room and watch the boys turn out for unloading of the train. She saw Bruiser put out his lantern and go off to the guard's van where he was to sleep; tent hands and grooms turn out from their carriages and set up a dixie. In no time the rails and yards were swarming with circus hands going about their jobs. Syd and Monty joined them.

From the moment the train stopped everybody was busy. Daylight came quickly. Jack had gone off to inspect the lot which was a little distance from the railway, while Dan, anxious that every detail of his plans and organisation should be carried out, bossed unloading of the waggons and cages.

There was some shunting and uncoupling of the passenger end of the train from the trucks which were

T

brought to a ramp. And presently elephants and their keepers were moving up and down unloading the gay red and blue waggons, drawing them out of the railway yards and along the road to the lot. Almost as quickly the town was awake and a crowd of men and boys had collected to watch the elephants and circus waggons.

On vacant ground Jack had leased for the show, Monty and Jack took their bearings. Monty was to be tent boss; but in these early days Dan had to have a finger in every pie. He had to teach the lads their game, he said, and see that everything was done with method, and an exactitude which would save time and trouble in the future. While the canvas was being unloaded, he had the ground measured. Canvas and stakes were spread out.

Gina watched holes dug for the king poles, the red and white of the big top hoisted and balloon against a background of grey shabby houses, smiling to see how Dan was at his old tricks, hailing an onlooker to give a hand hoisting the tent and driving a stake here and there, although he had thirty men to do all this work now.

The tent was up by the time townsfolk were having their breakfast; the waggons stood there on the lot, gorgeous in their new paint. The dixies steaming for breakfast, collected tent hands, grooms and keepers down beside the engines. The men washed their faces and hands in buckets of water set on the ground near by and went about whistling and chiacking each other. Mrs. Dennis, the clown's wife, who was to be cook for the family, served a meal in the dining saloon, coffee and omelettes, *cuit au point*, as she declared proudly.

Shaved and dressed, Dan sat down to his breakfast, as excited and jubilant as a schoolboy.

'I don't know what you call this egg muck, Gina,' he

said. 'I'd rather have the bacon and eggs your mother used to give us. But I suppose it's all right, eh? If only she was here to cook for us? But what price Haxby's with a French cook on the train? I told Dennis when he wanted to bring along his wife. "No hog-fats. There's got to be no hog-fats on the show!" "Madame is good cook!" he said. "Can wash and sew," he said. "Well that's all right," I said, "as long as she will." "Always we have been together," he said. "Right," I said, "we'll give her a trial." They tell me she liquors-up and has a temper. But she runs Dennis and the dogs. They'd be no good without her.'

He looked round the dining saloon with its half-dozen little tables, to see Lily and Jack sitting at one table, Gina, Syd and Bob at another. Les and his wife in the corner near the window. Max was to sit with him; but she was not up yet.

'It's going to be a damned picnic this show, I reck'n, Jack,' Dan chortled.

Les's wife was the only flaw in his satisfaction. She liked to dress up and play attendant to Les in his acts; but made the excuse of being an artist reason for doing nothing else. Dan had taken a dislike to her not only because she was sickly and useless, but because she was always complaining, and kept Les dancing attendance on her.

'Well Rene,' he would say, 'what's the growl this morning?'

And she was annoyed with him because he would not allow her to smoke on the lot, or outside the train.

'See here, my girl,' he said, that first morning in New-castle. 'I won't have women smoking on Haxby's, least-ways not outside their own quarters. It gives the show a bad name.'

'My Gord,' Rene exclaimed. 'Is this a damned Sunday school, or what? In America . . .'

'This is Australia,' Dan reminded her gently. 'And the show's Haxby's. Smoke as much as you like in your carriage but if you take my advice, you won't – and your health'll be better.'

He walked off, and Rene, who had been dancing with an American vaudeville company when Syd found her stranded in Sydney, looked after him, exclaiming, in a high stilted drawl.

Jack and Lily had told Dan of conditions in some of the rough-and-tumble smaller American shows they had worked with, and he was determined to run the larger Haxbys' with as much rigor as he had run Haxby's in the old days. In all these ways affecting his pride and sense of importance, Gina let him go his own way. She was anxious for him to keep the illusion of owning Haxbys' as he had done every other show which bore his name.

Dan had organised and run the show as only he could have run it with his years of experience and knowledge. Jack and she worked with him, learning from him, taking all he could give, grafting their own ideas on to his some-times. But everybody recognised that in these latter days Haxby's could never have been what it was without Dan. He was a master showman, knew his job from end to end, and he had got organisation and administration to a nice point. Some of his ideas were old fashioned; but he prided himself on a clean show. He would not allow filthy language among the men; women were forbidden to smoke outside their cars; and any groom or keeper found guilty of cruelty to the animals was warned that he would be sacked on the spot.

The American and foreign artists laughed at the

strictness of Haxby's regulations – the little tin god air with which Dan ruled the show, but La Stella, and those of them who had worked with Wirth's, knew the same rules were enforced there. A tent hand had been sacked for swearing!

Monty's wife was a very different proposition, a woman after Dan's own heart, a real plum of a little woman he called her. She worked with Monty in his juggling and Japanese turns. Made costumes for him, herself and the two children. Sewed and cooked for Bach, Joshua, and several of the other artists. And she was always good tempered: nothing ever seemed a bother to her. Everybody liked her, made a confidant of her. She was probably the most popular woman on the show.

After the circus was a week out, it was working on oiled wheels. As each act finished while the show was on at night, gear was collected, packed and loaded ready for moving; the acts were arranged to fit in with reloading the train so that a start might be made according to schedule. Every man had his job and went about it mechanically.

In less than an hour after the crowd had drifted away and a performance was over, the tents collapsed and all the stakes and gear on waggons, drawn by elephants, had been loaded on to the train. Monty, who was lot-boss, sent his men round the grounds to see no peg, stake, mallet or rope had been left behind, a couple of men gathered up the papers, and a little after midnight except for the mark of the ring and stake holes, a vague smell of wild beasts and horse lines, no one would ever have known a circus had been there. Tents, horses, keepers, the train itself, all disappeared, as if by magic.

Dan decided for awhile at least to keep to the old

system of a procession through the town, towards midday, whenever municipal authorities would allow it. The custom was falling out of favour; but as an advertisement, Dan declared, and almost everybody agreed with him, Haxby's could not do without it. The artists hated the procession, and all who could got out of it on one pretext or another. But Dan would not stand any nonsense these days. He was an autocrat in the sunshine of his power and determined to make the most of it.

Rene, who had been posing with the strong man, roused La Stella and the Americans against the procession. Dan declared they could have their wages and get out if they did not parade with the rest of the show. They paraded and no more was heard of the protest.

Dan's only edict which nobody paid any attention to was: 'Artists are forbidden to keep pets on the train.' Almost all of them did. Madame's cockatoo was eating the oilcloth from the floor of her kitchenette beside the dining car, and Stella's monkey was always in mischief. Monty and his wife had a couple of Australian terriers which slept with the children, and Lily refused to be parted from her Pekinese, Nanki-Poo.

'Good God,' Dan raged. 'These damned pets are more trouble than the whole of the menagerie put together! Destructive pests, making a mess and smelling the place out——'

Pets were kept out of his sight as much as possible; but continued to lead luxurious lives in nearly every carriage on the train.

Before leaving Sydney, Gina had induced Jack to engage a quartette of American trapezists to take the place of his own turn for awhile. It was an understood thing that after the opening season he and Lily would retire, but Dan was reluctant to drop the Fire-Flies from his programme. It had been one of the most popular items, and only when Gina insisted that Max was working too hard, could not stand the strain, did he consent to the substitution of La Stella and the Vaux brothers for a few months.

Although the trapeze work was so much easier and less dangerous than her work with the horses, Gina realised that Max's point of strain was there, and she must be relieved of it.

So La Stella, as Mrs. Jo Vaux was called, her husband and her husband's elder brothers, Jim and Harry, had joined the train. Stella, a hard-eyed, black-haired little woman, called herself American, because she was born in New York while her parents, Spanish acrobats, were touring with one of the smaller American circuses of their time.

Stella had been given a good name for programmes to begin with, and she had been wire-walking as long as she could remember – balancing on a wire stretched a few feet from the ground, and in the afternoons had worked with her father and brothers on the horizontal bar and trapezes.

From her first appearance when she was six, she had wandered all over the world. Falling in love with a youth in a rival troupe, she ran away with him and joined his partners in their trapeze act. The Flying Vaux, as they were called, had no woman as clever as Stella with them. They were glad to get her at any price. Jo was timid, but good-looking, and very popular with women and girls, so the two elder men put him forward, gave him the flash work and stood back themselves. Intrepid and shrewd, it was not long before Stella knew her man inside out. After a year or so she was ruling the roost; the two elder men deferred to her in everything. They respected her ability; she made Jo work; but was furious if she caught him eyeing the girls.

'But it's business . . . good business,' the brothers argued.

Stella, vindictive and jealous, unleashed the anger everybody went in fear of.

'I'll look after the business,' she screamed, 'I am the business. I'll drop him. I'll drop him one of these days, if I catch him glad-eyeing. See, if I don't.'

In one of their aerial acts, as she hung from a trapeze, swinging backwards and forwards, she had to catch Jo and hold him, swinging together until he flew off and caught another trapeze.

To fail to catch him, or to drop him, would mean a fall of forty feet into the net or a shattering death for the man. Nobody believed that Stella was quite capable of keeping her word. But she dropped Jo once, to prove it, and no one had been game to take any chances with her since. It was almost murder, but she had judged her time and velocity so that although Jo was shaken he was not much the worse for the fall.

'Next time you won't get off so easy,' she warned him.

Jo had lost his good looks after being married to Stella for four or five years. Although he managed now and then to go on a spree for week-ends, she kept beer away from him as much as possible and would not let him eat any of the food he liked best.

'A devil of a woman, a fair devil,' he wailed to everybody who would listen to him. It was certain if he had strength of mind for anything he would have left her. But he was too afraid of Stella to try to run away.

'You worm,' she screamed at him sometimes. 'You miserable worm!'

But he was her worm, what there was of him, and in her way she was devoted to him.

She fed him, worked him, let him have a few shillings of their joint wages occasionally. But The Flying Vauxes were no longer young. The time was coming when they would not be able to put up a performance worth looking at. Jo and his brothers were doing a clown turn to eke out their usefulness on Haxby's. Stella herself was getting fat. She was forty-five if she was a day, although still extraordinarily clever and agile.

When Dan was beginning to growl to the Vaux brothers that they must put a little more ginger into their act, attempt some new and more daring stunts, if they wanted him to renew their contract, Jim talked it over with Stella.

'The old devil,' she swore. 'I'll have a word with him.'

And even Dan Haxby was so afraid of Stella's tongue, that he renewed her contract with a few compliments, and a mild request for a change of the same old hard-boiled tricks they had been putting over ever since they joined the show.

'Sure, Mr. Haxby!' Stella promised. 'Sure. We'll give 'em something to keep the pot boiling. I'll drop Jo again one of these days if he don't keep his eyes off of your daughter, Max. That'd give you a nice little sensation . . . and all the advertisement you want.'

'My God, don't do anything of the sort,' Dan begged.

'She's quite equal to doing it, I believe,' he told the family afterwards. 'What a woman! I don't wonder Jo looks the poor-spirited mongrel he is. I'd drown her if she belonged to me.'

Stella was really a prey to her domestic instincts. Had saved money religiously for years and was looking forward to retiring and starting house-keeping for her husband and his two brothers. But she was not quite ready to start yet. It would suit her quite well to stick to Haxbys' a while longer. She did not know where she and the boys, as she called them, would get another job. They were none of them any longer young. And there were so many Japs and yellow skins doing the smartest trapeze and wire walking stunts for next to nothing, that it was difficult to get any sort of engagement these days.

Max and Stella hated each other at sight. They were both too used to their own way to get out of each other's. Honest and outspoken, used to say just what they thought, without consideration of anyone's feelings, they had exchanged candid opinions each of the other. If anything would induce Max to take up her work on the trapezes again, it was the idea that by doing so La Stella and Haxby's would part company.

Haxby's showed one night in Newcastle, a night in Maitland and went north into Queensland, playing the larger towns for two or three nights and moving on again. From Townsville, the train glided over the ranges and downs to Cloncurry, and south again by way of Longreach and the Darling Downs.

Gina's growing friendship with Bach caused Dan some uneasiness.

'What's the meaning of it,' he growled. 'I don't like Gina always prowling round with that damned lion tamer.'

'Oh, go on, Dad,' Lily replied. 'Leave Gi alone for goodness sake. She's not a kid. Can take care of herself, surely.'

Bach had been teaching Gina to drive the motor-car which travelled with Haxby's. It was more or less a family treasure; but like the circus, Gina's property as a matter of fact. Usually she enquired whether anybody wanted to use the car, or would like to go for a drive with her if the train had reached, or was not leaving some country town on Sunday.

Sometimes the boys and Max, or Lily and Jack, accepted an invitation and went with her; but as a rule they preferred to rest and loaf about the train. Circus folk are not sightseers. Besides, her excursions with Bach were recognised as Gina's perquisite. She and Paul went off into the country for dinner every Sunday, and brought back fruit and vegetables, or cream and eggs, home-made jam, asparagus, persimmons, or pine-apples: whatever they happened to find wherever they might be.

Sometimes it was no more than an opal or topaz, Bach had bought from some old hatter or prospector. Paul Bach had a passion for collecting precious stones in the rough. Everywhere he went in the back-country of New South Wales he asked about the gems; and liked to search for topaz pebbles and white sapphires in the dry creek beds.

In a small yellow chamois leather bag, he hoarded opal chips, potch from the Cliffs and black fired 'nobbies' from Lightning Ridge, topaz in dim translucent globules, pieces of amethyst and crystal. In Queensland he collected diamonds, emeralds and sapphires, none of any great value, just shards and fragments of light and fire.

'But why do you want them?' Gina asked once.

Paul shrugged his shoulders.

'Do not ask me. I like to have them. The buried beauty of the earth – perhaps.'

Bach had brought Gina out of her shell, Lily said. It was he who suggested that she should buy the big fur coat which disguised her shoulders so well, and he presented her with a yellow silk shawl to fold over and over and trail in long silken fringes down her back. Gina had begun to look quite handsome in consequence of his attentions.

The boys and Jack were as concerned as Dan. The intimacy between Gina and Bach had grown by slow and easy stages until it was a recognised thing on the show. Nobody quite approved of it. Everybody was a little apprehensive of the consequences it might have on Haxby's.

'Is he making up to Gina?' Monty asked Jack. And Les asked him. They realised Gina was a woman worth making up to these days and wondered what would happen to Haxby's if Gina married Paul Bach and gave him the whip-hand of them all. She took his advice a good deal. Bach had remained as much a stranger, a hard man to know, for everyone except Gina, as he was when he first joined the show.

There was some curious deep sympathy and understanding between Gina and Paul Bach. Their blood leapt and flowed towards each other; and they talked together with freedom and energy, Gina's intelligence thriving under Bach's bitter blazing at what he called 'the base virtues' which rule existence: the clap-trap of sentimentality, superstition and optimism which make for success in life. He appreciated a simplicity and solid worth in her; her capacity to absorb and respond; the fertile soil she was for any seed of the emotions he chose to sow. They enjoyed companionship, a unique friendship before the more subtle currents of sex began to run, tangling and entwining them.

'You hate women,' Gina said.

'It is so,' Bach agreed. 'But I cannot hate you, Gina. You have heard that Lisa, my wife, left me to go away with a Russian violinist. She left me, Gina. That does not matter. But the two children she left also. They are at school at present . . . at home in Hamburg. The youngest was not a year old. No, I do not like women . . . I prefer lionesses. The lioness is so much better a mother than most women. Would she leave her cubs for a damned musician?'

As Gina could not say, he continued:

'A woman who would leave her children . . . her baby for any man . . . is not fit to live. If ever I see Lisa again I will kill her.'

He said it in such a fixed and final way that Gina did not doubt he would do as he said.

'You, Gina,' he had said to her one night when they were eating in a city restaurant. 'You tempt me . . . you rouse my blood. You stand aside from life. You watch it. You do not give yourself to life. You do not live.'

'Oh, I——' Gina shrugged her shoulders. Her sombre gaze lighted to the fire of Bach's eyes. 'What else is there for me to do?'

His hands closed over hers, the primitive force of the man taking possession of her.

'If you will give yourself to me, I will show you what else,' he said.

Gina, raising mocking stirred eyes, murmured slowly: 'I'd be glad to.'

And so Gina and Bach became lovers. They went about much as they had done before. Greeting or indifferent to each other, with a friendly nonchalance; but there were days when they went away together, spent Sunday at some distant farm house, and Bach was known to leave Gina's car in the early hours of the morning. Both Gina and Bach seemed happy and satisfied in the arrangement; and the boys and Jack wondered what would come of it. They were indignant but could do nothing. Gina would not discuss herself or Bach with them. And Dan somehow never suspected the relationship.

To have a lover gave Gina a dignity and poise she had never known before. She was serene and tolerant of Jack's and Lily's dislike of the affair; but quite unmoved by anything they had to say.

CHAPTER 26

AFTER playing Broken Hill, 'the last place on earth, by God,' as Dan said, the circus train wound a swift wriggling course over red earth and blue bush country to Kapunda, where the copper mines had once supported a flourishing town and where great shafts and workings were now almost deserted.

Through Peterborough and the pastoral and wheat growing districts round about Quorn, showing for a night in the larger towns, Haxby's made south over the stark majestic ranges dyed azure, indigo and amethyst to Augusta and the sea; then West for the winter.

Between States there was all the business of changing trains to be negotiated; but Jack had gone days ahead to arrange for that. Across wide grey stretches of the Nullabor plains, for two days, the train stopped only to take on water or coal. All hands loafed and spelled luxuriously until tossed earth of the search for gold appeared again, with shafts, and the wandering herds of goats which always accompany them.

The goldfields of Kalgoorlie and Boulder were past their prime; but Haxby's played to record houses on Saturday night and for the matinee performance it gave in Kalgoorlie.

'Gold mines,' Dan chuckled, 'are always a nice little investment for us, although the days when a prospector paid for his seat with a bag of colours are long past.'

Dan remembered them though, and found old acquaintances to reminisce with at 'The Horse-shoe' about the
gay wild times when Haxby's had put up a little one-
poled tent and showed for a week on the Golden Mile.
Gina was riding then and Rocca had set the place roaring
with laughter.   Some of his jokes and sayings were still
remembered.

'It's a grand show you've got now, Mr. Haxby,' some
of the old timers said. 'But you couldn't beat the old
one! Remember the dwarf on the draught horse. Grey
Dawn wasn't it you called him . . . by Moonlight out of
Paddy Murphy's Plain? Gosh . . . a great go! You can
hear the boys talking and laughing about it yet, sometimes.'

But it was in Perth, where the lot was on green flats
overlooking shining stretches of river, that something of
its old gaiety came back to Haxbys'. Gina on the verandah
outside her room at the Esplanade Hotel heard Max calling,
as she came upstairs.

'Gina! Gina.'

Max came rushing on to the verandah. She was
radiant; her whole figure dancing.

'Who do you think's here?

Gina could not guess; but Max did not wait for her to
try.

'Lal! And we're engaged and going to be married,' she
sang. 'And Dad's going to give Lal a job on the show.
La-la-la, La-la-la. . . .'

She dragged Gina up and down the verandah singing
and dancing till Gina cried.

'Maxie! Maxie.'

'Oh Gina, Georgina Haxby, I'm that happy I could die!'

Max threw herself into one of the easy chairs on the
verandah and continued breathlessly,

'We were in the dining room, Gi. Dad and the boys and me . . . and Syd was just telling us about Brasapa's in Singapore and how you got the leopards, when Lal came into the dining room. Just walked in the door . . . like anybody else . . . walked in and stood looking round with his hat off. I couldn't believe my eyes. "Lally," I called. He smiled all over himself. I knew it was really him then . . . and I just ran, Gina, and threw my arms round his neck and kissed him . . . And of course when I woke up there was everybody in the damn dining-room staring and grinning at us . . . Dad purple and the boys as if they didn't know where to look or what to do. But I just hung on to Lal and we walked up, and I said: "Dad, it's Lal!"

'Dad bawled: "You better go upstairs my girl. You – You——".

'But I hung on to Lal. And he said :

' "I can't let her go, sir! I can't ever let go of her again – if you don't mind. We're going to be married, right away, aren't we, Max? And if you'll give me a job on the show, I'll be obliged, because I haven't a bean to bless myself with."

' "Well, I'll be damned!" Dad said, and sat down all of a heap. And Lally sat down on my chair and I sat on Dad's knee, and told him if he didn't give Lal a job at once, I'd run away and get married in the morning and where'd Haxby's be then? So Dad said all right . . . and it's settled. Only Dad says . . . it's got to be a real slap-up wedding. No hole and corner business.'

'Maxie!'

'What on earth's all the noise about?' Lily had come from her room in a pale blue silk dressing-gown edged with swansdown.

U

'My wedding!' Max replied.

'Max, are you mad?'

'A bit,' Max admitted. 'And I wish I could always stay mad, like this. Everything's fixed, Lil. No one can stop it . . . we don't want to lose any time. So you'll have to be bridesmaid, Gi, darling, and——'

'But Max, after what's happened. How could you?'

'I don't care what's happened,' Max replied. 'I've got him now . . . and I mean to stick to him. Lal says that red-head cow took up with another man on the train, and he left her there. He's been dying to come back to us, but was afraid I wouldn't understand . . . forgive him. All that——'

'But why all this hurry, why . . .'

'Oh, I don't mind whether we're married or not,' Max replied blithely. 'That's just to oblige Dad and Gina and the rest of you really——'

'Max!'

Gina laughed as happily as Max in the girl's defiance and triumph.

'She's just beside herself, Lil,' she consoled. 'Aren't you, Maxie? And it's worth anything in the world to have you like this.'

Looking at that lovely radiant face, the vibrating creature of tremulous happiness Max had become, Gina had no more uneasy thinking as to what was best to do for her. Before this combustion what could she do? What could anyone do? Max had solved her own problems. She was happy. As to the future that must take care of itself.

It was all very well to wonder whether Laller was worthy of her. Gina herself did not think he was. Laller Hayes was probably as weak and self-centred a young man as she imagined. He would give Max more miseries

than most men gave the women who loved them. And
Max was so young. Too young to know her own mind,
Lily said. Perhaps, Gina agreed. But to have found
and laid hold of happiness, even for a moment, was
something. Max should have hers. No one should
interfere or balk her of it.

Max did not intend that they should. She was passionate and strong willed, a Haxby in that, Gina recognised;
and so little disciplined except to her job, she would do
as she pleased in any case. She always had done.

Only Dan had any influence with Max when it was a
question of arranging for her wedding.

'No, baby. No,' he insisted, 'you can't be married till
it's properly billed. When we go east again you shall be
married. We'll have a real stylish wedding, supper under
the big top and all. It'll be a great ad. for the show.'

No amount of coaxing or wheedling made any difference. Max was not of age and could not be married
without her father's consent. And during the rest of the
tour through country districts of the West, she had to
make the most of sweethearting with Lal, and did, with
childish abandon.

Gina and the rest of the family realised Dan was
sparring for time. He had, as he said, put the fear of God
into the young cub: intended watching and studying him
closely to discover whether Max might be allowed to
marry him. Laller understood well enough that he was
on probation and did his best to convince everybody he
would be both a safe and suitable husband for Max and
a worth while addition to the show.

They began practising together at once. Max was
eager to rehearse the Fire-Flies again; and although Lily
and Jack were out of the running now, Syd and Bob took

their place, and Stella was given to understand her contract would not be renewed.

'The Last Links,' a comic trapeze act Max and Laller had invented between them from watching the antics of a cage full of the little sable South American monkeys, was revived. Max designed tight-fitting suits of silky long-haired brown stuff with tails attached, and caps which showed only their faces. She and Laller and the boys got no end of fun out of the high jinks they arranged together. When they had perfected the performance, they invited Dan and members of the company to a dress rehearsal. Max had made herself a little monkey doll which she carried in a pocket, hugged, played with and searched for fleas so drolly that everybody was delighted – and vowed 'The Last Links' was a genuine novelty and merited a rise of screw for its perpetrators.

Dan promised to put it into the programme right away and feature it as one of the attractions for the Eastern States season.

The trick cyclist, Ernst Jeck, and his lovely young wife, Lois Goyer, who was a Russian ballet dancer, joined the circus in Fremantle with a French bull dog and King Charles spaniel in their hat boxes.

Jack had seen Jeck in the United States and engaged him by cable for an Australian season. His wife assisted him in his acts; but the dogs Dan was unprepared for. He stormed about the dogs, and the liability of foreign artists to cart pets round the world with them: but he was so impressed by the skill and audacity of Jeck's work that he fell back on his pet word to boom the turn, and advertised Ernst Jeck as 'the octo-miraculous wonder of the world on wheels.'

And everybody fell in love with Madame Jeck at

sight. She was like a French doll in biscuit china with blonde waving hair, dainty, charming and sweet-tempered; and so good a little wife to her big husband, who on occasions showed the nervous strain of his years of strenuous and daring work. The folds of Madame's eyelids were pink with weeping sometimes, although she took refuge in a migraine, or some other little ache or pain as excuse for them.

When she showed Max and Gina some of the exquisite bizarre frocks she had danced in on the Riviera, in Paris and St. Petersburg, they were speechless with admiration. There was one lovely ballet dress of green ostrich plumes; another of rose petals. Still another, of moonshine tissue and dew drops. But Lois Goyer had made a love match, and given up her career as a dancer to follow her husband to Australia.

Persuaded by Max to dress up one day, she danced on the platform set in the ring for her husband's turn with the bicycles. So lovely and gracious a figure as almost to be unreal, she ran on tip-toe, posturing, whirling, pirouetting in the 'Coppelia' ballet and 'L'Oiseau de Feu' while Rabe played on his fiddle for her.

Max, who had never met a woman so exquisitely finished and fascinating as Lois, worshipped her with school-girlish rapture.

'Oh, can't we put her on, Dad?' she pleaded. 'She is so sweet . . . and there's nothing as beautiful as her dancing in the show.'

Dan, who had watched the dance in the empty tent, with only a few of the artists practising and ring-hands going about their jobs, had nothing but admiration for the dance and dancer.

'But this is a circus, Max,' he objected.

299

'It's not enough for work to be beautiful and graceful,' Gina said, bitterly. 'It's got to be hair-raising somehow, freakish, startling or dead funny, for us to put on. The public wouldn't understand, if we gave it something just beautiful to look at.'

'That's right,' Dan agreed. 'If she'd do that dance in the lions' cage now, there'd be something in it.'

'Dad!' Max explained. 'You'd never suggest such a thing!'

'By God, it's an idea——' Dan declared enthusiastic-ally. 'I'll see Bach about it. We want to get something new and sensational for Melbourne.'

He went off at once to interview Paul Bach about the possibility of Lois dancing in the lions' cage. Bach was not in favour of it. The young lionesses would be all right and Milli; but he was not sure of Rosa.

'Well – don't have Rosa in the cage for the turn,' Dan said. 'That's easy enough, surely.'

Paul grumbled to Gina that he did not like the idea of a woman in the lions' cage. And little Madame Jeck with her bare arms and legs, her perfumed flesh, looking like a bird of paradise – fluttering and whirling before the lion-esses, it might be too tantalising. Besides would she have the courage? It could be done, of course, but not if she were afraid, likely to faint or scream. If she tripped or fell— God only knew what might happen. Gina herself did not think there would be much danger with the young lion-esses who had been reared on the show; but she distrusted both Milli and Rosa, the beasts Paul had brought with him.

When Dan suggested to Lois half in joke, half in earnest that if she would do that dance he had seen the day before, in the lions' cage, he would give her a contract at a handsome figure, she exclaimed, startled, and almost too frightened to speak:

'Dance in the lions' cage? But you are joking, Mr. Haxby!'

The idea ripened slowly. It took the form of a rumour that Madame Jeck was going to dance in the lions' cage. Everybody, tent hands, grooms and performers began to talk about whether she could, would, should do such a thing.

Jeck discussed the proposition with Paul Bach. He discovered that there was little danger from the trainer's point of view with the young lionesses; but that Paul would not consent for Lois to appear with the older beasts.

Then quite suddenly one morning Madame Jeck confronted Dan on the lot. A slight erect figure, she said quietly:

'I have decided to accept your offer, Mr. Haxby.'

'That's a real plucky little girl,' Dan exclaimed delighted. 'What does your husband say?'

'He is willing,' Lois replied steadily.

Max was furious. She had a headlong affection and admiration for Lois and could not understand Jack consenting to the danger for her. No one knew better than the circus folk the risk and danger although so much had been said to minimise them. Even if he spoke impatiently and crossly to her sometimes, nobody doubted that Ernst Jeck was devoted to his lovely young wife.

'What on earth does he mean by it, Gi?' Max demanded. 'If Lal were ever so careless about me – I'd – I'd – drop him.'

Gina smiled, knowing how much more dangerous the work Max had been doing for years really was.

Max laughed easily, guessing the meaning of her smile. 'Of course—' she said, 'but it's different with us!'

'I don't know. I think it'll be all right,' Gina murmured. 'Paul says so. If she's got the nerve, to do it – he'll see she doesn't come to any harm.'

'Well, I don't like it, Gi,' Max declared flatly. 'And I think Jeck's a brute to let her go into the lions' cage. She didn't want to at first, you know. Thinks she's got to show she's not frightened. Stella says he's nervy himself. Thinks he won't be able to work much longer, and they might as well make all the money they can before they retire. And Lois is so sweet she doesn't like to let him take all the risks – he's as nervous as a cat before he goes on now, sometimes, and that savage if anything goes wrong with the gear.'

Max had her own dressing tent; but the rest of the women artists shared a large tent, to change from outdoor clothes to parade costumes, or ring tights. They dressed before up-ended wardrobe trunks with paraphernalia of mirrors and make-up spread out on them, and their show dresses on hangers, in calico bags, inside.

There were sometimes five or six women in the tent dressing and undressing, making-up, or chatting and mending clothes, between their acts. Max sometimes blew into the tent to yarn with Lois, or Connie and Anna while she was waiting for her turn.

Rene and Stella she could not endure and rarely spoke to. They went about a good deal together, were known as 'the fast set,' because they smoked, were addicted to high balls, 'spots,' and cracking jokes with the men whose dressing tent was alongside. Rene and Stella took a malicious delight in telling each other stories to make

Max glare, and remark blightingly: 'This place needs disinfecting when you two get going.'

'Well, child, you got your own tent,' Stella would say. 'Why not stay there?'

But everybody was more or less rattled and concerned, the night it was known Lois was really going to dance in the lions' cage. Max went to talk it over with Connie and Anna Molnar in the women's tent, while she was waiting for her turn with Monty and the Snowies.

Lois herself laughed at Max's distress, opening her pretty grey eyes wider when Max quite frankly aired a criticism of her husband.

The circus went north across the brilliant tapestry of the Western sand plains woven with wild flowers, to Geraldton – where the skies were bare, blue, and the sunshine hot and brilliant although it was supposed to be still winter there.

The train was drawn up near the sea, and all hands went bathing – men at one end of the beach, women at the other. Even Lal and Max were not permitted to disport themselves in bathers on the beach together.

'If that don't beat cock-fighting!' Rene exclaimed.

During the summer in Sydney, Gina, Max, Jack, Lily and the boys sprawled on the beaches, surfed and swam all day, most of their days together; and members of the company did as they pleased in the cities where they were not living on the show. But in towns, with the show, it was different. Mixed bathing was against the regulations.

'I won't have it,' Dan said. 'It'd give the show a bad name.'

Two of the lionesses distinguished themselves by escaping from their cages in Geraldton after the show. How it had happened nobody knew.

People going home from the circus were panic stricken to see Belinda and Sadie prowling off to the sand hills. Bach, Syd and half-a-dozen of the tent hands followed them; and after a chase through outlying streets of the town turned the great beasts into a stable at the back of a hotel yard, where Bach slammed the door and kept them, until Syd drove a waggon with a cage on round, drew the waggon up before the stable door, and opened the door of the cage. The lionesses leapt into it, cowed and terrified by the strangeness of their experience: the spectacle of shrieking and fleeing people, and flaring lights everywhere, the harsh cracking voice of their trainer raised in anger against them; the flail of his whip on their hides.

Bach was furious. He declared somebody must have opened the door of the cage or the lionesses could never have got out like that.

It was only when Gina told him she had discovered a little jeweller's shop in the town in which rubies from the north were for sale, that his good temper returned. They went off together to see them, and Bach bought half-a-dozen small rubies as well as a golden pearl from Shark Bay, two or three blisters and a small lustrous ash-grey nodule which he said was a black pearl and more valuable than all the rest put together.

CHAPTER 27

HAXBY'S was in Adelaide for the spring when the almond blossoms were out, the grass new green plush everywhere; the ranges and a wall of lavender and blue about the wide-spread white buildings of the city.

Bach had been training a couple of bears and two wolves for an act with his lionesses. Syd, helping him, was eager to work Sultan, the tiger, himself. Bach had taken Syd as an apprentice and was teaching him the management of wild beasts. He had promised Syd a trial performance in Adelaide, and agreed with Dan to have his own act with the lionesses, bears and wolves ready, after a few days' work in the big practising cage, which would be set up for him when the circus had settled down in Melbourne, a week or so before the show opened.

'If I am aten – well I am aten,' Lois cried cheerfully as she ran out for her dance in the lions' cage that first night, a wonderful head-dress of plumes flaunting about her head, her bare arms and bust, slender legs, emerging from the downy bouquet of her dress of green feathers.

She confessed afterwards that her legs trembled so she could scarcely make them move when first she whirled into the cage. But Rabe had given the music she loved. There was nothing to do but dance to it, even if she were dancing to her death. She had forgotten where she was as she danced. Then she flashed out of the cage again.

The dance was a triumph. The beauty and grace of the dancer might have been almost lost in that narrow space behind the bars of the cage; but her spirit flew thrilling and dazzling everybody. So ethereal a creature Lois looked, and was, in the exaltation of her surrender of personal feeling, and flight above it, as she moved before the five great yellow beasts seated on their pedestals, or racing round the cage about her.

From the clamorous applause of the great crowd, with her arms full of flowers and boxes of chocolates, Lois ran to her husband.

'You are pleased with me, Ernst?' she asked.

He, proud and exulting, held her a moment, and could not speak. Who could doubt that he loved her?

Soon the dance of the Russian ballerina in the lions' cage ceased to be a nine days' wonder. The circus people took it much as a matter of course, forgetting all the foreboding and consternation there had been when it was first mooted. Lois herself ceased to mind it very much, although she did not sleep well at night, and shivered all through when yellow fur of the lionesses brushed her bare legs as they ran past before bounding into their cage. Once Belinda had got down from her pedestal, snarling, as Lois entered the cage; but retired at a word from Bach, his whip cracking beside her.

It was forbidden, an unheard-of thing, for a lioness to do, to get down from her pedestal. Belinda's temper had not improved since she was taught to jump through the fire hoops. Bach did not like it. He was more concerned than he cared to say. And hoped that the dance of the 'Bird of Paradise' in the lions' cage would not be required after the Melbourne season.

'It is all very well, for a while,' he said. 'Lois is a brave woman. But I do not think she can stand the strain for long.'

Max's wedding was the next sensation of that year. It was a 'slap-up affair' as Dan had promised.

The trouble at first was to decide of what religious persuasion the young couple were; where they were to be married and how.

Neither of them knew anything of God except as some thing you exclaimed by, and the devil as the embodiment of vexation and nastiness. In the wandering life they had led, courage and stoicism had been the supreme virtues. What anybody imagined, or believed about what happened to you after you were dead did not seem to matter much.

God, devil, hell and damnation were words which slid lightly through almost every conversation on the circus. But nobody bothered much about what they meant; and nobody, that Dan could see, was any the worse for that. His children were courageous, clean-living men and women; trained hard, none of the boys smoked or drank intoxicating liquors, having pride above everything else in their physical fitness, although they were good-natured fellows, kind to their animals, to any creature in distress, and a fine affection held brothers and sisters together.

Dan had a respect for God as an accepted idea; but he had never found time he said to go into the differences of religious opinion. He tried hard to remember what sort of a church he and Lotty had been married in; but all he could recollect was that it had been an unpainted little wooden shed in an up-country town, Methodist or Presbyterian probably. But that would not do for Max. Nothing short of a cathedral would be worthy of Max, he thought, and Haxby's.

Laller said that he did not mind where he was married

so long as he got Max; and Max said she did not mind where she was married so long as it was to Laller. She had never been baptised and he had no clear recollection of any ceremony. But as St. George's was nearest to the lot, they decided to be Anglicans for the occasion. A date was fixed; Dan interviewed the clergy and a choral service was arranged for with all honours of 'The Voice That Breathed' and the Wedding March from *Lohengrin*.

So that to the cathedral which reared its classic pile from traffic of the city streets, Max went in her satin and orange blossoms, half hidden by her great bouquet of white roses and veils of misty tulle. And so lovely she was that, as Paul Bach said: 'There's something to be said for religion after all.' Everybody felt it; Dan himself was almost converted.

The service in the gloom of the great grey stone building with its stained glass windows hung like jewels against the light, the awe-inspiring strains of the organ, fresh young voices of the choristers, all impressed him as a first-class show. He promised himself to go to church more often.

Monty's two little step-daughters were bridesmaids and Syd and Bob walked beside them. Gina and Lily had front seats with Jack, and Monty and Les and their wives. The women's dresses were all described in the papers next day. 'Miss Georgina Fay in golden brown velvet and furs of tawny marten carried a bouquet of yellow pansies and golden fern, while Mrs. Jack Dayne wore a smart suit of sapphire armure cloth, with close fitting hat to match and a bouquet of delphinium and forget-me-nots.'

A proud man, Daniel Haxby walked up the aisle to the

great altar, starred with candle lights. He looked pale and trembled almost as much as Max, who had never been so nervous in all her life. She felt as if she hardly knew Lal when he came towards her, very bland and debonair, rather like a tailor's dummy, she thought, and wished she could just clutch his arm and bolt for her life.

It was a curious experience for the family, this dip into the ways of what Dan called 'stick-in-the-mud society.' All the company in best clothes and hundreds of strangers were there in the audience to see Max married.

'Like being the whole circus ourselves, wasn't it, Lal?' Max queried afterwards. 'But I'm glad we haven't got to go on again. You only have to be married once, after all. I was never so scared in my life . . . rather work with Zuki any day. My knees trembled so as I could hardly walk.'

After signing a lot of papers in the vestry, a clergyman told Max she was really Mrs. Laller Hayes at last. Lal and the boys kissed her, and when Max and Lal stood on the church steps, everybody surged forward to shower bride and bridegroom with rose leaves and confetti. Newspaper men beside tall spindling cameras held back the crowd, as the bride stood a moment in the church doorway on the arm of her good-looking bridegroom, saying : 'A moment! Just a moment please!'

So radiant a little creature, Max shone in her white dress and flowers that members of Haxby's were beside themselves with admiration and excitement. Lois and Anna threw their arms round her and kissed her. Stella pushed forward to embrace her; Stella in black satin and diamonds; and Madame Dennis whom you would scarcely have known for the new curled black wig she was wearing and rouge she had rubbed into her wrinkled cheeks.

Laller picked Max up in his arms to escape from the crush and carried her to the carriage Dan had ordered the white horses to be harnessed to, with Bruiser and Charley in uniforms and wedding favours to drive. So Max had gone through the street, people cheering and calling to her, as if she were a fairy princess with her Prince Charming. And then there had been the wedding breakfast in the big circus tent, a wonderful spread for the whole company, at which only two outsiders were present, Auntada and Uncle George. So closely knit was the family that there were scarcely any people outside the circus world whom they called friends.

When Max cut her cake, Princess was led in to take her morsels from the bride's own hand; and all the horses and wild beasts were given carrots and an extra feed in honour of Max's wedding day. A flashlight photograph taken at the moment appeared in some of the papers next morning, over the note: 'Maxine Haxby (Mrs. Laller Hayes) feeding her favourite horse, Princess, with a piece of wedding cake at her wedding breakfast which was held in the tent at Haxby's circus yesterday.'

It was Max's own idea that every girl at the show that night should be presented with a tiny piece of wedding cake, done-up in silver paper, 'to dream on.' And a great idea it was, Dan chuckled.

The tent had been packed to overflowing; and it was just as well Jack, with great presence of mind, had ordered half-a-dozen extra plum cakes, because women of all ages claimed the privilege of 'a piece of cake to dream on,' and Max's wedding cake, huge as it was, would have vanished like snow under the demand.

There was no doubt about it, Max's marriage had been

a great advertisement for the show. All the papers gave accounts of the ceremony at the church and breakfast in the circus tent afterwards. Max's presents were described: diamond ear-rings, a baby Austin from Gina; cheque from her father; case of cutlery from the boys; silver vases from Auntada and Uncle George; tea set from Bruiser and Charley; travelling cases of crocodile pointed with silver from the company; a tiny platinum moth set with diamonds from Paul Bach, and a gramophone with all his pet records from Rabe.

And in it all Max was so happy, Gina was troubled for her.

'When people are happy like that I'm always afraid,' she told Bach.

She was happy too. She had overlooked that in her concern for Max; and it was at her that the black hand of Fate struck, when the show went on its way again, making inland and across country, through all the blaze of early summer, red earth and yellow wheat fields, under turquoise pale skies to Sydney where Haxby's was due to appear again at the end of the year.

CHAPTER 28

It was in Sydney, a week after the show had opened, and Haxby's was drawing good crowds with that dance of La Lois, as she was called, in the lions' cage, and Bach's act with the lions, bears and wolves he had trained to climb a ladder and play ring-a-rosy together, that Paul came to Gina, as she stood in the darkness behind the tents, watching assembly for the grand march, one evening.

His reserve and dignity, the bitter cynical humour which had held him apart and always a stranger on the show were gone. He was like a jelly which had set and was melting. A man broken, a little insane, he seemed as he paused beside her; and he had not been drinking.

'It has been good, our time together, Gina,' Paul said. 'Not good enough for you . . . But what does that matter? It is always the unequal . . . the ephemeral things that are most beautiful in the world . . . Lisa, my wife, and the man she left her children for, are here. To-night I saw them in the hotel together.'

He had left Gina as Dan's whistle shrilled, and music for the parade blared, gay and cacophonous, with its jumble of airs and instruments. Elephants, camels, horses, their riders and attendants, lurched forward in all the tawdry glory of their trappings. The Arabian Nights procession was still popular. Its eastern splendours had been renewed and added to, and Dan was satisfied nothing more effective as a spectacle could be devised, although Gina herself was beginning to think a change of dress and turn-out was needed.

When the parade had swung its course and lurched into darkness under flare of the kerosene torches again, she went into the tent to watch Bach in his act with the lions. She was troubled and apprehensive but could not allow herself to accept the significance of what he had said. A consciousness of doom weighed on her. She did not know what to do; how to fend it off.

Bach exercised all the lionesses for the first part of his turn in the big cage set up in the ring. Put them through hoops and making figures together. Ordinarily his voice was harsh and resonant; he moved briskly, a smart, well-set-up masterly figure among the tawny beasts, in his dark blue uniform braided with gold. But to-night Gina sensed a difference in his whole bearing – a looseness and indecision. He flung his whip carelessly; his voice grated without carrying any will behind it.

She turned to send word that Lois was not to dance to-night. An explanation could be made that she was ill. But Lois had darted into the cage and was whirling before the lionesses, as the resolution took shape. Gina watched her. Never had she known such apprehension and terror in the circus before. Jack and Syd standing beside the cage shared her anxiety. They knew something was wrong with Bach; he was behaving in such an erratic way.

For the first nights of Lois' dance, Gina had insisted that Jack and Syd should stand beside the cage with loaded revolvers in their pockets to use immediately if danger threatened the dancer. But the act had gone so quietly, everybody lost fear for Lois. Gina knew that neither Jack nor Syd carried a revolver to-night.

Bach seemed to pull himself together while Lois was

in the cage. His voice rang out harshly as he called the lionesses by name. They scampered past Lois in the last phase of her dance, romping for the cage on a waggon beside the ring cage. When Lois had slipped out, Gina looked at Jack.

'Thank God – that's over!' she breathed.

As Bach came from the empty cage, Gina went towards him.

'Paul,' she cried, 'What's the matter? Paul——'

He stared as if she were a stranger and brushed past her.

'Oh, go after him, Jack,' Gina begged, 'and see if you can't make him take hold of himself.'

An acrobatic turn and Stella's trapeze act, which did not necessitate moving the big iron cage from the ring, came on next, to give Bach a breather; then he was due to appear with the six lions, two bears and wolves he had trained to perform together. As the cages on waggons with their beasts were wheeled into position beside the sliding door into the iron barred enclosure, Gina herself went to look for Paul Bach; but he avoided her and was behind bars of the cage before she saw him again.

Dan had gone over towards the cage and, urbane and loquacious, was telling the audience about the act, as the animals were released and loped to their white pedestals, set at intervals from each other.

'Here, ladies and gentlemen,' he explained, 'you will see not the lion and the lamb lying down together, but lions, wolves, and bears playing ring-a-ring-a-rosy – and enjoying themselves as much as you did – once upon a time, not very long ago.'

The band played the Ring-a-ring-a-rosy music, very slowly as Bach faced the beasts before him, his long whip in hand. He called them by name, cracked his whip and they circled the cage, the bears dancing on their hind legs, while the lionesses and wolves revolved on all fours, and all sat back on their haunches at the 'pop down a posy!' The audience laughed and cheered.

But Bach was working as if the nervous control and restraint of years had broken down. He flung his whip recklessly. The animals sprang from him and trailed back to their places, sensing slackness and disorder in his method; removal of the will in those eyes which had always been iron and ice to them. Bach seemed to forget the system of their work, put their tricks out of order, hazardously. The beasts rushed to him and back to their stools, nervous and distraught, not understanding this change in the rhythm of their performance. Once Rosa got down from her pedestal, eyes phosphorescent, fur rising; Gina watched panic-stricken. Bach's whip cracked. Rosa slunk back and mounted her stool again.

'By God, he's drunk,' Jack whispered coming to Gina. 'That beast'll get him if he's not careful.'

'Hell, what's the matter with Bach?' Dan demanded, going to Syd where he was standing beside the cage.

'Drunk . . . he's so drunk he can't stand,' Syd muttered.

'Get him out of the cage as fast as you can. Tell Rabe to finish the tune.'

Rosa had sprung snarling again towards the blue-clad figure of her trainer. A woman in the audience screamed. Exclamations of horror and alarm flew out and grew with many voices to a chorus, although only the circus people knew the danger; how unrehearsed and ominous the behaviour of the lioness and her trainer were.

Paul flourished his whip and staggered, called Milli and Rosa to pose on the ladder he held for them. But they ran round him jostling each other, distracted by his strange behaviour.

Gina went to the ring and stood beside the cage.

'Paul!' she called. 'Paul!'

It was obvious that Bach had lost all sense of time and place. He was lashing about him as in a nightmare. To get him out of the cage was impossible.

'Open the cage doors,' Dan called to the men standing beside the smaller cage. They pulled back the iron doors which held the cage on the waggon beside the enclosure in the ring. The two lionesses in their terror and disorder rushed past it at first. Then seeing the trap-door open, Milli bounded towards it and Rosa followed. Just as they sprang up the ramp, Bach moved forward blindly and fell. At the same moment, Rosa turning, sprang snarling, and was upon him.

In a blinding flash, through the panic and uproar of the crowd, the door of the big cage opened and Dan, seizing an iron bar, entered and beat Rosa over the head with it. Retreating with a howl, she fled up the ramp to her cage and the boys slammed the doors. Jack and Syd ran into the cage and dragged Bach, who was unconscious, out between them.

The three younger lions, the wolves and bears had sat patiently blinking on their pedestals. Dan stood facing them Bach's whip in his hand while the ushers tried to keep order in the crowded amphitheatre behind him. Never before had he handled wild beasts in the ring except old Hero, and that was years ago. He did not know now whether the lion and the bears would obey him and what would happen, if they did not. A very gallant, sturdy old man, he stood there while the other cages were wheeled into position, the doors opened.

'Polly, Belinda, Sadie, my girl,' he ordered with a flick of his whip. And the young lionesses dismounted and ran off to their cages.

Only the wolves and the bears were left.

With the loud, sharp voice of command which had dominated Haxby's all the days of its existence, Dan ordered them in turn to their cages. The bears first and then the wolves. And the beasts obeyed him.

When he stood alone in the empty cage, Dan was quaking like a leaf, he admitted, although he disguised the fact by a little more than his usual swagger, bowed and withdrew, waving his hand to Rabe. The band struck up for the next item of the programme. Dennis and his dogs held the floor while Dan swallowed a couple of stiff whiskies in his tent. Then he went into the ring again as if nothing had happened.

'What was the matter? What in God's name was the matter with Bach? Was he drunk?' he asked Gina, later.

'No, he wasn't drunk,' Gina said.

Paul was not seriously hurt, the boys said, when they talked the catastrophe over after the show. He had a nasty gash on his cheek and Rosa had torn the flesh along his back and shoulder. But he was dazed, as if he were doped, or out of his mind. He was all to pieces anyhow.

Jack and Monty had driven him to the hospital. A doctor put half-a-dozen stitches in the torn flesh of his back. But Paul refused to stay in hospital; and as the doctor said there was not really any need for him to remain there, Jack had taken Paul to his hotel, put him to bed, and arranged to go and look after him in the morning.

But in the morning some one brought news to the circus that during the night Paul Bach, the lion tamer, had shot himself. He had shot also a woman staying in the same hotel. She had arrived the day before with a man who was playing first violin in the orchestra of the Grand Opera Company, whose opening night would be at the end of the week. Bach was the woman's husband, whom she had left years before, it appeared. He had vowed to greet her in this fashion should they ever meet again. She had been taken to a private hospital, but was not seriously injured. Bach was dead.

The inquest and inquiry which were held next day brought no further light on what after all was a very common-place tragedy as far as the news was concerned. Every week or so the newspapers related some such incident, in bald, matter-of-fact terms; there was nothing remarkable about it, except that the man who had done the shooting was the lion tamer at Haxby's.

Mr. Daniel Haxby, of Haxby's circus, stated at the enquiry, he believed Bach's mind to have been unhinged at the time of his death. Events at the circus immediately preceding the shooting seemed to point to that. Ordinarily the most self-possessed and cool-blooded of men, on this night he seemed suddenly to have lost his nerve; to be working mechanically, as if he did not really know what he was doing. There had been an accident. Bach was attended by a doctor before being taken to his hotel by members of the company, having refused to go into hospital.

On the circus, tent hands, grooms, keepers and electricians, who talked over the fatality, were sure Paul had brooded until the idea of revenge took possession of him. Everybody knew he had vowed to kill his wife if ever they met again.

'You know how it is,' he said to Gina once. 'You

play with an idea. Then it hypnotises you. The comedy becomes tragedy.'

Gina understood Paul had been impelled to keep faith with himself. It wrecked him to do so. His repressions shattered, the fixed idea had taken control and driven him relentlessly to the goal of vengeance – or justice, he set himself.

'Vengeance or justice?' Dan grunted. 'The one's too bad and the other's too good for this world.'

He was exceedingly annoyed with Paul for having messed up the show the way he had done, by going and shooting himself, and putting the lions out of action.

'Beats me,' he growled, 'why an ordinary sane man wants to go potty like that and bust things because a woman turns him down. Besides, I thought . . . he was a bit keen on our Gina.'

Bach's little bag of rough gems had been found done up in a package addressed to Miss Georgina Haxby. Inside on a sheet of hotel notepaper there was a line in the fine German script which read: 'For you, my dear, who were the most precious of them!'

At the end of the week, the show went north along the coast, and a little distance inland.

Max and Laller had a carriage to themselves on the train now. They came sometimes to the dining car for meals. But Max liked to amuse herself with a chafing dish, making strange messes of beef-steak and tomato and onions which Laller declared were scrumptious. But she hated washing the greasy dishes. So, as Lal had to do them he tried to restrain her efforts at domesticity.

'Oh, darl, don't you bother,' he begged. 'I hate you to get all het-up and – perfumed with onions – let's go and eat with Gina and Dad.'

Dan did not approve of these half-hearted measures of house-keeping even on a circus train.

'See here, Max,' he said. 'You got to learn to cook and sew like any other decent married women. Connie – now – there's an example for you!'

'Me?' Max gurgled happily, throwing her old childish joke at him. 'I'm an artist. I'm not going to wash dishes?'

'Well – see to it,' Dan warned. 'I won't have any of these new-fangled marriages on my show, no babies – no——'

'How many grandchildren would you like?' **Max** warbled.

'Eh?' He looked at her sharply.

But Max had run off with her gay, fluttering little laughter.

'What do you think, Gina?' Dan asked eagerly. 'Do you think she means——'

'I don't think so,' Gina said. 'She'd have told me. She's only teasing you, Dad!'

'Oh well,' he muttered, disgruntled. 'You see there's no funny business, Gina. Max stops work at once – if – I never thought of that. We'd better hang on to Stella – after all for a bit, I suppose. I'll have a word with Jack about it.'

He went off to where the tents were thrust against timbered ranges, steeped in purple mist, the wide scattered houses, shops and buildings of an industrial town spread about them.

CHAPTER 29

Organisation of the circus worked with a precision that would have done credit to a military camp, every man had his job and was responsible for it. Monty and Jack were overseers in their departments; but Dan never relaxed a watchful fussiness the years of his strenuous days on the road had inculcated.

Circus-goers exclaimed to find the menagerie tent empty as they went home to bed sometimes. They hung about to see the tents dismantled, the elephants at work hauling heavy waggons containing the canvas, stakes, poles, seats and electric supply gear to their allotted trucks on the long train which lay waiting and lighted, declaring it was as good as the show to see the show pack up and get under way again. But Dan knew every detail of the business so well that he fumed if the boys dawdled stacking the seats, disconnecting the lights, or put one elephant on a load when they should have used two.

Usually he was up as soon as the train stopped in the early morning; and tramping along beside the carriages in a dressing-gown and carpet slippers, kept an eye on unloading, although there was not the least necessity to. Trucks were brought into position, the train shunted, elephants released and their keepers took charge of them. Skids were laid from trucks to the railway sidings; the elephants brought into position, to the cries of their keepers: 'Ully! Ully!'

'Alice! Bertha! Ully, Ully!' went up with a chinkle of chains and slow creek of wheels, as the blue and scarlet waggons emerged from the inert chrysalis of the train; moved across to the green carpet of the lot, or along the wide street of a country town where some suitable site for the show had been rented. Dan was never quite easy in his mind unless he was watching to see every cog of his machine moving with the regularity he demanded. At night, urbane and handsome in his dress suit, with the medals he had won in his youth for swimming, riding, and life-saving, pinned across his breast, he stood at the door of the tent, thanked visitors for their patronage and directed them to their seats, kept a sharp eye on programme and peanut sellers, and in the ring was as brisk and lively as ever.

Jack and Gina went over the night's takings at ten o'clock; took them over to her car on the train and put the cash in the safe there. Dan wanted to know what Haxby's had earned each night; but did not concern himself about the business side of the show much beyond that.

At night he would not sleep until the lot was cleared, the train loaded again, and Bruiser had come along with his report: 'Train goes in ten minutes, Mr. Haxby. The lashings are all fast and all's well.'

But Rabe was concerned. 'The old man's breaking up,' he said. Dan was more fussy, crotchety and impatient than he had ever been.

Hustling embarkation, in a thunderstorm, up north, he caught a chill. 'Got a touch of dengue,' he said, and could not shake off the cough it left.

He barked a good deal and complained of a pain in his chest. But for no amount of talking would he take any care of his health. Laughed at the idea that anything could ever be wrong with him. 'Never had a day's illness in me life,' he boasted. His only illness, it seemed, was his last. That cough clung and plagued him. Stubbornly, he went on with his work, convinced the show could not get on without him, until he was not able to get out of his bunk one morning.

'It's this damned cold, Mont,' Dan said. 'Don't seem to be able to throw it off. Stiff nip of whisky'll sweat the thing out of me.'

He refused to be moved or to see a doctor; and no one dared to go against him, until he was delirious and in such a fever that the boys decided on calling in the only medical man in a small seaside town.

His verdict was pneumonia – double pneumonia – and a serious outlook.

Gina had Dan's carriage on the train run off to a side track in the goods yard, and a nurse installed. Gina herself remained with her father when the circus train went on; but he died three days afterwards.

Conscious a little while before his death, he was annoyed to think of dying in such an out-of-the-way place.

'Don't let me die here, Gina,' he gasped, when he realised his strength was failing, with a flare of his old spirit. 'Get me back to Sydney . . . Let's do the thing in style . . . like Max's wedding . . . It'll be . . . a good ad. for the show.'

But he could not be moved then. Dan talked in a rambling, half conscious way, a few hours before he died. Gina heard him say 'Lotty', as if he were speaking to her mother, telling her something.

'Oh well,' Gina caught the low incoherent muttering, 'suppose he's gone too . . . had to shoot him . . . didn't like to tell me. Gina——'

Gina knew he was thinking of Phil, trying to ask about the pony.

'Yes, Dad,' she said. 'Uncle George thought it was best——'

Dan moved his head ever so slightly in assent and seemed comforted to know Phil had travelled the road he was taking. He did not speak again.

There was no show on the night of Dan Haxby's funeral. Crêpe draped placards on the circus tents announced that: 'Owing to the death of Mr. Daniel Haxby there will be no performance this evening.' Mourning notices proclaimed the desolation of his family, and there were write-ups of Dan's career and sterling character in many newspapers.

Gina and the boys grieved that their father had been denied the public honours, pomp and ceremony of the splendid funeral he had so optimistically planned for himself as the creator of Haxby's. They knew how it would have pleased him if his wishes could have been carried out. But the show was billed for towns, far and wide, in northern Queensland. Its course could not be deflected.

So Daniel Haxby was left behind on a quiet hillside overlooking the Pacific Ocean. All the company that could be spared from minding the animals came to say good-bye to him there, and people of the surrounding towns and countryside were surprised to see men among the circus folk weeping: Rabe and Dennis embracing each other beside the grave. Joshua, the strong man, who was a German, soft-hearted and sentimental, blubbered as he clasped Syd to his mighty bosom exclaiming:

'*Leider Gottes!* But he was brave – a good showman, Dan Haxby.'

The circus went on without Dan, much as it had always done, except that Monty became ringmaster; and Bruiser reported to Gina at night when the train was ready to move: 'Train leaves in ten minutes, Miss Haxby. The lashings are fast and all's well.'

The season in Brisbane was disappointing, as city seasons usually were. Monty, new to his work as ringmaster, would never be the showman his father was, everybody said. But then Dan Haxby had been a born showman, at home with any audience, as jolly and happy-go-lucky cracking jokes for children and country-folk in the ring as he was out of it. He understood the knack of poking fun at the slack, work-worn, city-dwellers, jibing them into forgetfulness of their shrewdness and perspicacity, as Monty would never do. But then Dan had been at the game nearly all his life. Forty years on the road and in the ring, he boasted. And Monty, though entitled to step into his shoes as the eldest son, was still too stiff and polite with a crowd to make much headway against its sated appetites.

Besides, without Bach and his turns with the lions, and other wild beasts, the programme suffered considerably. Lois could not dance, and although Syd was still working Sultan, the young tiger, there were no crude thrills to put before an audience to make up for the exploits with wild beasts which had been advertised months ahead.

Syd was eager to have charge of the lions as well: Gina reluctant to let him take on the added responsibility. He was too inexperienced for the job she thought, although he had fed the lions and looked after the cages since Bach's death. The beasts seemed to recognise an apostolic succession in his authority over them. But the scars

Bach's breakdown had left were too fresh in her mind for Gina to consent to her young brother practising and exercising Paul's big cats for a while.

'You'll have to get somebody to work them, then,' Syd insisted angrily. 'Our beasts are all right – but Milli and Rosa and Rex'll get out of hand in no time.'

'I suppose so,' Gina agreed indifferently.

CHAPTER 30

NOBODY knew quite what to make of Gina during those months after her father's death. She seemed to have lost interest in the show, although she was really the Boss now. Haxby's belonged to her more than it had ever done during Daniel Haxby's lifetime when Gina had wished him to enjoy the sweets of office. She drifted about the tents and the train a morose, gloomy figure, brooding and lonely.

Max was happy now and did not need her. Determined not to be a shadow on Max's happiness, Gina kept out of her way.

That she missed Bach was taken for granted. They had gone everywhere together with a good fellowship rather than loverliness which impressed everybody. The boys thought Gina was taking her love affair with Bach, its break-up, more to heart than they had imagined she would.

There was something more in it than that Gina herself realised. She was suffering some deep dissatisfaction, unrest and discouragement with life. Withdrawal of her father's strong personality had something to do also with this breakdown of her will and resistance to misfortune. Odd man out, she roamed and glowered on the outskirts of all the closely-woven days and doings of the circus, although the reins of its existence were knotted in her hands.

Y

At night she had become a prey to terrible dreams. They drove down in avalanches upon her. She wakened, crying out and squawking with terror, from a nightmare in which the train had bolted down some steep mountain side, the carriages came all rattling and smashing open – cages of wild beasts and elephants' loose boxes so that the lions, bears, wolves, tigers and elephants whirled among helpless sleepers on the train. Or again, the electric lights had failed for a few moments in the crowded tent while Paul was working the lions, or Sailor the elephants. There was a stampede in the darkness, shrieking of women and children, the trampling, cracking and smashing of tent poles.

'Oh my God!' she sobbed as she wakened.

And sometimes she was riding again, riding joyously, gaily, then falling – falling to that abysmal pain and bewildering torture. Or Rosa was attacking Paul. She could see the great beast's yellow fur rising, fluffing, the turn of her head, that lurch and spring like lightning, and her fall on the prone figure of the man. Moaning helplessly, she had watched Rosa gnaw, as if she were eating into Paul's back again. Gina had been so filled with·the yellow baleful glare of the beast's eyes that she could not go near her in the menagerie for days after the dream.

And sometimes she dreamed that all the beasts in the menagerie had escaped from their cages; rushed, over-whelming their keepers and trainers, mauling and devour-ing them ruthlessly by way of wreaking vengeance and justice for the captivity they had suffered so long. Monkeys chattering, elephants squealing, lions snarling rushed everywhere, trampling and laying waste as they escaped into the dark outside country.

Again and again the dreams came, racked and pursued her, until Gina was afraid to go to sleep. She could not imagine what was the matter with her that she should be the prey of this phantasmagoria of horror. In her waking hours she had never imagined such things – taken the outside chances of circus life matter-of-factly and not bothered about them. Of course everybody knew if the lights failed during the elephant act, or the turn with wild beasts, there might be trouble. That had been her father's one fear in all his circus life. Electric light the one fault he had to find with the new show.

The lights had gone out, unexpectedly, once or twice; but never during those turns, happily. The chances were a hundred to one they ever would. And there was that hundred to one chance of danger in everything you did in the world. But to make a nightmare of it! To let it make nightmares for you – Gina could not understand herself – and these nights of fear and misery. Thought of them haunted her during the day; but she could not bring herself to talk of them to any of her family.

It would be thought there was some madness of grief for Bach in it, she guessed. And she knew it was not that, but a curious breakdown of her will in sleep which released this horde of repressed fears. That and the clamorous instinct of her senses to be released from the oppression of too much brooding. Not only about Paul, but about the world in which the game of life was played at such cross-purposes.

To admit that she was afraid: did not want to be left alone at night, was out of the question. Gina began lulling herself to sleep with beer or whisky alone in her car at night; and tried to read till she lost consciousness.

Seeing her light on in the small hours, one of the

grooms who had been sitting up with a sick horse, in a town where the circus was showing three nights, went to speak to her about the animal. Gina asked him to have a drink and he stood talking awhile.

'By gosh! You have got nerves, haven't you?' he remarked sympathetically.

'I can't sleep,' Gina confessed with bright eyes – 'and when I do it's all rotten dreams, Jim.'

A good-looking youngster who had knocked round the world and knew his way about women, Jim Bailey said that he always met his luck half-way. And the Boss of Haxby's was a feather which he saw might adorn his cap if he went the right way about putting it there.

From calling after the show, when everyone else had turned in, to see if Gina was all right, he stopped to yarn for awhile: 'cheer her up,' as he said. They had supper and slept together for a week or so. But Jim wore his feather too blatantly: boasted about it among the men, and in a month found himself sacked, with a couple of weeks wages in advance. The Boss of Haxby's had done with him.

Anybody who had known the Gina of Haxby's in its early days – Gina at eighteen – would never have recognised her in the fat, middle-aged woman who was known as the Boss, when Haxby's came down from the back-country of Queensland and New South Wales and went south to Tasmania and then New Zealand, the year after Dan's death.

No one who had known Gina as a girl could understand her these days. Her whole nature seemed to have changed. Her temper flared passionately, unexpectedly. She was fond of beer, drank too much; and again and again, during the following year, a passion for some good-looking boy in the band, or among the keepers, made her ridiculous in everybody's eyes.

Only one person dared remonstrate with her. Jack Dayne talked to Gina much as he had always done, a savage hurt expression in his eyes.

'What on earth's the matter with you, Gi, running amuck like this?' he asked, finding her after a banquet and riotous night, heavy and red-eyed, in her apartment on the train one morning.

'Damned if I know, Jack,' Gina replied. 'I want to know if there's anything in this business of living, I think.'

'Do you imagine you're going to find out by getting drunk and making a fool of yourself with a rotten dog like Cyril?'

'Yes.'

'Well, you're not.'

'You know . . . I don't. That's the trouble. And I want to know, Jack. What's the use of standing off from Life, watching it all go by. Three-quarters of my life I lived that way. Then I wanted to feel something for myself. There's no reason why I shouldn't really.'

'It's the blasted money's destroyed you.'

'I think it has, Jack. Billy was right after all. He said to me once: "Life's a three volume novel, Gina. The first's the book of ideals and illusions; the second's the book of realities and noble resolutions; the third's the book of the senses and breakdown of the will." I think he was right, Jack. It's the third book I'm up to now.'

'Gina, I'd give anything on earth if you'd pull up.'

She looked at him with the eyes of a subtle unfathomable affection.

'No, old dear, I won't. There's a sort of misery and despair eating my insides out.'

'I know. I understand, Gi.'

'It's much better this way.'

'But——'

'Is he in love with you, this little beast, Cyril?'

'In love with me?' Gina's eyes had a serene mockery. 'Men do not love me, my dear. They like me – and use me. I like them and use them. Why not? You can't, as Paul said, always stand on the brink of life, wringing your hands.'

'But Rocca——'

'Oh yes, he really cared, I suppose – but I was as bad to him as everybody else. Couldn't get over – how he looked. Quite right too. Yes, I reckon. But this isn't love . . . it's taking from life all I can get. And why shouldn't I? It hurts no one but me.'

'It hurts me, Gina.'

'You?'

'To see you like this.'

'Oh no . . .'

'I've always thought you, as Rocca said, "the most perfect soul".'

'Perfect soul – my God!' Gina's eyes were dark in their disgust and bitterness.

' "If you were perfect – you would not be perfect".' Jack quoted. 'But to squander yourself like this.'

Aged and humble, Jack looked as he talked to her. Gina stared at him as if she were seeing him for the first time. They had always been good friends. She admired and thought the world of Jack Dayne. There was no one whose word about anything she valued so much.

'I must be growing old,' Gina mourned. 'Billy used

to say that we should die young. I hate age. People
are like fruit, they rot as they grow older or wither up.
The world would be a more beautiful place if young and
vigorous people ruled it – with their generosity and
impulses. Not the old by their weakness, and fear——'

'That's right,' Jack agreed. 'There's not many men
and women keep sound to the core when they're old.
Only the very healthy ones and hard-workers – like your
old dad perhaps. Oh well, we're not going to say he hadn't
his faults. But he was tough and straight, Gi – and game
as you make 'em.'

Gina's thought flew ahead:

'It was all the show with him.'

'That's right.'

'What Billy used to call "a purpose in life" – something
outside himself – kept him going!'

'Oh well, we've got to keep fighting – even if there's
nothing worth fighting for. Look at me – I've lived like
we all do when we're young and working, trained hard,
ruled out drink, rich food, too much of anything. But
now I'm old, the show's done with me. What does it
matter? I'm not proud of my strength and muscle and
will any more. I'd like to crock up and run off the rails.
It'd be relief somehow; but I won't let life beat me that
way. I've got to stand up to it, somehow.'

'That's because you're Jack Dayne,' Gina said. 'All
grit. I can't see you crocking up and running off the
rails, Jack——'

'Well you, Gina . . . you've stood out for me, as something so good and solid . . . something that all life could
do to you wouldn't destroy.'

'It can't——' Gina replied sullenly.

'If only we could go on the road again, Jack,' she

went on after a moment. I liked it with the waggons and horses. This is all right, I suppose. It's success, and a great thing for Haxby's – the big tents and all the elephants, grooms and keepers. But I liked the old life better. . .

'Coming down to a town in the early morning, with the mists rising, cuckoos calling, the earth all shining after rain. Paddocks green in spring time, and the country the colour of baked bread at the end of the summer. Wattles yellow with blossom beside the road, and the sky pink at sunset when we were camping up near the Murray, the trees dark and Mum roasting teal or black duck over a bit of a fire near the waggons. Remember the smell, Jack? Good, wasn't it, eh? But now it's all racket and rush and rattling along . . . I suppose it's all right. Only I wish we were on the road with horses and half-a-dozen waggons again . . . A fire of mallee roots and blankets under the stars'd do me on a night like this.'

'It was a good life, all right, Gi,' Jack agreed. 'But there was the wet weather, don't forget, and floods – we couldn't go back to it.'

'I suppose we couldn't.'

'We wouldn't make a living that way, these days . . . and Max and the boys have to be thought of.'

'Of course, but——'

'The question is what are we going to do about the show. It's not what it was, since the old man went. Mont's not the ringmaster he was, nor ever will be. And something's got to be done about the lions.'

'Syd wants to take them on.'

'Well, why not let him? He knows them and he's not a kid any longer.'

'I'd forgotten. How time goes.'

As Gina seemed lost in thought Jack went on.

'And the clowns. . . . We'll have to get a lot more fun into things or we may as well shut up shop . . .'

'Sounds quite like Dad talking,' Gina murmured.

'Oh well, we've been losing money for the last few months. Something's got to be done and you know it.'

There seemed no shaking her from the heavy thoughtfulness.

'Unless you're thinking of closing down——'

'Goodness, Jack, what are you talking about?' Gina sat up, startled. 'Haxby's closing down?'

'Well, it's either that or – wake up,' Jack said grimly.

'I see.' Gina spoke as if she were really seeing a long way and a great deal.

'Even Charley's concerned about it. I heard him giving a lad he's taken on to help with the horses a dressing down the other morning. "There's too many b's flying about. Not a bloody bee left in the hive," he said. "The old man'd turn in his grave if he heard the way some of you chaps go shouting around on Haxby's these days".'

'Charley?' Gina smiled.

'But one of the men said something to me, that stuck more than anything else. I didn't mean to tell you . . . but perhaps it'll show what I mean, about things going to pieces.'

Jack hesitated as if it were really difficult for him to tell Gina what he had heard. It might hurt her too much; yet there was the need of rousing and attaching her to work of the show again.

'I heard one of the elephants squealing the other morning when we were unloading, and went over to see what was the matter. It was that big soldier chap from

British India was handling them. I saw him jab Alice with the bull-hook three times under her front leg, so I went over and had a word with him.'

Gina knew of course that an elephant's hide is tough except over the stomach and intestines, where it is as thin as silk, and that one of the most sensitive parts to strike an elephant is under her front legs.

' "Here," I said,' Jack continued, ' "that's not allowed on this show." Solly wanted to know who the heil I was and all the rest of it, and told me I wasn't Boss. "No," I said, "but I know who is, and I'll have a word with her about this." Then he laughed and said: "That stuff used to go when the old Boss was here . . . but she don't care a monkey's hang about the show or the animals." '

'Did he say that, Jack?' Gina was disturbed.

'He said it,' Jack replied, 'and that's the feeling's got hold of everybody. Things were strict in the old days . . . but foul things are happening on the show every day and night, and you don't know. You don't care, Gina.'

'Jack!' Gina protested.

'Oh well, the men hit it up in Bury last pay day, you know. We got out of a shindy with the police by the skin of our teeth; and there was that business of the girls some of the chaps took along with them on the train. "Kidnapping" it was called – one of the girls was under age – and it was the devil's own job to fix things with her father. People are beginning to say again: "Shut up your chickens, the circus is coming".'

Gina exclaimed to herself.

'Well, you do mind?'

'You know I do,' Gina said.

For several weeks after that Gina gave herself to tightening up and straightening out the discipline of the circus, seeing that every detail of its complex machinery worked with the exactitude Dan had required. If Daniel Haxby had been a martinet, his daughter could be no less a stickler for the hard and fast way of doing things, it was discovered.

During practice in the tent one morning, a month or so later, Gina remarked quietly: 'Got a new clown for you, Mont.'

'Go on?' Monty stared his amazement. 'Remember Dad used to say? "Clowns? There's no bloody clowns these days. They've gone out of fashion. Don't breed'm!" Where'd you get him? What's his line?.'

'He'll be all right. I reck'n he's what we been looking for. I'm working up an act for him. Want him to be a surprise for you,' Gina said. 'Told Jack to bill him for Saturday. He'll just toddle in and out, fool round and try to imitate everybody, like Rocca used to . . .'

'Is he a dwarf?' Monty asked, his eyes brightening.

'Oh, deformed,' Gina turned to go out of the tent. 'I think he can get things going, anyhow.'

There was a good deal of joking about Gina's dark horse, the real old-fashioned clown she had found who was going to cry: 'Teapot!' and reduce a city audience to laughter and tears.

The new clown had been given a try-out one afternoon when nobody was about. Rabe had been there and said he was all right. Rabe had rehearsed the band on the act.

On the night of the new clown's first appearance, Jack was the only man in the audience who did not laugh. Gina herself was the clown. It was true, as she said, she did nothing much. She just ran on, clumsy and lumbering, parodying the juggling and tumbling act with a gleeful cry: 'I can do that!' Or, ' Show you how it's done!'

making herself look as ungainly and repulsive as possible.

She was billed as 'Punch, The Hunchback Clown,' and got-up to look like Mr. Punch with a little dog which was supposed to do tricks, and never did any, making people laugh as much by his failure to do as he was told, as if he had been the best trained dog in the world.

The Punch and Judy act Gina put on with Dennis who owned the dog, beat out something like the old hearty laughter for which Haxby's had been angling for so long. It flew gushing and unrestrained. Punch had only to stand and show his hump, run across the ring, or fall sprawling on the ground, for laughter to neigh out and bellow round him.

'By God, you done it this time, Gina,' Monty cried coming into her tent. 'I'd never've believed it was in you. But you got the real thing. The real clown's just got to stand and gawp, and the crowd'll roar at him. There's others, no matter what they do, they can't raise a laugh. They're too funny to be funny . . . work too hard. Course it's born in you, I suppose. Dad used to be a first-rate clown himself, Rabe says.'

'Oh, I remembered something Billy used to say,' Gina told him.

'What did Rocca say, Gi?' Monty asked.

'He said,' Gina murmured, a slow smile covering her thoughtfulness, ' "All you got to do if you want to make the crowd laugh, is stick out your belly, and shake your back-side at it." '

For days and nights Gina had wrestled before she could throw herself to the crowd to laugh at. That was the way Rocca had redeemed himself, she remembered: blighting laughter and exclamations of surprise had lost their sting for him.

338

Max and Lily hated Gina to make a guy of herself; but everybody realised how Haxby's would benefit by getting some humour into the show. Gina herself, with her showman's instinct, was compensated by the thought of what skinning of herself had achieved. When it was done, she was not sure that she would not get as much satisfaction out of her clowning as it gave. In a way, she was happy to be performing again: somehow, anyhow, to be on the strength of the circus. It was good to have got that laughter of the city crowd; to have won the applause it was so chary of.

She began to enjoy a sense of power. The circus, and every detail of work on it, moved as she directed. Jack Dayne was her right hand man; but before long he was surprised to find he was only that. Gina developed an executive and organising ability which amazed him. They worked easily together, each falling into the place designated by their natural capacities, recognising each other's strength and superiority.

Jack's was the business mind which weighed and costed every enterprise Haxby's embarked on. He kept a firm hand on expenditure, costs of up-keep and transport. After a few years, he was telling Gina she had paid out over a million of money for railway facilities, and that the show was costing her about £1,000 a week. They took as much as that in a country town for one night, sometimes; so Haxby's was doing all the old man could have expected of it, and still carrying its banners.

Only Monty took less kindly to the new position. He and Gina had two or three rows in the first months of her renewed activity. But Gina made herself clear. Haxby's was to be her show during her lifetime, although members of the family were all shareholders. After her death, the boys and Lily and Max might carry on as they thought fit.

Gina liked her food, grew fat and fond of bright colours. Usually during the day she wore black satin or a dress of figured silk and heavy jewellery, her amber necklace and ear-rings and two or three diamond rings. An exacting taskmaster, very strict and finicking about her instructions being carried out, she raged, as Dan had, at anybody who slacked or did not train systematically.

Every artist had his or her hours for practising. In the morning from eleven until twelve, if the train was early on a lot, she exercised the children who were learning to ride, or tried out some new stunt with the clowns.

More placid, good-humoured and jolly, as she grew older, at forty-five she was very like Dan Haxby.

'A chip off the old block, Gina, if ever there was one,' Monty cried bitterly after a difference with her at lunch one day. 'It's all the show with you – the damned show.'

'Too right, Mont,' Gina agreed. 'But I love garlic. God, how I love garlic . . . and beer, and a bit of fresh bread and cheese.'

She seemed happiest really when, in her clown's dress, made-up with plastered face and rouged mouth, she waddled into the ring and tumbled about, making herself grotesque and hideous, to get the brittle crashing merriment of the crowd that could hurt her no more, in whose laughter she could join, at the order and harmony of a world to which the circus held the dim surface of its mirror.